Old North Side Cafe

Stories, Essays, Homilies,

and Sayings

Jim Dunn

For Jane, from Liberty schools, William Jewell and now with the retired teachers group, I am always amazed at what you can do! Jim Dunn

For Zachary and Matthew

Old North Side Cafe

Special thanks to Joe Wally and the Sun Newspapers
for giving these characters a home.

Thanks to Dean Dunham, Bruce Ehlenbeck,
and the Presbyterian Ladies Power Group
for being the First Readers.

Thanks to the Missouri cities of Savannah, St. Joseph and Liberty
for creating such wonderful places and times
in which these characters could live.

Thanks to Doug and Shera
for giving me a place to write, and for their encouragement.

Thanks to Sandy at the Corbin Mill and
to William Jewell College for taking me in.

And, of course, thanks to Kathy Dunn.
This book, these characters, the author and cafe
all rest on her shoulders and live in her care.

Chapters

Prelude

You probably have been to the Old North Side Cafe once or twice a long time ago. You will remember the vinyl-covered booths and Formica counters that are throwbacks to another era. There was a time when every small town had a cafe where men came to talk, socialize, and drink coffee. If they were lucky, they had a waitress like Stella who had perfected the dual arts of pouring coffee and serving pie, never missing a heartbeat or comeback. She also served as mother, cafe spouse, and could-be-but-never-will-be girlfriend.

The Old North Side Cafe slips easily into cliché now, branded with stereotypes and familiar situations. There is a Boss Hawg who holds commanding court at the Liar's Table. There is the weathered collection of men, and a few women, who visit the Cafe for morning coffee, an afternoon break, or a Saturday escape from the inexhaustible list of household chores. They are the town merchants and service people, farmers, professionals, retired-but-searching, not-yet-old men, and anyone lucky enough to have free time for coffee. You will recognize all the men, their wives and children; Stella, the cook, and the cashier. You have known each character in one form or another your entire life.

Cafes exist wherever there are stories. The Old North Side Cafe is one of a million campfires, saloons, beauty shops, feed stores, church basements, libraries, and now, fast food restaurants or grocery stores, where people gather to form their life's narrative. The setting, technology, context, and culture continue to change and evolve, but the need to tell and hear stories never goes out of date. Life and death, love and sacrifice, sex and sin, all abound in the North Side men, the full-leaded coffee they drink, the thick-sliced cured bacon they crave, and the peach cobbler with ice cream that tops every afternoon. It all comes with a heaping helping of Stella, and an unquenchable thirst for the company of friends.

The Old North Side Cafe on these pages is a mixture of 1950s Hatfield's Sporting Goods in St. Joseph, Missouri, the original North Side Cafe on the north side of the square in Savannah, Missouri, and a Waid's (later Trail's End) Restaurant in Liberty, Missouri. The stories are from the 1960s to the present, pretty much as they were first told in a local weekly newspaper column. The men are my dad, father-in-law, and my grandfather. They are the guys I knew in five different churches and three towns, and a lovely waitress I hold in my heart to this day.

The stories are pretty much exactly as they were told – sometimes to the entire group, but more often among two to five men. Some stories I witnessed. They actually were never shared at the Cafe. I swear, some of these stories were hilarious the first time around. Some, like the ones about drinking and people with different lifestyles, cannot be understood in today's "modern" sensibility. Drunks, thankfully, are no longer as funny as they once were. People with disabilities and alternative lifestyles are now better understood and appreciated … at least in some places. On the other hand, in today's world, folks sometimes wonder about the kindness the Cafe characters so openly shared with strangers. We don't do that so much anymore. Almost anything you are about to read about politicians and politics, taxes, government regulations, and lawyers has not changed since the first curmudgeonly cave men found a fire to sit around and complain. From that day to this, many people still think they know what life is about, what's <u>right</u> … but Cafe boys know better.

Stories define our lives. How you tell a story can change the whole meaning. Stories are more powerful because the narrative lasts longer than the facts, and is easier to believe. The characters live out the same plots with different outcomes. Nothing is new, but everything is different when a story is told well. The Old North Side Cafe is the day-to-day story of a time and place that is always retelling and reinventing itself; always thinking in a new way. Life's old stories are some-how told again and again, but each becomes its own truth.

Come on in! Do you smell the coffee and hear the clinking of porcelain cups? The background hubbub of voices permeates the air. Stella, the lovely waitress, grabs your elbow and leads you over to Water Street Pete, the Boss Hawg. "Wel-come stranger," Pete says pointing to a chair. "New blood is always appreciated. Just be sure you don't take anything anybody says too seriously. Half these boys forgot to take their medication this morning."

Someday you will hardly remember your first introduction to the crew. Later, you might meet Larry, who owns the Cafe, and the kids who come and go washing dishes. There are Stella's gay friends who help put on the Thanksgiving dinner. The hubbub rises, and you settle into your chair and take a place. Like most new things, it will require some time to know what's really going on. At the Cafe, the men call this "intuitive, longitudinal learning," and if you believe that, Water Street Pete will have your lunch every day. However, things will gradually make sense. Day-by-day-by-day, the Cafe talk, the unsaid acts of kindness, the piling on of meaning and experiences all add up. Pretty soon, you are all friends who actually care about each other. It isn't like blood family, or the guys you knew in high school and the military. It is a softer, more flexible kind of connection. If you let them, the stories and storytellers can begin to create something more than the sum of their parts.

"I once saw a tree explode into flames," Gladstone Gus said, rubbing a napkin across his mouth. "A hyperactive woodpecker started that fire." It takes a while, but slowly some of the men finally get the joke. This is the kind nonsense that you must put up with if you come to the Cafe. In time however, real things happen. Nobody ever sees it coming. You won't see it either. That is how stories usually work.

Yep, people think they know life. They don't! It is hard to look past behaviors and bravado to the feelings inside. It is feelings – things like heartbreak, fear, sorrow, longing and joy – that run the human show. You can't know how folk "feel" about things without putting in a lot of time and effort, and banking a load of pure trust. Stubborn, crotchety, and insensitive old codgers sometimes carry buckets of hurt and burlap bags of hope in every step. If you really want to know life, you must come to the Cafe where the stories never end, and woodpeckers burn down trees.

Cafe's Cast of Characters

Water Street Pete

Pete once predicted his victory before winning a hotdog eating contest at age six (22 dogs). He got moderately rich selling candy bars out of his backpack in sixth grade. By the time he graduated from high school, he ran a junk food empire with representatives in seven different grades. Pete's senior year included a fast car, a white sports coat, and a basement room filled with music, cigar smoke, every magazine on earth, and a giant easy chair from which he ruled a considerable kingdom of juvenile delight.

Pete served in the Army and saw action in the Pacific Theater during WWII. He does not talk about that time in his life. Eventually, Pete supplied sports equipment and medical supplies to high schools and colleges across Missouri. He knew every coach and cafe in every town. He was an avid sportsman who hunted every nook and cranny of Missouri. Every man he met became his friend. Pete paid a lot of coffee tabs that were not his own, and kept track of every small town athlete, prom queen, politician, and entrepreneur. He read newspapers and followed a thousand sports teams. Pete always had a dog.

Pete also attended every event for which he had an invitation. He had charm and a way with words, and soon enough, he was well known throughout the state. There was a collection of buddies with whom he traveled the world hunting and fishing, going to sports events, trying out restaurants and even playing some golf.

Pete learned to cook, and set up his own kitchen in his basement. That kitchen was far nicer than the one his wife used. Once a year he hosted a "Wild Game Feast" that featured all sorts of exotic meats (all shot by Pete and Friends), good whiskey and cigars. Pete said he made the "Worlds' Best Chili" – and probably, he did. Pete loved to tell his famous chili story. After cooking his famous chili for about six hours, Pete left the enormous kettle on the floor to "rest". His dog caught the scent and started eating the chili. Pete then had to decide if he could go ahead and serve the chili to his friends with dog slobber in it.

As he got older, Pete lorded over the "Liar's Table" at the Cafe. One fall, the *Kansas City Star* newspaper did a big feature story (complete with pictures) on Pete in which they called him the "Boss Hawg". Pete could not have been more proud. Pete was never mean, but he did not tolerate stupidity of any sort. Liberal or conservative, young or old, man or woman, the Boss Hawg would keep you in line. He loved a joke (dirty jokes too) and he told a thousand stories that could take your breath away. As for politics, Pete was the sort of Conservative who never wanted anything done for the first time.

Pete ran the show wherever he went. He knew and cared for every member of his tribe. When the conversation broke down at the cafe, he picked it up. He was so well read and knowledgeable, Pete almost single-handedly educated the cafe crowd on the issues of the day. More than any other person, he made the North Side Cafe one of the very special places on earth. He was that kind of man. Yet, and unfortunately, Pete, like a few men of his era, could be a bigot, an unexplainable blind spot in an otherwise good man.

Water Street Pete ate too much, partied too hard, and burned his candle from both ends. He got fat. His knees went out, and he went from one cane to two; then a walker, and eventually an easy chair where he lived out the last days of his life before his heart finally just quit. Pete slipped away.

In his day, Pete's place was at the head of the great Liar's Table where he commanded respect and allegiance. The men all loved him. Stella, however, and a lot of other women, was not so sure. Pete could make anything interesting, and then he could make it controversial. He knew how to get people revved-up, and/or shut-up. You can see him now – both hands in the air, an infectious smile on his face, a born leader able to make the world turn at his will. He was the Boss Hawg! And YES! Of course he served that chili with the dog slobber still in it. Then he told the men the entire story. It was the best chili they would ever have.

Manor Hill Mack

Mack was a poor farm boy from Northeast Iowa. During the winters, he moved into town with another family so he could attend public school, a common practice in those days. His friends called him Dynamite because he was strong and could fight hard, despite his small size.

After a major dust-up with his brother, Mack left his home at age 16 and eventually joined the Air Force. He became an assistant to a colonel, and spent WWII flying around the United States carrying important papers and running errands for his boss.

Mack never got to compete in high school sports because they interfered with chores, but he was the fastest man in his Air Force unit. His considerable athletic skills would one day repeat themselves in his sons, one of whom became an all-American in two sports.

While Mack was stationed at Rosecrans Airport, then located in Missouri before the river flooded and placed the airport in Kansas, he had a blind date with a woman from St. Joe. She was the love of his life. Mack labored the next 40 years fixing furnaces, checking for gas leaks, reading meters and becoming the comforting human face of "natural gas" to a small country town. Each day at 10 a.m. and 2 p.m., Mack had coffee at the local cafe.

Mack was a deacon at the First Baptist Church, a member of the Masonic lodge, and the heart and soul of fast pitch softball in Northwest Missouri. Pick a Friday or a Saturday night in the summer, and he was at a rural ballpark umpiring three or four games. When Mack called a pitch, he would turn to his right, point his finger smartly in the air and call for all to hear, "Sttrrrrriiiiiiiike one." He was famous, and often more fun to watch than the softball game itself.

Mack attended every sporting event his kids ever participated in, and started coaching a little league team two years before his first son was eligible to play so he could get the "coaching thing" down. Pete gave him the sports equipment. When his children left home, Mack created the first-ever T-ball and then pitching machine leagues in his town so his grandkids (girls included) could learn to play baseball. It was during this time of his life Mack achieved his greatest accomplishment. Mack was an extraordinary grandfather! He bought bikes just to have them around in case the grandkids came by. He poured a cement slab at his back door that worked as a patio/basketball court (then he put bars on the back windows because so many got broken). He coached each of his grandkids in every sport, and they all became famous high school athletes.

Mack never bought a mutual fund, never had tax shelter, never took a fancy vacation and never got the things money can buy. Mack was a simple farm boy from Iowa. He was a union man and a fiscally conservative Democrat. He did not tolerate bigotry in his home, and was known to provide meals to people in need (much to his wife's chagrin). He often served as the town nut! He wore bright, spray-painted green boots on Saint Pat's Day, and dressed up as Santa at Christmas to hand out presents (presents he could not afford) to children going through hard times.

Mack's flaw was his temper. All his life he struggled to keep it under control. He was known to just get up and leave the Cafe when he was about to get mad.

One early summer day, Mack bought a new wheelbarrow and shovel to start digging, by hand, a basement under his termite-ridden house. The dirt from the basement leveled his back yard. Mack learned how to jack up his house, lay concrete block, pour a cement basement floor, and repair termite damage. His handmade basement was a testimony to a grit and resolve few folk today can comprehend.

Mack was solid. He was a doer, and he loved kids and sports with a tender passion. It seemed like the entire town came to his funeral. People like Mack don't exist so much anymore. Our modern culture doesn't have much room for a man who cares deeply about other people's children, just as much as his own.

City Hall Sam

In another day and time, Sam would have been a self-made millionaire. He could do anything. He made people feel safe, and they instantly trusted him. He had an ability to stay calm in times of crisis. Nobody ever saw Sam lose his cool. Eventually he was elected to the City Council where he seemed to serve forever, always providing common sense guidance to his town. His children went on to become very important people who ran large companies, served on important boards and made big money.

Sam was an African American. He was a Negro. He was black. As a result, in those days, he was the head custodian at the junior high school, and not president of some company. Sam was so competent, so good at his job that the school's shiny, well-kept presence and calm atmosphere permeated every aspect of the education his school provided. Everyone – teachers, students and parents – knew it was Sam's School. Sam, who never had a chance to attend college, took what was possible and made it work.

Today we understand there are all kinds of intelligence. There is book learning, conceptual skills, social intelligence, the ability to focus on a problem until a solution is reached, and so on. Sam had the entire package. Sam used his skills and talents to rise above the subtle racism that infected rural, small-town life. He was the Jackie Robinson of Cafe history. Sam was such a good man he forced everyone to meet him, and his race, on a higher plain.

Sam's greatest loves were his church, his faith and his family. When Sam prayed, you wanted to be standing close to him because you knew he had a direct line. But here is the most amazing thing about Sam. He was humble. He was the most unassuming, gentle, treat-everyone-with-respect-and-kindness person you might ever meet. He was a graceful man with a slight body, easy movements, and a voice like molasses. Not many (none) cafe crews included an African American in their group during this time in small town Missouri. He was an anomaly of immense significance. Sam was a minor miracle for his time in more ways than most Caucasians could ever know.

Camelot Bob

Bob was a Navy educated, blue-collar worker, who held ultraconservative, racist, and male-chauvinist opinions. He had a big mouth and often did not think before he spoke. He liked to say things like, "This is just the way I am, take it or leave it!" And, "The peace sign is the footprint of the American chicken." And, "God made Adam and Eve, not Adam and Steve!"

When Manor Hill Mack's long-haired son came into the Cafe one afternoon, Bob asked him if he "squatted to pee?" Bob did not worry about facts, feelings, or how much things cost. His plumbing/construction business grew into a mighty empire when Hallmark Cards hired him to build all of their stores. By the time he got to the Cafe, he was the richest man in town. There was not a close second. Bob bullied or bought his way into just about everything and that includes the Cafe. Here is a sampling of some of Bob's most famous quotes:

Concerning "Mexicans" coming in to work at the local hog farm: *"For the last 35 years the USA has aborted more than a million babies just so liberals could import foreigners to be our workforce."*

Referring to Clinton's impeachment: *"This idea about not kicking someone when they are down is b.s. Not only do you kick him, you kick him until he passes out— then beat him over the head with a tire iron—then roll him up in an old rug—and set him on fire."*

While explaining his support for Israel: *"The Holocaust happened because God allowed it to happen… because God said, 'My top priority for the Jewish people is to get them back to Israel.'"*

On how to protect our children from violence: *"This Christmas I want you to do the most loving thing I can think of… I want you to buy each of your children an assault rifle, 1000 rounds of ammunition, and teach them to shoot straight."*

On how to fight terrorism: *"America's increasing decadence is giving aid and comfort to the enemy. When we tolerate trash on television, permit pornography on the Internet, and allow babies to be aborted, we are playing into the hands of radical Islam."*

On women's liberation: *"Women cry rape when men dump them."*

Only one man, Water Street Pete, could handle Bob. He did it by making Bob look like an idiot when he got too far out of line. Pete would roll his eyes and say something like, "Bob is that the same mouth you eat with?" The men laughed and Bob would sit quietly and fume.

Camelot Bob and Holly Lake Jake were the two polar opposites at the Cafe and their arguments were legendary. Bob hated welfare, climate change, rebellion of any kind, male hairdressers and florists, any soft and cuddly creature, and above all things, Democrats. Bob was so outrageous he became a caricature, a cartoon replication of himself. That was Bob's saving grace. He was obnoxious and narrow-minded to the point of being plain funny.

Every day Bob arrived at the Cafe in some outrageously expensive Eddie Bauer outfit, said stupid things, and Water Street Pete eventually slammed him to the mat like some heel in professional wrestling. It was hilarious, and it never got old.

There was one other thing. Bob was a member of the Cafe family. So, no matter how out-of-line he got, he always had a "family" card he could play. That is how it works at a small town cafe. The rules aren't much for kicking anybody out, and it's standard for there to be one upstart in the group. For his part, Bob slipped men money when they had hard times, no questions asked and no repayment required. He visited his buddies in the hospital, and he brought excellent wine to the Wild Game Feast. If all this sounds amazing to you, ponder this. Bob and Jake would do anything for each other. In the Cafe family, they can fight like mad dogs, but let something happen to either one outside the Cafe and they are there for each other – with the care and will to make things better.

Holly Lake Jake

Jake is religious, very religious; but he is never obnoxious or "holier-than-thou" about it. He prays before every meal. He studies his "marked-up" Bible, and he rarely misses church (where he teaches an adult Sunday School class, and has been known to be a stiff critic of weak sermons). He gives 10 percent of his income to the church, and then gives more money to any cause that helps the poor. Jake is also a poet, storyteller and a preacher who tries hard to do the right thing. He gets upset when he doesn't meet the high expectations he has for himself.

Jake is a bleeding heart liberal through and through. There was never a labor union, a government program, or a school tax that he didn't champion. Education was a great, important thing to Jake, and he believed in helping everyone get the best education possible. Jake also loved books. In his mature adulthood, he would take to his back yard to sit underneath a pear tree and read. He always had his trusted jelly jar glass, filled with lemon tea and ice, to slowly sip the afternoon away.

Because Jake was of Arkansas hayseed heritage, he understood and loved hot and humid weather, the glory of a fish on-line, and he could spit a mean watermelon seed. He also knew one measure of a man was how he "showed up", and so even on the warmest day of summer, Jake mowed his lawn wearing a tie.

Nothing about Jake was fancy or ostentatious. He liked life simple and plain. His claim to fame, however, was a creative streak, his stories and infectious laugh. Jake actually thought about things; so, when he talked, the men never knew exactly where he was going to come from, or just where he might go. Jake would start out talking about men making moonshine whiskey in some backwoods hollow still near the river back of his farm, and then end up talking about bombing Iraq – somehow he always made sense.

Jake and his daughter had a special relationship. He loved that girl and would do anything for her. When his daughter asked her dad to watch her kids, fix her car, loan her money, or take her to the store, Jake was there. As a result, Jake ended up spending a lot of time with his two grandsons. On a Sunday afternoon after church, they would "make camp" in his backyard, which means they cooked hot-dogs over an illegal fire and then "marched" around the sand box doing "drills". He loved those boys!

Jake spent WWII picking mosquitoes one by one out of a trap to help researchers find a cure for malaria. He did not like the idea of killing things, but he would sacrifice a mosquito or two. Jake liked a great choir, a violin virtuoso, theater, opera and all things literary. Single-handedly he raised the artistic IQ of the entire Cafe.

Far and away, Jake was the best storyteller at the North Side. He had stories the men asked to hear over and over. When Jake and his daughter took the oldest grandson to his first year of college, Jake calmed the nerves and stopped the tears by telling one amazing story after another – an eight-hour story tour de force. You will read a lot of Jake's work in this book. Jake was the quiet confidant of all the Cafe men, but he selected Camelot Bob as his special project. The men all wondered how Bob and Jake became friends. Well, they became friends because Jake willed it to happen.

One more thing. Though he was extremely tight with his money, Jake always tipped Stella way more than the check amount, because that was the kind of person he wanted to be.

Gladstone Gus

Gus was a bit younger than the other men, and more a product of the Vietnam era than WWII or Korea. Gus often wore his hair a little long and sometimes had a beard. He played guitar, had smoked dope, and liked to camp out with his kids on a mountain pass or lonely beach. He drove a small grey pickup truck. Gus wore shorts, sandals and a necklace with some kind of foreign gold coin he claimed was minted the same year he was born.

Gus was spiritual and sometimes religious. He had a gentle soul and a naïveté about things that did not square with a few people, or his experiences, or places he had been. Gus liked folk music, dancing, riding around in his truck, and for a real good time, he might go watch three movies in one day. He was born country and had blacktop roads, corn silos, river fishing and John Deere tractors imprinted deep into his soul. He had milked cows by hand, made real churned butter, played small-town Friday night football, and gotten arrested for throwing toilet paper in the trees around Andy Anderson's house.

Gus would have been an authentic, Good Ole Boy if it had not been for books and having his knee blown out by a vicious football hit. The books, which he read voraciously, made him want to see the world, and the bad knee gave him the freedom to explore something besides sports. Gus was in San Francisco for the Summer of Love and in New York City at the Whiskey a Go-Go the night Martin Luther King was shot. Gus was camped on the Big Thompson River above Fort Collins, Colorado, the day Nixon resigned from the presidency. He was in a small town school, sitting in study hall, when he heard the announcement that President Kennedy had been shot dead. His school chums stood to cheer when they heard Kennedy had been assassinated. Gus walked away and played hooky from school that sad day. His disappointment and disbelief in his peers left him bewildered.

Gus eventually settled into a high school teaching career, and then went into communications and public relations work. Gus liked people and he especially enjoyed kids. He volunteered for every public service position his city had to offer, and for much of his life was a fixture at the local Presbyterian Church. Gus, along with Jake, kept the Cafe honest. They kept the Cafe, and this is important to know, from tilting way too far to the right and a narrow, conservative take on things. Gus knew nothing was as black and white, as some people thought, and he was able to give everyone the benefit of doubt.

Finally, Gus got a little extreme with his emotions at times. The boys understood this, and let some things pass now and then. Still, nobody could light up a room like old Gus when he was on. His stories of travel and adventure riveted men to their seats, and left them staring in disbelief. At the Wild Game Feast, Gus would break out his guitar and sing original, and hilarious songs. His kindness, sincerity and willingness to help, put the best face possible on his annoying and naïve, liberal ways.

Ridgeway Ron

Ron was the oldest guy in the group. Nobody ever knew just how old he was until he died, and they learned he was 96. He did not look or act that old. Ron was a farmer. He had lost several fingers to a farming accident, and had permanent "farmer stripes" (sunburn lines) on his forehead and forearms. Like every farmer who ever walked a field, Ron always thought things were about to "Go to hell in a hand basket." If it did not rain for a week, he thought a drought was coming. A few sprinkles meant floods. He was perpetually "broke" though he lived in a giant house (at least five additions) and drove a new red or black pickup every year. Ron carried around a wad of cash rolled up in a rubber band that he used to buy a new 70-inch TV or Weber BBQ grill on a whim.

It's cliché, but Ron actually wore a seed cap, a blue-collar shirt and overalls. In his overalls he kept a pencil, notepad and pocket watch. He wore boots, sported a blue and white Big Smith handkerchief, and never went anywhere without his pliers and Buck pocketknife. Ron never admitted he was sick, never complained of aches and pains, and got up every morning at 5:00 a.m. He was a farmer! He liked dogs but would never let one in his house; and, truth be told, Ron would die before he would let a dog lick his face. He liked eggs and hated chickens (farmers know the truth about chickens). He thought cows were amazingly dumb animals and wondered why anyone would ever, and he really meant "ever," romanticize them. Cats were sneaky, but useful on a farm.

Lunch in Ron's world was called "dinner", and dinner was the big meal of the day. For almost 50 years Ron ate a giant (starch imbued and mostly fried) dinner and then immediately went back to backbreaking labor. Ron ate bacon, eggs, toast, grits, molasses and/or jelly every morning. He drank a gallon of coffee each day and actually liked buttermilk. His arteries remained wide open, he stayed skinny, and slept like a baby every night.

Ron does not understand antiques and wonders why anyone would have old, broken-down furniture decorating their house. He thinks putting an "antique" butter churn or milk can on your porch is stupid, and he will tell you so. Ron likes big trucks and green farm machines. He likes toy tractors, 4-wheelers, his easy chair and a goodnight snack. The men all love Ron, but he has no idea what that means. His stories are as dry as Oklahoma dust, and he still would rather talk about the price of soybeans than just about anything else, except a football game he did not have time to watch. He is a master of understatement and wit. Ron likes to check the sky and then look at the pocket watch he keeps in his overalls. He keeps track of things. He knows everything that is going on and every bad thing that could happen in the next few hours. Ron is a living, breathing example of what a Missouri farmer used to be.

Stella the Waitress

Stella had it all for the first part of her life. She was married to a big-time farmer, had four children and a big house, and took vacations on "cruise" ships. She drove a huge van with swiveling captain seats, Bose stereo, leather trim, smoked windows, and at least 30 cup holders. Stella was the consummate gentleman farmer's wife. She was beautiful, adorable, and always just on the plump side of perfect. Her hair was big and stiff, her make-up just a bit caked, and her heart was pure as Spanish gold.

Stella hosted giant breakfasts in her home for every major holiday. Everybody was invited and everyone came. She was a down-home Martha Stewart with a recipe for everything a farmer ever raised or wanted to eat. Stella was president of the PTA, head of the church hospitality committee, and chair of the sesquicentennial cookbook. She had one foot on the farm and one foot in town society, and the stretch marks to prove it.

Stella did not know how unhappy she was with her "great" life until her no-good husband up and left one day with another woman and a new family. There is always more to a story like this, and not much is accomplished by placing blame. But here's what happened. The no-good husband used the legal system to get the farm, the money, and the "farm sale" proceeds (he had deeded everything in the new girlfriend's name). Stella and the kids moved to a small house in town where they learned to live cheap.

Stella took the job as the Cafe waitress and all her varied skills began to shine. She could pour coffee with one hand while she served pie and ice cream with the other. She directed traffic with her head while her eyes controlled conversations and told men where to sit. Not even Pete could best her in slinging just the right insult to shut somebody up or make a crabby old man laugh. The Old North Side was strictly a man's world, but it was ruled by a woman.

Stella could be angry at times, but the scars left from her marriage became her reminder to stay soft and kind to others who were not as fortunate. She was always no-nonsense smart and efficient as she fed the homeless and cared for the hurting. She also had an unnerving, almost spooky ability to know what would happen in the future. "I can tell that's not going to work," she would predict about some hair-brained scheme Jake might come up with, and she was always right. The men all loved Stella.

Stella had lost a child to a car accident. She felt she was to blame, and that is a significant part of her life's arc. It may explain some things about her altruism and endless sense of duty, and why she hated mirrors. Yes, the men all knew her story and that knowledge gave her a vague authority. It also served to keep the men tender and protective with her. Larry, the man who owned the Cafe, let her slip food to the needy and open the North Side on Thanksgiving. Stella used that holiday to feed those who were not wanted by their families or had no other place to go.

Stella was really something in her early life, but after her dark night(s) of the soul, she became a true force of nature. She filled rooms with joy, she inspired generations of young people who came through her home, and she became a saint to the outcast and the poor. Stella's children grew up strong and confident. They all learned the value of a dollar, how to work hard, and the importance of family. They will sacrifice for each other and stick together now even when controversy would tear some siblings apart. After her sorrows, Stella did not find herself a new life, she created one. Watch for her in the background of every story. Everywhere you look, you will find Stella.

Chapter 1

Philosophy

René Descartes walks into a restaurant and sits down for dinner. The waiter comes over and asks if he'd like an appetizer. "I think not!" Descartes says, and POOF, he disappeared. City Hall Sam tells that joke at the Cafe every few years, and nobody ever gets it.

If Descartes had been correct about, "I think, therefore I am", the Cafe would be empty most days. Thankfully, you don't actually have to think to come to the North Side. Most Cafe guys build their thoughts from watching TV, listening to Rush Limbaugh and Glenn Beck, or playing the old tapes of what they heard their parents say when they were little. That is as far as their philosophizing goes. The Cafe believes academic philosophy is best kept in college classes and out of real life. Personal philosophy and truth, on the other hand, are the lifeblood of the Cafe. Within this framework, there is actually some individual contemplation that truly borders on thought.

Camelot Bob believes the Bible is very clear about the earth being 5,000 years old, and that means Jesus rode dinosaurs. Bob also knows climate change is nonsense. Ridgeway Ron is not sure we ever went to the moon and cannot believe Lee Harvey Oswald acted alone to shoot John F. Kennedy. City Hall Sam believes in aliens. Manor Hill Mack believes in the unions. Nobody believes in Allah, but they all believe in God, except for Gladstone Gus, who thinks it is complicated.

No one at the Old North Side Cafe, with the exception of Holly Lake Jake, would ever think of himself or herself as a philosopher, and for good reason. As a rule, philosophers usually end up dead before their time – just ask Aristotle. Philosophy scares people half to death, and the conversations at the Cafe bring witness to this fear of "thinking too much about things". What you believe is actually a personal choice not based on fact. In fact, a belief does not necessarily even need to be true. That makes your personal philosophy a wonderful and unique thing. Personal philosophy is worthy of hours of wrangling over made-up facts, debating nonsense, ignoring truth, and delivering sassy comebacks concerning one's purpose in life and place in eternity.

On another level, however, the day-to-day philosophy of life that permeates the Cafe is remarkably rigid, timeless, and understood. The old guys talk it into the ground until life's truths are a fine dust that settles on every concrete item and intangible idea.

- What is God?
- What is love?
- What is real?

All of these impossibly difficult questions have been meticulously worked through in discussions ranging from ghosts and fortune telling, to unfaithful wives and dying pets. Men mull over memories and the nagging complexities of time and begin to understand it is better to let some things be. Truths worn thin by tradition, ritual and Bible study mean these men don't have to think too hard on life's thorniest problems; the final "truth" has metastasized into deeply held feelings that are harder than Camelot Bob's head.

When the men talk of their families, their faith, and friends, a stunning bit of passion and resolve colors every word. The things that are true to them are filled to the brim with honor and sacrifice. This intangible truth is then born again in action. They sit with one another at the hospital, they gather for the rituals – feasts (Wild Game Feast), the clashing of wits (cards), birth, baptism, and marriage. They come by when they fear something might be wrong with a buddy, and they stick together when someone is challenged. They compromise their strongest beliefs each day in order to stay together. Like most men their age, they like to act tough and impermeable, but their hearts are tender, and their emotions leak through their eyes and hands, and, eventually, into their actions. They "opt for the relationship". They choose people over process. What is "real" to them is a genuine love for one another. And, that in turn, is what they know of God.

Now, philosophy takes a natural curveball in politics (more on politics later). There are, of course, two camps: liberals, who mostly vote the Democrat ticket, and conservatives, mostly voting Republican. Your philosophy on life dictates the camp. Those who favor order, good business, the death penalty (but oppose abortion); and are for swift and certain retribution, secret sex, following the rules, Ronald Reagan, and never doing anything for the first time, are the conservatives. Liberals are for partying, forgiving, moving on, tolerance, flexible rules, sex, and endlessly reinventing the wheel. These different positions give all of them plenty to talk (argue) about.

Philosophy as a sport, complete with all the sports metaphors, means they figuratively run over, drill, crush, and pancake each other. It is a beautiful thing to watch, depending on your testosterone level. Camelot Bob can live forever on a good, personal philosophy fight; Holly Lake Jake – not so much. Therefore, as usual, the Republican conservatives take the day. They just wear the poor liberals out. That means Camelot Bob gets the last word every time:

"Boys, you may remember that on July 8, 1947, several eye-witnesses claimed an unidentified object with five aliens on board crashed on a sheep and cattle ranch just outside Roswell, New Mexico. You all know of this event. It has been talked about for many years. I am here today to tell you this actually happened. The truth has been covered up long enough by the U.S. Air Force and the federal government. Here is the truth about that incident; you can look it up yourself. The spaceship, with all those aliens, actually landed in March 1948. That is exactly nine months before the births of Albert Arnold Gore, Jr., Hillary Rodham, John F. Kerry, William Jefferson Clinton, Howard Dean, Nancy Pelosi, Dianne Feinstein, Charles E. Schumer, and Barbara Boxer." Bob now gets deathly serious. "My fellow Americans, we have been infested, and then inbred, by alien liberals. No wonder our poor country has gone to hell!" Bob doesn't seem to be kidding.

Stay Busy and Have Fun

A recent study of around 400 schoolchildren concluded that at this age, real happiness doesn't lie in wealth or celebrity status, but in doing something that is fun or worthwhile in and of itself.

The psychologists, who were studying the beliefs of these children (between the ages of nine and 12), also found that depressed children were more likely to think that happiness/fulfillment came from the acquisition of money, fame and beauty. Children who tended to value things like wealth and appearance, over actual talent or achievement, were at greater risk of being depressed. Better-balanced children were more likely to believe that feeling good came from having lots of friends and doing activities that were fun.

Manor Hill Mack could have told you that and saved the experts a lot of trouble and expense. Holly Lake Jake, Water Street Pete, City Hall Sam, Stella the Waitress, and all the gang know about happiness because, unlike the pundits and academics, they actually are happy people. Holly Lake Jake leads this discussion, "Most research on happiness is done by 40-something-year-old men and women who are scared silly by death, or it is the product of 'market research'. No advertiser will pay money for research that concludes we don't need money, toys, celebrity, physical beauty and personal power to be truly happy. The youth and beauty worshipers promote a vision of beauty that is actually unhealthy and a regimen of physical fitness that defies logic. Nobody NEEDS to run a marathon or have perfect skin to be healthy." Jake is on a roll.

Here's what the Cafe crowd knows about happiness:

- First, it is not for sale; it can be rented for short periods, but that's it. Once you are above the poverty level, money might actually make you less happy. This certainly is true for a majority of lottery winners.

- People who are super-conscious about their health, or possess great beauty, are not any happier than the rest of the population, and interestingly enough, happiness is by far the better indicator of who will live a long life.

- What really makes a difference is a reasonably good and stable marriage, good friends, a willingness to help others, and yes, a spiritual life. People who put their efforts in these areas have a much better recipe for growing old well.

- Being neurotic about your health is actually a threat to a long, healthy life.

- Also, attitude is, as they say, everything. Glass half-empty people are not only unhappy, they are at greater risk for all kinds of diseases.

"If you want to be happy and give yourself a chance for a long life, there is irrefutable, fact-based information to guide you," Jake concludes. "You will never see this on TV or hear it from anybody trying to sell any product, however. If you want to have a long and happy life, use your life to do something that is fun or worthwhile. There are happy people who have overcome unimaginable obstacles, because they still do things that give them joy and have meaning."

Overcome now with how happy he feels, Jake orders a piece of coconut cream pie. He plans to go to church on Sunday. "Learn to laugh at yourself. Help others, stay busy, and make it fun. It's a good life!" Jake pontificates.

Water Street Pete and Camelot Bob, of course, want to throw up.

Where To Go When Something Is Wrong

A lot of jaw flappers haunt the Old North Side. As a result, some pretty incredible stories drift around the tables now and then. Mostly, just silly stuff like the time Holly Lake Jake found the dog. Actually, Jake's grandson found the dog, but the dog ended up with Jake when the boy's mother ruled out any possibility of her boy keeping the dog. It was obvious to Jake the dog was a purebred, and his suspicions were confirmed by a local veterinarian who said it was a pointer of worthy lineage. Jake took a shine to the dog. Nothing could prepare him, however, for the amazing event that was to occur.

It was a lazy spring evening when Jake took the dog for a walk in the country. Without warning, the little puppy went on perfect point. His body was rigid with expectation. Jake knelt down to get a direct sightline on what the dog had found. Jake was bitterly disappointed. There was no game. In fact, there was nothing but a dusty road and an abandoned mailbox. Jake scolded the dog that still did not break point. In a moment, however, Jake understood the true brilliance of the dog. The name on the mailbox was "Bob White." When men tell such stories at the Cafe, a shower of napkins cascade onto the perpetrator. "It's the truth, I swear it," said Jake, as a wadded napkin hit his coffee cup and splashed his cuff.

Then Jake started again. He put on a serious voice like he was going to say something special. "My older brother is like a dad to me. I don't really remember my dad much. He died when I was young. There were a lot of us kids, and this brother; he was the one who took care of me," said Jake. Somehow, the mood changed at the Cafe. Jake's voice held a tender edge. You could feel emotion slipping through the inflection of the words. "He was the first one to ever tell me that story. He could tell stories better than anybody I ever knew," said Jake. That was all Jake said, but to these men, they all knew something was wrong with Jake's brother. Jake did not talk that way unless something was wrong. That's the way it is at the North Side.

That night, Jake's buddies began calling, and one-by-one, they happened by, for no real reason, just to say hello. They talked about the grass they had planted or how the Royals were doing. Sometimes, they did not talk at all. Jake knew why they were there, and it made a difference as Jake worried about his older brother's illness.

If the North Side was just a place to flap jaws and tell stories, it wouldn't be worth sour grain. But the North Side is a safe harbor. It is a campfire, a tree house, and the hidden fort for aging men. In a nation enamored with self-service, these guys like looking out for each other, and they do. They make a joke about almost anything, but they hold together in times of trouble. Some say that's smarter than a mailbox-reading dog.

Jake Finds Andrew's Rock

First, there were the robins, and then the crocuses. A surprising swarm of bugs flew by in a mating frenzy back by where the pear tree used to be. At twilight, wild geese now call on the downwind, moving north. At the back door, muddy shoes gather after a surprise rain, and closed cars are surprisingly hot. It's still light at 8:30 p.m., and keeping the grass mowed is a growing concern. Spring has come at last to the old Cafe.

Holly Lake Jake slipped on his gloves and surveyed the battlefield. Jake has never known a time of peace. His battle against crabgrass, dandelions, nut grass, grubs, and weather has been a life's undertaking. His father before him knew no peace. Johnson grass, push mowers, drought, and gophers plagued Jake's dad as far back as memory served. The power of weeds, pestilence, blight, and natural elements is far too great for any mortal. Jake, like his dad before, is bound for defeat. All fall eventually to their lawns. Still, it's a glorious struggle with a few minor victories. One year, Jake actually had apples. Two years ago, the tulips were glorious. Perhaps this would be the year for roses or – and this is a thought to treasure – irises. It is not winning or losing but the <u>doing</u> that counts. It is nurturing the good and making a commitment to try.

Today, Jake made his first foray into the winter-plagued rock garden. His Japanese yews were still growing, but that was about it. Jake carefully moved the rocks out, ready to rake and spade. The ground was moist, and the clean smell of freshly turned earth lifted his spirits. He was glad to be back in the garden. His spade turned up a rock just slightly smaller than a softball. It was gnarled on one side with worn gray and black bumps. Heavy like granite, yet more smooth and illuminated like quartz, Jake lifted the rock for examination. He remembered this rock. The rock was from Malvern, Arkansas. It was from Andrew's grave. Jake's grandson, Andrew, was born prematurely, before his lungs had a chance to finish forming. He lived just a few days. Jake helped dig the baby's grave in the rocky Arkansas soil. The rock came from the soil of that sad day.

A robin, chirping merrily from a nearby pin oak tree, broke Jake's thought. He weighed the rock in his hand and turned it over. "Andrew," he said the name out loud and liked the sound. An easy breeze was rattling the last rusty leaves in the oak, and a second robin flew in. "Andrew," he said again, softly. Jake put the rock with the others he had found and went about raking and spading. He noticed red peony shoots were budded. He liked peonies; big fragrant flowers with a thousand ants crawling over them. "There's not a little kid around who doesn't get a thrill discovering ants on peony buds," he thought.

The day wore on as Jake raked five giant bags of leaves, dug in the garden, and checked the hostas and ferns on the east side of the house. Eventually, he got back to the rock pile in the front garden. Each rock had a spot. He put Andrew's rock over by the peonies; it would do well there.

Years ago, he had wondered why he kept the rock. Now maybe he knew. What a season this is, filled with surprise and wonder; life all around. Who knows what treasures are buried, waiting to be found.

War Is A Weapon Of Mass Destruction

by Holly Lake Jake

"The belief in the possibility of a short decisive war appears to be one of the most ancient and dangerous of human illusions." — Robert Lynd

Our country needs an intervention. We have put ourselves in a box. We are about to go off to war with another nation. Some of our oldest and dearest friends are openly pleading with us to at least wait. Polls show support for war is dropping daily. Good people, who love our country, are facing ridicule, harassment, and charges of cowardice, because they cannot support a war without doing every last thing for peace.

Caring, thinking people should not lightly join the executioner's side. I'm afraid our anger and frustration over the events of September 11 have left us brittle, half-cocked, and trigger-happy. This machismo, war-mongering rhetoric is not who we are. Our own Civil War, the most costly in U.S. history, took our will and stomach for killing long ago. Somewhere, deep inside most of us, is the notion that we only fight when cornered. We are not aggressors or bullies. Our mistakes in Vietnam demoralized a generation. Sometimes, the generals are wrong. War itself is an abomination; children are the first victims. Fifty percent of Iraq's population is children. Our children will also die in war. Can we visit their graves not knowing we made every sacrifice possible for peace?

The United States will need every modern, industrialized nation to join us in the world-wide effort against terrorism. We simply can't go it alone into war and claim the high ground of moral right. If we are to lead the world, it must be with a solid reputation as peacemakers first and warriors last. Good friends, nations who have had their citizens die with ours in battle, friends who also have children and families and dreams for peace, are asking us to go slow. Fellow Americans are calling us to seek peace first, even at some sacrifice. Peace is the harder, more courageous path. What good will all our wealth and power be if there is no Earth left?

The sacrifice of war is so great. That wild card, once played, can have catastrophic implications. Will we be safer from terrorists by attacking back, when even our close friends are pleading with us to hold back? Will other nations, fearing aggression, only want more weapons of mass destruction to protect themselves? Will the forces of war, confusion and uncertainty, strengthen evil's presence in the world?

Violence does not produce justice. It only weakens our chance to live in peace. Using violence to solve problems only creates bitterness and despair. Soldiers and bombs won't end terrorism. The seeds of the next war are always planted in the blood of the war before. Could we be making a mistake? Have our friends and allies really lost their gumption and their resolve? Is waiting no longer worth the risk? I'll listen a little more. I'm not ready, not yet, to pull the trigger on war.

"Jaw-jaw is better than war-war." — Harold MacMillan

Ghosts Tell Gus Not To Worry

Cafe wisdom says the best way out of difficult times is through them. Gladstone Gus was trying to remember that. "Behind bad luck comes good," Gus kept telling himself as he surveyed the damage wrecked on his holiday season. First, his oldest son's car had broken down twice in the middle of Iowa on the way to and from school. Just as Gus got the car home, the timing belt fixed, and the alternator replaced, the clutch went out. Gus was stoic. Then things got worse.

Gus's wife's car started veering violently to the left, and the repair required three trips to two different mechanics to finally get the car to go straight down the road. His second son's car had been to three different mechanics, and had three different "car operations," to end the banging that came out of the front end. It still bangs; in fact, it is worse.

Gus also had lost his glasses, giving his vision an annoying fuzz. His dog growled whenever he walked in the room. Technology stocks, Gus's only claim to financial glory, explored new lows. "Life is a long lesson in humility," somebody said. Gus learned there was termite damage in his living room, and the new floor tile in the bathroom had cracked. His dog chewed the exquisite leather jacket, a Christmas gift of some expense, he had bought for his son.

Gus sat on the edge of the bed thinking of Job. "Job feels the rod, yet blesses God," his father-in-law likes to say. "The Lord gave, and the Lord hath taken away; blessed be the name of the Lord," is recorded in Job 1:21. Pity parties are not Gus's nature, and he was more upset with feeling sorry for himself than his afflictions. That's when he learned he would need to buy a new refrigerator and stove. Both were "before marriage" appliances that had served the family well for over 22 years. Gus felt his savings hemorrhage. A savings artery had been cut, and the bleeding was coming in gushes. "Misfortunes always come in by a door that has been left open for them," Gus whispered to himself, just as his grandmother had done years before.

The cold and dark of wintertime was no help. With that, the phone rang, and Gus held his breath. He knew another shoe was about to drop, an axe fall, and an ill wind blow, but Gus smiled and found his cheer. Something fundamental in Gus was about to take hold. Its origins he did not know – maybe church, family, or a good gene, but it was there. Gus chose not to worry. Here is a basic truth that is both Gus's curse and blessing and the object of his smile: "The misfortunes hardest to bear are those which never come."

"Good morning," Gus said into the phone. "It's another day in paradise."

Waste Not, Want Not

by Water Street Pete

If you combine the Constitution, Bill of Rights, Bible, Koran, and Boy and Girl Scout creeds, and look for the most commonly used expressions to define "good character", here is the list you will get: loyalty, responsibility, perseverance, optimism, trustworthy, honesty, courageous, respectful, compassionate, adaptable, and contemplative. These values are so embedded in our culture they form the backdrop of what we once were supposed to be like. Think about it! These are the characteristics you would want for a neighbor, co-worker, in-law, or politician.

Baby Boomers grew up with these values. Each night at the dinner table, at family gatherings, or riding in the car to grandma's house (the only vacation we ever took) messages were drilled into baby-boomer noggins. We knew how life was supposed to be. People make fun of us now, but every Baby Boomer knows how to finish these sayings:

Money doesn't grow on _____.
There are starving children in _____.
Don't ever go out wearing dirty underwear; you might be in an _____.
Waste not, want _____.
I'm doing this for your own _____.
Someday, you will _____ for this.
Use it up, wear it out, make it do, or _____.

These, and a thousand more, were hammered deep into our subconscious. Remember TV in the 1950s? *Leave it to Beaver, Father Knows Best,* and *Sky King.* Almost every show reinforced this list of values.

Let's not glorify these times too much. There also was vicious racism; women were treated abysmally in the workplace; and a veil of silence covered important issues like mental health and domestic abuse. But we did have access to some consistent teachings on values. Some TV shows today reinforce these values, but they are not the shows that kids like to watch. Today, there are more TVs in homes than we had channels when we were younger. Those TVs are often tuned to reality shows where the person who cheats and lies the best wins the most.

Kids today just do not have the access to help, guidance and reinforcement that Baby Boomers did. We learned values at home, and not just from our parents. We learned them from relatives and neighborhood adults, and they got reinforced at Sunday School and public school. Where do kids learn character today?

There was a time when 98 percent of our population stayed home and worked on the farm. The farm-based economy changed, and dad left the home to work in a factory. Then mom had to leave the home to go to work. Now children are so involved in activities and school, they are gone from home, too. Our relatives live further and further away, and schools can get in serious trouble if they even mention values or character education that conflicts with special interest religious groups.

Some believe that the freedom of the 1960s, without the balancing effect of responsibility training at home and institutions, took us off course. Others point to studies that TV viewing has fundamentally altered perceptions and values. Some blame Watergate. Whatever you believe, please consider our children now need adults and values training in their lives as much as any generation ever has.

None of them can know what they have not been taught. If we want them to be loyal, responsible, perseverant, optimistic, trustworthy, honest, courageous, respectful, compassionate, adaptable, and contemplative, it is up to all of us to teach them. Our parents were not asked to do it all alone. At stake is the kind of world in which we will get to grow old.

A Bad Moon Rising

Drawing out his tattered piece of legal size paper, Camelot Bob announced the end of the world. "Before you start laughing, listen to this," Bob said, and he began reading in a solemn voice the summer's list of natural catastrophes. "There was the drought, then last week, we had the worst hurricane floods of the century. Earthquakes have made Turkey and Taiwan a massive graveyard. Pine beetles are destroying the Rocky Mountains, dead rats and hypodermic needles are washing up on our beaches. I tell you, something is going on, maybe the end of the world."

"It's the ozone layer," said Water Street Pete.
"It's nuclear weapons testing," said Ridgeway Ron.
"It's an ancient prediction coming true," said City Hall Sam.

Gloom and doom took hold, each man telling his story. That's how it went until the conversation wound its way to Holly Lake Jake. Jake told this story.

He had taken a call from his daughter last evening asking him to come over and talk to his eight-year-old grandson. When Jake arrived, the boy was in bed with the covers pulled up to his chin. He refused to study his spelling and had his school clothes on, including his shoes.

"What's going on?" Jake asked.
"Nothing," the boy replied.
"Why are you in bed with your clothes on?" Jake asked.
"No reason," the boy said.
Jake's daughter was listening at the door, and Jake turned to her. "Why don't you let us men be alone for a moment," he said.
"You know, I went to bed once with my clothes on. I was afraid I would be late for school, but that's not the reason you're here is it, boy?" Jake said.
The little boy shook his head.
"I didn't think so. You probably have a better reason than I did. You want to talk about it?" Jake asked.
The boy shook his head and said, yes. Then, in a whisper he muttered, "I'm scared."
Jake slipped into the bed beside the boy and asked, "What's scaring you?"
"The kids at school say the world is going to end tomorrow. They have a book, and in the book it says the world will end, because God is coming back. I read it, Grandpa," the boy whispered.
Jake didn't say anything as he stroked the boy's hair.
"I don't want the world to end. I don't know what to wear. I don't want to go to Heaven in my pajamas," wailed the small voice.
Jake felt like crying and laughing at the same time. "Is that why you got your

clothes on?" he asked.

"Yes," the boy said. "What do you think we will be doing after the end of the world?"

"I don't know," said Jake. "I suppose we will spend a lot of time meeting new people and learning answers to questions."

"Are you scared the world will end, Grandpa?" the boy asked.

"Yep, I suppose I am, but I'm not sure the world will end tomorrow," Jake said. "Once, when I was about your age, the moon came up bigger and more yellow than I had ever seen it before. One of the boys in the neighborhood said it was a sign the world was ending. I spent a night, like you're doing now, worrying about the end of the world. I prayed and asked God to save the world 'til at least Christmas. He did that, and it was one of the best Christmases I ever had. You never know how much you can appreciate something you fear you might lose."

The boy snuggled close to his grandpa and talked for an hour about the end of the world. Jake let him talk and answered his questions, even the silliest ones, like he was talking with his equal. Finally, the boy was quiet and then looked at Jake.

"Will you quiz me on my spelling words just in case the world doesn't end?"

"Sure will," said Jake, and they did.

The Great Gift We All Can Share

by Gladstone Gus

All but Death, can be Adjusted—
Dynasties repaired—
Systems—settled in their Sockets—
Citadels—dissolved—

Wastes of Lives—resewn with Colors
By Succeeding Springs—
Death—unto itself—Exception—
Is exempt from Change—

I was young and in college when I first read this poem by Emily Dickinson. Lights went on, bells rang, and my first real thoughts about the true nature of forgiveness began to develop in me. To this day, when I'm teaching Sunday School, I know one question will always get an amazing response from kids. Here is what I ask them, "If somebody honestly says, 'I'm sorry', and asks you directly for forgiveness, is it your duty to forgive them? What do you think?" Before you read what kids say, here are a few more interesting ideas from others about forgiveness.

Eric Hoffer said: *The remarkable thing is that we really love our neighbor as ourselves: we do unto others as we do unto ourselves. We hate others when we hate ourselves. We are tolerant toward others when we tolerate ourselves. We forgive others when we forgive ourselves. We are prone to sacrifice others when we are ready to sacrifice ourselves.*

Hillary Rodham Clinton, who must know something about forgiveness, said: *In the Bible it says they asked Jesus how many times you should forgive, and he said 70 times 7. Well, I want you all to know that I'm keeping a chart.*

John F. Kennedy said: *Forgive your enemies, but never forget their names.*

Some of the great thinkers offer us some unique ideas on forgiveness.

Robert Frost wrote, *Forgive, O Lord, my little jokes on Thee - And I'll forgive Thy great big one on me.*

Sir Francis Bacon wrote, *We read that we ought to forgive our enemies; but we do not read that we ought to forgive our friends.*

Voltaire says, *No snowflake in an avalanche ever feels responsible.*

William Blake wrote, *It is easier to forgive an enemy than to forgive a friend.*

What did the kids say? You might be interested to know that the kids in my class most often make a great case for forgiveness. They are much more tolerant and willing to accept an apology than my generation.

They are willing to drop old grudges and look for compromise. In an age of bitter contention on so many fronts, our young people seem to be much more tolerant, accepting, and forgiving than the culture they are inheriting. That gives me hope.

Should we all be more willing to forgive, maybe even forget?

My favorite quote about forgiveness, and a quote I admire for many different reasons, comes from Reinhold Niebuhr. Here it is:

Nothing worth doing is completed in our lifetime,
Therefore, we are saved by hope.
Nothing true or beautiful or good makes complete sense in any immediate
context of history.
Therefore, we are saved by faith.
Nothing we do, however virtuous, can be accomplished alone.
Therefore, we are saved by love.
No virtuous act is quite as virtuous from the standpoint of our friend or foe
as from our own;
Therefore, we are saved by the final form of love, which is forgiveness.

Have You Heard The News Today?

by Gladstone Gus

So much of her story was like a fairy tale, the ending is hard to believe. Dawn Black married her high school sweetheart and was a Courtwarming Queen. She had three beautiful daughters. At age 43, blonde hair and beautiful eyes all shining, she could still turn heads. It is a mystery and with sadness, the way things ended. It is unfair and senseless, even cruel. Her death is like strange, urban legend. Almost everyone knows the story.

In the early morning of January 24, Dawn was on her way to work when she had a flat tire and pulled her car off the side of the interstate. We must be careful not to second-guess a mystery we cannot solve, but for inexplicable reasons, Dawn chose to walk across Interstate 35, maybe looking for help. As she did, in the pre-dawn darkness, she was hit and killed. From riding in a car, to a flat tire, to a date with eternity, her life was gone in a matter of minutes. The bad luck cards fell in an impossible straight chain reaction of events that mocks common sense and tests every fiber of faith. That impossible scenario ended a life.

The word of a pedestrian death on Interstate 35 ricocheted from media to media, across radios, TVs and phones. Traffic backed up for miles on the interstate. Dawn's death marked the morning for thousands. Around water coolers, and as secretaries gathered opening the morning mail, the strange events of the morning were the topic of conversation. Until the name was released at about 10 a.m., the Northland held its collective breath. Too many husbands send wives to work in the city on that stretch of road. Mothers and fathers knew their daughters were on that highway.

Events such as Dawn's death test the meaning of our living. When planes fall from the sky, because of a chain reaction of minor mechanical failures, or the roulette wheel of cancer points its arrow at the brightest and best among us, we cannot help but wonder what little meaning, if any, there might be to these few days we have for a life.

The startling morning news story, the one that gripped an entire city, was personal to us who knew Dawn, her husband, and her mom and dad. We can't comprehend what happened.

Maybe we should all remember to use cell phones, or carry CALL POLICE signs in our cars for the one time our cars fail us on the early morning drive. Maybe we should remember to tell our wives that we love them each morning or tell our children what they mean to us more often. Maybe we should remember there are no guarantees. Maybe we should think about not postponing our dreams. There must be something in this senseless mess, but I don't get it. The sun should not come up nor should the clocks keep turning. But the clocks do run, and the story goes on despite us.

I just want you to know that I knew Dawn. I know her husband, her mom, and her brother-in-law. The woman in that big news story was a real person, and she is missed.

Dawn Black died January 24, 2001; have you heard the news today?

Sing It Out Brothers And Sisters

by Holly Lake Jake

GOD OF GRACE AND GOD OF GLORY

Cure Thy children's warring madness
Bend our pride to Thy control.
Shame our wanton selfish gladness
Rich in things and poor in soul.
Grant us wisdom, grant us courage,
Lest we miss thy kingdom's goal.
Lest we miss thy kingdom's goal.

> Words: Harry Emerson Fosdick
> Music: John Hughes

We sang this hymn in church Sunday. While we sang, I couldn't help but wonder what has happened to our world's faith communities. In polls of those who call themselves Christians, and according to news media reports from many and varied houses of worship, from the mouths of good, God-fearing people, the world is at war, and we're right to go forth.

So many people, both here and abroad, think the Christian faith now stands for a political agenda that is almost the opposite of what Jesus preached. They think Christians increasingly have embraced a theology that is pro-rich, pro-war, and pro-American. And, to this end, many Americans believe Muslims embrace terrorism as a basic tenant of their faith.

Listen carefully to the arguments from faith communities to justify striking first in war, killing innocents, women and children, or spending billions of dollars on the military industrial complex. People of all faiths are being called to remember their dead and to give death back in kind. "We must hunt them down and kill every one of them," is a quote that has found sympathy among faith communities across the world. Sensitivity or mercy, they say, is weakness, and some even call it treason.

Does this kind of talk sound like it is born in faiths that honor life, love, forgiveness, and renewal? Some faith leaders see merely opposing war and, therefore, the killing of innocents as treason. Questioning the wisdom of bombing the children of civilians, thereby causing more hate to flourish, is considered aiding the enemy.

"Cure thy children's warring madness"

We sang this hymn in church as we have done for over 80 years, no matter the president or political thought of the day. What has changed? How many in our faith communities here in the United States, both Democrats and Republicans, now embrace the use of negative campaign ads, fear mongering, and the utilization of wedge issues to paint our presidential candidates, as bad – maybe even evil – people? Depending on which ads you watch, our greatest leaders are: unable to act in a crisis, stupid, cowards, liars, misleaders, weak, uncaring, capable of being used by others, and waffling. These ads are talking about two great men. Both love and pledge to defend his country. Is it any wonder so many people are absolutely sick of politics? You would think people of faith, no matter where they stood in the political spectrum, would denounce slander, hate, and false accusation. They don't. Polls show the faith community seems eager to choose sides based on these ads.

"Shame our wanton selfish gladness,
Rich in things and poor in soul."

Faith communities are almost always born among the poor, the oppressed, the hopeless, and the suffering. All of our great religions, and especially Christianity, call us to care for each one of God's children and all of God's creation. This notion that God is a Democrat or a Republican demeans and weakens the very idea of faith. Faith is for all people, and gives hope and meaning to all. "It breaks down the walls that divide us, so that we are no longer strangers, but fellow citizens and members of the household of God." Faith, not hate, is our chance for peace. The shrill voices on the radical edges of the world's faith communities are all defending their wars.

"Grant us wisdom, Grant us courage,
Lest we miss Thy kingdom's goal."

Shoot That Pig! Shoot Him Now!

Holly Lake Jake looked over his family. They were gathered around the old pine wood box that had been salvaged from the back porch of his mother-in-law's house in Malvern, Arkansas. It was over 80 years old now and served as a coffee table in his daughter's home. Everyone was eating Tippin's pies, drinking coffee or wine, and laughing as they shared family stories. It must be noted here that Jake does not approve of alcohol in any form. Jesus most certainly had created wine from water for purely medicinal reasons only. Jake did not fuss, however, at his kin's supposedly sophisticated wine consumption. Every family has some fallen angels.

It was a stunning mix of young and old, talkers and thinkers, prim and proper, and Jake's questionable son-in-law, who gathered around the pine wood box this night. Moody teenagers ("If I can't have a Hollister sweater in orange, my Christmas will be ruined."), cranky seniors ("Who ate all the smoked turkey?"), and, of course, harried parents ("Please, sweetie, I'll drive to St. Louis next week to find you a burnt orange Hollister sweater.") and, ("I'll get you another smoked turkey on Monday.") all seemed to relax for a moment.

The conversation starts slowly and negatively, as is the custom of our culture.

"Is that a real fire? I hate artificial fireplaces!" is the first word out.
"They just don't make pumpkin pie like they used to!" says another.
"What time does the football game start?" every male seems to ask at once.

It's a bad start. Conversation is a challenge in the new century.

Then, Holly Lake Jake tells a story.

"In another age and time, the days of pump handles, real cream, and wood stoves, there was a pig that crept each night into my grandma's watermelon patch for some good Arkansas Black Diamond watermelons. Grandma had lost Grandpa about a year earlier, and with the help of two grandsons, was trying desperately to hold onto the farm. The watermelon patch was her one nod to her late husband. Paw-Paw's family always loved a good Black Diamond melon. The family owned an old shotgun, and Grandma announced to her terrified young grandson that they would wait in the patch that night to feed that rascal pig some buckshot."

Now, at this point in the story, nobody is fidgeting or talking about football games. All eyes and ears are on Jake. Half eaten pieces of pie, steaming cups of coffee, and an occasional wine glass are all neglected. Everybody wants to know about the pig and its date with Great Grandma's gun. Jake continued his story.

"Sure enough, through the darkness you could hear the old pig a coming, snorting through the tall grass into the melon patch.

'Get the gun,' Grandma said to her petrified grandson. The pig came into view, silhouetted in the moonlight.

'Draw a bead and fire,' Grandma ordered.

'The grandson froze.

'Shoot him,' Grandma said.

'I can't do it,' the grandson muttered, still shaking. Grandma turned hard and cold. Her voice was like iron.

'Shoot that pig! Shoot him now!' she ordered.

"Scared into submission, the grandson fired. The pig squealed and snorted, then blistered a path out of the melon patch and was never seen again. Billy, the grandson, talks about it to this day.

"That's a true story. Of course I can't tell it like 'ole Billy can," Jake says. The family laughs and wonders how the story could be told any better.

Then, for a while, they are a family like from some Norman Rockwell painting. All of them gathered around a simple antique wood box, fire blazing, eating pies, and telling stories. No television, no video games or radio, and no little cliques of people off in different rooms ignoring each other. No martyrs out in the kitchen cleaning up. Nobody left out. Everybody gathered around and listened to everybody else. They entertained each other around an old pine box.

An old Irish proverb reads, "It is in the shelter of each other that people live."

Jake's family, and his God, are his shelters from the storm.

Reading Too Much Thoreau

*"Talk of mysteries! Think of our life in nature – daily to be shown matter, to come in contact with it – rocks, trees, wind on our cheeks! The solid earth! The actual world! The common senses! Contact! Contact! What are we? Where are we? – *Thoreau

City Hall Sam edged his way off Kansas Street onto Mill Street, heading downtown. With the return of warmer weather, he was walking again. It was the menacing palpitations of his heart that first forced him to the road, but it was spring that kept him there. That and the familiar path he had come to follow.

Sam loved the house at the junction of Mill Street and Liberty Drive. Down farther, the Corbin Mill reminded Sam that he had never sent a note of thanks to Sandy for the way she had thought to restore the beautiful old mill. The top floor of that preserved mill was still the most wonderful spot in town to City Hall Sam.

"I have traveled a good deal in Liberty," mused Sam, remembering an old line from Thoreau. Almost every town block offered memory and beauty. Sam turned north on Jewell, heading toward the college campus. The Minors were repainting their sky blue house. Judy Minor is one of those unsung heroes who, each morning, rises early to run a swimming program at the Mabee Center. Her classes are baptism to new life for many senior citizens of the town.

*"If one advances confidently in the direction of his dreams, and endeavors to live the life which he has imagined, he will meet with a success unexpected in common hours." – *Thoreau

The steps up to Jewell Hall were the test of Sam's old legs. At the top, Sam laid his hands on the historic white columns and viewed the magnificence below. It was here, at William Jewell College, where Sam had been shown the vistas of the mind. Professors like Dean Dunham and Don Geilker, Tom Willett and David Moore had taught him to love questions, ideas and a search for wisdom…to live life near the bone where it is sweetest.

Marvelous lines of tulips greeted Sam as he descended the steps of Jewell Hall. Here was Pooch Robb's old house at the corner of Franklin and Jewell. Pooch had once sold hamburgers to college students from the living room. The great artist Patric Shannon had once lived there as well. Sam admired them both.

*"This world is but a canvas for our imaginations." – *Thoreau

At the end of Franklin Street, on top of the city's western hill, Sam viewed the site of the old Liberty Ladies College (now a public middle school). Once, beams of light between Jewell Hall and the Lady's College flashed coded messages from young lovers. Sam liked the possibilities of that thought.

Two hours later, Sam was sitting and talking at the Old North Side Cafe.

"Sam, you old duck, please tell us you are finished reading *Walden,*" begged Manor Hill Mack. "We can't stand another lecture about the meaning of life!"

The men laughed, and so did Sam. His old romantic heart, palpitations and all, felt strong and secure. Heaven was under his feet, as well as above his head, and so he leaned back to smile.

"If a man does not keep pace with his companions, perhaps it is because he hears a different drummer. Let him step to the music which he hears, however measured or far away." – **Thoreau**

The Rough Places Shall Be Made Flat

A couple had never been able to marry on earth but wanted to be married in Heaven. Saint Peter granted the couple's request and said he would make the arrangements. It took him a thousand years, but he got it done. A hundred years passed, and one thing led to another. The couple realized the marriage was wrong and once again went to Saint Peter.

"Will you help us get a divorce," they asked, and they were so sincere. Saint Peter, however, said he wouldn't do it.

The couple pressed Saint Peter for a reason, and finally, in a moment of exasperation, he replied, "It took a thousand years to find a minister up here; we'll never find a lawyer!"

The men chuckled and slapped Mack on the back. They like a joke at the Cafe. They especially like a good lawyer joke; nobody likes those peckerwoods. Pretty soon, they were back to politicians, China, sports, and the weather. Jaws were flapping and accusations flying. Coffee cups clinked and chairs shuffled. Time escaped through the conversation. There was not a thing extraordinary or momentous in this day, and that was its miracle.

Holly Lake Jake marveled at life away from the edges. Though the extraordinary path of life leads through death and divorce, injury and accident, decision and dismay, it has a way of swinging back to the middle and becoming ordinary again.

The collective history of the Old North Side Cafe includes unspeakable occurrences and choking sadness. There is injustice, and problems so complex that they stagger any understanding. Human relationships take everyone to the brink now and then. Life is messy, but each morning, a sun rises. Days gather into weeks and change to seasons. Years go by. Things scar over and sometimes heal. Men joke, tell stories, and find they are smiling in spite of themselves. Lawyers and ministers, bless their hearts, take abuse and the coffee flows. Everyone is forgiven, and then it is forgotten. It is all just a story in the end.

Those who stay on the road find it flattens now and then. The return of the ordinary, the blessing of consistency, and the passing of time are the comforts of the Old North Side Cafe.

Riding the Orphan Train

by Manor Hill Mack

It was a rainy and cold Saturday morning. A carpet of soggy leaves layered the lawn, announcing the end of another spring storm. A cold mist crept through the backyard, looking to bed down in the creek below. The day belonged to drizzle and things indoors. Planting beans would have to wait.

In older days, farmers gathered at a feed store just down from the pool hall when nature claimed a Saturday morning. The men walked old oak planks packed with grain dust and gathered around a coal stove. A bare light bulb battled helplessly against stacks of leaking, dark brown gunny sacks. An army of cats sneaked in the stacks where the hunting was good. Back by the counter, chairs drawn in a circle dictated by the stove's heat, the men talked and lied, poked fun, and stayed warm. Laughter was the common bond among farmers worried about crops and drought.

Not many remember those days. Those that do, come to the Cafe on a rainy Saturday morning with a heavy load of memories. Packed down with stories, they speak to honor a time that is fading away. On these rainy days, you will hear the great stories of life. Hear one now. Pull your slat-backed chair closer to the stove. Shake off the cold, and taste the smell of grain in the air. You are among friends.

Water Street Pete is telling again about the Orphan Train. Yes, it's all true.

"My great-grandfather was one of six brothers. They lived back East. Orphaned young, Grandpa was put on a train full of other children heading to Kansas. A family picked him up at the train station, and he worked on a ranch until he was old enough to leave. Orphan Trains, they were called. That's how Gramps got started.

"Later in life, he began a search for his family. He had a vague memory of his brothers and looked up old records. The search was a series of closed doors. He learned his brothers had all died. One-by-one, they slipped away, and he never knew them.

"He did find something extraordinary, however. Grandpa found his mother. She was very old, but still alive. She told him what happened. His father died just after the sixth boy was born. The loss of a husband and the weight of six children was too great for her. She was sent to an institution, and her boys were put on the orphan train. The government split them up. That's how it was done in those days. She thought she had lost her boys for good. My great-grandmother lived for two more years after Grandpa found her. He took care of her. She lived at his house, and Grandpa buried her in his family plot."

The specks of grain dust swirled around the old feed store, given life by the bare light bulb. The orphan train story will take you to the old feed store. It is etched in a farmer's heart. The harvests of living may not come for many years.

Pete's grandfather gave his mother what she had not been able to give him. The last two years were not magical, they were simple and plain as Grandpa tells the story. They were the final mending and ending in the wonderful full circle of life.

Chapter 2

Family, Life and Religion

The secret to a happy life, the old story goes, is to have a very large, loving and caring family – in another city.

A pastor announces he is resigning. A lady cries out, "Please, no!"
The pastor responds, "Someone will come who is even better."
The lady replies, "That's what they told us the last time."

These are the two least offensive jokes about family and religion I know, and both got a nasty letter of retort from a time when I slipped them into print. Nothing makes folks angrier more quickly than a careless comment about religion or family. We can't talk about them. We can't even joke about them. Not even a non-funny, totally innocent, page-filler can fly under the religion and family radar of censorship. When did we get so touchy?

Still, you are about to read some stories straight from the Cafe's repertoire of family and religious moments. Somehow, they talk about religion and family all the time down at the Cafe. Fights are rare, and usually the men nod their heads. There are a few exceptions. Camelot Bob could not understand why anybody would get upset when the city council put up a billboard that read, "Jesus is Lord of Our City."

Holly Lake Jake explained the sign was offensive to different religions and atheists, because it was their city, too, and Jesus was not their Lord. Bob didn't care. He liked the sentiment and accused Jake of being "politically correct."

"If you mean I have some manners and tolerance, then yes, I'm politically correct," Jake said. "Proud of it."

Now, if they ventured into rape, abortion, birth control for single women, Planned Parenthood, abstinence training, or turning off life support, it would be Katy-bar-the-door! The old boys have learned what they can and cannot talk about and how to address these issues.

Here, the Cafe's stories get very simple and are filled with heartfelt truth. Nobody defends their position; they let the story speak for itself. That's how they do it. Because these men are actually friends, they are willing to compromise their beliefs to accommodate another point of view. And, more importantly, because they are honorable friends, they stick together when times get difficult. They respect each other, and they want to have a relationship more than they want to be right.

Both religion and family are on our culture's slippery slope downhill. Neither will get more than lip service as long as some people continue to think they somehow have a deeper understanding of God's will, or that God shares information with them that is not available to other good-thinking folk.

Family and religion at the Cafe are strictly about loving each other, being kind, being there for each other, not giving up, etc. Rules about genealogy, baptism, communion, church membership, God's favored political party, and so on, are kept in boxes on a dusty shelf in Cafe storage and very seldom opened. One story in the coming chapter, however, does break the rule and will undoubtedly make somebody very mad.

You will love this chapter if you generally believe there are some forces in the universe we don't yet understand, and that kindness, forgiveness, patience, love, peace, and honor are good things to strive for. You will like it if you are not too keen on telling others what to do or think; you believe the forces of good can handle themselves pretty well; and you would never call a woman a bad name to score political points no matter what end of the political spectrum you champion.

Don't be fooled, however. These are not homey stories to make you feel good. These stories are actually dangerous. Remember, if somebody gives you a library card, you might end up checking out some books.

Candy At Church?
Are You Kidding Me?

Things have taken some strange turns over the years, but nothing is stranger than what's happened to food. Last Sunday, Manor Hill Mack stuffed his pockets full of caramels to give kids after church. He remembered a man at the Third Street Presbyterian Church in St. Joseph who did the same thing. It was a good memory. That caramel was the only thing that made the sermon worth sitting through. God knows the most direct way to a young boy's soul is his stomach. He made kids that way, so after church, Mack handed out his first caramel.

"Mommy, Mommy!" the little girl screamed. "This bad man is trying to poison me!"

Mack, now in shock, was flummoxed. Capitalizing on Mack's bewildered look, the indignant mother attacked.

"You ought to know better than to offer raw sugar to a little girl," the mother said snarling. "What kind of man are you? Come on Lauren, did that big, mean man hurt you?"

So much for caramels and a sacred childhood memory. Plagued with guilt, Mack searched for redemption within his own family. He offered to take his grandkids to a hamburger place.

"Do you know the saturated fat content of a cheeseburger and french fries?" his daughter asked. "Honestly Dad, I'm disappointed you would even ask." The snarl looked strangely familiar.

Mack sought refuge in the most sacred sanctuary of American culture and cuisine, a ballpark. An avid Royals fan, for years Mack had gone to cheer the Boys in Blue and eat hotdogs. But, baseball and food are out these days too. Mack was joyfully in the middle of a krautdog, and a "Hey ump, it's a good game. Too bad you can't see it!" when his daughter-in-law shamed him. "Hotdogs are nasty. Do you know what's in there?" she said, pointing at the hotdog like it was big slug. Three rows back, young rowdies were flashing flab, swilling beer, and swearing, but it was Mack's hotdog that was nasty.

"I miss food," Mack said telling his story at the Cafe. Mack missed the old days. The days of Tupperware-housed leftovers and green beans in cream of mushroom soup. Ahh, crockpots, and yes, more cream of mushroom soup. Mack longed for real whipped cream on sugar-laden cherry cobbler, and backyard barbecues where real men threw hunks of greasy meat on hot fires. As for "light" food… well, a "light" is what you give a buddy for a smoke.

Then the thought struck. Our country builds enough nuclear weapons to destroy the earth 125 times, makes and stores chemical weapons, continues to dump toxic waste in its streams, promotes violence and death in its media, has the highest infant mortality rate in the industrialized world, champions weapons systems over health care, and this same country is scared silly over saturated fats and sugar.

It is time to bring out the Butch and Sundance theory once again. In the movie, when Butch Cassidy and the Sundance Kid jump off a cliff into the river far below, Sundance worries that he can't swim. "Hell, the fall will probably kill you," says Butch.

That's what Mack thinks about the fuss over food. Better to look at the big picture. It doesn't hurt to be sensible, but the worry will kill you before the food.

The Peace That Passes Understanding

Holly Lake Jake came down to the Old North Side Cafe for a little inspiration. The pastor called and asked him to give the congregational prayer on Sunday. Jake said "yes," but didn't know what to pray. He was eyeing his coffee, wishing he had said, "no," when Camelot Bob popped in. Now, if two men are different, it is Jake and Bob. Jake swings liberal and from the heart. Bob was a Navy officer in WWII and talks military, corporate, and conservative.

"Can you believe this autumn," offered Bob. "I can't remember when the trees were so beautiful. I think it's ironic considering all that is happening in our country."

Jake nodded in agreement and then caught on to both the warmth and worry in Bob's voice. Almost 40 years ago, it was Bob who helped Jake paint the back bedroom in his old house. That was the beginning of an unlikely friendship. It was Bob who called when Jake's dad had died, and it was Bob who remembered the special events in the lives of Jake's kids. Jake noticed the brown spots on Bob's hands and gathering wrinkles around the eyes.

"Do you remember painting that room in my house?" Jake blurted out. "Why did you do that?"

Bob thought a moment, then said, "I saw you at church, and some of the guys said you were working on that old house. You had a little baby, and I figured you could use some help," Bob said. "Besides, I kind of like painting."

The conversation quickly turned to kids, on to the president, then the war and elections. Bob and Jake were good for an hour and a half of talk. Being together was a blessing for both men.

Sunday, Jake prayed this prayer in church:

"Father, we ask Your presence and blessing for our worship today. I know we act pretty confident and self-assured, all dressed here in our best. We are proud of ourselves that we made it up this morning. You know we've got a knack for seeming to be in control. The truth is, a lot of us worried from time to time. We are afraid for our country. We don't know about our jobs, and we get scared for our kids. Sometimes our friends and family get sick, and we feel concern for our parents and children. We rush past moments of peace and beat our heads against walls of obligation. Lost in our precon-ceived notions, we miss you, Lord. For a moment, we would like You to sit with us. Please join us to hear the prayers, sing the songs, and share a sermon. We also want to say thanks. Thanks for being there when we feel lost or overwhelmed. Thanks for

coming when we need assurance or even when we need something small like getting the back bedroom painted. Come again now; we worship in your name. Amen."

There was silence after the prayer. Jake saw Bob touching the edge of his hymn-book. His eyes were soft and glistening. Prayer and a tear are tribute to an old friendship at the Old North Side Cafe.

Buy Him Anything He Wants

Camelot Bob was beside himself with joy! Missouri beat Kansas in the Big 12 Tournament, the Royals are back, and it had rained on his fertilizer.

"What more could a man ask," cried Bob.

A jocular mood permeated the North Side. Men drank their coffee with caffeine, and Stella kept busy serving coconut cream pie.

"I'm in such a great mood, I'm even taking my grandson shopping for some Easter clothes," said Water Street Pete.

Pete is hopelessly old-fashioned when it comes to church fashions. His idea of proper attire for kids is a nice pair of slacks, white shirt, clip-on tie, parted hair, and polished leather shoes. Last year, Pete's fashion sense had caused some problems with his grandson. Pete had to learn a lesson about kids.

"Yuck-O," said his nine-year-old grandson.

The grandson's idea of church clothes were frosted front jeans, a Duke basketball jersey, and silver and blue, slip-on, high-top basketball shoes. Properly regaled, the grandson hoped to slouch his way into church, display divine indifference, and ask again about the possibility of a tattoo or body piercing.

"I'm not buying you ripped jeans, with or without frosting, to wear to church," said Pete.

"I need to be comfortable, dude," the boy smiled. "You're just too old to understand."

Pete blamed his daughter. She had taught this child clotheshorse to be fashion's slave. She claimed she, herself, was deprived as a child. Her self-image was destroyed because of the cheap, out-of-style, hand-me-down clothes she was forced to wear.

"Why, when I was a boy, my mom bought me my clothes, and I was proud to have them," snorted Pete eyeball-to-eyeball with his grandson. Two hours and seven stores later, Pete walked out with ripped-knee-frosted-jeans, a Duke shirt, and silver slip-on shoes.

Ravaged by guilt, Pete was a defeated man. Desperate for some dignity, he begged his grandson to at least properly comb his hair when they went to church. Maundy Thursday, Pete met his family at church. His grandson sat beside him.

Pete eyed the tender young boy he had once bounced on his knee, now slumped into a pew. His hair was gelled into submission; the smirk was gangster hip. Pete wished he could change the channel. His grandson looked like the kind of kid that would enjoy scaring old people.

"Hey, Pop," the boy said holding up his hand for a high-five!

Pete patted his spiked, gelled head instead and gave a worried look at the program. They would have communion. Communion was important to Pete. The grandson crunched his "cracker" like he hadn't eaten for a week and threw back his head when he drank the grape juice as if taking a shot of stronger stuff. Pete was mortified! Outside the church, Pete stopped his grandson and challenged him with a question.

"What did you think about when you took communion," Pete asked.

"I dunno," the boy mumbled.

"Didn't you think about anything? I mean like about God or Jesus or church?"

"Yeah, I guess," the boy said. Pete was glowing a faint red, and the boy sensed his grandfather's anger. "I was thinking about kids my age in Afghanistan."

"Why would you think about that," asked Grandpa.

"I was thinking that I wish I could help them," the boy said, his blue eyes thick with meaning. "I was thinking about all the things people do for me – like Jesus and you and Mom and Grandma."

Pete lowered his head and felt a shiver of shame. He should have known better than to second-guess his grandson.

So Pete sat at the North Side, savoring coconut cream pie, talking of sports, and Easter. March Madness is coming! The Royals are back! A spring rich with flowers and green grass is coming! Most of all, he looked forward to shopping with his grandson and buying him anything he wants.

The View From The Porch Is Very Good

The evening closed, charged with excitement and wonder. Headlights cut the massive sheets of rain looking for the watery realm of Main Street. Their passing rear lights left the streets a shimmering red. It was a night of liquid diamonds and rubies, and at long last, rain. Manor Hill Mack took his lawn chair to the front porch to watch the show. The air was cold and filled with the rich smell of ozone. His winter ears had forgotten the sound of rain. The countless syncopations and splashes, the dripping, the cars plowing through puddles, all found him on the porch.

Young Moderns have forsaken the porch. They set up a small slab of concrete outside the front door and stick an old milk can or something else equally stupid, on it; that's what they call a porch. People sink $250,000 plus into a home and leave it suffering the spiritual deprivation of no front porch. Mack's house might bring $82,500, but it knows the worth of a proper porch. Mack's swing alone was priceless. How many summer nights had he sat gently swinging, greeting passersby; the cool motion and steady creaking noise turning back worry and the summer heat.

It was a playground for his kids. That swing was their Ferris wheel. The front rail was a tightrope. The front hedge was perfect for Olympic leaping. On summer nights, Mack's kids sat on the front steps and shot watermelon seeds across the sidewalk or told spooky stories, their faces an ashen yellow from the porch light. It was here they laid plans so exciting and filled with wonder that no TV program ever won them away.

The porch was the staging area for lemonade stands, base for hide and seek, a stage for fashion shows, and safe refuge when mother got mad. For as long as he could remember, Mack had surveyed the world from the porch each day before walking out to get the morning paper. As the kids grew older, nights changed on the porch. Here, young lovers held hands and stole kisses. With June bugs and crickets rattling in the silence, Mack would "accidentally" turn on the front porch light, a clear signal for his daughter, and the young man with her, that it was time to go home. It was on this porch Mack had quietly cried the night his young daughter married. Few people knew Mack's softer side.

Memories swirled like the early spring rain that evening on Mack's front porch. Soon enough, the grandkids came out and played on the swing. After that, they raced back and forth from the porch into the yard trying not to get wet. Mack scolded the children, laughing inside at their playful spirit. It was soon too cold, and the kids went in. Mack sat for a while longer, sizing up the spring. The tulips were up. The forsythia was especially beautiful this year. Some redbuds were blooming. His lawn would soon need cutting.

The rain circled around streetlights and car headlights, continuing to fall steadily. There was a familiar comfort in this rainy night. The view from the porch was very good.

Do Not Negotiate With Terror Tots

by Camelot Bob

True, the Teamsters Union is a formidable force at the bargaining table. They proved that a combination of negotiating skill, effective public relations, and steel will can buckle management and bring it to its knees.

Teamsters are rookies, however, when it comes to the truly hard-nosed, no-nonsense, prisoner-killing tactics of the world's fiercest union. I'm talking about the brotherhood of children under 14 who feel somebody has promised them something before summer's end – a trip to the lake, Royals game, night fishing, car races, or camping out, makes no difference. If you even slightly muttered within earshot of a child that there was the slimmest chance of doing any of these activities, you are doomed. Unless you completely comply within the next 72 hours, an all-out strike looms. "Grandpa, you promised," a seven- year old would whimper, then grow her eyes to the size of cantaloupes, and water them down for effect.

"I thought we had a deal," an enterprising thirteen-year old will say, stealing a page from used car sellers. Suddenly, a father's integrity is called into question. You can't fight it without serious consequence. The kids' union holds all the cards, and they are ruthless. Should you fail to acquiesce at the first round of talks, they simply increase the stakes and call in bigger guns.

A seven-year old will think nothing of announcing at your most public function that you promised to take them to the amusement park, and now you are breaking your word. If you try to defend yourself, the young lawyer-to-be will announce dates, times, and names.

"June 13, 8:30 a.m., when I was helping you in the garden, you promised to take Shelly and me. I know you remember!"

If public shaming fails, the cold shoulder begins. They don't eat. They sulk. When you try to explain that there are just too many unforeseen things going on to take them camping, they stare right past you, eyes upward as if searching for a higher truth in the disappointing summer.

"That's ok, Grandpa," they say, and they make you know it's a lie. They also make you know they are somehow a better person than you for telling such a lie to get you off the hook. Still, everyone involved knows you are lower than sheep droppings.

Promises to children are sacred, everybody knows that. We worked it for all it was worth when we were children, and now it's our turn to pay the piper. Adults should know better than to promise. In June, we were weak. Summer spread out before us like a picnic, and promises of ball games, fishing trips, and drive-in movies rolled out much too easily. Our only advice now is give in, and get it over with. You are not so busy that your word must take a second seat.

"Thanks, Grandpa, for taking me fishing." "Thanks for the ballgame, Uncle Bob."

These are the sweetest words of summer's end. But next year, keep your big mouth shut.

All You Ever Need To Know Comes From Cartoons

"Grandpa, come over quick; the cartoon is going to start," whispered a small voice on the other end of the line.

"Sure thing," Manor Hill Mack said, "I'm on my way!"

It was early on Saturday. Everyone was gathered in the basement to watch. The lights were dimmed, and the show began.

Something about all this seemed very familiar to Mack. Kids gathered around the TV, the low lights, excitement in the air; this was the way TV used to be. Mack, who grew up well before TV, regularly got up to watch cartoons with his kids in the 1950s. Yes, on Saturday morning, they sat around watching a test pattern before the show came on. Many mornings, he sent his oldest son up on the roof to turn the antenna for better reception. A lot of shouting went on in those days. Mack shouted to his youngest son at the window, who shouted up at the oldest son on the roof, then everybody shouted back.

"Good, good! NO! You lost it. Snow, still snow. YES! The picture is CLEAR! NO! You had it! Go back! You're not listening!" The "you're not listening" always made the oldest son mad and was the start of a family feud.

"You get up here and turn this antenna!" the boy shouted back, and the ruckus began.

The shows in those days were really good shows: Sky King, My Friend Flicka, Howdy-Doody, Buster Brown (remember the magic twanger?). The cartoons were sumptuous: Mighty Mouse, Porky Pig, Mickey Mouse, Tom Terrific and Manfred, and George of the Jungle. These were shows you could give a Saturday morning to without regret. Commercials were better too! They were live. The dog they brought in to eat the dog food was real and did real things, like not eat the food – or worse.

Because early picture tubes were not very bright, the rooms were dark, and on top of every TV was a TV lamp – a great looking animal-like base, or a Conestoga wagon with a small lampshade. The cabinet itself was enormous with a tiny little green screen. People actually put colored plastic over the screen to create the illusion of color. Mack even ordered a magnifying glass to make the screen appear bigger.

Mack was elbowed from his nostalgia by a boisterous kindergartner. Little kids dance when they watch TV, they crawl over the furniture and stand on their heads. They knock over anything that is not tied down and chew on their t-shirts. Kids also eat nonstop. Mack once put down blankets and issued orders about eating over trays and not spilling. Now, spilling seems to be part of the fun. One little boy stuck an elbow in Mack's eye, and started chewing on his shoe, when a tree frog appeared on the screen.

Mack still liked the cartoons, but the public service announcements between the shows gave him pause. Do young children, like seven-year olds, have to deal with friends pressuring them to do drugs? Do 10-year-old kids really have access to crack? Are older kids giving drugs to their little brothers and sisters? Mack came back to the present. Here was a Saturday morning public service cartoon message opposing drug use. To end the public service message, a little cartoon guy says he respects his body too much to do drugs. Mack wished we had a culture that respected its young children so much that anti-drugs messages on Saturday morning cartoons were not necessary.

The "Peckerwood" Connection

A line of Canadian geese edged their way south over a soccer field filled with first grade boys, just learning the game. Camelot Bob noticed them first and pointed up. Soon, all the fans were marveling at the flying wedge honking its way into fall. The red soccer team saw their parents looking up and glanced up, too. They hardly noticed the blue team break down field and swamp the poor goalie.

"The little boys just stood staring at the sky, looking stupid, while the other team scored," Bob, a very conservative Republican, told the guys at the North Side. "I tell you, we are raising a generation of sissy boys!"

Bob had taken his first grader to the soccer game, because the boy's mother was off doing her New Age stuff again. He acted like he was angry with the boys for not paying attention to the soccer game, but he was really mad at his "Alternative Lifestyle" daughter.

"She gets together with a bunch of kooks who call themselves sophists, and they go to something called a dervish", explained Bob. "They all carry around quartz crystal rocks and listen to music from Africa".

Bob looked up the word dervish in the dictionary. A dervish is a ceremony where participants achieve communal ecstasy through whirling dances and the chanting of religious formulas.

"I knew they would all go nuts again," said Bob. "In the '80s, they were wanna-be hippies, grunge-balls, or gang members. Now, they are Yuppie, New Age, ultra-liberals trying to pawn their kids off on us."

Most grandparents are not as vitriolic as Bob, but many actually are trying to save their grandchildren from the current generation of parents. They think today's parents have lost sense of middle ground and forgot to grow up.

"They work too hard. They play too hard. They give their children everything and then won't spend any time with them," grouched Bob. "It is a good thing I'm around. My grandson wouldn't know anything if I didn't teach it to him."

Holly Lake Jake sat quietly, stirring his coffee and taking it all in. Jake wasn't sure what he thought about his son-in-law. The young man was growing his 14th beard in 10 years and still playing protest songs on his guitar. Jake did love his grandson, however. About once a week lately, Jake would take his three-year-old grandson down to the woods behind the house, just past the pear tree, and have a cookout. His grandson gathered up sticks in a little bucket for grandpa to make the fire. Usually, they had a hotdog and a marshmallow washed down with Kool-Aid from an old jelly jar glass. They carefully poured water on the campfire when they were done. It would be a sight if the police ever tried to make them stop. Jake is called "Pop" in his family and knows lot about fires, frogs, bugs, birds, pears, trees, saws, nails, flatulence, and theology. Just the stuff little boys like.

"That is a peckerwood," Jake would say hauling his grandson up in his arms and pointing to a bird. "Over there is a granddaddy long legs, and you are a little boy – about the best thing God ever put on this old earth."

Jake's backyard was a mess of swings, jungle gyms, and sandboxes, all homemade. Jake's view was to keep it simple. Neither he nor his grandson played too hard or loafed too much. A few little rituals like the campfire, hello hugs, and afternoon naps were just fine. They kind of liked it "middle of the road." Jake could get a little wild, however. Sometimes "Pop" and his grandson would "March, March, March" in a circle from the kitchen to the dining room, to the living room, and through the hallway back to the kitchen. They lifted their marching knees up to their chests and generally acted very important and smug, just marching around the house.

Jake wondered if his little grandson would ever stop in the middle of a soccer game to watch geese fly by. Would he risk missing the action and let the other team score – all for a bunch of passing birds? Jake kind of hoped he would.

Mission Accomplished, Mickey Dog

by Water Street Pete

Mickey the Wonder Dog's mission was to raise two boys, keep them safe from harm, and be a force of love in our family. I am proud to report Mickey has completed her mission with honors, the last year performing her dog duties in intense pain, without complaint or loss of disposition. In the last week of her life, as she lost the ability to get up at will or walk without falling, Mickey Dog never whimpered and tried with all her might to rise when any family member entered the room to give proper greeting. The last day of her life, she gave comfort and then left with a grace and dignity befitting her rank as a purebred Golden Retriever and revered family member. Let it now be known she is worthy of honor and accolade, fond memories, and our most grateful tears.

In her youth, Mickey raised two boys with an ease that made days and weeks go by without thought or care. Boys and dog chased each other endlessly in the back yard, roamed empty lots and the church grounds down the street fearlessly seeking adventure. The day four-year-old Matthew sneaked down to the church playground looking for his older brother, it was Mickey who signaled danger. We walked toward the church together until Mickey sensed a menacing, larger dog was threatening her boy. Her usual Golden Retriever prance turned to a dead run as she became a golden bullet aimed squarely at the head of an enormous Black Labrador. Mickey struck the Lab at full force, both dogs rolling in a heap. The Lab's retreat was instantaneous.

The best stories are the little ones, however. Her demands for attention, the circuit she made at night so she spent time in every bedroom with every family member, the quiet patience she used as she waited for a door to be opened, and – please forgive our family secret – the four of us and Mickey crowded in a tiny bathroom in the morning, all of us talking and preparing for the day.

Mickey never got tired of watching me mow the lawn, weed the garden, wash the cars, or take out the trash. She could watch me work for hours and then lick my hand to say, "good job." When my wife and I fought, Mickey barked at us to shut up, and if we didn't stop, she would try to pull one of us away.

Mickey drank champagne with us on Christmas Eve (that's my little secret; I'm not sure my wife knew). Mickey loved enormous snowstorms and actually tunneled in drifts. She ate vegetables and won my mother-in-law's heart. Mickey was the only one among us who could ever tell Nana what to do and get away with it.

If this were not enough, Mickey had a behavior that made her memorable to anyone she met – she went wild around light. Shine a flashlight on a wall and she would climb it to get to that spot of light. She stood endlessly in the front yard waiting for the door to open and the reflection off the glass door to move across the lawn. She NEVER tired of chasing it.

Words will never capture the countless little moments that a good dog gives to the life of a family. Mickey could tell when we were sad and gave comfort. She shared our joy, never complained what TV show was on, and listened to my crummy guitar playing for hours and years. When the boys got sick, she never left their bed. The boys are ages 21 and 15 now. Mickey gave them 12 years. She was no great hunter or mighty guard dog (she liked to lick strangers); Mickey was just a family dog. She loved us unconditionally and taught us all to calm down and enjoy the little moments that mark the passing of a family's time together.

So, here is her tribute. I will never again see a shooting star and not imagine Mickey chasing the light across the sky. The Greeks had their gods to fill up the night sky and tell their legends. Our family had Mickey the Wonder Dog! Her mission complete, she is now free for all time to roam our best memories, chasing the light of remembered joy.

The Checker Match Massacre

by Water Street Pete

Many years ago, in a summer of continuous 100-degree days, I took my son to Fairfield, Iowa, to visit Aunt Marie. Marie's house had been built by her husband, Merlin, a life's dream, and a labor of love. The result was a two-story, stucco house with a flat roof and Spanish design. There was no air-conditioning.

The local "misery index" was 110 degrees when we arrived. Within minutes, a sticky layer of sweat oozed out on our bodies looking for moving air. Annoying rivulets began forming in private places. Our arms stuck to the plastic table cover.

If you have ever wondered how people lived before AC, we can offer some insight.

Rule 1: Find a fan. We instinctively edged our chairs in front of a fan. In other days, there was a fan in every room. Some had two.

Rule 2: Get a cold drink. In the old days, iced tea was a passion. The body craves liquid, and a man's passion is ice. Today, people don't much care if the ice tray does not get filled. When we were young, you got whooped for forgetting to fill the ice tray.

Rule 3: Wear cool clothes. Yuppies with their ties, suits, and long-sleeved shirts will die in un-air conditioned hot weather. A power failure in Kansas City today would kill at least a million people; all dead in pools of starch and Coco perfume.

Rule 4: Don't exert or upset yourself, and keep your mind off the heat.

Conversation was a survival art in the old days. Not dwelling on petty irritations can be liberating. Even at 105 degrees, I began to feel comfortable, but my 10-year-old son was wilting. Maintaining one's cool is a learned art.

"How about a game of checkers," I asked, hoping to pass the time. The boy nodded yes. I poured my son an iced drink, moved him by the fan, and the game began. The heat made me mean. My son lost three straight. Then Merlin took over. Though 81 years old, almost paralyzed with Parkinson's, and hurting from arthritis, Merlin wanted a piece of me. We moved to the porch. Here, an evening breeze might dim the heat or divert a passing friend's attention. Fly-swatters in hand, the family headed out for the showdown.

Merlin played checkers like he built his house. He was relentless. There was nothing fancy, no frills, only a grim determination. The ice clicked in the glasses as new rounds of tea were poured. Bugs met a crushing end, and so did I. Unable to even move a checker (Aunt Marie could somehow read his hand signals on where to move a checker) for three straight games, Merlin took me to checkers school. He showed no mercy! My son shared the triumph and marveled at the strange man in the wheel chair. It is a great memory to this day.

Even heat has its blessings. As night falls, depression fades. Now it is time to leave the house and take a walk. Streetlights can make leaves look magical. Shadows add incredible depth and mystery to any object. My son and I kicked dust and talked. I remember telling my son the family stories about Grandma's cinnamon rolls and Dad's dog, Queen.

That night, we slept on pallets on the floor. There was a fan blowing at each end. Still, the heat kept us awake, and so we talked some more. "How did we ever live without air conditioning," someone always asks.

Maybe the old days weren't so great. We wouldn't glorify them now. But some still long for a night in an old home playing checkers on the porch, drinking iced tea, and sleeping by a fan. And talking with a son.

Oh No! Men's Day At Church

by Camelot Bob

It was Men's Day at church. That must give one pause, considering most days in our culture already are "Men's Day." Still, it is significant when any group takes it upon themselves to examine their being and consider how they could be better.

The surest sign that it was Men's Day was the odor from the church kitchen. The smell of burning food (sorry guys) is a sure sign that men are in the kitchen. Men's breakfast in the church basement is revealing, in a cultural sense. Table decorations aren't considered. "Basic" is an understatement. There's coffee, orange juice, pancakes, syrup, and sausage in roughly that order of importance. For those with more exotic tastes, there's non-dairy creamer and packaged jelly. Eggs are available upon request; you can order them any way you want, but they usually come out scrambled.

Cleanup is no-nonsense. Everything that can be rolled up in the paper tablecloth goes into the trash. The rest is put through scalding hot water. Food is either permanently baked on the plates or melted off. That's how men like breakfast – efficient and simple. If anything causes trouble, use Tabasco sauce or bolt cutters.

Conversation turns to weather, politics, and health. Today, it is mostly weather, because if it doesn't rain soon, the entire Kansas winter wheat crop will blow across Missouri in a giant grass fire.

Another sure sign of Men's Day is the worried looks of the women and pastor. Imagine how men would feel if all the church women, dressed in overalls, went to overhaul the church van. About the time wires and transmission parts started flying, men would get jumpy. Watching men snoop around the kitchen, fiddle in the nursery, and take over the primary Sunday School classes makes a woman edgy in the same way. As for the pastor, he knows there is no way the church service is going to come in under 90 minutes. By then, half the pot roasts in the county will be burnt to a crisp, and the back pew where the young people sit will be one major squirm.

Actually, the service wasn't bad. The all-male choir was admittedly good, and the male duet, superb. There was trouble in the children's service, however.

"Imagine what school would be like with all teachers and no students," the leader said, aiming at the importance of education. The little kids pondered this and fidgeted around without answering.

"Now, imagine what school would be like with all students and no teachers," he said.

"Cool," said a very young man in the back, who suddenly was quite interested.

"You guys wouldn't learn very much, would you?" the man asked, and you could almost hear the kids thinking, "Double cool!"

Still, the man finessed it with a very astute reference to a church dedication party. Parties mean a lot to kids. By now, however, the service was hopelessly long with two men left to speak.

Women understand lists, and men understand schedules. Being in charge and running overtime is hard on men. Men measure success by how fast they get places, getting done early, and working overtime. The men's service was in trouble, but Chet saved the day.

"I've got some things to say that have been on my heart, and we may just run over. I'll try to be brief," he said honestly, with feeling.

WOW, a man speaking from his heart – rare, even in church! Suddenly, everybody relaxed. The tension broke. Chet saved the service.

After the worship, all the men stood about congratulating themselves. The preacher relaxed, and the women smiled. Men's Day had come and gone, and the church still stood.

Gus Stops Sleeping For Ten Years

Exhaustion filled the old North Side. Bodies with sunburns and aching muscles shuffled their way around tables and sat in a daze before half-drunk cups of coffee.

"Can you believe this weather?" offered Manor Hill Mack, trying to jump-start some sort of conversation.

It didn't work. These men were tired. In the great spring battle of lawns, cars, gardens, and cleanup, old age had lost.

"I'm so tired my teeth hurt," moaned Holly Lake Jake.

"I'm looking forward to death," added Camelot Bob, trying to clean garden dirt out of his fingernails. "It's cheaper to go to the Farmer's Market than plant a garden."

Of course what Bob said and what he did were two different stories. Bob was still roto-tilling a newly-added section of garden 45 minutes after the sun went down. Cafe men are proud of being honorably tired. It's a side effect of testosterone. Gladstone Gus knew all the fussing was a ruse. Like all the others, he had his own story of what "tired" really was. Here is his story.

It was almost springtime, and his wife was very pregnant. She took sick in her eighth month and spent two weeks coughing in bed until Gus packed her off to the hospital. His wife had pneumonia. As soon as the I.V. was in, contractions started, and their baby was born three weeks early. The doctors said both baby and wife had some sort of virus, however, and would have to be quarantined. That's when Gus quit sleeping altogether.

With one son at home, Gus alternated time between house and hospital. The baby was now in an incubator. His wife's liver count had gone abnormally high. A week later, Gus brought their baby home. His wife stayed in the hospital. Gus fixed the formula, changed the diapers, rocked the child in the night, and prayed. One morning, as he was cooking pancakes, the phone rang. Gus was so tired he couldn't figure out what was ringing. His son answered and handed him the phone. The voice was weak and sounded far away, but Gus didn't have any trouble understanding who it was.

"Can you come and get me?" his wife asked. "The doctor says I can come home."

Gus was tired, but for the first time since the birth, he relaxed. It was at least a month before his wife got some strength back. Most of the memory is a blur. Gus learned just what it means to take on a baby full time, and his respect for mothers knows no limit.

"You guys don't know what tired is," laughed Gus. "Let's go play some golf."

A salvo of wadded napkins hit Gus as the men adjusted their aching bodies in waves of moans and heavy sighs.

"Can it, Gus," said Jake, trying to soothe a sunburn. "You're as worn out as the rest of us."

That night, Gus slipped into bed, laughing at the feel of cool sheets and a quiet night. He wouldn't ever want to relive those days when the baby was born, but he wouldn't give them up either. He who has come through the fire will not fade in the sun.

You Just Never Know

by Gladstone Gus

"You never know," my father-in-law likes to say. If time is a teacher, he should know. Last week, David O. Moore celebrated his 92nd birthday. In his life, he has been a teacher, preacher, carpenter, writer, father, husband, grandfather, farmer, and general nuisance to all who can't take a joke, are self-righteous, or think they somehow know more than anybody else.

A commonly held belief in our family is that I always manage to show up at his house when it is time to eat.

"Well, my boy," D.O. Moore says to me, "I see you have managed to appear right at lunch time, again."

"Yes sir," I say, "and just what are we eating today?"

"You never know," he says.

But I do know, because I keep track of when he smokes a turkey, makes bread, or cooks soup. I know he will badger me, but the food is worth it. Pop can be cantankerous, impervious, and irascible, and when he is, we say it is the "Norman Syndrome," kicking in. Norman is the crotchety old curmudgeon in the movie, *On Golden Pond*.

Pop and I once drove together to Phoenix on Christmas Day. We made it to Oklahoma City, where we bedded for the night. Pop took me out to eat at the Waffle House diner and said, "Get anything you want, it's Christmas."

The next morning at 2:30 a.m., I heard Pop shouting, "Are you awake???"

"I am now," I replied.

"Then we might as well get going," "Norman" declared, and that was the end of that night's sleep.

Turns out, there was a blizzard bearing down on us, and if we had not left when we did, we would have spent two more days of Christmas break in Oklahoma instead of Phoenix. You never know.

Pop is a master storyteller, and he has more stories than a hound dog has ticks. There is the story about the guy who raised worms. Every night when he fed the worms, he sang the song, "How Great Thou Art." The worms began to associate the song with food and would come to the surface when he sang, ready to eat. To impress his friends, the guy would sing to the worms, and the worms would rise out of the ground as if in homage to God. The guy was a worm evangelist. Pop swears that is a true story. You never know. (Side note: I took his college course in religion at William Jewell College. That is why he questioned half the town about me when it looked like his daughter and I were getting serious).

You are probably wondering when I'll start to say something nice. After all, it is his birthday. He is 92! Forget that! John Barrymore said a man is old when his regrets begin to outnumber his dreams. My Pop is a kid. He doesn't need any sweet talk yet.

As for you, David O. Moore, I'll be over for lunch today, and I expect some nice soup, homemade bread, and a good story or two. And, if you get to speculating why your son-in-law ended up as cantankerous, impervious, and irascible as you....well, "You just never know."

Selling A Farm On The Courthouse Steps

Holly Lake Jake wandered off to a side table and set alone nursing coffee he did not taste. The hot wind that ushered him into the Cafe held on as sweat pasting his body to the vinyl booth. The drought had claimed another record high for the day. There was nothing for Jake to do but wait and worry and wonder.

On the courthouse steps, his sister's farm was being sold that day. The house she had brought three of her four children home to had fallen into the red column of a bank ledger. Today, it would be sold to consolidate the loss. Jake's brother-in-law had worked 14-hour days for five years trying to beat this day. He had long since taken a job in town to make ends meet, but the red ink won.

Jake didn't know what to do. If it had been a tornado or fire that took his sister's home, he would have been there, and they would have cried together. They would have prayed thanks that they were alive and well and could go on. Uncle Jake would have lifted his nieces to warm family hugs and bought them ice cream at the Dairy Queen. But that's not how it is when a farm goes bust. Tragedy takes so long, it comes as an afterthought. Jake's sister just wanted it done without a fuss. People sit in silence, as scattered as the dust in the drought.

Jake remembered a story about his grandfather's farm in Iowa. He was four years old when it happened. It seems Grandpa and Grandma were out milking in the small lean-to attached to the side of the barn when a tornado hit. Gramps watched the side of his barn lift into the air about 30 feet and explode. The milking lean-to was untouched. Jake's dad had to borrow the money to go home and help Grandpa clean up and build a new barn. The whole family, two brothers and a sister, loaded up and went along. When your family is in trouble, you go to help. As a four-year old, he carried wood to the giant bonfire that was the old barn and gathered eggs for his grandma.

Today, farm tragedies are so common people rarely give them a second thought. A way of life is slipping into history just as surely as the old riverboats and cowboys of yesterday. Once the ethic was family first, the land second, and money last. Now all that counts is the money. But those who remember a family farm will have treasure. The walk to the barn in the morning to milk, nursing a sick calf, guiding a cultivator down majestic rows of beans, the smell of fresh cut clover, and raising kids on open land are memories too rich for letting go.

Jake penciled in a field of flowers on his napkin. In his mind's eye, they were bright with color. Sitting alone in the North Side, it was all he had to offer his sister, but he wanted her to have them. They could take the farm, but they could not take his family. The land would change, but not the memories.

In his way, Jake was at his sister's side all day. He cried for her and said prayers of thanks that they could go on. He held her and cared for her kids, just as if a tornado had struck.

That's what old country boys do at the North Side Cafe.

The Family Farm Fades

by Ridgeway Ron

Some things don't change. Rainy, autumn days still pull men like magnets to the Cafe where old farmers still complain as if their bad moods were a religion. To hear a farmer tell it, everything is a catastrophe waiting to happen.

On the first rainy day, they start talking flood and gripe, because they can't get in the field. When the sun shines, they talk drought and whine about the heat. They say they never make any money, though they all drive new trucks, have big combines, watch satellite TV, and bustle off to Las Vegas or take cruises every other year. Anyway, that's how it used to be.

Now, most people say the family farm will pretty much dry up and blow away in 10 years. The big farms will have it all. Landed gentry will own everything, and hired hands will work the old plots. Modern farms will be run by men in suits and college trained bean counters. An employee will drill seed, layer it with fertilizer, bug and weed killer, and just wait for harvest. That's how we like it in these United States – cheap, fast, and easy. Sam Walton and McDonald's taught us that. Rainy days mean nothing to suit and bean counter farmers. No magnet draws them to the old Cafe. Griping doesn't even mean much to these guys. They just cut losses and move stuff to Mexico or wherever else it's cheap at the moment. That means it's mostly the old guys who come to the Cafe on a rainy day. To the suits and bean counters their stories must seem quaint and old-fashioned. It's easy to poke fun at old farmers.

Sure, the old farmers griped and moaned, bellyached, and whined, but down deep they were venture capitalists of the most extraordinary sort. Who else would bet their life savings they could beat nature's full hand? Farmers yearly put it all on the line, and when the floods came, the droughts raged, bugs flew, and prices dropped, they simply tightened the belt. If it meant bumping a 16-hour day up a notch, running cattle, selling seed, or using bailing wire for a cheap fix, farmers knew how to take up slack. Farming wasn't just business, it was a life.

Now, the rainy days are older and grayer at the Cafe. The griping has slowed like the tick of an unwound clock. Let the big boys have a turn at it. Farming was always laced with change. These old men once drove horses and picked corn by hand. To them, 200 acres was a big spread, and milking 10 cows was a lot. They gathered eggs for breakfast and chopped chicken heads for Sunday lunch. Plowing straight and true was their symbol of good farming.

On this October day, the wind whips up darker clouds around the Cafe, and the old farmers huddle closer. Somehow, their grizzled lines break into smiles, eyes dance with laughter, and there is a mirth no bean counter will ever know. Their sense of survival carries a confidence that brightens up even rainy days. They wait for fate's next best shot. These old farmers have stood up to it too many years to back down now. Optimism is in their blood. No matter what the suits and bean counters do, there will always be a farmer in the American spirit.

When greed and callousness do their damage, when fast and cheap have done all the damage they can do; and then moved on, folks'll start looking around for help. Someone will have to step forward to pick up the slack. Help is waiting, biding time, at the old Cafe.

Too Fast For Fast Food

Today, the Old North Side is discussing fast food restaurants. It is not pretty.

"The other day, I pulled into the drive-up window and asked for a simple hamburger and soft drink. Well, you would have thought I asked for the moon the way the girl acted," said Camelot Bob. "First, she can't hear. I practically had to spell hamburger for her. Then, she gave me the wrong thing and acted like it was my fault."

A lot of the older generation thinks the younger generation is "snotty." Manor Hill Mack honestly believes his fast food waitress gets upset because he uses a senior citizen discount. This diatribe goes on for hours, drifting and winding further and further from the truth. Finally, Stella, the waitress, decided to add a dose of reality to the discussion. Her daughter, who works in a fast food restaurant, smuggled a voice activated tape recorder to work. Here is the unedited transcript of an actual fast food exchange:

Teenager: Good afternoon, can I help you?

Customer: Uhhhhh, yea. I want a hamburger…. something to drink…. some French fries.

Teenager: Regular hamburger, small French fries, and a small Coke; is that ok?

Customer: Is that hamburger with cheese?

Teenager: No, but we can put cheese on it.

Customer: NO, no cheese. The doctor said I have to cut down on dairy products.

Teenager: So, a regular hamburger, small French fries, and a small Coke; does that sound ok?

Customer: I don't want a Coke, I want 7 Up.

Teenager: Is Sprite ok?

Customer: Is what ok?

Teenager: Sprite. Is it ok to have Sprite instead of 7 Up?

Customer: No, give me a Coke.

Teenager: That will be $2.57.

Customer: Do you have a senior discount?

Teenager: Yes sir, I gave it to you.

Customer: I wanted a large fries.

Teenager: I'm sorry, let me get you some large fries.

Customer: No, no, I'll eat these. Do you have ketchup?

Teenager: I put it on your tray, sir.

Customer: Oh, I forgot. I have a coupon for the fries.

Teenager: I'm sorry, this coupon is expired, sir.

Customer: Oh, it says it's good for August.

Teenager: It expired several weeks ago, sir.

Customer: Well, ok, how much is it?

Teenager: $2.57 with a senior discount (*she does sound tired*).

Customer: Look, young lady, you don't have to get snotty about this. I've earned this senior discount.

Fast food is a hard go for everyone. Some young people are rude. There is a shortage of minimum wage laborers, and there are not enough quality kids to hire. Part of the problem is the fast food atmosphere. Customers are expected to be fast, too. Last, expectation has outstripped capacity. Even with five lines six deep, each customer expects everything fast and easy.

Sadly, it was fast food that reduced the North Side to an antique. Once it served family food. Now its function is coffee and talk. Kids really haven't changed that much – the world has changed around them. That's what happens when things move too fast.

Did You Say, "Gay Marriage"?

by Holly Lake Jake

I'm sticking my neck out today. I don't understand why people have their panties all in a wad over gay marriage. Why does anybody care if two people want to pledge their love for each other and promise to help and support each other for the rest of their lives? No institution or group of people own the exclusive "rights" to marriage or its definition. I generally support anything that brings love, happiness, justice, and peace into the lives of people. I think there is enough injustice, hatred, prejudice, and evil in the world as it is. I don't feel any need to work up anger over gay marriage, or institutionalize prejudice in the Constitution.

Most people think homosexuals should have the same rights in housing, jobs, and public accommodations and should have equal access to government benefits, equal protection of the law, and the freedom from harassment due to their sexual orientation. As gay people age, they value the same things straight couples do: loyalty, devotion, and the security of a committed relationship. They want a rich family life, are generally religious, and are committed to being good neighbors and law-abiding citizens. In short, they want the same things straight people want. Gay people make valuable contributions to their communities, serve on boards, volunteer, lead charities, and generally try to make life better for everyone. Why is marriage such an emotional issue?

Perhaps some people still believe gay people have a choice about their sexual orientation. Many people actually believe that gay people could simply choose to be heterosexual if they wished, but the reality is gay people have as much choice in picking what sex they are attracted to as straight people do!

Homosexuality is really not about sex. That's why the argument that gay people are trying to somehow "recruit" is so absurd. Gay people know there is no choice in attraction, and therefore, recruiting is a waste of time. The real issue with being gay is the isolation, hostility, and the constant misunderstanding faced each day. I hear a lot of vague arguments, but the opposition to gay marriage stems ultimately from a deep-seated homophobia in American culture, borne out of prejudice.

In anybody's book, prejudice is a bad thing. Because of this prejudice, gay people cannot make medical decisions for their partners in an emergency. Gay people can be compelled to testify against partners. Wills and durable powers of attorney often do not stand up to a family challenge. Custody decisions, exclusion from a funeral, or the right to visit a partner's grave can all be denied. Property bought jointly can be sold quickly at a huge loss.

These are the actual stories of gay couples. It is not a matter of special rights to ask for the *same* rights that other couples enjoy by law. No matter how we feel about homosexuals, the rights of life, liberty, and pursuit of happiness are for all the people in our country.

Mice, Men, And Martial Arts

It is a dry winter. A yardstick will go down seven or eight inches in some cracks. No water means no seeds, and that means the birds are starving. Animals that usually winter outside are coming indoors to find water. They are drawn to the water that condenses on foundation walls. Bugs and mice are thirsty, and that thirst makes them brave. Holly Lake Jake knew all this and was sitting in the back bedroom reading one of his Christmas books when the phone call came from his granddaughter.

"Papa!" she pleaded. "Come quick! It's a mouse!"

Jake knew his granddaughter was "Home Alone" during the extended school winter break. He also knew she would be hysterical at the sight of live mice. Jake understood her fear. All her life, Jake had warned her about the dangers associated with mice.

There are believed to be about 300 separate varieties of house mice in the United States. Mice have great balance, enabling them to walk along telephone wires, ropes, and similar thin objects. They can jump 12 inches vertically. Mice can run up almost any vertical surface – wood, brick, weathered sheet metal, cables, and can easily travel for some distance hanging upside down. They can swim and travel through pipes!

Mice breed all year and can get pregnant within 48 hours of producing a litter of six. Female mice may crank out as many as 10 litters (count 50 young) per year. Gestation is 18-21 days, and 35 days for a mouse to mature. Most mice live from 15-18 months.

Mice like to live in stoves and under refrigerators. They eat 17 times per day and can chew through insulation, wires, sheet rock, and cereal boxes. Mice nibble and graze all day, but really chow down when the sun rises and sets. They must eat about 10-15 percent of their body weight every 24 hours. In six months, two mice eat four pounds of food and leave 18,000 fecal reminders.

This was Jake's moment. He hurried over and found his 13-year-old granddaughter standing on the kitchen table with a butcher knife in one hand and a hammer in the other. She was crying. Apparently, the mouse was under the stove.

Jake got a broom handle and gently pushed a very frightened mouse out from under the stove. He then pinned the mouse down with the broom end, picked it up by the tail, and threw it out the back door.

After the commotion, Jake took his granddaughter to the hardware store where they found a plethora of mice deterrents. Jake promised to come back regularly to check them. He also promised to come whenever his granddaughter might call.

Jake is now his granddaughter's hero for life. She bakes him cookies, gives him hugs, brags about him to her friends, and defends him against her own mom and dad. Jake had to admit, he had gotten a lot of mileage out of mice. His young wife, his daughter, and now his granddaughter all consider him the bravest, most wonderful man on earth since the day he saved each of them from attacking mice.

By the way, has Jake ever told you that mice who eat the brains of mice that have been taught how to do a task will learn that same task 50 percent faster than the first set of mice did? Mice are formidable and voracious foes! Good thing brave Jake is around to protect the women of the world.

Life Flight Saves Jake

It was, at long last, a beautiful, shimmering morning at the Old North Side Cafe. The light reflected off counters and glanced about the room, illuminating all that was bright and clean and clear. Stella dashed among the tables pouring coffee, vaguely flirting with the overlords of the Cafe kingdom. The ubiquitous tinkling of cups, whispers and laughs formed the backdrop of the day. It was a fitting setting for the return of Holly Lake Jake.

Three weeks ago to the day, Jake had suffered a heart attack. Coming up the basement stairs, he felt a sharp pain. His wife recognized the signs and hustled him to the emergency room. They, too, saw the signs, and it was a fast helicopter ride to St. Luke's Hospital in Kansas City. Common modern miracles saved Jake. All of that was over now as Jake eased himself into the gleaming silence of his old, familiar table. His buddies sat proud and smiling. They waited for Jake to speak.

"So how's it going?" asked Jake the men assembled around the familiar Liar's Table.

"Been kind of slow," answered Camelot Bob. "We haven't had any bleeding heart liberals around to pick on."

"Just as well," replied Jake. "They would have made a fool of you anyway."

The laughter eased up and floated like light across the room. Stella suddenly appeared.

"Jake, how you feeling?" she asked. "I hope you didn't give those nurses as much trouble as you give me."

"If they had been as good looking as you, I might have," said Jake. "And I'm doing fine. Thank you for asking."

Anytime a North Sider spends time in the hospital, several mandatory discussions must follow. First, nurses must be rated in ways that cannot be shared with the outside world. Second, the men must expound on the degradation of bedpans, urinals, open-back hospital gowns, and cold operating tables. Men must then better each story of hospital woe until Gladstone Gus tells his about his urinary tract infection. Then the men shudder and the stories stop.

Finally, they must discuss the mysterious food. People lie about hospital food. Jake's daughter would take off the plastic cover to his meal and tell a sinful lie.

"Dad, this looks really good. I'd like to have some for my supper," she'd say. That was a lie, and Jake knew it. Under the plastic cover was a congealed, dough-looking thing with a piece of wilted parsley on the side. It was barely organic. If it was supposed to be chicken, the gravy was white. For beef, the gravy is brown. Italian food had red stuff on it. All possible taste had been extracted from the mashed ball except for the salt-less sauce which identified the meal.

All lies are essential in a hospital. Jake continued the lie. When the rehab nursing tag-team came in to practice their throws and punches, Jake said the meal was "fine." Then, doctors came in and lied about when Jake would go home, and hospital bean counters lied about how much it all cost. The insurance company lied about how much they would pay, and the nurse lied about coming back with the pain pill. Everyone lies in a hospital except for one person. The person who comes to take blood tells the truth.

"This may hurt," he says, gouging around for a vein. That guy is always honest.

Such talk twisted and turned over an afternoon. Jake laughed, and the men enjoyed a return to the way things should be.

"Look Jake, next time you want a helicopter ride, will you just call and we'll get you one. You don't have to pay $2,000 for a ride to the hospital." That's actually coded North Side Cafe language telling Jake he was loved, and they had been worried. Jake knew the meaning, and he felt the calm that comes from being with friends.

The light still danced on the counters long after the men left. The long gloom was lifted from the Old North Side Cafe.

Farm World Seems Lost

Sometimes, the dust particles drifting through shafts of sunlight, or the clink of porcelain coffee cups, call up a memory at the North Side Cafe. Lace window curtains drifting in a slight summer breeze, the smell of mowed grass, or the clunking sounds of machinery are sensory bookmarks to the old guys. They say the early memories are the last to go.

Manor Hill Mack grew up on a farm in northwest Iowa, located north of Cedar Rapids, roughly between Spencer and Manchester. He remembers places with musical names like Strawberry Point and the Wisconsin Dells. It was a life filled with the distinctive chug-chug of an old John Deere tractor, small round bales of hay, cats in the milk house, and early mornings in the chicken house to gather eggs. It is a world away from today.

There were white lace curtains above his mother's kitchen sink. Each night before supper, Mack washed his hands at the sink with well water drawn with a handle pump. The pumping sound, the gushing cold water, and the movement of the handle up and down all combined to create a routine marked by the rhythms of farm life. Sudden Iowa storms, or the lazy drift of heavy summer air sometimes blew through the kitchen window lace, creating shadow dances on the wall. Those dances are now etched deep into a small farm boy's recollection. Mom's kitchen was a lock box for the smells, textures, sights, and sounds of a time we will never know again.

Mack vividly recalls the musky odor of wet feathers and the comical sight of headless chickens taking a last romp before being cooked for supper. Sharp knives, cutting boards, ice picks, and porcelain wash bowls were the utilitarian tools of the kitchen, not decorative announcements of status. That old kitchen and mom's calloused, loving hands spark up in Mack's mind from time to time. The fluttering lace, the pump handle racket, ripe food fresh from a garden, and a sudden death on a worn kitchen counter are all gone now.

It is amazing how the past can come back so easily, but so changed, like the appearance of a friend who has also grown old. Nothing is ever as it was. That's true of memories, too. The line between reality and truth blurs, but nothing is more honest than a farm memory. The child locked in Mack's old body still can recall the familiar crunch of cold snow as he walked to the pond to chip holes in the ice to water livestock. (What a treasure that axe would be now). Then it was up to the cobweb barn, steaming with ripe manure in the cold morning, and home to the endless battles between cats and mice. Thirteen cows were milked, and the heavy milk buckets carried to the separator. All the sights and sounds – dusty hay, the sweet odor of ground corn cobs, and breakfast cooking on a wood stove on cold mornings – all are memories. Mack remembers with a broad smile how cows were both so dumb and so majestic at the same time.

Everything seemed to come in extremes on a farm. The weather was hot, and the iced tea was cold. By breakfast you were starving, but the meals were huge. The work seemed overwhelming, but at times, driving a team of horses, you felt like the king of the world. Memories soften the hardships of that life. Mack enjoys his visit to a world of lacy curtains, pumped water, autumn harvests, musty barns, and memories of life on a family farm.

Time To Walk The Fields

The farmer spirit in Ridgeway Ron knew it was time. He rose early and packed a thermos. There was an edge of frost on the dead heads of marigolds. Just last night, Ron had seen the flying V of Northern geese swooping low along the tree line. The morning air was cold now, and the sun seemed to save its energy for an afternoon's burst. It was the season of soft flannel shirts and light jackets with warm pockets. The furnace came on regularly, leaving the faint odor of burnt lint throughout the house. Yes, it was time.

On an autumn day, Ron will drive alone, or with his grandchild, along the back-country roads, just looking. The search is for leaves and trees, but the treasure is the season itself. Eventually, back roads will lead to river bluffs and the true splendor of autumn. Nature's art is random and wild. Driven by instinct and physics, not motive, forests wrap themselves in color, unaware of the combined majesty of their effort. Ron likes morning on a river bluff best. He likes the slant of sunlight and the shadows. He likes the glistening film of frost and the dew that sparkles in the leaves.

Older men feel lonely and lost at times. They miss having years to spare; and they sometimes search for the sound of geese in night flight, and powerful pull of change as it sweeps across a season. They long for the miracle of "one more day." There is no magic in autumn's spell, no answer to the hard questions; but there is comfort. Tall, golden aspen; burgundy and orange maples; the magnificent mixed colors of sweet gum leaves; and the rusty yellow of elm fill up the eye. Leaves are nature's most powerful metaphor. In concert, their eruption of color is an inspiring symbol what could be — we could be constellations of colors, our lives filled with diversity and amazing transformations. Our last stand can be a good one.

Autumn is also the simile of decay. One leaf falling diminishes the whole. Unchecked daily subtraction leaves us stark and bare. Similar in our loss, we are like the leaves in a falling symphony of orchestrated despair. Ron feels these things and understands them, but not as thoughts. He is a farmer connected to the land and all its ways – all its memories. Wisdom is a powerful thing.

From his view on the river bluff, Ron remembers leaves. From those first days in elementary school when his mom ironed golden maple leaves between pieces of waxed paper to the save their color, to those daring days when his rural farm chums raced bicycles through piles of burning leaves as a death defying stunt, Ron remembers leaves. He remembers catalpa trees, their huge leaves and those mysterious long cigars that he and his sister tried to smoke. As a father, Ron raked huge piles of leaves and then dragged the picnic table over so his boys could run across the tabletop and leap into childhood. They sunk to their heads with grins shining across their faces. Then, there was the great discovery! The dog liked the leap as much as the boys! Those days were so fine!

Ron remembers trees. There is the giant sycamore by the Second Baptist Church, the maples at the college that turn early, still healthy elm trees – somehow spared – in a pasture north of town. The list is long and growing.

By noon, the moment has ended. Ron touches a last hickory tree on his hike back to the car. He loves the smell. Ron does not wonder if this will be his last fall – he is so much older than most people think. He just rejoices that he has been able to answer the call to walk his fields for another autumn season.

Ron, like most of the aging around us, is a man of many colors, golden in years. Such a great presence among us can splash our mornings with unexpected vibrant colors, and the common joy of a season's end.

Chapter 3

Teaching and Learning

"The Colt .45 pistol was the great equalizer, but education is what won the West," says City Hall Sam.

In a glorious age of excess, the United States Government gave away millions of acres of land. It paid railroads to push their rails across the continent on land, with all its resources, free for the taking. What a deal! It worked. The country grew and prospered.

"We did the same thing with education," and now Sam is all worked up. "Free land was set aside for public schools. Public education worked better than anyone ever could have imagined. Educating the young ushered in an era in which the United States became the world's most important nation. The greatest American achievement is its public school system. There was good reason for such a noble experiment. A democracy depends on people smart enough to vote." Sam now is downright giddy with excitement! "You can see what happened when we finally ran out of free land. The country stopped growing, and we have been fighting about it ever since. People bought up the land, and they have the power. Now that they have discovered how much money is in public education, people want to grab it, carve it up, and control it too."

Liberals Holly Lake Jake and Gladstone Gus think public education is now under siege. "Politicians want to gut it and take the money."

Conservative Camelot Bob thinks the following (word for word): "Teachers are a drag on our economy. Teachers don't work for three months, their pension funds are too generous, and the kids they teach are not learning anything anyway."

Here is how Bob proposes to fix it. "First, we find a way to make sure public funds are shared with private schools too, so those parents can stop paying that damn tuition out of their own pockets. Next, we shuffle all the good kids off to nice private schools where they will have lots of fine resources and will not have to deal with the troublemakers, the poor, the challenged, the violent, mentally ill, and parentless. We'll stack 'em deep and teach 'em cheap in public schools. Hopefully, they will become invisible."

Bob is rolling now. "Some of the good loser kids will be put into charter schools where we can make up all new rules for testing and success. Kids will show some progress, because the new rules will guarantee it. Again, the charter schools will get first pick of students and take the money off the top. Then, the news media will compare the test scores, and sure enough, the private and charter schools will do better. Charter schools will ease the public conscience, and public schools will get even less money." Bob openly admits the real agenda is putting more money in a few pockets. It's all business, after all, and business is the American way.

"Oh, and one other thing," he says, "those baggin' and draggin', Ebonics speaking, scary looking, gangbanging, welfare babies will get just what they deserve. At last, the good kids will be safe."

Jake wonders, "How did public education, the greatest achievement in the history of our country, get into such a bad spot? How did we forget, in three generations, that public schools for all are the only hope for our democracy and our way of life?"

At the Cafe, every man will tell you his parents made huge sacrifices to put him through school. Many even sent their children to live with folk in town to get schooled. They paid a higher percentage of their income for public education than anybody does today. They voted for schools that are monuments to education's worth and place in our society. The first thing they did after World War II was make damn sure people could go to college on the GI bill. They valued public education for all. The GI bill worked and ushered in another age of prosperity. Public education works!

Ninety percent of the North Side crowd supports school bonds and levies. They support teachers and principals. They love all kids. They are Americans. How could they not? Bob just honestly believes the public education beast has gotten too big, too expensive, and too out-of-touch with the values he holds dear. He wants to starve it. He sincerely believes the private and charter schools can do a better job, and he is willing to risk a generation of children to prove it.

For What It's Worth, Free Advice

The Old North Side Cafe

Kids with backpacks and the first rounds of big yellow buses about town signal a new season at the Cafe. Summer is giving way to the start of school and coming autumn. Grumpy old codgers hover over coffee clouds, anticipating cold snaps in the weather and the smooth textures of flannel and fine wool. The start of school is a very distant memory for them, but the feelings of a new season filled with promise and expectations are as common as autumn's harvest.

Too often, it seems, the aging offer their criticism, but not their help, when it comes to children and schools. Water Street Pete wanted to change that. Watching children board their bus one morning, he devised a plan.

"Boys, I think we should come up with a few tips for parents and their teenagers on how to be successful," Pete said, and was answered by a general moan.

"I can't even tell their sex anymore," said Camelot Bob. "How should I know what to tell 'em to do?"

Pete would have none of that mumbling nonsense. "Just living as long as you have means you have something to offer," said Pete. "I admit, however, that if it is only to gripe, well, that isn't much."

Slowly, they came around, and here it is:

The North Side Cafe's "School Tips for Success"

One: Enjoy every day you have – it flies by fast. Tell that girl you're interested in her. Go see that mountain. Learn to play that guitar. Go for something or you will be stopped by everything.

Two: Learn! There isn't a one of us who doesn't wish he had learned more when he had the chance. Everything is important. Everything comes back to help you someday – even English class and fractions.

Three: Be your own person. God made you special; act that way.

Four: Don't do anything now that you can't change down the line. Grow or color your hair any way you like. Dress how you want, play in a band, jump out of planes; we don't care. But, don't mess up your brain and/or gene pool.

Five: You won't believe this, but it is the gospel truth. You will probably get exactly what you want from life. Be careful what you want (this includes being that "oh so good looking, but stuck up" popular queen or king).

Six: You only fail when you give up. The only mistake you ever make is doing something wrong twice.

Seven: Never, ever badmouth your own family in public. Nobody trusts a person who betrays his kin to strangers – that includes your little sister!

Eight: Be known for the good you do, not the bad. Be known for what you support, not what you are against. Bad reputations become a ball and chain quicker than anything we know.

Nine: Give older people a chance. We know how to protect you from your parents.

Ten: Get good at something that doesn't get you into trouble with the law. Sing, write, work on cars, kick goals, do math, paint, help others – just learn to do something well.

Eleven: Do basic things for yourself. What you don't know (like laundry and cars) gives people power over you.

Twelve: Almost everything you see on TV is not real. If TV started showing reality, you wouldn't need these tips. All TV wants is your money.

Thirteen: Always over-tip the waitress, start saving money, call your mom when you're real late, keep gas in your car, learn to enjoy good food, and take free advice for what it's worth.

How to salvage a kid. Say and do things that make him/her feel special, worthwhile, capable, and good. Look past behavior to the feelings inside, and give them a chance to be a success. Fortunately, God's quality control is pretty good. Most kids are fixable if you try.

God Bless Garrison School

by Gladstone Gus

Let's have a history lesson. Lewis and Clark floated by our neck of the woods sometime in 1804. Settlers arrived in 1817, and Clay County was formed in 1822. Liberty, the county seat, was incorporated in 1829 becoming the second oldest town west of the Mississippi River. William Jewell College in Liberty, Missouri, founded in 1849, is one of the oldest colleges in Missouri. February 13, 1866, Jesse James supposedly robbed Clay County Savings Bank in the nation's first successful daylight bank robbery. Built in 1858, that bank is now the oldest building on Liberty's Historic Square.

Fortunately, Liberty was prepared for criminal activity; Liberty Jail was built in 1833. Joseph Smith, first president and prophet of the Church of Jesus Christ of Latter-day Saints (the Mormons) was held in jail there in 1839. Smith was saved from death by Colonel Alexander Doniphan who disobeyed a direct order to have him executed. It is our county's "Profile in Courage." In 1846, that same Colonel Alexander Doniphan began an historic land march to participate in the Mexican-American war. *The Liberty Tribune* published its first issue in 1846 and staked a claim to history. Lightburne Hall, was built in 1852. The legendary S.P. Boggess opened a Ford dealership in 1908 near the Liberty Square. That's a nutshell version of our local history.

The sad thing about Liberty and Clay County history is that one of our most significant, historic landmarks is never mentioned. Perhaps we are missing something important in our county. Here is a statement concerning Garrison School, issued by Liberty Public Schools at one of their September business meetings. Read it carefully:

"Garrison School is a symbolic, cultural center for Liberty and Clay County, as well as a continuing reminder of the heroic contributions and incredible spirit of African Americans in their long journey to freedom.

"Our country did not allow African Americans to be educated until 1865. Somewhere around 1873, Garrison School was founded, and by 1910, 117 children had attended the school. It was here in this small schoolhouse that a continuous struggle for an equal place in the great American experiment was played out. For nearly 100 years, Garrison was the only place African American families could go for an education. Because so many black families attended the school, its history is actually the history of the African American experience in Liberty and Clay County.

"The building itself is a bookmark for countless families as they trace their ancestry and celebrate their heritage. So many significant African Americans, including the first African American pilot, were Garrison graduates. The roots of African American education in this area grew from seeds planted in Garrison School.

"For its history alone, we should seek to preserve Garrison School. Today, there are precious few landmarks to remind us of the struggles African Americans faced in our community and to celebrate their achievements. The area around the school is designated as the Garrison Historic District and dates back to 1843. Garrison is an historic building that anchors an important historic area. Garrison can speak eloquently to children of all colors about freedom, perseverance, and the importance of education in America."

Liberty and Clay County have Jesse James, for whatever that is worth. We have Lewis and Clark and Joseph Smith. We have Alexander Doniphan, who really is a hero and could be our greatest claim to real fame. The jail and William Jewell College hold prominent spots in our history, and they should. It is Garrison School, however, that may one day be our most important landmark. Should we choose to save it, years from now, when we have finally conquered our old prejudices and tunnel vision for all things white, we may take another look at our history.

At Garrison School, there are untold magnificent stories of courage, dedication, perseverance, and our American spirit. I can see the tour bus unloading and the tour guide walking up to what is now hallowed ground. "Garrison School is where a small band of dedicated American families made a stand for freedom. Facing overwhelming odds, they stood up for human dignity, hope, and the power of education," the guide might say. "It was here we examined the depths of our human spirit and found greatness in our soul."

We Raise What We Praise

by Ridgeway Ron

Here is what we know about television and violence.

- If a child lives in a home where problems are solved through reason and discussion;

- If hitting is an absolute last resort, and ugly shouting and name-calling are uncommon;

- If kids feel safe in their own house;

… then television violence does not seem to have a major impact.

On the other hand, children who live in homes where violence "solves" problems, ugly behavior is the norm, and fear rules, then television's impact is unmistakable and powerful. Television tends to reinforce what is already in a child's home. Violent homes become significantly more violent when TV viewing increases.

That brings us to a bloody school sidewalk in Arkansas with children and teachers dead. All were killed by two boys, ages 11 and 13. Not since Kent State when our own National Guard gunned down four college students have we been so bewildered by senseless violence. What has happened that white, rural kids, supposedly the flagship of family values, have come to embrace ambush murder?

In the media, we hear it is our culture gone awry. Movies and TV have corrupted our children and our soul. Pundits say it's because guns are too plentiful and too easily obtained. We hear we should charge parents with the crimes of their children; perhaps capital punishment for 11-year-olds will deter kid criminals. Some whisper it is the dark side of Southern life. Most frightening is the notion that even our schools are no longer safe.

Let's be reasonable. First, there is nothing wrong with most kids. They are responsible, caring, decent kids. This notion that kids are somehow flawed bothers me a great deal.

Second, some kids are so miserable at school it is hard for us to imagine their pain. These students are unconnected and broken, capable of great harm to themselves and others. The result is schools are more concerned about violence than ever before. School officials know that safety is every parent's first concern, and schools too have made it their top priority. Every teacher realizes they cannot leave children unsupervised for even a moment.

Despite the huge effort by school leaders to keep kids safe, there is no quick fix to violence. Less entertainment that glorifies violence is a start. More training for teachers, and controlled access to schools will help. So will keeping an ear to the rumors that float around schools. All, however, are at best, bandages.

I'm told that in the minutes after the Arkansas shooting, the road to the middle school was clogged with parents desperate to reach their children. In that moment, parent priorities were made straight. What mattered most were children, and that they were safe. Home by home, heart by heart, if that thought spread across our country, school violence would diminish.

Help A Kid The First Day Of School

by Gladstone Gus

The North Side tradition is to tell a school story at the start of each new school year. Old stories include the time I watched a teacher wait patiently to be cussed out by an angry young student who stuttered and how that teacher and I became friends. Of course, some will remember my own Fruit of the Loom incident. As a grade schooler, yesterday's wadded up underwear was still in my jeans, and I pulled it out for all my third grade class to see.

My favorite start-of-school story is about a student other kids considered a loser. One day in class, she told us about being born prematurely and how she was brought home in a shoebox and had to sleep on her father's chest for two months to stay warm enough. She then looked the entire class in the eye and told us God had saved her for a purpose. She would make something of her life yet. That girl is now head of a pediatric unit at a Kansas City hospital.

This year's story is about Ben. Ben was an eighth grade student at East High School in Kansas City in 1972. Ben was not an honor student. I am not sure he could even read. Ben was small. He was quiet. He never caused any trouble, and nobody paid the least attention to Ben, including me. I started my job at East in mid-October. The class had reportedly already run off their first two teachers. I could understand why. They walked in and out of class at will. They talked without stopping. I dreaded any day apples or oranges were served at lunch. If you can picture fruit flying around a room, you can imagine why. In the chaos of trying to bring order to eighth graders (some of whom were about 100 pounds heavier than me), you might understand why Ben slipped through the cracks.

This class once threw a desk and all my papers out the third floor window, and the principal came to chew me out for not being able to control my class. Finally, I lost it. One day after ten minutes of "apple dodge ball," I hurled my book against the back wall and screamed I'd had it. It was them or me! I faced them with murder in my eyes. They laughed! They jeered! Some wanted to actually fight me. "Get out!" I screamed. To my amazement, they all got up and left. Everyone, that is, but three girls and Ben.

I went to the principal. The principal asked me if I really wanted to teach. I said, yes. He told me to draw up five rules (no more), and he would back me up. If a student broke a rule, the principal would send him/her home and s/he could not come back until there was a parent conference. I kicked out 26 students and had 26 parent conferences. Some nights, I stayed at the school past 11 p.m.

I never kicked Ben out. Ben never caused any problem other than he was absent every other day. Finally, one night on my way home from the last of my parent conferences, I stopped by Ben's house to see what the problem was with his attendance. Ben did not come to school every day, because every other day his younger brother wore his shoes. The two had only one pair of shoes between them, and on the day his brother wore the shoes, Ben stayed home. The principal found Ben some shoes, and Ben came to school every day after that. I don't know what happened to Ben, but I know Ben's story is not over.

Every school year in your hometown there is a long list of names of kids just like Ben who really need some help with basic back-to-school supplies. Responding to this basic need is a small effort for you, but with more impact on the recipient than you will know.

It's "Sr." You Idiot, Not "Sen."

by Gladstone Gus

Garrison Keillor tells a hilarious story about a young man who borrowed his uncle's motor home to go ice fishing on a Minnesota lake. After a wild night of fishing and partying, the young man failed to notice they were the only ones left on the lake. Sure enough, the ice was breaking up. The boys survived the melting lake, but the motor home did not. The young man spent the next three years paying for the motor home. While friends went off to college, or had youthful adventures, the boy worked two jobs paying off every penny. It was a very hard lesson. A few years later, however, the boy remembered the cost of that commitment and got out of a relationship before it drifted into a marriage that neither really wanted.

Spring of the year 1967, I, too, went to the school of hard knocks. Thinking to leave a legacy, but actually not thinking at all, I joined some friends in spray painting "Senior '67" on the swimming pool dressing rooms in Savannah, Missouri. Being stupid enough to vandalize was not enough for me! I also abbreviated senior as "Sen." instead of "Sr.", forever cementing my reputation as an idiot and a bad speller.

The law caught me, and I personally paid for repainting the entire swimming pool complex with no help from anybody. It took every penny I had ever saved and a summer of hard labor. My dad was mortified. He made no excuses for me. His disappointment showed, and I felt awful. I grew up a lot that summer. My dad handled things just right.

That brings us to an old story about a group of young people who vandalized public property. Their youthful rampage ran into a lot of money for repair. A story made the rounds that some parents went to the prosecuting attorney asking what it would cost to get their son or daughter off the hook. The parents apparently felt justice was for sale. Like about everything else in our culture, some kids and their parents counted on daddy's money and influence to settle the issue.

Responsibility is fleeting among some young people and their parents in our culture. Almost as often as not, when I was in my teacher role and called a parent about something their child had done in class, I first had to defend myself. Parents have a lot of excuses and rationalizations: "The rules aren't fair." "Other students get away with the same thing." "Do you have proof?" "It's your fault, because there is a 'personality' conflict." "My child has never had a problem with any other teacher." Or, and teachers hear this one with regularity, "You are just picking on my child," the parents say. I have heard parents say all these things. With attitudes like this, you can imagine what their kids are like. Personal responsibility is not a high priority in our culture. My dad told me to get along with teachers, even if the teacher was wrong. "You might as well learn to get along with people," he said. It was valuable and responsible advice.

Life once taught responsibility in natural ways. On a farm, if you did not take care of livestock, or you put off doing your work, the family suffered. Excuses and rationalizations didn't mean much if the hog died, or weeds took the beans. Today, for some, showing up for work is optional, being on time is negotiable, and excuses pardon responsibility.

Before this paintbrush gets too wide, I want to also say that there are a lot of responsible parents and young people. I just wonder how many seniors today would pay off a motor home before going to college. How many parents would let their children take a degree in the school of hard knocks? How many young people have any idea what a commitment like marriage really means? I hope, at least, my students learned how to abbreviate "senior."

We Need A Terrance In The Class

by Gladstone Gus

"Tell me and I'll forget; show me and I may remember; involve me and I'll understand." - Chinese Proverb

"You are rewarding a teacher poorly if you remain always a pupil." - Nietzsche

"There are three things to remember when teaching: know your stuff; know whom you are stuffing; and then stuff them elegantly." - Lola J. May

My teaching philosophy can best be described by a story. In December of 2009, my college liberal arts communications class of first-year students was preparing for a "culminating" activity. Most were giving speeches. Terrance Masters was struggling.

A favorite of the class, Terrance was witty, unabashed, and intellectual. He was a refreshing change at a religious-based college where most students wanted to give their testimony of faith more than any other speech. Terrance had something else in mind for his culminating activity. About a third of the way through, I saw it coming. Terrence was coming out. "I am gay," he said. "I am gay." It was a curtain being pulled back. For the next several minutes, Mr. Masters mesmerized his contemporaries with the gentle eloquence of his truth, his place in life, and his fear that he would be rejected. He gave a great speech and put to extraordinary use the learning we had shared in class.

At William Jewell College in a small Midwestern town, many of my students had never heard those words before; never experienced anyone say, "I am gay." Many students stayed after class to talk. Seeds went into brain soil; lights of new experience were shining for the first time. There were no "black or white" absolute dictums. Old assumptions were challenged. Fear sat in the back seat of the class, and then was expunged all-together, when an African-American star running back declared, "Now, that took guts!" I could have been fired that night. Instead, it was another day of class.

Learning can happen when people feel safe and respected. Young people will respond to the most challenging issues of the day with dignity and grace if such behaviors have been modeled all through the class. My philosophy of teaching is to trust my students and turn on the lights. If I can impress them with how much I work and care, they will give it back to the entire class in greater proportions. Teachers plant, drip ideas, cultivate the soil, chop the weeds, and get out of the way.

Terrance wrote me last week that he is a finalist in auditions for new members of the cast of the TV show *Glee*. He wanted me to wish him luck. Truth is, he hasn't needed me since December of 2009. But because I teach, I will always need a Terrance in my class.

Teachers Know

by Gladstone Gus

Teachers know the unexplainable excitement when a bell rings to start teaching; the amazing joy of welcoming a child to class. Teachers know chalk dust on their pants, gum on their shoes, paper cuts on their fingers, and ink stains on their front right pocket. Veteran teachers know how to teach in the dark, in construction zones, in closets, and in fear. They know death, violence, inexplicable anger aimed at them for a parent's failure, and how to eat lunch in 10 minutes. They know kids who work harder to just get on a bus each morning than some kids do to make straight A's. They know kids who sleep in cars, on the floor, in a different house each week, in the back room at a fast food restaurant, and in class. They know kids who have never worked for a thing in their life and who don't expect to work for a grade; their parents back them in this assumption. Teachers know parents who want every other child in the school disciplined, but not their own; parents who expect the truth from school, but will lie on a note to protect their child. They know the alive sound of a full hallway of laughing kids and the splendid silence of an entire classroom of students reading a great book.

Teachers know questions to make a seasoned detective blush. "Did you have toilets when you were young?" "Did you ever smoke dope?" "Is that ketchup on your tie?" "Do we really have to do this?", and the always-exasperating, "Is this for a grade?"

Teachers know how to diagnose illness, react to multiple emergencies, fix Spider-man's broken arm, counsel love-sickness, duck and roll, and clean-up anything. They know when to hold 'em and when to scold 'em.

Teachers don't know about having money or getting thank-you's. They don't know about greed or people who leave their work at the office. They don't know about business flights, luxury lunches, junkets, or expense accounts. They don't know how people can vote against a child's future to pay for their own luxuries. They don't know how politicians can cut school budgets to pay for their own ineptness, and they don't stop teaching well when their salaries are frozen or their fellow teachers are laid off.

Teachers know what it is like to make a difference; to touch the future; to do important, worthy work; and they know they cannot care too much, give too much, or work too hard. Teachers know the joy of driving the oldest car in the parking lot, getting a slightly used set of dictionaries, receiving notes with their name misspelled, and hearing their students talk about a vacation they can never take.

Teachers know the joy of a needy hug, being led by the hand to see a picture, the power of "You can do it," and the gratification of a child bragging on himself to his parents. Teachers are negotiators, motivators, referees, event planners, ministers, lawyers, set designers, cooks, psychiatrists, stain specialists, odor supervisors, critics, academics, and cheerleaders.

Teachers know the pain and joy of the last day of school; the names of their kids now in Iraq or Afghanistan; the hurtful snub at parties when they say they teach; and the vague, negative innuendo of an old friend asking, "Do you still teach?"

Teachers know that being with the kids, getting to teach, and feeling proud of what they do is something only they can understand.

We all need to remember what teachers know.

Best Friends Forever

The Cafe men stopped and stared as the woman in the wheelchair entered the cafe. She looked about 30, blond hair and well dressed.

"She is a person who has cerebral palsy," said Ridgeway Ron. He recognized the behaviors.

"Poor thing," Camelot Bob, muttered under his breath. "I know I would hate to be stuck in a wheelchair."

"You know what, Bob," Ron said trying to keep his voice even, "she isn't stuck to that chair, and I doubt very much if she feels like a 'poor thing.' "

"What are your talking about?" Bob countered. "She's handicapped, an invalid in a wheelchair."

Ron did not want this conversation, but it was too late.

Ron squared his shoulders toward Bob.

"The word 'handicapped' dates back to England when persons were licensed to stand on a corner with a cap in hand to beg for money. People with disabilities don't want charity. They want to participate, to be included. The word 'invalid' literally means 'not valid,'" Ron said. "Don't use it on her!

Bob, of course, got mad.

"Ron, I did not take you for a bleeding heart liberal. Tell me, what makes you so sensitive about cripples?"

It was Judy who caused Ron to be sensitive about the physically challenged. Judy was a little girl who came to Ron's first grade class in an era when a child with cerebral palsy was banished to remote institutions and separated from the other kids. Somehow, Judy got through.

Judy was born blue, and doctors all but left her for dead until Judy's mom intervened.

"Call her Judy! Say her name!" she ordered. The doctors were stunned but tended to Judy. They saved her life. Judy's heart was beating, but the lack of oxygen in those first moments left her with cerebral palsy.

That first day in first grade, the teacher told the class not to stare at Judy. So, the class put their heads down on the desk and pretended to sleep when Judy walked in. One by one they looked up to find Judy was not a monster.

The kids figured it out. They were the ones who insisted Judy join them on the playground. The kids wanted to know why Judy was not in the Christmas assembly (an administrator wanted to 'save' her having to stand on the stage.).

Then there is the great Halloween story – the best Halloween of Ron's life. The seventh grade girls had a slumber party. The boys were waiting for them on the town square. Mischief was in the air. Soaping windows and throwing toilet paper called for fast action. But, there was no way the girls would leave Judy behind. They found a wagon, and one of the girls rode with her. Judy handled the TP and soap. At the square, the girls flirted shamelessly. Judy was part of the gang, a friend; it would not seem right without her there.

Judy needed no pity. She gave more than she ever got. Most people with disabilities do if given the chance. Today, some expert might call Judy's inclusion, "natural support." Ron found that it worked both ways.

"A person with a disability is not brave or heroic because they are in a wheelchair. They are not special gifts from God. They don't always need a compliment. They just want to be a person and be included," Ron said to end his Judy story.

Bob scratched his head and stared again at the woman in the wheelchair. A lot of years of conditioning were being challenged. Giving another the dignity of personhood, beyond labels and pity, is a very freeing and rewarding experience. Judy had taught Ron that lesson in the wonderful days of youth when he and Judy were best friends.

More Than Names On A Page

by Gladstone Gus

It was a last snow before spring. The dark skies created shadowlands on the white tapestry of winter's end. Daffodils and crocus, tulip shoots and forsythia joined with leaf buds and green grass to splash the landscape with colors and the fore-shadowing of spring. Winter's last words were in black and white, stark against a gray cold sky. Brown corn stalks, worn out by winter, rattle in the chilly wind.

All the unexpected, heavy snow is my reminder that before spring, there is a final bit of work that must be done. For me, these last days before spring are sacred. This is the moment the earth has been laid bare before a new season. These are my days to remember and reflect.

Teaching school for 26 years means students have given me so many days of joy I can-not count them. Memories come in waves and permeate my thoughts. Those lucky enough to have taught can recall countless stories of student success, achievement, laughter, and learning. Seeing kids achieve is what makes teachers tick. On this last fling of winter, I take a harder count and remember names so cherished I cannot write them now without tears. These are the names of children and my students who died young. Their gift to me is to remember to enjoy my life while I have it.

Amy McGuire, Mike Penton, and Andrew Farnham are more than names on pa-per to me. They are bookmarks to the page I can turn when I forget my blessings. I can see Scott O'Dell, Dana Hadden, Kevin Barry and Beverly Lee clearly in my memory. Those memories on this last day of winter's reign mean more to me each year. Patty Robertson, Jamie Baxter and Julie Adkins; every young person's life has a story. Some details of their deaths are so sad they test my faith to this day. Some of the stories are how other young people rallied together at the time of their death. I know I will hear from old friends and former students just from the mention of these names. The remembrance is that strong.

Other stories are of love and grief. I know parents whose love has never dimin-ished. Reading their child's name again will be bittersweet, but my hope is they will forgive me for the sadness of seeing the name again. My own story is deep and complex. I was close to many of these kids, and at least four I counted as dear friends, as old teachers tend to do.

Natalie Goodnight's walk across the stage at her graduation, carrying the love of an entire school and a terminal illness, was one of the most courageous things I have ever witnessed. That walk comes back to me in my own times of doubt and worry. Thank you again, Natalie.

Against my judgment and wishes, my students insisted we include Kevin Barry's picture in an all-school slide show after his death. That slide received a standing ovation, and I learned it is important to both acknowledge and remember by name and face the children who have died young. My students taught me that.

Be encouraged to read the names aloud and remember others that you alone may know. Then keep watch. We do not know the day or the hour, but we all have this moment to reflect and renew. I'll take this moment to remember these great kids and their lingering gifts to me.

Good Kids Are Coming

by Gladstone Gus

Meet a group of some very nice young people. They will be graduating from your high school in the next month or two. According to historian and author William Strauss, Millennium children were born from about 1980 through 2000 and grew up during the 1990s and the 2000s. They were raised on technology, parental guidance, and a new national appreciation for children. Do you remember these bumper stickers, "Babies on Board," "Have You Hugged Your Child Today," and "It Takes a Village to Raise a Child"? The children those bumper stickers talked about are now graduating from high school. All that attention and good self-esteem, all those new schools and good teachers our culture gave to them seems to have paid off.

Here is the story of the Millennium Generation. The Millennium Generation was born at time when our country put a real focus on improving the lives of kids and their families.

The Gen-Xers who grew up before them were not treated nearly as well. Many Gen-Xers were Latchkey kids, the children of divorced parents. They were, for the most part, kids with two working parents who found themselves home alone way too much. With only pop culture to keep them company, and an amazing amount of unstructured, unattended time, Gen-Xers were left to fend for themselves. Gen-Xers learned to cope. They should receive more credit, but they smoked more, had more abortions, committed more crimes, and they drank a lot more alcohol than previous generations.

The Millennials are very different. Children born in the '90s saw Las Vegas become a family resort town. Parents and grandparents did not leave these children home alone; they brought the kids along as they traveled and went out to eat. The family outing and the family night dinners returned. Fathers started watching their children be born, and the mothers of these children were older and wiser and more ready to have children. Parents as a whole were more mature and ready to become caregivers, teachers, and mentors.

The Millennials were busy little kids, too. Mom and dad put them in camps, organized sports teams and gave them lessons in just about everything. They did not have free time, because they were busy keeping their new day-planners full of activities.

The result is that these kids are different. Our 2005 graduating seniors have more interracial interaction among themselves than any other generation. They have seen first-hand what hate and violence can do. They witnessed the bombing of the Murrah Federal Building in Oklahoma City. They watched in horror as two Columbine High School students killed and wounded their classmates. Then, they lived through September 11, 2001. On that day, they saw there are still American heroes. Policemen and firemen replaced rock and movie stars, sports heroes, and rebels as a deeper and more substantial kind of hero.

As a result, the kids became more patriotic than any other generation and led even their elders to a new appreciation for the U.S.A. You know what, the Millennials even like their parents, and their parents like them! These kids smoke less, have fewer pregnancies and abortions, commit fewer crimes, do fewer drugs, and drink less alcohol, for the most part, than ANY generation we have records for. These gains are sustained in EVERY ethnic, gender, and racial group.

Just how cool are these kids? Consider this: Nine in 10 describe themselves as "happy," "confident," and "positive." Teen suicide rates are now falling for the first time in decades. They're cooperative team players. They like doing community service, and they like working in groups. By a huge ten-to-one majority, they believe it's their generation – and not their parents' – who will do the most to help the environment over the next 25 years. A recent Roper survey reveals Millennial teenagers blame selfishness more than anything else when asked, "What is the major cause of problems in this country?"

We need to brag about our kids! People who make a living putting down our young people (politicians, preachers, and fear mongers) need to get their facts straight. The Millennials may very well become the best generation our democracy has ever produced.

You can give them a graduation present if you wish. When you hear some uninformed person talking about how bad our kids are, set them straight. Parents and schools have done good work. Give credit where credit is due!

Graduation Ain't What It Used To Be

by City Hall Sam

I went to three graduation ceremonies, and spoke at one, this spring. I never get tired of seeing happy kids having their moment of recognition. Ok, maybe after 500 names have been called, I get weary. But the walking across the stage, the faces and the smiles, still inspires and gives me pleasure.

If you haven't been to a graduation ceremony in the past 20 years, you probably don't know that modern graduation ceremonies are a now a cultural battleground. On one side are the armies of decorum, respect, formality, and dignity in celebration. A far larger army of jubilant, self-centered and self-absorbed, party-bent, noisemaker- and foghorn-equipped individualists are on the other side. Somewhere between these two camps are a handful of people who just want to hear their child's name called, and see him or her walk across the stage.

The war features staging skirmishes when academic teacher-types turn into quasi-burly security guards, searching bags for noisemakers and making stern warnings about ejection, diploma withdrawal, and arrest. The party crowd could care less. Foghorns in their underpants, they have come to rock the house. All this tension between warring factions leaves everyone exhausted. The most prevalent comment I heard this graduation season, and I heard it from parents, graduates, relatives, and friends alike, was, "I'll be glad when this is over!"

As a result, the war got ugly! People wore their crude t-shirts and flip-flops, they knocked little grandmother types out of the way running for a seat. Then, after their child's name was called, they got up and left. People blatantly, even conspicuously, ignored pleas to hold the noisemaking down so every family could hear their child's name called. The decorum folk and the palace guards seethed with anger and forgot to smile.

In the end, graduation is no celebration for many people. It is to be endured. It is no mystery why graduations have lost their luster. We have already celebrated graduation from nursery school, kindergarten, fifth grade, middle school, and junior high.

Martha Stewart, celebrity chefs, party planners for children's birthdays, and outrageous decorum at sporting events have raised/lowered the bar on celebration to unattainable and absurd levels. Nobody is supposed to be uncomfortable, patient, forgiving, considerate, quiet, or put upon at any public gathering anymore. You would think simple hospitality and some self-sacrifice was a new form of torture.

We won't turn off cell phones, we have to park close by, and we don't sacrifice for the greater good. At one graduation, people simply ignored emergency officials who asked people to clear an area to get a gurney through to a heat-attack victim.

Fixing food for others, hosting a party, putting up with relatives, having to clean the house, spending money on someone else – you ought to hear the griping these days. Sometimes one must wonder if we are truly able to be really happy for another person's moment of celebration.

All that said, the best graduation I ever saw was truly a celebration. There were noisemakers, and people yelled from the audience. Dress was everything from suits to sandals and shorts. Some graduates actually drank champagne during the ceremony. The only difference was everyone – from president to faculty to parents to graduates – was smiling. I don't know how it happened, but it was clear that everyone wanted to be there; they were happy for these college graduates, and they did not want the moment to end too quickly. Everyone called off the war for a day. They looked for the good thing to happen, and it did. People honored all the graduates, and not just their own.

Real ceremony can still happen. I think I'll celebrate that!

Take Your Child To College

by Camelot Bob

Here is the drill when you take a child to college. First, months of planned shopping using discounts, coupons, and rebates have created an enormous pile of material items almost all of which you never had as a young person, period. Irons, padded hangers, microwave, food pantry, and the all-the-latest-in-college-fashions will fill one corner – or entire floor – of your home.

In a dazzling display of Martha Stewart Living, towels are coordinated with bed-spreads, wastebaskets, toothpaste holders, and Kleenex dispenser. You will only wish your own home or office was so nicely appointed. You must never question the necessity of any item, however. Questioning a college student is considered a lack of confidence by the parental unit; questioning is degrading, insulting, an-noying, and so "out of touch!" If you do not already understand why a young person needs three pairs of expensive athletic shoes, you are obviously too dumb to understand the explanation. Your opinion on how to pack all the things you paid for into a car is also not necessary. Your help will be needed after there is a full-blown crisis. Then, you will be expected to take the blame for the crisis, solve the crisis, and certainly praise your child for handling a difficult situation so well.

Taking a child to college requires a plethora of touchy-feely interpersonal skills. First, your child should drive, and you should be quiet. Crossing yellow lines, speeding, braking for no reason, and playing the radio extremely loud are just part of normal teenage driving behavior and should be quietly overlooked. Your child will need to stop often for food and nature breaks. Stop for them with a cheerful heart. Your own hunger and natural needs are irrelevant, however. Never, ever ask to stop for yourself. You will be ridiculed for old age, faulty bladder, and general geezer malaise.

It is also a good idea to look at a map and actually find where the campus is located. Accept the fact that your son or daughter will think they know where the campus is located and drive aimlessly for about an hour before you meekly suggest a correct route. This servant role is required, because your son or daughter needs to feel they are grown up and ready to handle living on their own. You must not make a mental list of all the things you are paying for, so they can live "independently".

Your job, once you arrive at the dorm, is to carry everything up four flights of stairs, move it at least four times, then put together the bed, dresser, and desk without mak-ing it appear you are dictating how the new room should look. You are not to speak to possible collegiate friends roaming the dorm, but you must somehow appear "cool" and "with it." This is most efficiently handled by handing out large sums of cash.

Now comes the hard part – the trip to WalMart. You will believe that you have already bought every item a college student could possibly need for the next four years. Wrong! You have bought nothing! Now, you must join hordes of harried parents at the local discount store for all the wires, rugs, cleaning supplies, health products, clothing racks, toilet paper, decorative items, storable bins, and necessities you thoughtlessly forgot to purchase earlier. Be prepared…the line will take a minimum of two hours. Your bladder will know.

Once the purchasing, packing, and setting up is over, you are officially useless. Your job is to melt into the background, eat lunch with the other parents, comment on how nice everything is, control your emotions, and then leave gracefully. If you went off to college in the long ago, leave your first day story at home. Last words of advice are not well received. The last hug and the last kiss with mom will be tolerated, just barely. Your child doesn't want to know how hard and lonely the trip back home will be.

When you get back home, you will go into their old, empty room, and sit on the bed. It will be one of the worst moments of your life. Of course, it is not as bad as all this, really; it just feels that way. Your child is growing up, and that reality makes you crazy. Back in the dorm, your son or daughter is sitting on their bed, too. You are both feeling alone.

A Goodnight Goodbye

by Gladstone Gus

When Natalie Goodnight was a sophomore, she wore the best hats to school. That was before I knew her story. I'd see her in the halls, her hat cocked to one side, and I thought she was a model, or a free spirit. I don't know what I thought really, except she was special.

Natalie had an artificial leg. Some months she had hair. When she had chemotherapy treatments, she lost her hair, and then Natalie came to school with nubs and hats. She was New Wave kind of punk. I pictured her as the lead singer in some alternative rock band, or the muse of a fashion designer. She seemed so daring, so avant-garde, and mysterious. Because of her leg, she rocked just a little when she walked. Natalie's walk was her own.

Her junior year, I didn't see her as much. Kids began to tell me her story. There were the continuing bouts with cancer. I didn't know what to do. She wasn't in any of my classes. I tried to say hello in the halls now and then. I was afraid she would think I was some kind of weird dork or stalker if I just walked up one day and said something like, "Hello, I'm Mr. Gus. I teach here and think you are about the most courageous person I've ever met. And I want you to know I feel like this school is a better place, and I'm a better person just watching you walk the halls." People don't do that. I didn't.

Her senior year, Natalie was back. Her hair was long and thick, and she had a smile that filled up a room. That first semester, I began to hope the cancer was conquered. Natalie had lots of friends; she seemed to be on top of the world.

The last semester of her senior year, Natalie enrolled in my Mass Communications class, and I at last got to know her. She was quieter than I thought. She wasn't the punk rocker type at all. Natalie was sweet. Natalie was nice to everyone. She was nice to teachers and her classmates. She forgave the kids who were afraid of her and didn't know how to act around her. She handled her fame pretty well. The girl had a sense of humor, too. She was elected one of the producers of a big TV show we made in the class. I'd write her these long notes with all this work she had to do, and she asked if I got writer's cramp. That TV show was the best one we ever made. Then she was gone. Natalie went back to the hospital for more tests and more operations. The cancer was back. I saw her twice after that.

On graduation day, she unpacked a hat, her big smile, and famous walk one last time. Despite a great deal of pain, she marched with her classmates to receive her diploma. Her mortarboard had that familiar tilt. She walked the stage like she walked the halls, with courage and spunk. When they called her name, the entire senior class rose up as one. Their ovation rocked the house.

Natalie came up to school a few weeks ago for a short visit. She looked tired. We made some small talk. I told her I needed her back to produce this year's show. She told me I'd have to find somebody else to do all that work. Then she said to call if I did need some help.

Natalie Brook Goodnight, 18, Liberty, MO, died Monday, September 18, 1995. Our lives are not endless cycles; they are winding roads to a set destination. Natalie walked her road with a style and grace I will not forget. Good job! Well done, kid! You left things better, because you were here. May we all do as well.

It Took A Teacher

by Gladstone Gus

Shirley Swisher was my first grade teacher. She was young, and new, and oh so pretty. She didn't know I was almost legally deaf. One day, she slapped me hard across my face for not listening in class. Then she yanked me by my ear out in the hall. I cried hard, saying I was so sorry. Miss Swisher listened, and then she cried too. I eventually got help with my hearing. Later that year, she asked me to light candles at her wedding.

Mrs. Dobbs hugged me every day of my third grade life. They were big, slobbering hugs that seemed to engulf me. From her arms, I looked out at a world that seemed doable. She was one of the first people to tell me I should write.

Mr. Boringer was a small man with a moustache. He had more energy than ants and taught algebra with passion. I grew up in Missouri when the legal drinking age in Kansas was 18. One very windy, blustery March day, Mr. Boringer looked out the window and said to a class full of 18-year-old senior boys, "Whew, how would you like to be in Kansas on a windy day like this?" The class collapsed in laughter, and Mr. Boringer acted like he didn't know why. Mr. Boringer took my brother and me to movies, and when I blew out my knee in football, he brought over his portable stereo and left me the Beach Boys. The Beach Boys stayed forever.

Mr. Kelum taught social studies and didn't care that much about discipline. His classes were wild. He loved saying things like, "I disapprove of what you say, but I will defend to the death your right to say it," and, "Nature and books belong to the eyes that see them." I actually remember "thinking" in his class. He gave me Voltaire and Emerson and direction for my life.

Mrs. Claibourn completely covered my papers with red ink. She took no nonsense – even forced Gary Davidson, our school's resident rebel, to do homework. She was so mean, she made us memorize huge passages of American and English literature. I can still quote entire poems by Byron, Tennyson, Shakespeare, and Poe. It has been a burden to have to carry so much great literature around in my head all these years.

Glenn Zahnd was my high school Sunday School teacher. He was a lawyer and must have owned seven black suits, all exactly the same. His shirts were starched, and he was not noted for brevity. Somehow, Sunday mornings became our safe harbor, Mr. Zahnd our mentor.

Emerson said, "Shallow men believe in luck," or so Mr. Kelum said he said, but I don't know how else I got to have such wonderful teachers in my life. At college, dumb luck struck again. Dr. Dean Dunham was my advisor. In those days, Sigma Nu's at William Jewell College were not especially known for academic rigor. My "brothers" majored in CliffsNotes, habitual socialization, and Zetas. Dr. Dunham gave us the high country of the mind, and our first views of an examined life. We talk about it to this day.

"We must cultivate our garden," Voltaire said. Teachers rise each day to such work. It is their way. Thank you, teachers, for all you did and do for me. Thank you for the work you will do today on behalf of children and learning.

Once a year, schools all across the United States celebrate American Education Week. It is literally true you could not read this message if not for the teachers you have had. Take a moment in the next week to send a note to a teacher who made a difference in your life. Write a letter to the editor thanking a teacher, or give a teacher a call and say thanks. Or, better yet, spend a moment being a teacher yourself. Don't let the exterior fool you. Our children need caring adults now, more than ever.

"The true test of civilization is not the census, nor the size of cities, nor the crops – no, but the kind of man the country turns out." – **Ralph Waldo Emerson**

School's Out

Holly Lake Jake thought it was one of the strangest phone calls he had ever received. School was officially out for the summer at 12:45 p.m., and at two o'clock sharp his grandson called.

"Grandpa," he said. "I'm, uuuhh, bored. Can you come get me?"

The grandson was stuck at home by himself on the last day of school. An hour of freedom, and the child was bored. "What did you do for fun when you were a kid?" the boy asked when Jake came to pick him up.

Jake didn't know where to start. He made whistles out of mulberry sprigs; they spun tops and used magnifying glasses to burn holes in leaves. He packed lunches and headed for the woods where they built forts. On the banks of the Grand River near Pattonsburg, he made magnificent mudslides, built castles on sand bars, cooked frogs legs, and chased snapping turtles.

"Well, we got up, did our chores, and then went on adventures," said Jake.

"Like what?" asked the boy.

"Once we dug a fort out of a hill in the vacant lot just down from the church. It took us four or five days of digging to get a hole big enough that we could sit in comfortably. Then, we scavenged the neighborhood for lumber and put a top on the fort. We covered the inside with soft, dried grass and the outside with branches. We made a tin can phone to the outside and set up peepholes for light. We even built a fireplace to cook hot dogs and marshmallows. Of course, the dried grass caught fire when we tried to cook the hot dogs and the fort burned down. We barely escaped with our lives."

"Didn't you go to movies or day camp or watch TV or hang out playing video games at the mall? Maybe go to a concert?" the boy asked.

"Nope, we didn't do anything that cost more than we could make collecting pop bottles," said Jake. "We listened to radio and had baseball heroes. We all wanted to be Stan Musial, Mel Ott, Ralph Kiner, or Ernie Lombardi. We loved baseball."

Suddenly Jake was 11 again and about to relive the most precious of his boyhood memories. No kid does this now, but Jake remembered how each summer started with the creation of a ball field. They mowed out the base paths, build a precarious backstop, and used squashed tin cans for bases. What games they had. A smash down the right field line was an automatic double, because it hit the old cottonwood that hung over in fair territory. Hitting a foul in the creek was an out. There was the famous continuous play rule that squelched fighting by making players do it over if they could not agree. The object of these games was to play, not fight over rules. Goodness, what a memory.

"Pop, will you buy me a Coke and rent a movie?" the grandson asked.

Jake sensed sadness in them both. The world had changed. Parents could no longer give their children the freedom he had known. Kids have money instead of freedom. Money for Cokes and movies, video games, day camp, and concerts, but they don't have empty fields or mud slides, burning forts or packed lunches, and days spread out before them to do exactly as they please.

"No Cokes," said Jake. "How about a game of catch?"

With that, the summer began.

Chapter 4

Storytelling

Great gospel singers have the "hum." When they are not singing the words, they are swaying back and forth humming, and in that "hum" is so much passion and emotion, you don't need, as they say, "nothing else."

When they tell a story, Holly Lake Jake, Water Street Pete, and Manor Hill Mack have all got the hum. Pete can make you feel mad when you really have nothing to get mad about. Jake makes everything mushy and fuzzy, dripping with over-sugared Kool-Aid, but he's got the hum.

Those who have the hum can tell stories about rivers, and you hear the water drifting by. The clocks stop. Facts become irrelevant. Stories offer meanings without making the unbearable mistake of defending them. Unlike any other form of communication, stories become epic, because they contain wisdom. When the really good storytellers at the Cafe get going, when they get their hum on, they can cure the deaf.

Thank heavens we are coming out of a dark period for storytelling. At last, we are remembering again that learning must be passed through the heart. All those bulleted facts, concrete sequential thinkers, quick one-page-reports are dangerous and insulting, colorless, and two dimensional! It is big corporations, like FedEx and CVS, who are leading the way for stories and abandoning their mission statement for their corporate story.

Stripped of emotional intelligence, facts lack wisdom. Good Lord, facts are the tools of bullies and unthinking brutes on their trivial pursuit's power trip. Facts alone, without interpretation and the filter of feelings, rip the hearts out of learners, tie them down, and squelch the life out of 'em.

But storytellers are transformational teachers. Please, this cannot be overstated. The loss of wisdom, thought, and civil discourse in our country is directly related to our abandonment of stories. Stories tell both sides without being coercive. Stories carry deeper, better-remembered lessons that are easier to pàss on, and move through the brain on swifter, more reliable channels.

Stella and the Cafe boys are our modern day Shamans. Almost single-handedly, they are keeping the story-telling tradition alive, after it was abandoned by the movies for special effects and by TV for gratuitous adventures in voyeurism.

Be warned, the chapter which the reader now holds, from start to finish, is a very explosive document. As a whole, and in its details, are the meanings of life, the coming of angels, accounts of all things rotten and decaying, and the triumphs of chance love and things wild.

Stories always have been, and are now, the human translation of daily life into an understandable form that is more powerful, beautiful, and coherent than the events themselves. Stories are the currency of meaning and understanding.

The first rule in storytelling is to leave a story better than when you found it. Everything here is fair game for you to tell again. If we are going to save the world, it is time to get your "hum" on.

Freaking At The Frog Hop

by Water Street Pete

Moonlight Serenade. The words move across the imagination like eddies of light dancing on a lake. They swirl and dip as moths circling the soft play of a porch light. Sweet spring rhythms dance with them in memories so fine they have crossed the lines between dreams and time. The high school jazz musicians took their places. The advertising read, "Moonlight Serenade Tea Dance, Sunday, 4:00-7:00, at the Middle School." None of the young musicians knew what secret messages from another time were written in those words. For them, it was just a dance to raise money for the music booster club to send kids to summer jazz camps. It was a gig, a chance to play, and their last time together as a band before the end of school.

Their audience moved slowly. Most men wore coats and ties. Women wore dresses. Many leaned as they walked as if the weight of years shifted with each step. Their hair was lean and white, sometimes traced with blue. But they knew music.

Fifty years ago and more, some had come to the Frog Hop Ballroom in St. Joe, Missouri, to trip the light fantastic. Big bands and their famous leaders were on stage to play music born of slaves and the roaring twenties; ties tempered by the Depression, and finally shaped by war. In memory, the Frog Hop was not the creaky building with a low ceiling that serves some business now. Before the fires, the Frog Hop was a real ballroom with high ceilings covered in silver leaf. A mirror ball broke the light into thousands of tiny dots, endlessly circling the floor and walls in hypnotic displays of motion.

One couple, just entering this Middle School-located Moonlight Serenade, thought a record was playing. For them, it was all there…the big horns, rhythm, bass, and a sound so large it filled the entire room. A huge crescent moon graced a corner of the room; candles lit the tables. The Frog Hop was back…the stuff of miraculous transformation.

Among the would-be dancers, one couple stood out. He was tall, lanky, with a shuffle walk and the grind of years around his belt. She was shorter, and seemed cautious. Her face held back, and together they were just waiting. No one would guess for what.

The band struck up "Fernando's Hideaway", and the couple strolled to the floor. In the music, both were born anew. His head flew back, and his foot kicked in a strut so sharp that this one mere movement claimed the entire dance floor. She edged sideways, her back rigid and serious. The music moved upwards from the floor into her legs, and she snapped her chin high in the air and matched him move for move. They seemed to be one living moment gliding on the dance floor, kicking the teeth of time.

Others played to them in crisp turns and flipped hands. The dance floor swelled with blue hair and ties swinging in the music.

Suddenly, it was before the war. The light played off the silver leaf ceiling, and the young musicians knew they had caught music's night train. Such dancing! And not an old bone in the place.

Farm Fears

by Ridgeway Ron

A farm can be a frightening place. All that heavy machinery whirling and clanking, looking for fingers, feet, and bits of clothing to clip off or pull in, combine with countless sharp objects and uneven, slippery surfaces to make the farm a bit more dangerous than you might imagine. Ridgeway Ron has finger nubs to prove it. Cattle get persnickety and defensive. Manor Hill Mack has broken ribs, a smashed foot, and a bad eye (yes, a cow's tail can even be a hazard) to offer up as anecdotal proof.

Farmers need to know how to handle harsh chemicals, 220 volts of electricity, suffocating grain, and a tipping tractor. Things are always falling out of haylofts, slithering into the milk barn, flying out of the Power Take Off (PTO) or ready to blow over.

Weather issues are magnified on the farm. Barn lofts can quickly heat up to 130 degrees. Chipping a drinking hole in a frozen farm pond almost cost Camelot Bob his life. Lightning, floods, tornadoes, mud, and ice make farms miserable and deadly.

Believe it or not, many farmers will tell you the most dangerous part of farm life is isolation. Farmers work alone a lot. If something happens, it may be hours before help finds them, and hours more to get to a hospital. Farmers are nosy people, but part of that snooping around is to make sure everybody is ok. In town, neighbors can watch your property or run for help. Police, firefighters, and paramedics in full gear are just minutes away. Explosions, loud noises, and flashes of light can go unnoticed on a farm.

Intruders are a horror all their own. Nobody dreads the "knock in the middle of the night" as much as a farmer. Now that so many farm dads have to work in town (sometimes at night) to make ends meet, their wives and children face unique dangers. Manor Hill Mack's granddaughter was home alone with her two small children when a woman started banging on her door. "Let me in NOW!" she screamed. "I know you are there, let me in!" The screaming woman's car had run out of gas. She got lost on her way home and had a panic attack.

Mack's own daughter, Cindy, tells a story about an early morning visitor. She and her husband got up each morning at 4:30 a.m. to do the milking. One morning, the alarm clock did not go off, and the hired hand knocked at the door to wake them up. The next morning, there was knocking at the door again; Cindy assumed she had missed the alarm and the hired hand. It was not the hired hand. It was a woman, obviously confused, with a message: "I am here to bless your land," she said. "The Lamb sent me."

By this time, Cindy's husband had made it to the door wiping sleep from his eyes. "What is it?" he asked.

"It's a woman here to bless our land. The Lamb sent her." Cindy calmly said.

Turned out the woman was mentally ill. She had run her car in a ditch, found her way to the barn, and fed a baby lamb. Her footprints showed she had circled the house five or six times before knocking on the door. Every farmer has stories like these – strange events in the dark of night.

Once again, farm life has much to teach us about living in our modern world. We can learn a lot from farmers about how to handle and face fear, but still live a normal life.

Bathroom Humor Stinks Up Cafe

It was an Indian summer morning at the North Side. The first frost came, taking with it bugs, pollen, and allergens. It was a nice day – that is, till Camelot Bob came in. First, he told his usual rude joke.

"Boys, what's the difference between a blimp and 365 bowel movements?" Bob asked. Nobody dared guess.

"Well, the blimp – that's a Goodyear," Bob said. "And 365 bowel movements – now, that's a Great Year!" A storm of wadded napkins flew through the air to a chorus of moans.

"Say it ain't true, you constipated old buzzards," Bob said, laughing more than anyone else. "You know that was funny."

"Maybe that joke's funny if you're eight years old, but most of us think bathroom humor went out with moose-gooser poems," said Holly Lake Jake. Then Bob got feisty.

"I'm sick of everybody always being offended. Hell, some people can't even take a good lawyer joke anymore," Bob said. That's when Jake started in on Bob.

"Bob," Jake inquired, "have you taken your pulse lately?"

"No," Bob replied, somewhat perplexed.

"I think you should. There's a rumor that you're dead."

"What?" Bob asked.

"Bob, in the past 10 years, you haven't discarded a major opinion or acquired a new one. I was wondering if maybe you were dead, and we just didn't know," Jake said. The boys laughed, and Bob threatened to stab Jake with a fork.

"Jake," Bob said, "when you are as perfect as me, you don't need to change."

Jake smiled. Bob needed a lesson in how the world had changed. People don't see the world the way the boys at the Cafe do. For example, most people we meet don't remember the American Bicentennial Celebration; 33 percent of the people living in the United States think people have always been on the moon. Almost everyone is too young to remember the assassination of John F. Kennedy. Nobody remembers the Korean War. Ninety percent don't remember "before TV." Now Jake spoke directly to Bob.

"We're saying you need to change, Bob, and not just your underwear. The world has changed on you."

The Cafe got quiet. It is hard to be reminded that the world is changing and that people who want to be a part of it must change, too.

"Oh, I get it. You're saying I need to change my jokes. I need to be more politically correct and contemporary," said Bob. "Well then, did I tell you my grandson was going to college to study mustard? Do you know where?" Bob asked looking around the room.

"Poop-on U," he said with a very smug grin.

Fortunately, Bob would never change.

Nude Night In Weston

It was a Friday afternoon and Camelot Bob seemed jumpy.

"What's up, Bob?" asked Holly Lake Jake. "Looks like you got feisty britches."

"Nothing," said Bob, but you could tell he was lying.

"Come on, out with it. What's going on?" said Water Street Pete. He wasn't asking.

Bob looked around to make sure nobody was listening, then he motioned the boys in close. "You got to swear to keep this secret," said Bob. "I mean it. This is real."

The boys fixed their most solemn faces and nodded their pledge to silence. Bob was clearly shaking. This had to be good.

"It only happens when two events coincide. First, payday must fall on the last day of the month. Second, there has to be a full a moon. I'm telling you that's how it has to be."

A car horn sounded from the street outside, and the men jumped. It was the end of the month, and the moon would indeed be full. Bob's eyes searched the Cafe again, and he leaned in even closer. Silence held them all in its tight grip.

"Even the most stable people have moments when they lose the connections that keep them sane. Sometimes, the regular codes of behavior don't apply. When the moon is full and payday falls on the last day of a month, there is a town where the rules are different," Bob said, but he seemed to hesitate. He put his hand by his mouth as if to hold back what he was about to say. Then he spoke.

"Tonight is the night," he said. "It's Nude Night in Weston."

The men gasped. Bob quieted them with a gesture.

"Maybe it's the money. Maybe it's the moon. Maybe it's the cork in the bottled despair of farm life exploding from the pressure within. I don't know, but Nude Night in Weston is like nothing you have ever seen before," Bob said, and his eyes glazed.

Vivid, disturbing images danced in the gathering dark of the old Cafe. The men were sweating. Their breathing labored under the spell of Bob's story. They all knew where Weston was – a quiet farm town up north. Surely, this was a mistake. Bob put a sharp edge of urgency on his whispered voice.

"It starts with a bow dropped from a woman's hair. Men loosen a tie and unbutton their collars. Soon enough, kids walk barefoot, and respectable ladies are driving breathlessly without significant articles of clothing. It isn't low-life, mind you. It's fine, upstanding pillars of the community – members of boards, church officials, ladies aide societies, and gas station attendants. They all just seem to lose control. People who don't usually speak to each other drive up and down the main road honking. It's like snakes shedding their skins for the new one that lives inside. It's Nude Night in Weston."

Something in the way Bob said the last line put a shiver through the group, and Jake dropped his coffee cup with a resounding clang.

"You're lying through your teeth bigger than a yellow dog," said Jake. "The people of Weston ought to sue you for telling such a ridiculous tale. Nude Night in Weston! Why, I never heard such a preposterous story in all my born days."

Bob laughed. "I had you going for a few minutes didn't I?" he said. The men groaned and filtered out of the Cafe.

That night it started. One by one, engines fired across town, and headlights blinked on. Pretty soon, a trail of beady lights cut across the back roads out of town. A caravan was forming. The thick night closed on a small of line of cars going north. Ribbons were falling; ties loosened. The moon was full, and money burned to spend.

It's Nude Night in Weston.

What's That Noise?

This is not a story for the faint of heart. Camelot Bob slept soundly. He seldom dreamed and almost never moved once he was asleep, but tonight the splashing of water called him to awareness. At first, he thought the bathroom stool was running and contemplated going back to sleep, when a low bang and following splash cut the silence. The noise woke his wife.

"Bob, Bob, wake up! Did you hear that?" she said jabbing him in the ribs.

Now Bob had no choice. He rose for an expedition into the unknown. A momentary silence created a still tension as Bob walked the hallway. He stood at the open bathroom door listening, gathering courage. Amazingly, the lid to the bathroom commode lifted slightly then banged down on the porcelain rim. A splashing noise followed. Bob was shaken. Carefully, he switched on the bathroom light and approached the stool. A faint gurgle told him clearly something was wrong. Bob was not prepared for what was under the lid. There, swimming frantically, was a huge sewer rat! Bob yelped and slammed the lid down. Then Bob did what all men do in times of terror, he yelled for his wife.

"There's a rat in the stool," he called to his wife. "A rat!"

Bob's wife came running and found her husband holding down the commode lid. "Get encyclopedias!" cried Bob.

She ran off looking for the "R" as Bob yelled, "We need at least six books!" Moments later, the books weighted the lid as the rat continued a frantic swim for freedom. Bob began flushing the stool, but it was no use. It only made the rat mad.

Soon it was apparent. Bob would have to do battle with a rat. He retreated to the basement. His wife followed, arms clutched to her stomach. Bob put on heavy electrical gloves, two long sleeve shirts, steel toed shoes, brush pants, a breathing mask, and stocking cap. He grabbed a hunting rifle.

"You can't shoot him!" cried his wife, "You'll break the commode!"

"I know that," Bob lied.

Upstairs, Bob, now dressed for battle, assessed the situation. A huge rat. His toilet. The middle of the night. Bob picked up fireplace tongs and began to think.

"Get me the can of Drano!" he commanded, after braving a look at the rat's beady, red eyes. Acting with incomprehensible bravery, Bob lifted the lid and threw in the Drano. Water churned and a noxious fume rose. The rat splashed.

"Why don't you put the Drano in the tank?" his wife said. "And flush the water down on the rat."

"Shut up!" Bob said. He was frantic and beginning to sweat. Then Bob had the brainstorm. "Go boil water, at least three pans," he declared.

In no time, pans of boiling water covered the stove. Bob and his wife hauled the steaming pots of water into the bathroom. Bob was battling for family and home. He would not risk the water cooling down. He flung open the lid, shrieked, and poured in the scalding water. Three great heaves, and it was all over. The rat's nervous system simply shut down. The creature lay motionless. Bob used the fireplace tongs to put the rat in four heavy duty plastic leaf and lawn bags, wrapped it with duct tape, then took it to a dumpster by a local shopping market.

"Is it gone?" his wife asked.

"Yes," Bob replied, and they were quiet.

The next day, Bob called City Hall. "Sewer rats will do that," they said. "Next time, put the hot water in the tank and flush it down on the rat."

"Next time!" screamed Bob. "You mean there could be a 'next time?!'"

Men sat in shock as Bob told his tale. There are a million stories at the North Side, but none strikes more terror than the night a rat attacked Bob's commode. Rats in the toilet mean no one will ever again sit easy in the night.

Mothering A Child Like A Sunny Day

Wind and freezing rain stripped the last leaves of autumn creating a brown mush on the streets as Stella walked to the old Cafe. Autumn's end, with its bare trees and the coming winter, play hard on Stella. Divorced, children grown, Stella walked through a hard season on her way to work

"What'll it be boys?" Stella asked, swinging pots of coffee and a giant smile.

"Stella, did you have Cheerios for breakfast again?" asked Manor Hill Mack, mocking her usual exuberance even on a cold, wintry day.

"Anybody can be a sourpuss, Mack. When it rains, you got to turn it up a notch," Stella said with a laugh. "Now, you want your coffee in a cup or on your head?" Stella was never bested, but her tongue always cut toward a smile.

A cold draft moved across the Cafe as the door opened and a couple shook off the mix of snow and rain. They headed for a table and sat alone, unspeaking.

"Good morning," Stella greeted the couple. "What will you have?" The man ordered a standard breakfast. The woman had nothing.

"Something the matter, honey?" Stella asked.

"I'm not eating this morning," the woman replied. Stella wouldn't let it be.

"Are you ok? You look like something is wrong." Stella's extraordinary step into another's private life would have come across as intrusion by anyone else. From Stella, it was an act of kindness. The quiet woman lifted her head and smiled just faintly.

"I'm having an operation this morning; I've been hemorrhaging. We live in Texas and are here on vacation. I'm a little scared," the woman said.

Stella embraced the woman with her eyes. "Why, you're going to be just fine," Stella said. "Don't you worry another moment. People over at the hospital are the best around. You watch, everything's going to turn out exactly right."

From that moment on, Stella mothered over the young woman like a sunny day. Stella didn't hear how the operation turned out, but she said a prayer for the woman that afternoon and went on with her 12-hour shift. Truth is, the operation did turn out fine. A doctor's skill and Stella's kindness pulled the woman through. Back in Texas, the woman wrote her friends about Stella. "We were strangers, and she took us in."

Stella never knew how her little act of caring moved through the season, but she does know kindness gives comfort both ways. Walking home that night, a freezing rain washed the trees, creating silver webs against the street lights. The leaf mush glistened as cars splashed by. The world was draped in diamonds for Stella. We never know the good we do, but feel it as a dim reflection – in a stranger's smile, in sparkling lights across the night sky, in simple pleasures. Little joys are the reflections of kindness.

A Tree House, Playboys And Cigarettes

A single robin offered its greeting to a new morning as Holly Lake Jake walked his back yard inspecting spring. His maple tree was tipped with the reddish buds of future leaves. The oak was about two weeks behind. The stump of his old tulip tree, cut down to protect power lines, still haunted Jake. He wished he had not given permission to cut that tree.

Jake has always been a tree lover. The family farm in Arkansas had a brittle silver maple he would climb to pass the time. From the tree's top, he could see a farmland valley spread out beneath him as the thrill of dangerous heights coursed through his young limbs. When the wind blew, he swayed with the branches and became part of the tree – heady stuff, being one with the wind. Trees were Jake's link with nature. Some choose flowers or majestic mountains. Some need clouds, waterfalls, the ocean, an open meadow, or a desert to make the connection. For Jake, it was trees.

About age 12, Jake made his first tree house in the woods behind an old mill. It was a summer's work to scavenge the countryside for discarded boards, nails, and furnishings. There was not a right angle in that tree house. Each board had at least 15 nails in it. None were hammered all the way in before being bent over. Each board was placed at angles only a 12-year-old would understand. It had a marvelous ladder (two rungs were decidedly dangerous), peep holes on every side, a lookout nest, trap door, and a rope hoist. Better yet, it had a roof full of holes for viewing the sky.

Before long, the local boys outfitted it with all the essentials of a proper tree house: pillows, blankets, drinks, candles, scandalous magazines, and cigarettes. Jake learned about moral decay in that tree. He uttered his first cuss word and explored the mysterious world of macho boyhood. In the evening, with lightning bugs floating on the darkness, Jake huddled with friends and told spooky stories. There, he heard the first of many lies about the forbidden world of adults. Once, when the moon rose full and red, Jake feared the end of the world was coming and ran to the tree for safety. Conflicted and afraid, Jake threw out the magazines and cigarettes and prayed for his soul. Still young in his theology, however, he retrieved the magazines and cigarettes the next day. The tree house is gone, but that tree still stands, as does the silver maple behind the mill.

Though fall is often more closely associated with trees, for Jake spring is their season. Out in his back yard with the tulip stump, the oak and maple, his precious pear and apple trees, Jake finds the season he loves most. His fingers explore the rough, tactile feel of the maple. His eyes drift up, and for a moment, he is swaying with the wind atop the tree. The old fright of free fall, while clinging precariously to a branch, puts a tension in his grip.

It is said the majestic redwoods of California were already tall when Columbus first came to the new world. Some trees still alive today date back before Christ. Trees link us with the past. They grow on every continent, in every land. Their seeds are an assurance of the future; they breathe out oxygen cleansing the air. Jake seldom thinks of this during his backyard stroll. He takes the season, with its trees, for what it is today…then sits with the wind, watching the world.

God Calling Me

by Gladstone Gus

I now have a new candidate for the most embarrassing moment in my life. The clear winner had always been streaking the congregation of the First Presbyterian Church in Liberty. I was then the church's youth director, and the church's youth, as a joke, had stolen my clothes as I showered at church camp. Instead of just waiting for somebody to come by and asking that person to get me a towel and some clothes, I snuck out a back window and ran through the woods to my cabin. Please, remember I was young, and I honestly believed I could make it back to my cabin without being seen by anyone. Unfortunately, some church elders were taking a nature walk at that exact moment. Our paths crossed, and I had some explaining to do.

Now there is a new candidate. I don't know why my most embarrassing moments take place at church. Regular readers will remember I attend Chandler Church where my brother is the preacher. Fortunately, it is a wonderfully forgiving and tolerant congregation. I always sit in one of the first few rows, so I can hear the music. Our little church has a full orchestra and is always recruiting more. Some mornings, I feel like I am at the Metropolitan Opera; it really is that good.

I also sit near the front, so I can watch the children during the children's service. The children's service is as much fun as the music, because our children are so earnest. The more they get involved in whatever is being said to them, the more they squirm and fidget, poke and tug, giggle and make noise. You never know when some five-year-old might embarrass their poor parents; it is just a hoot!

So, I'm sitting in church, up front, and………My cell phone rings! I thought my phone was off, honestly. I wanted to become invisible. You could hear gasps coming from the congregation.

A loud voice in the back, that I recognized as one of the most influential church elders, said, "I think it is a cell phone!" Then things got worse. I could not get the cell phone out of my pocket to turn it off.

"It's the preacher's brother," the voice said. Every eye in the place was on me.

I sputtered, "I'm so sorry," as the phone rang again. I felt naked.

My older brother, the preacher, gave me a very stern look as I finally got the phone turned off. Then, from the pulpit, my brother says, for all the congregation to hear, "After all these years, my brother finally gets a phone call from God, and…. HE HANGS UP!"

The congregation laughed, and I was off the hook, just a bit. Of course, I still get kidded, but I deserve it.

Later, I checked to see if there was a message. There was no message, but the call was from some place in California. I guess God needed a tan.

Giant Sign Glows In The Night

"Raking leaves sure isn't as much fun as it used to be," Holly Lake Jake thought to himself, rounding up another pile of yellow, hard maple leaves. In the old days, it was a matter of pushing the pile curbside and burning the leaves. This took skill, engineering acumen, and a healthy respect for wind. When the kids were little, they jumped through the burning leaf piles in tests of bravery.

"Get back from those burning leaves," Jake would yell. "You'll catch fire."

Those were the "good old days" of leaf raking – the soft colors of fall, the kids playing, the scent of burning leaves wafting over the town. Jake remembered autumns when hot chocolate called him and the kids in from leaf raking. Now there is too much bending and stooping to leaf raking. Lordly leaves ask you to bow before packaging them in expensive, disposable bags. There is less energy for re-raking scattered piles where children play.

"Stop jumping in those leaves," grown men yell to startled children.

Leaf piles are the swimming pools of autumn. You are supposed to jump into them. Sadly enough, after raking 27 leaf bags full, one does not appreciate children or the color of leaves. Men begin thinking about cutting down perfectly good trees.

Jake missed the fire and smoke. There is something responsible and manly about fire. Fire stupefies men. Flames licking through leaves, destroying a season's work, call up a vague memory of creation – this burning of leaves is important work. Now all Jake could smell was his sweat.

It was in this instant that Jake noticed the first hint of new color across the draw in back of the pear tree. A sudden gust and a cloud of leaves revealed more color. What was it? A sumac grove? A magnificent maple or oak? Jake was sure he had never seen it before. His pulse quickened as his eyes strained to solve the mystery.

Another gust and leaves fell, the answer, hidden all summer by leaves, came screaming through Jake's brain.

"Egads!" he yelled, "it's a BILLBOARD." The monstrously garish sign peaked over the top of the ridge and into Jake's old heart. He felt violated by the mountain of modern marketing.

That night, he dreamed the revenge of the old and powerless. A wind whirled across town collecting every leaf from every tree, a tornado of color, which suddenly swirled, gathered and died on the BILLBOARD sign. Then Jake stepped forward with an old stick match to do the honor. Flames engulfed the BILL-BOARD as the old North Side gathered to dance in primeval glory. Ah, it was a wonderful dream.

Tomorrow, when he rakes leaves again, it will be with a smile. There was still some magic in autumn after all.

We Taught Him All He Knows

by Gladstone Gus

Last Saturday afternoon, former Northland football star turned Kansas State Wildcat, David Allen, returned a punt for 74 yards and a touchdown against Texas University.

David's touchdown sparked Kansas State to a 35-17 victory over the Longhorns and gained the Cats undisputed respectability. Now everybody from Goodland, Kansas, to Hannibal, Missouri, is claiming to have discovered David Allen. Major sports writers are gushing. TV broadcasters are subtly cozying up to David's Kansas City football legacy. Even the incomparable Joe Cook is trotting out his David Allen stories.

All this is well and good. David deserves all the attention he is getting and more! But move over sports media. The North Side Cafe knew him first! David Allen may be your latest story, but he is our local hero!

I watched him on the playground in fifth grade at Ridgeview Elementary School. He was brutal at four-square and unstoppable in the afternoon football scrimmage, which in those days was played to the death, or at least until Mrs. Phelps said recess was over. At one time, the entire record board at Ridgeview had his name on it. David Allen was our star in elementary school! Top that, Mr. Major Kansas City Sports Columnists.

In eighth grade football, David scored nearly every time they handed him the football. He was a man who made defenders look like they were in the Pee-Wee league. In high school, I not only watched him lead the Liberty Blue Jays to three years of amazing glory, I had him in class! I personally told David Allen to stop thinking about football and start thinking about his homework. "Football is nice," I told David Allen, "but a good education is your ticket." So, when David Allen was interviewed on national television after the game Saturday and came across as the intelligent, articulate young man we taught him to be, I was certainly glad he stayed with studies, as well as his football.

One-dimensional sports writers will dull you with their limited view of the world (there is more to life than sports) with articles like this: "David Allen is a punt return god. The prince of juke and the duke of jive – Allen is a winged warrior wonder, a galloping gridiron ghost, and I tell you this because I know both football and alliteration. Tell your friends you first learned about David Allen from me!"

BALONEY! Meet the real David Allen – David is a nice kid who overcame a lot of adversity and worked incredibly hard to win his recognition. He can be a little hard headed, but that's good (David could play without a helmet if necessary). He has a great sense of humor and once played a righteous, overly zealous pastor in one of our mass media productions. I have the video tape to prove it. David has earned what he has with talent and work. His personal life is personal, but the young man had no silver spoon.

So let the sports writers have their fun. Tell the world about David Allen, the great punt return specialist from Kansas State University. I'm the mass media teacher who told him to study, so he could look good in the interview after the game. David, we were great!

She's In The Freezer With The Door Closed

Today at the old Cafe we are talking about life and death. It is not a discussion for those with a delicate stomach. In fact, Holly Lake Jake lost his once voracious appetite for the day's Blue Plate Special (chicken fried steak) after Camelot Bob gave a graphic description of the incidents surrounding the passing of Mrs. Alance Candever.

There was once a time when manhood required some discretion among men. If there was a car wreck, a man would shake his head and say, "It was bad." And the gore would go unsaid; there was no need for descriptive detail. Where the puncture wound was found, or how deep the cut was made into the muscle, was mercifully left out. TV news and the movies have changed that. The newest mark of manhood is to endure the most horrific scenes of violence imaginable, and act like it was nothing. Limbs chopped off, blood squirting, bones crushed, and people dead – this is entertainment?

That brings us to Alance Candever. Jake was just about to take his first taste of Blue-Plate mashed potatoes and gravy when Bob started talking about Alance. Alance Candever was a woman in her 50s. She had two grown children and a truck-driver husband who took to the road quite often. Listen to Bob's account of what happened.

"Alance Candever is dead," Bob said, and stillness jolted the room. "Suicide…. they found her this morning."

"How'd she do it," asked Manor Hill Mack.

Bob eyed the crowd and then lowered his head, shaking it side-to-side as it went down. "The freezer. She climbed in the freezer and shut the door."

It was at this point that Jake gave up on the green beans. His fork fell to the plate with loud bang. In the old days, men would have let it go and wondered in silence, but today's new manhood demanded titillation.

"Was the freezer plugged it?" asked Mack.

"No, but maybe it should have been. It was out behind the barn in the sun. You could have put a fork in her, if you know what I mean."

Jake watched the steam roll of his hot mashed potatoes and wondered why the grisly details were so important.

"They didn't find her for 26 days," continued Bob. "They know it was suicide, because she left a note."

Suddenly, a couple in the next booth over got up and left abruptly, food uneaten. The woman gave a quick glance to Bob's table and said, "This town is weird! Don't you have anything else to talk about?"

Bob and the boys looked a little surprised and sat in silence while the couple walked out.

"What got into her?" asked Bob.

Jake broke the silence. "We're sitting here in a restaurant talking about a woman locking herself in an unplugged freezer, and you wonder why people get up and leave?"

"Doesn't bother me," said Bob. "I was just wondering if she changed her mind once the door was closed."

With that, Jake gave up on lunch and headed for the door. Back in the Cafe, they talked about Alance for hours. They decided it was a pretty frightening way to go.

Jake drove home thinking that more people than we care to think about shut the door on their own lives. Alance was just more obvious about it.

Women? Yep, We Got A Few

Yes, there are some stories about women at the Old North Side Cafe. There was the time Stella arm-wrestled Camelot Bob. And who can forget the stories about Manor Hill Mack's granddaughter, Jodi. The six-year-old once informed her minister, during the children's service, she was sick of stories about sheep and wanted to hear something about pigs.

Most famous, however, is Water Street Pete's amazing mother, Zelda. Zelda and her twin sister, Zena, were from Arkansas. You never met two zanier, God-fearing, man-crushing women in your life. They weren't "liberated" or any nonsense like that. Zelda and Zena came to understand early in life how basically worthless men are. Armed with that insightful knowledge, they laid a path of broken hearts from Little Rock to Kansas City and back. Unlike many women of their era, Zelda and Zena knew you did not have to marry a man to enjoy one.

On rainy afternoons, the men will huddle close, chewing the fat of old age. Sooner or later, a lull comes in the conversation, and someone will ask Pete about Zelda and Zena. Pete will massage his double chin a moment as a broad smile sneaks across his face. The men lean in close as Pete clears his throat to speak. They know this story will be good.

"Did I tell you about Mom's feud with the self-service gas station attendant?" asked Pete. "Well, it was back in the early '70s..."

Zelda disliked cars. Turning the key was as much as she ever wanted to know about them. Zelda especially hated self-service. Gas pumps were malicious, nasty things. Pumping gas was cheap, meaningless labor best performed by low-I.Q. brutes stinking of sweat and grease. In short, pumping gas was man's work.

Zena and Zelda were women of the Depression, however, and that meant they knew the value of everything. If gas was cheaper at self-service, that's where they went, hating every minute. One day, it happened. Zelda filled her car with gas and went inside to pay.

"I don't like this," she told the man behind the counter. "What is the world coming to when a woman is reduced to pumping her own gas? Why, something should be done!" The man offered a typical, worthless man smile.

Driving away from the gas station, Zelda felt a tug. Not much of a tug, but enough that she gave her car more gas. The tug grew stronger, and the car momentarily hesitated before suddenly lurching forward, the pedal now down to the floor. Zelda had a sense of something dragging behind her car and smelled gas fumes. Bchind her car a gas hose dragged along, the nozzle still firmly planted in her gas tank.

"Oh my," said Zelda getting out of her car to watch the show.

"Lady, you ruined my gas pump," the attendant screamed running after Zelda's car.

Zelda was unruffled. "Young man," she said, "this is the risk you take by operating a self-service station."

The explosion shook the town and truly unnerved Zelda and Zena. Word got around what had happened. The girls never pumped a tank of gas again. You would think they had planned it.

Snakes At The Big Apple Salon

It was a slow day at the Big Apple Hair Salon. Camelot Bob was in for his regular trim. Lovely Aileen was doing the job. Life got more interesting for Bob once he decided to come back to the forbidden world of the beauty salon. Bob liked being served by a woman. He believes in a Biblical hierarchy that places man just below angels and above women. He thinks men do the hard stuff. They make the money and compete for power and position. When snowstorms hit men shovel the walk. Men fix the car and furnace. Men take mice out of traps. Men serve on the front lines in war, drive on the ice, do the plumbing, and tighten their belts when resources are scarce.

Women are soft and feminine. They are genetically and spiritually engineered to offer support, to be caregivers. Women go in the lifeboats first. They are the keepers of life. Men are their defenders. Women are the castles, and men are the knights. When there are no savages to defend against, men deserve a rest. There is no rest for women.

Bob thinks it is just about right that he sits on his throne while a subservient woman massages his manly hair. He gives orders and offers wisdom to the collective bunnydom around him. Of course, when Bob leaves the beauty shop, the women offer a collective sigh of relief and have him for lunch. Not that Bob is totally naïve. He knows Ashley, the manicurist, carries the full armor of women – sarcasm, feinted helplessness, and sexual tension. Ashley will occasionally tweak Bob's ego; not enough to lose his business, just enough to get his goat.

So, here is what happened. Bob was on his throne, with lovely Aileen running her long, sharp nails through his thinning hair, when an alarm sounded. Ashley's daughter was coming toward the salon with something in her hand. "I think it's a snake," Ashley squealed.

Sure enough, a nine-year-old girl was standing at the front door holding a live snake. Panic gripped the salon.

Bob snorted and laughed out loud. "Women," he said with obvious disdain. "Afraid of a little snake."

Aileen dug her nails into Bob's scalp and considered nipping his ear. Then Ashley calmly stepped forward.

"Why it's a lovely snake," she said to her daughter. "Can I see it?" She deftly held the snake up for inspection. "It's a nice snake," she said moving toward Bob. "But, ooogh! It has sharp fangs!"

With that, she lightly dropped the snake in Bob's lap. They say his scream was clearly audible down at the Cafe. Bob lurched backward, launching the snake into the cash register. Bob leaped up and ran out the door, hair half-clipped, still wearing the cape. Aileen and Ashley stood at the window watching him go.

"It's a shame. Who will we talk about?" Ashley said.

"He never tipped anyway," said Aileen.

"What was wrong with him," the little girl asked. She was again holding the snake.

"Testosterone poisoning," Ashley said. "Makes men crazy every time."

Stella's Valentine Surprise

Valentine's Day comes to the old cafe. Little candy hearts are dancing around, creating grins as the messages are read. Stella the waitress is giving them out.

"True Love," reads one. "Be Mine," "Hug Me," and "Rowdy Girl," read others. Stella knows how to shake things up for Valentine's Day. The old guys are reading their candy hearts and passing them around like grade school kids.

"Kiss Me Now," "Lover Boy," "U2R Mine," "Girl Crazy"......

Laughter erupts as the secret messages are read. Stella fends of some saucy comments.

"Stella, darling," says Camelot Bob, "I've just got to know how you get the energy to work here all day and dance in my dreams all night."

"Bob, darling," Stella shoots back, "any dream you're in is a nightmare!"

"Stella," says Holy Lake Jake, taking a turn. "You've been taking your 'Good Looking Pills' again, and they're working just fine."

"Jake, the only pills I take are aspirin for the headaches you give me," Stella says, pouring some more coffee.

Finally, Water Street Pete offers his best line. "Stella, as many hearts as you've stolen, you should be in jail!"

"You can't steal what people give away," Stella says with a grin.

"Sexy smile," "Joy Boy," "Love 4 ever," and "Miss You," the men read on their candy hearts.

Stella is on a crusade to break down the walls that divide people. Divorced, children pretty much grown, brothers and sisters spread out – she knows anything divided by two comes up less. She has had enough of division. Stella is into addition and multiplication. On Valentine's Day she passes out hearts, hers included, and hopes they keep on moving down the line.

"Come on Stella," says Ridgeway Ron. "Tell us how to get to your heart."

Stella laughed and was going to say something like, "The road to my heart leads through the bank," or "Talk is cheap, new cars are better."

Then she had a memory.

One February day before Valentine's, she went to see her father. Her mom had died the summer before and he was lonely. Stella was lonely, too. They talked, and then Stella's dad said, "I want you to have something." From the hutch, he picked out a marvelous old vase. It was about 15 inches high, long and slender. The vase was fluted glass, ribbed, and the base was decorated with intricate designs.

"As far as I know, this is the only thing I have left that belonged to my father's mother. I want you to have it," he said. "You are the one who always loved flowers."

Stella put the vase on the counter and reached out to her Dad. They hugged without talking and shared tears.

Stella told the story, and suddenly she realized her eyes were wet. She stopped and felt foolish that her heart had slipped to her sleeve. The men were quiet until Jake broke the awkward silence.

"Heartbreaker," he read on his candy heart. "That's you Stella."

The men laughed and Stella flashed a smile. "Better to break from use than rust away," she said.

Stella spent the rest of the day passing out her hearts, picking up dirty silverware, and keeping the cafe in line. Toward dusk, the florist van pulled up out front.

"Stella, you done hit the jackpot," said Murray, the florist, handing her a bouquet of exquisite red roses.

Stella gasped and ripped open the card. "You always were the one who loved flowers," it read, signed by the boys at the old cafe. On the bouquet was a large candy heart: "If kindness were pillow, you would be a cloud." Stella didn't know whether to laugh or cry, so she did both. Multiplication and addition had worked again.

Chapter 5

Seasons

Every season is their favorite at the Old North Side Cafe.

The Cafe is more fickle than a sweet little February valentine all decked out in curls and swirls, wearing a fancy, frilly dress, and ready to break your heart. Sweet candy and tantrums, flirts and snubs, the seasons always offer more than they can deliver, and then give back more than they take. It's a roller-coaster ride in life's amusement park; smoke and mirrors, delicious fears, and miraculous moments from the most unexpected things.

Seasons become a paradox, a conundrum. For most of their lives, the aging boys mock snowbirds until they become one. A March day calls creaking, old bodies to work, and then throws the old boys in a heap, suffering and sagging, into bed. Like the "heel" in professional wrestling, malevolent, uncaring, immoral spring loves to ruin them.

Then there is June. So beautiful and so dangerous, June lures the old codgers into their past youth. Spring softens the boys up, and then June finishes them off.

Summer crushes whatever romanticism they have left, and, dear friend, there is no crank like an old crank sweating off summer.

Thankfully, summer finally relents and offers autumn. The Cafe does love autumn. The Cafe loves the clothes – mature men like a loose fitting sweatshirt and khaki pants. They like the food, the harvest, the sports, colors, and comforters. And so it is, that while spring comes in a day, autumn lurks slowly into winter and the four great holidays of life: Thanksgiving, Christmas, New Year's, and Valentine's Days mask winter's terrible cold and snow.

Every season, in the end, marks itself with a feeling and moment. It is a snow-drift or a snapdragon; a sumac leaf, or heat rising off the pavement. The seasons are moods and memories, smells and touches, all poured-over with sticky emotion – all hopelessly entwined and impossible to sort through. Only the fleeting, ethereal snippets of life are eternal.

The four seasons form a ritual so manifest in Midwest culture that it drives every instinct and behavior. The circular movement of the seasons lures the old boys into a comfortable notion that nothing really ever ends; there is only the cycle of life. How wrong they are. Spinning tops wobble, then roll and rest. It ends. The sun is always rising someplace, but time, with death, brings darkness to us all.

Einstein said we have time, because otherwise everything would happen at once. Old guys who know they rushed through their lives now can't figure out what to do with the time they hurried to get. They think they are just killing time, but the opposite is true. Some, like Camelot Bob, think the past is not just a guidepost to show the way – it's a hitching post to tie down the horse. He thinks nothing should ever happen for the first time. For those who take time to smell roses and keep thought scrapbooks, time is both passing and still infinite. Time is the gentle friend who allows them to grow old, to experience each moment as infinite, and then allows them to fade, like a fire burns down to be forgotten.

Isn't it interesting we know about the past, but have no control over what has been? We can control the future, but who knows what the future brings? Old men talk about these things, but not directly. God no, not directly! Ain't any college professor's bullarky creeping into the Cafe, not ever! Nope, the meanings of life all smell like a story, and a story about the seasons is always brewing, fresh and aromatic, at the Old North Side Cafe.

Green, Green Grass Of Home

The ubiquitous hum of lawnmowers permeated the neighborhood as Camelot Bob stepped off his back porch to survey the damage. His worst fears had come true. There in the lawn were the telltale stripes of improper lawn fertilization.

"My God, the wife is going to kill me," mumbled Bob as he counted the brown rows in his once verdant Kentucky bluegrass lawn.

Bob was a country boy, raised on an American ethic that says more is better, and biggest is best. When it came time to fertilize the lawn, Bob bought the cheapest, strongest, biggest bags of fertilizer he could find (10-10-10 from Sutherlands Lumber), and then tripled the recommended dose. For extra measure, Bob opened the spreader too high and hit the trees and shrubs twice. The results were horrific.

"Went a little heavy on the fertilizer, didn't you Bob?" asked Holly Lake Jake surveying the brown-and- green striped yard. "Did you try watering it?"

Bob had watered daily, hourly even. The result was abnormally fat green grass shooting up above the brown stretches. Bob looked pretty silly riding his lawnmower across the striped wasteland. Bob's wife could not help it; he had offered her a free shot.

"I told you to use the lawn service," said Bob's wife.

Bob's logic had been that for half the price he could do the work himself. In fact, as he poured on the fertilizer, he pictured himself the envy of the neighborhood with a homegrown lush stand of dark green grass.

"We once had so little, we learned to make do with what we had. We changed our own oil, ironed our own shirts, cleaned our houses, and kept our own yards," said Bob that afternoon, defending himself at the North Side Cafe. The men nodded their understanding. They tried to make him feel better.

"When I do the laundry, I use too much soap," Water Street Pete said.

"I scorch my shirts, because the iron is too hot. I think the linen setting must do the best job," said Jake.

"…and I brown-and-green pinstripe my yard. Excess is too easy for us," moaned Bob.

"Organization and control have replaced labor. Don't work harder, work smarter," interrupted City Hall Sam, "and when all else fails, read the directions."

The men replied by wadding up their napkins and throwing them at Sam.

"Read the directions my foot (except, they don't really say 'foot'). Whoever heard of such a thing," Gladstone Gus said.

That night, Bob started the work of verti-cutting and reseeding his lawn. He did all the work himself, toiling 7-8 hours a day. He worked too hard and hurt his back. He ignored his wife's icy stares. He cut his hand twice and lost his pliers trying to adjust the seeder.

Come the end of June, however, when the katydids sing softly to summer, and a full moon rises over our lush humid plains, Bob's grass will be standing tall and green – the product of stubborn excess and the old country boy ways.

Apple Picking Time

Though aging comes with growing aches and pains, there's a better side. Still waters run deep. Beneath those sore muscles and short breaths, understanding and appreciation are about as good as it gets. As folks grow older, emotions come easy, and the richness of simple moments unfold.

In nature's cycle, autumn is that final burst before winter. It is the best! Grumpy old men grow smiles in the quickly darkening evenings. They hear the wind song of birds gathering in fencerows. The gold and orange splash across the deep blues of autumn and say it's time for another fling.

Such an autumn day demands a trip to the apple orchard. Apples are as crabby and sweet as old men. Like older folk, apples require a period of dormancy. They must be fully ripe when harvested because immature apples ripen poorly after picking. Stored correctly, apples can remain fresh up to ten months.

Apple trees do best planted on slopes and hilltops where cold air moves down the incline before blossoms on young fruit can freeze. Every apple variety has its own moment when it is most ready. The famous Arkansas Black isn't ready until late October, but the Empire and Jonathan have come on earlier, for instance.

Most people don't know this, but the Delicious apple came from a seedling found in Iowa in 1895. The Stain apple came from the seed of a Kansas Wine Sap apple in 1866. John McIntosh in Ontario discovered McIntosh apples in 1796. No seed exists that will grow these apples today. Every new tree must be grafted.

Apples and apple cider were mandatory for early settlers. One rotten apple really does ruin the rest. Apples are good for teeth, every apple has a star inside (cut it sideways), and just thinking of apples means you must have one to eat.

Manor Hill Mack, Holly Lake Jake, Camelot Bob, and Water Street Pete drove out to the country and loaded in an old farm pickup for a ride into the orchard. Two rode in the back of the pick-up, their feet dangling from the tailgate. Riding "open" on a farm reminds a man of his youth, and kids riding with their feet dangling off the hay wagon or bouncing on the fender of a tractor. The old truck crept down the hillside with the men stopping to polish, then taste, the different apples. Kids don't know what "apple polishing" means anymore. Grocery stores stole it, but when an apple is picked right off a tree, a dull film hides its beauty. Farm boys, hoping to get in good with their teacher, brought her a fresh apple and polished it up on their sleeve to make it shine. "Apple polishing" seems so much a nicer term than the word kids use now when their classmates play up to the teacher. Anyway, riding on the back of the pick-up, their feet dangling, their pockets bulging with apples, the old boys were having a fine day.

At the barn, it got better. A fresh batch of cider was cooling.

"Have a taste," Mr. Girven said.

"Much obliged," the boys answered.

They drank a lot of cider, and with the apples they had already eaten, nobody had to guess why they didn't make it to the Cafe the next day.

Autumn's like that, sudden special moments followed by a hard snap. Still, there are times when old kids rub fresh Jonathan apples on their sleeves as they gaze across a field down to a stream below, and it seems like yesterday, only better.

The crunch of an apple, the spice and soft sweetness with a hint of tart; these are the tastes of a fine autumn before a winter comes.

Mum's The Word

Word is out along the treetops and down the fencerows. Autumn is coming. Kitchens, long abandoned because of the heat, begin to simmer with the rich aroma of chili and baked cornbread. There is no other season like autumn. Resplendent in color, charged with a sense of fulfillment, and edged with ending, fall draws men to the old Cafe. The stories get longer and bolder, the bets bigger, and smiles easy to find.

Holly Lake Jake felt the Cafe call, but autumn has its list. The furnace needs inspection, windows need cleaning, yards need attention, and a memory needs tending…the memory of Arnold Schumacher.

To know Arnold, you first had to know chrysanthemums. Chrysanthemum comes from two Greek words meaning, "golden flower." They are autumn's gift to summer's end. Chrysanthemums explode with color as the days get shorter.

That brings us to Arnold, though everyone called him "Doc." For as long as anyone could remember, Doc raised a field of chrysanthemums on the edge of Liberty. Those in the know walked the field with him, and they picked their plants together. Doc dug up your final choice right then, and tied it with bailer twine in a big sheet of brown paper. Then you talked.

"Yes, it was a dry summer, and the flowers are about two weeks late," Doc said. "See the grass edge? Over the years, I've lost about a foot of soil."

It was in Doc Schumacher's chrysanthemum field you would find real, true lasting autumn. Here was the quiet harvest of tradition. Memories lingered in the brilliant colors and worn hands. Flower power ruled in this field of dreams. Sometimes, Doc ordered your wallet back in your pocket; his gifting born of a spirit older than the field.

Like their flowers, Doc and his wife Lillian (Liberty has an elementary school named after her), were explosions of kindness. Flowers loaded safely in the trunk, you backed out to the main road, and Doc watched for traffic. Back home, chrysanthemums lit up dying flowerbeds for a final fling.

You could travel a lot and never find better than what's out the back door. Schumacher's chrysanthemum field was like that. It was the Northland's little gift for those with the good sense to find it. Many are the houses around Liberty that still have a perennial chrysanthemum marking a friendship grown in Doc's field.

People in Asian countries have cultivated chrysanthemums for over 2,000 years. In October, the Japanese celebrate the Feast of the Chrysanthemums. At one time in their history, the Japanese ruled that only royalty could grow the chrysanthemums.

No wonder the flowers from Schumacher's field once made Jake feel like autumn's king.

Ghosts, Dust And Wood Plank Floors

by Ridgeway Ron

These are the days of slush and potholes, windshield wiper fluid, and the salty white residue of a fading winter. Gray days and endless, meaningless, spits of snow ache their way into the simple routines of work and home, and leave us longing for spring. Expectation exceeds reality, and we are out of tune with life.

The Cafe's cranky, curmudgeons have worn their welcome at home, and are shooed out to make their own way in the gray chill of sandy streets and muddy snow. They are a hacking, sniffling, congested lot of aging men. Old stained parkas and canvas coats, belts stretched and marking the excesses of inactivity and appetite, shoes scuffed and neglected, the men come to the Cafe. An old mentality draws them there.

In their youth, ragged ruffians in galoshes and long underwear tagged behind Paw-Paw to the seed store. These same gloomy days called an older generation to walk plank wood floors, lit by bare hanging light bulbs, and rest on rickety, wooden chairs and metal stools, all circled around an old coal stove. This was their gathering place – their clubhouse and sanctuary of rural life. Haphazard stacks of feed and seed bags created a labyrinth of cobwebbed, shadowy tunnels and passages in which cats and mice played out an endless game of life and death. The ubiquitous dust claimed every inch of a feed store leaving a tactile and olfactory signature that every farm boy knows and misses now and then.

This was the golden age of storytelling – an ancient, oral tradition combined with the unfathomable magic of radio to create an era when imagination and sound trumped the visual chains of reality. Gathered around hot glowing coals, the dust forming halos on hanging bulbs of light, and the calico cats sneaking in shadows, our great grandfathers created a tradition so rich and full of comfort, that it is part and parcel to who we are even now. That is why the old men come to the Cafe on a gray day. They wedge close on the Naugahyde seats and clank porcelain cups on chipped saucers. They run rough, wrinkled hands through the steam rising from hot coffee, and they begin to thaw. Somewhere, the slight smell of an old feed sack drifts into their memory, and the light dims showing the dusty shadows of prowling cats. The faint popping and clinking of an ancient hot stove, and a memory of Paw-Paw's easy laugh and huge calloused hands gesturing to make a point, all cloud the moment and form a familiar, alternative reality. The old boys are home.

Stories of who is related to whom, when people married, and the names of their children mix and churn, cutting passages to hidden memories and old stories. They talk and laugh as kin, and the cold, gray of a loitering winter fades. The inexplicable magic happens again – Paw-Paw is alive; Uncle William, Walter, Grandpa Charley, Art Decker, Sam Ehlenbeck – all the names come back. Their laughter fills the old Cafe. Their mannerisms, voice inflections, how they sat on the rickety chairs – it all drifts in the dust that fills the plank flooring. Imagination and the spoken word are working again. It is a fine day after all. Glad you came by!

It's A Twister Mister

Tornado season. The words cause reverence at the old Cafe. Mystic winds that somehow blow up from Oz, and then down the back alley of the Midwest, dominate spring. Usually confident and jocular, the old-timers speak in reverent tones of tornados, and each year the myths grow bigger.

"My Dad was milking when the storm came up. The milk parlor was just a lean-to on the side of the barn. We had eight cows. Mom ran out to the shed to warn Dad and just as she stepped in, the tornado struck," said Manor Hill Mack, wringing his napkin in his hands.

"Dad said it got deathly quiet, and the barn just started to rise. It lifted vertically off the ground about 40 feet and then dropped straight down. The milking parlor was untouched. The cows, locked by their heads into wooden stalls, hardly moved." Ohhh, the men liked that story. In a world we wish was orderly and structured, capricious winds separate life from death on a whim.

"I couldn't have been more than 10," said Ridgeway Ron, gesturing with a finger stub, a telling reminder of farming's dangers. "It got dark like it was night, and the birds stopped singing. It was more quiet and eerie than I ever remember. The tornado came from out of the southwest, and my dad scooped me up and took off running to the cellar. For the next few minutes, I felt the cellar door heaving against the wind and was afraid the storm would rip it open and suck us out to die. Then it was over.

"Outside was chaos; boards and tree limbs were strewn about. And this is the truth – one of our chickens came squawking up with no feathers. The storm had plucked every feather out of that chicken, and it was still alive." Whoa, the men cringe at that story. Stories start spinning now, taking on a life of their own.

Holly Lake Jake told of a pickup truck that was carried in the sky five miles and put down on K-Highway, facing the right direction. Water Street Pete says there's a statue in Oklahoma with a piece of straw sticking out of the soldier's ear. A tornado's vacuum drove it there like it was a nail.

The stories whirl, and the Cafe gets dark and apprehensive. A killer tornado crested the hill over Topeka and then plowed into the city. Another lifted the roof off a school building and dropped it back on helpless children. A string of three marched over Kansas one spring, leveling one town. A seven-mile long and one-mile wide path of destruction destroyed half of Joplin's schools and killed over 160 people.

Noooo, the men whisper as the stories turn gruesome and close to home. Winds are gathering from back in time, heading for the present. The men sense the Cafe windows beginning to rattle as a spring storm closes in.

Camelot Bob remembers, but does not tell of his tornado. He lived on a large hill overlooking St. Joseph. Dad was gone, and Mom was frantic to get her three children to the basement. Bob didn't go to the basement. He walked outside and stood frozen as a whirling black phantom roared over the town. The sound, the majesty, the overwhelming force of the tornado shrunk the boy. It was as close to God as he had ever been. There was no meaning in the wind – it just was.

The wind rattles the Cafe windows once again, and spits of rain streak the glass. The men huddled close, sipping coffee, and twisting napkins.

Knee-high Corn Meets Burma Shave

by Manor Hill Mack

"The corn is knee-high on the 4th of July." My Dad used to say this as we chugged two-lane black-tops in an old Plymouth, heading for his parent's farm outside of Manchester, Iowa. This was when car travel could still be a little "iffy". Tires could blow, the engine might overheat, and a water pump or a generator might give out and strand the family on the side of the road. Saying "Knee high on the 4th of July" must have given my Dad a sense of confidence, and renewed his faith that all was well in the world as we headed north and east from St. Joe, Missouri. Dad said it a lot. I know his dad, my grandfather, said it. "Knee high on the 4th of July" was an insider farmer saying. Of course, corn is always waist high, at least, on the 4th of July.

When I was a little kid sitting in the back seat, with a 55 mph hot wind blowing in my face, I used to wonder what kind of giant had knees so high. Thankfully, advertisers solved that mystery with the introduction of the Jolly Green Giant ads of my youth. Riding in the back seat of a Plymouth, with my older brother and little sister, I needed the diversion of growing corn and Green Giants. My dad smoked unfiltered Camel cigarettes, and casually offered his ashes to the wind whizzing past his driver's seat window. Those ashes blew in my face. My older brother, of course, had claim to the prime window seat behind mother's window where it was sweet perfume blowing back, or mother asking, "Is this too much wind?" and rolling up the window just a bit. My little sister was put in the middle of the back seat (the pit of long-distance travel) where she was systematically tortured by my brother and me. She got back at us by telling outrageous lies to Dad who would then say, "Boys, you don't want to make me stop this car!" Dad never did stop the car, because the threat alone petrified us with fear. I ate windy cigarette ashes and stared out the window at the corn and read the signs.

When super-shaved
Remember, pard
You'll still get slapped
But not so hard
Burma-Shave

Violets are blue
Roses are pink
On graves
Of those
Who drive and drink
Burma-Shave

A lot of my philosophy of life is deeply tainted by Burma-Shave.

The trip up to the farm was never so bad, however. I loved the farm. On Grandpa's farm, I hid out in the chicken coop where it was hot, but strangely exciting to be surrounded by so many living things, all clucking and laying eggs.

But nothing compared to getting lost in the corn. I understand why crop circles and corn mazes can be so intriguing. A healthy corn plant can get seven or eight feet tall. The leaves have an edge to them, and the green is so true. You are in a different world in the middle of a cornfield.

The corn brings back a lot of memories. Yep, I can still hear my Dad saying, "Look, the corn is knee high on the 4th of July," and Mom would say it back to him. In the back seat, my brother would say it, and then I would say it; even my little sister would repeat, "Knee high on the 4th of July." Off we went into the mighty corn belt of the earth, our car chugging, the family reading signs, playing the Alphabet Game or 20 Questions, feuding, drawing boundary lines on car seats, and then falling asleep in each other's laps.

"Knee high on the 4th of July," heading to Grandpa and Grandma's farm. "Hey Dad," I whisper now, with two grown sons of my own who have been properly taught about corn. "The corn is knee high on the 4th of July."

More Than A Season Of Old Men

by Holly Lake Jake

It is the great season at the old Cafe. Autumn feels comfortable to those on the happy hour side of life. They understand harvest. They understand aging has a beauty. They know Thanksgiving is the best of all holidays, and they appreciate the swirling excitement of leaves against the coming gray and glistening skies. And so they gather around the Cafe's old Formica tabletops with their collection of steaming, porcelain cups. In these moments, the old friends edge closer together.

This is their season and their harvest. There is a majestic beauty to the earth that they understand and see in one another. Stella, the waitress, moves easily among the tables, a coffee pot in each hand. The extra crowds of autumn give new life to the Cafe. She likes these days; she likes the people who stop in for coffee and conversation.

Over in one corner, the workers from In As Much Ministry, and others from the food pantry, quietly visit, talking about the day. The bad economy has caused a tremendous demand for food. At the big table, the hospital volunteers gather. A cup of coffee is a small pleasure for them. Here are the unpaid servants who are asked daily to soothe coarse nerves before a surgery, or give directions to worried parents. The hospital could not operate without them. The housing ministry group will be in later to take their break. Their group is called Habitat for Humanity. They build houses to sell interest-free to deserving families. Volunteers from Hillcrest Ministries were in last week. They work without pay to help put homeless people back on their feet. Some of the Cafe regulars are now volunteering their time to gather and sort supplies for hurricane victims in Florida and Haiti. A particularly happy bunch serve as volunteers called Youth-Friends, and read books and visit with local elementary school students during lunch. A couple of very serious looking men and women talk over autumn plans at the nature sanctuary. A group of women go over Saturday's menu at the food kitchen. The Meals on Wheels team comes in the same day and time each week. Two members of that team also volunteer for a hospice.

Stella knows all the stories, and more. It is a sadness to her that our culture and the media are more interested in death and rumors than the real stories of life and survival. One couple, the man and wife just paying their bill, opens their house to a college student who needs a home. A woman goes daily to her daughter's house to be with her grandchildren after school. A dollhouse, rich in labor, is built for a granddaughter who lives many miles away. The church library is cleaned. A phone bank for a community blood drive magically fills every available slot. Quilts made, cookies baked, rides given, and patients visited — the autumn spirits move.

There is a beauty and worth to this season that few stop to know. It is not just the turning leaves, or the stands of corn waiting for a combine, that give these days such enormous beauty. It's not just the geese going home, or the flocking clouds of sparrows. Nor is it the sudden thrill of a first frost or the cold taste of fresh cider. It is more.

Autumn is the season of life giving itself back to life. The kids are grown; the career is winding down. The need to be "first, best, or most" grows dim. Autumn is a last season of care; the harvest of life. Trees are planted now to give shade to children these good folk will never know. If you look, you can see, and if you ask, you will learn. The real beauty of autumn is that people still care. Those who have lived the longest and known the most live these days helping others. Their autumn harvest is good works and deeds, and their thanksgiving is for the time and health to keep on helping doing good deeds and acts of kindness.

Autumn is the great season of land and life. The Cafe is its home – a refuge of beauty for the good, gray spirits of fall.

Jake Gets Mad As #$%%

Holly Lake Jake first noticed a splash of color driving down Ridge Street. A scarlet red, burning with orange flame, shimmered in the breeze, whispering autumn. Summer has fallen. Autumn with its brilliant death charm was calling for a new celebration, and all earth answered with an obedient technicolor burst of life.

Jake drove Highway 291, going south out of town. The river and its majestic cottonwoods called him. The hard maples, rich with yellow and red, stood out on the hillsides in welcome. A thick, scarlet shag of sumac left blistered red lines along forgotten easements, railroads, and utility lines. Jake was alone, driving nowhere special, off to look at America. He was overcome with the season. Rural homes, decorated with multi-color sweet gum trees, announced autumn with hay bales and corn shucks. Hapless scarecrows, their pockets stuffed with straw and necks cut with red bandanas, ushered him past farms and fields toward the river. Jake read the Missouri River had once been over a mile wide with islands of color reflecting light into the slow moving lake-like water. It must have been a magnificent sight. Hedge apple trees, and their seasonal harvest, dotted a clearing with textured spring green. Their wood supposedly burns so hot it can consume an unprepared fireplace. Jake's friend called the fruit Osage oranges and said they kept bugs out of basements.

Jake admired his moment with the river and autumn, then turned north to Watkins Mill. He sat at the lake and heaved rocks into the mystery of murky water. Geese saw his play and advanced; gaining power and speed, they launched before him into the sky. Jake was finding the America he loved.

A beer can broke the trance. A giant blue pick-up truck roared into the clearing. Three men emerged, tossing off their excess for others to pick up. The bumper sticker on the back of the truck gave these men away. "Don't like my driving, Dial 1-800- Eat #%&@," it read. Here was the other side of America. Jake would not take away these men's freedom of speech, but he resented their insult to freedom. Jake abhorred the rude mockery of decency, made public for even the most innocent eyes. People who put such stickers on their vehicles are a cheap form of mean. They are desperate, inadequate people consuming their own freedom, parasites feeding on themselves.

When the men wandered off, Jake could not restrain himself. Picturing himself as the Osage Avenger, he took tape from his trusty toolbox and covered up letters and words. His pen did the rest. Now, the violation read. "-------Like my driving-----I ----eat #%&@."

Jake is not a perfect man. His act of vandalism costs autumn a little of its splendid edge. Yes, the Missouri River is no longer a mile wide and is laced with progress and poison, and yes, today's birch gliders spew dioxide. Yet, Jake lingered by the lake, gathering a sack of Osage oranges. He liked their tactile elegance and dense form. They were his symbol of autumn. The trees they came from were so hard their wood ate chain saws. But when it did, the flame was hot and intense. Jake was like that as well.

No Lie Like A Winter Lie

These are the days of remembrance and recollection. Men gather in the comfortable warmth of the Cafe to spin yarns and tell their stories once again. Nourished by friendship and hot, fully-leaded coffee, they crank up memory's old engines and travel the roads of youth. Selective recollection ensures happy endings and increasingly heroic deeds. Winter always does this. Cold winds and blowing snow sound the bell to gather together. Graying men haunt old seed stores with potbellied stoves and the rural, county cafes – the word gets out, and the men come, full of tall tales and life's amazing anecdotes. Winter makes men consummate liars.

Water Street Pete claims he kept an old John Deere bailer working five years with chewing gum and rusted wire. Our friend Ridgeway Ron remembers the time he poured plant fertilizer on his zinnias each week for three months. Those magic seeds, of course, came from a borrowed seed catalogue, and their secret identity is forever lost, but Ron swore those zinnias were a foot across and grew six feet tall. Come fall, Ron says he had to cut them down with an axe.

Then there are the car stories. City Hall Sam once drove from Denver to Kansas City on 13 gallons of gas. A 50 mph wind blew him downhill the entire way. Sam says he had enough gas left to drive to work the next day. Gladstone Gus, in what is widely considered the most outrageous tall tale ever told at the Cafe, swears that during a drought, he drove his Jeep across the Missouri River – catching four catfish on the way.

That, of course, leads to stories about snow and ice.

Up by Pattonsburg, Missouri, there was once an ice storm so bad that everyone had to wear ice skates to get around. "I swear it's true," says Camelot Bob. "I skated to school for a week before there came a thaw." Men remember when they had to tie a rope from the back door to the outhouse, or you could get lost in a blizzard. "Old Chap Winger was found frozen stiff down by Rushville one winter, his hand still on the rope. It snowed so hard he couldn't make it back in, and he died right there. He was still standing two weeks after the blizzard when Russell Anderson found him. We can only guess why he died smiling," says Holly Lake Jake.

Camelot Bob tells about a pig that fell in love with him. Seems Bob always had a way with pigs – his nieces called him Uncle Porky. Whenever he came to visit, the hogs would come up to the fence to snort and bay for him.

Anyway, one very hot summer day, a pig was so enamored with Bob she broke free and headed his way at full-on pig speed. Bob stayed treed for two hours before the pig burst its heart hankering after what she could not get. They butchered the pig on the spot, and Bob had his lover's bacon for breakfast the next winter.

Sometimes the stories take a different turn. They get spooky. Manor Hill Mack was only four when his grandfather died back in Manchester, Iowa. His family left for Cedar Rapids, Iowa, early the next morning. Mack's parents found his grandma crying hysterically. His dad took off to the funeral home, and his mom got busy cooking and cleaning the house.

A confused, little Mack wandered into the dining room alone and started to cry. It was there, in the dining room, that an older man came in, picked up the young boy, and dried his tears. He told Mack that Grandma would be ok, and his mom and dad hadn't forgotten him. They were just busy helping Grandma. The man also told little Mack that Grandpa was in Heaven and liked it very much, and then showed him where some of his Dad's old toys were stored. At the funeral home the next day, Mack saw that the man who came to visit him in the living room, and the man in the casket, were the same person.

Most amazing, Gus also tells that there was once a President of the United States who repeatedly lied to the American people. That president governed over a time of great job loss, economic hardship, and increasingly bitter division among all people. During his tenure, the poor and the middle class lost jobs, their life savings, and a sense of hope. At the same time, the very rich were made even wealthier. That president even took us to war without a plan to keep the peace.

"You know what? The guy got re-elected! Go figure," said Gus.

Men tell these stories with a straight face, and though the wind blows outside, inside it's warm and cozy. Truth spins its way in and out of fantasy like steam drifting off cups of coffee.

This is February, the time for tall tales and odd truths at the Old North Side Cafe.

Another Day In Paradise

A chorus of chirping birds and the distant chugging of lawns mowers gave the day away. Spring in all her finery had whispered in on the edge of a cool morning breeze. Slanting sunlight etched out shadows along leaf and flower as the collective countenance of a fine May morning made its case for perfection.

Manor Hill Mack was a convert. He wondered how a day could be much better. Warm sun, cool shade, a yard to mow and the energy to do it; he would put this moment in Missouri against any. Such days liberated Mack. He was not born to do the work that goes on inside houses. He hated vacuum cleaners, pine scented cleansers, mildew restrainers, and abrasive powders. Mack had never appreciated a hanger in his life and could care less if wet towels got in the clothes hamper. His idea of cleaning the bathroom was wiping up hair. As a boy, he had once cleaned his room, only to find he had been sleeping on his dresser. Yard work was his medium. Here, dirt was the substance of life. From it, grew his true calling. In the yard, he did all the things that were forbidden inside. He splashed water, tracked mud, laid his sweaty body against the cool comfort of trees, and properly cursed the small nuisances of life.

"Mack, will you clean the bathroom? I have to get my nails done," interrupted Mack's wife. Mack cringed and said yes. He had no choice; she did everything inside while he piddled around among the impatiens, red oak, and hearty fescue. To refuse the bathroom would mean an outbreak of cold war. Mack liked peaceful coexistence.

He had to admit the stool and tub were especially bad. A film had collected on the tub, and even his super-chlorinated-bleach-abrasive powder was challenged.

Mack dived into the chore. Like a fool, he wore one of his best shirts. Growing up, he didn't have a lot of clothes, and "A little dirt never hurt anybody," so they said. Much to his wife's consternation, Mack still wore whatever he had on when the notion to work struck. The chlorine bleach, however, had spotted his new shirt. Worse yet, his wife was looking at him. It was obvious she was ready to pounce.

"How many times do I have to tell you not to wear your good shirts to do housework in?" she exclaimed.

Mack grabbed a wet rag and started wiping the shirt, but it was no use. Five minutes later, his wife came in holding the wet rag. This time, she was really mad.

"Don't you know wet rags leave stains on the furniture? I found this on the table!" Mack swallowed. It was best to shut up now and repent.

That night, he worked till 9:30 washing the driveway, planting a few flowers, cleaning the deck, and trimming bushes. The lovely day faded to darkness, and an occasional lightning bug challenged the night. Mack's wife brought out a glass of iced tea. She said the bathroom looked good.

"I'm better with the yard," he said.

"I know," she replied, and life closed on another day in paradise.

June Brides, My My

Camelot Bob couldn't help laughing when he saw it. There on Barry Road, just east of Metro North Mall, a jalopy was parked proudly outside a church for all to see. Beer cans festooned the rear bumper, and a skull-and-cross bones flag fluttered from the antenna. There were other decorations, but a large banner on the passenger side door was the central feature of the wedding car: "SHE MAY NOT BE THE MAYFLOWER, BUT SHE'LL COME ACROSS TONIGHT," the banner said.

"Ahh, marriage," Bob whispered with a chuckle. He thoroughly approved.

Marriage's history gives insight to Bob's attitude concerning weddings. Many of our current customs reach back to 200 A.D. when wives were scarce in Northern Europe, and real men carried big clubs. A man in search of a bride often found slim pickings in his tribe, so he got the fiercest warrior he could find (called a "best man") and headed out to the neighboring village for any young girl who had strayed too far from home. This "thug" approach to marriage not only gave us the best man tradition, but led to the symbolic act of carrying the bride over the threshold of her new home. Kidnapped wives rarely walk willingly into marital bliss.

Weddings were especially fun in 200 A.D. The church altar held a cache of arms for use against angry in-laws whose attacks were understandable and frequent. The best man stayed by the groom's side to keep him from getting killed, and the bride stood to the groom's left to give his sword hand free movement in case of an attack.

Even the lovely wedding ring, supposedly symbolic of never-ending love, may be disputed. Some believe, with good evidence, the ring is symbolic of the fetters used by barbarians to tether a bride to her captor's home.

The ring finger has a history, too. In India, nuptial rings are worn on the thumb. Early Hebrews placed the wedding ring on the index finger. Credit the Greek's failure to understand anatomy for our modern "ring finger". They believed a "vein of love" ran from the third finger straight to the heart, and therefore should carry a ring symbolizing love. Christians worked their way over to the vein of love during the wedding ceremony by first placing the ring on the top of the bride's index finger and saying, "In the name of the Father," then the middle finger with, "In the name of the Son," and the ring finger with, "and the Holy Spirit. Amen." Call it the Trinitarian formula.

Now, for the honeymoon – please read with discretion. "Honeymoon" comes from the practice of "hiding out" after abducting a young wife from another village. Attila the Hun gave new meaning to the word "honeymoon". Following a practice of drinking alcohol sweetened with honey for a month after marriage, Attila remained indelicately soused after marrying the Roman Princess, Honoria, sister of the Emperor. Fittingly, three years later, Attila had drunk himself to death.

As for veils, they, too, are man's creation. Designed to keep women obedient, servile, and humble, veils date back to early Muslims who expected their women to keep their heads covered. Yellow was the favored color of early wedding veils.

So it was that Bob laughed at the "Mayflower" and her journey into a new life; it's in his ancestral memory. Oddly enough, in Europe they now decorate marriage cars with flowers. Here, we do beer cans, condoms, and poison symbols. Modern-day "Attila's" forget the honey and just drink. No wonder 50 percent of our marriages end in divorce. Still, 93 percent marry again – and their divorce percentage is even worse.

Bob wished the newly-weds luck and drove on. His wife (also known as "She Who Must Be Obeyed") expected him home. Bob's Mayflower was now the battleship "Missouri" and nothing to mess with.

Finding Fault With Home Cooking

A thankful euphoria settled on the edges of the Old North Side Cafe. Nowhere was it so noticeable than by the rusty temperature gauge on the east window.

"Boys, I want you to know that four years ago today, the temperature was over 100 degrees. Our yards were already burned up, and by-in-large, most of us already had planned a trip to Colorado to beat the heat," said Camelot Bob, who tracks such things.

Keep in mind, most North Side conversation is, shall we say, negative. What fun is there in sitting around talking about how right everything is? It implies God, elected officials, women, lawyers, SUV drivers, and college graduates actually know what they are doing. But with the record low temperature last week, it became apparent that at least a few moments of bliss had settled on Northwest Missouri. What were the men to do but actually try saying something nice? Everyone except Manor Hill Mack, of course....

"By God, I hope my furnace doesn't have to come on," said Mack, who could find fault in home cooking. "They get you anyway you go; this June we don't have to turn on the AC, instead we got to turn on the furnace."

So much for a positive attitude. Actually, sitting around the old barbeque grill on a cool evening is when the ginger in these men actually does begin to mellow.

Before air-conditioning and a heightened fear of bugs drew us all indoors, there was a time when the cool nights of June drew young men outdoors. Slick hair, a fresh shirt, and a few gallons of gas called them to shadowy country lanes. Cars with V-8 engines, summer jobs you could do in your sleep, and the friends you never forget formed the backdrop for careless joy.

After those nights, the moon would never be so full again. Memories wait just below the surface on a cool June night. After a rain, they grow again. Small lines of corn, edged by the giant shadows of tall trees – all shimmering and lush in a buttery moon – crop up from the past as the smell of sumac dances with lightning bugs in the air. These were nights of promise and assurance that somehow things end up right.

"Good weather we're having," says Water Street Pete. "I tell you, there's nothing like an early summer night in Missouri. I've seen it all – the mountains and the oceans – and I'm here to tell you that few things match early summer in Missouri."

At this time, you can't help but love these old jaw-flappers. For all their crusty cynicism, they have selective, sentimental memories. Four years ago, they were sweating and cussing anything that moved. Today, all they remember is a June dream they had 40 years ago.

Masculine Splendor

Camelot Bob swaggered into the Cafe, his face flush with manly pride. It's deer season in these parts, and when a man has that look, you know he's made a kill.

"Ten-point rack," said Bob. "He came pretty as you please; couldn't have been more than 30 yards away when I shot him."

Ah, the masculine splendor of fresh meat. It was once a rite of passage when a boy bagged his first deer. Even now, these men have an odd reverence for "the kill." Not that the deer had any chance. Bob carries around a $5,900 rapid-fire cannon to do his work. In the woods, he is a walking hunter's catalogue. Bob wears:

- The Maine Warden's Parka (the same parka chosen for winter used by the men and women of the Maine Warden Service), $469.75;
- The sport-tech glove system, $59.75;
- The Jim Whittaker cap, designed by renowned American mountaineer Jim Whittaker (the first American to reach the summit of Mt. Everest), $69.75;
- The "briar resistant, 16.7 oz. per lin. yd. wool reversed whipcord" Bird Shooting Pants, $94;
- The famous Gore-Tex Field Boots (machine tested to simulate a lifetime of use under water without any apparent leakage), $208.75

For dangerous moments in the wilds around Chillicothe, Bob has a mini-pocket survival tool, $51.50, and an alpine lantern with a spring-loaded candle, $49.75. Not since Indians painted themselves and strung feathers in their hair have the local deer seen a sight such as Bob.

That's exactly what a 10-point buck was thinking when it saw Bob sitting by a tree, picking briars out of his pants. By the time the deer caught scent of the sweating bundle of Thinsulate, it was too late. Bob had fired off enough rounds to defend the Alamo. One caught the buck in the butt. The rest of the story is hamburger.

"I like deer meat in chili," says Bob, which is another way of saying he can't stand the taste of wild meat and has to hide it under as much pepper as possible.

Still, there was that moment of memory when Bob saw his dead deer. "Congratulations son, your first deer," he heard his dad say. It is hard to underestimate the emotional impact of a deer with its butt blown off.

So, the following morning, he told his story at the North Side. As he spoke, his hands danced to articulate the hunt. Bob paid homage to the size and beauty of the deer. In secret ways, he explained his own cunning and courage. With a dramatic gesture, he relived the moment of death. It was a fantastic story – they always are. Hunters must gather to describe their deeds. So it has always been; so it was today at the Old North Side Cafe.

Go Big Or Go Home

"Who wants to get a pumpkin?" asked Holly Lake Jake.

"I do!!" screamed three young voices.

"Get your shoes and coats on then," said Jake as the room turned into a mass of flying tennis shoes and jackets. Moments later, the two oldest rushed out to fight over the car window seat.

"I can't find my shoes! Grandpa, wait for me!" cried a small voice, tears streaming. One shoe was by the trash can, the other was in the bathroom. Jake had to dig some mustard yellow socks out of the dirty clothes hamper. Then it was out the door.

"I thought we could go up to the Sibley Orchard by Fort Osage and the honey farm," offered Jake to a chorus of cheers. The tears on the youngest had turned into a full-on smile of pure joy. "Are you going to find a nice pumpkin?" Jake asked him, as he buckled the car seat.

"I'm gonna find the biggest one," was the answer, with arms stretched to the limit to hold a huge, imaginary pumpkin.

"You are not!" shouted two voices from the way back. "Grandpa, you aren't going to let him get a bigger pumpkin than us, are you??"

"We'll all get the same size pumpkins," said Jake. This was a side of humanity he did not like.

Ah, it was a splendid fall day; the colors were right and stood out in three-dimensional glory against a deep blue sky. The talk was about the kind of face each would put on his pumpkin. Imaginations were running at full speed.

"Grandpa, will you, will you put a scary face on mine?" stammered the youngest, with visions of wide-eyed horror filling the sweet human face.

"Sure will," said Jake.

At the patch, frenzied activity burst from the car. The two oldest shot off to the farthest part of the field, lifting and inspecting as they went. Neither would make a choice for fear the other would find a bigger version a second later. The youngest chased after them, but took about three steps before he fell over the first pumpkin vine. It was a hard fall, but because nobody seemingly saw, he dusted off, got up, and charged on. Three steps later, and boom! This time, it hurt. Jake ran over and lifted up the crying boy for a hug.

"You know, I saw a pumpkin over here that would be perfect for the scariest face you ever saw!!" whispered Jake. The tears stopped as the boy dug his face into Jake's shoulder. Off they walked, a boy and his grandpa. The pumpkin they found had deep ribs and a knot that looked like a wart. With pointy eyes and sharp teeth, it would be "really scary", according to Grandpa. The boy nodded, sensing the possibilities. Jake negotiated the decision between the other two boys. All they really were interested in was dominating by size.

Three pumpkins rattled around in the trunk on the ride home. If anything, the fall colors were more beautiful. The youngest slept an innocent sleep. The terrors of this world held no sway for him beyond the face on a pumpkin.

That night, in the dark of his basement, Jake lit a candle in the face of a truly scary Jack-O-Lantern. Pointy eyes, sharp teeth, ugly wart, and a slit for a nose. It was gruesome. It was perfect. Jake and his grandson never do anything halfway. That's why they like each other so much.

Snow Days Rule

Stella stood at the back window watching the snow pile up. It was the biggest snow in 60 years. You might know it would happen on her one day off at the cafe. The radio was filled with reports of traffic accidents and closed schools. It was a day to stay inside. Stella clutched her arms close to her stomach as she stared out at the snow. There is a strange excitement to the way nature can rise up and flick away the schedules and routines of life as if they were crumbs on a pair of pants. For a moment, Stella's house seemed so empty. Something was wrong. The pace of the snow picked up. Wind whipped the edges of a spectacular drift that was forming across the driveway. Shoveling out would be chore.

Stella turned and wandered into her kitchen. Aimlessly she opened the cupboard and stared at the shelf where she kept cooking supplies. At first it seemed a vacant behavior. Then it hit her. Stella was checking to see what she had on hand to make cookies. She laughed at herself. She remembered the feeling. For a moment, she was a young mother again. School was called off, and the kids were home. Dripping snowsuits hung at the back door and little faces were demanding hot chocolate and telling sledding stories.

"Honest Mom, I shot down the hill," the youngest said. "We must have gone 10 feet in the air when we went over the jump. I'm not kidding."

Her boy's face was right red and his eyes sparkled with a delight only a little child can know. The oldest was making a fire in the fireplace and listening again to the wonderful list of closed schools. Stella wondered if she knew then how precious those days were.

Back in the present, her inventory was complete. Chocolate chips, flour, baking soda, butter, sugar, vanilla, salt, eggs – Stella had everything she needed to make cookies. It wasn't long until that old familiar aroma filled the kitchen. Cookies baking, coffee brewing, Stella glanced at the patches of frost on the windows and thought they would be perfect place for little boys to scratch their names – that's how it was.

On the really bad weather days Stella played Chinese checkers with the kids and then passed out big yellowing sheets of construction paper for refrigerator art. She still has those priceless picture of Mizzou football players with giant shoulder pads and almost no head.

An empty house in a snowstorm is the deepest kind of quiet. There were no piles of brown cotton gloves to put in the dryer, no pools of melting snow to wipe up, and no shouts to, "Close that door! We can't heat the whole neighborhood!"

Stella slumped as she walked back to the bedroom her boys had shared. They were gone. The forever days had ended. Stella wandered back to the kitchen and was about to call the little girls down the street to come over for cookies when the phone rang in her hand.

"Hello Mom," her youngest son said. "I was just thinking about you for some reason and decided to call. Is it snowing hard there too?"

"Snowing real hard. They closed the schools."

There was a long pause.

"Gosh Mom, remember when we used to go sledding down Kelley Hill, and you would make cookies and hot chocolate. You were always yelling at us to close the door and not track snow all through the house."

Stella laughed to hide her tears. She felt worse and better at the same time. A good snow day can shake up everything -- even a memory or two.

Rub Old Hands In Dirt

Break out the liniment; the Cafe's got a serious case of sore muscles. Spring is a hard season for these old men. Cooped up for a winter, they emerge from hibernation driven to sweep the garage, mow the lawn, dig the garden, prune the trees, and suffer.

In younger days, these men greeted spring with 18-hour days. Their bodies were weapons fired with devastating accuracy against unplowed fields, broken plows, unpainted barns, and manure in the feedlot. Some nights, they walked in from the barn near midnight, counting tomorrow's jobs. Every muscle was sore, and deep exhaustion crept into every joint. To understand farmers, you have to know this moment…life was real for them in this moment. There was a sense of importance in those days, a sense of being where one was supposed to be; a sense of art. Hard work was the brush that painted the plowed fields, fed the cattle, and milked the cows. At the end of a day, a man stepped back and surveyed his creation. The work was unbelievably hard, and only he saw it. It is no wonder the Cafe's aging men tear into spring. There is something out there they miss; something they need. As a result, they overdo.

Camelot Bob raked the garden, cleaned the garage, mowed the yard (after picking up every stick, of course), raked out the side flowerbed, planted some seeds (he knew it was too early, but couldn't resist), and started building a compost pile. Every bit of logic chastised him for working so hard. He was too old, too fragile, too susceptible to injury. Worst of all, Bob knew logic was right.

Still, spring leaped out of the night. The red bud tree glowed in the twilight. The smell of cut-grass and turned-earth drifted from the yard. A simple breeze lounged out by the red oak and then moved toward Bob. Bob remembered again he was alive. He remembered the simple joy of doing what was possible with a day and saying good night tired. He remembered his farmer's heart. He rubbed his hands, as farmers often do, and held them up for inspection. Yes, they were old, but so is the earth.

Each spring, the earth comes back, and so do the souls of men at the old Cafe.

Chapter 6

Cafe Politics

The Old North Side Cafe was the original "tea party" some 30 years ago.

Government funding? When it comes to money, the boys are so tight you can hear them squeak when they breathe.

Social justice? Sure, it's just to have women's work and men's work. They don't know who is gay among them, and have never considered it might be a possibility.

Armed Forces? This is the key foundation for American influence and success. War is a bad deal, but our country is worth it.

Arts and culture? "Nice if you like such things, but what's the point?"

That's how it is at the Cafe on most social and money issues.

Here is a tip to understanding Cafe politics. If you want to understand how the old boys view the world, you need look no further than how they think about pets.

First, the only real pet a real man can have is a dog. How you handle your dog determines your political persuasion. Conservatives like big dogs that are loyal, well trained, and obedient. They think a dog has to have a reason for being, so their dogs are hunters. Their dogs "heel, come, sit, and stay." They ride in the trunk, stay in kennels, get their ears twisted if they misbehave, and are respected for their beauty, breed, and work. The dogs of conservatives stay in the yard, eat only dog food, wear shock collars, and have electric fences. How much they cost, and their purebred heritage is important. These dogs know their place and stay there. They live the life they were bred to have. When they get old or sick, they are put down. Their owners like the word, "bitch."

Liberals like smaller dogs with personality and a little rebel spirit. Their dogs come inside the house and jump on the couch, bark at strangers, eat snacks of all kinds, and are trained with treats. These dogs get "groomed" and wear bandannas. They sleep on the bed with their own pillow and blanket. They still jump up on people, bark at the doorbell, take over your favorite TV chair, and go to the vet if they have a cold. Dogs become members of the family. Their deaths to this day bring tears. You will find their ashes buried in the back yard.

"If you ever saw how a dog lives on a farm, you would never let one lick your face," Camelot Bob likes to say. His dog wears a shock collar and is extremely well behaved. "Buster knows who the boss is. I am the alpha dog," Bob says, and that is the gospel truth. Buster, who clearly knows his place, is a happy dog.

Pache Nova (supposed Latin for "New Peace") belongs to Holly Lake Jake. Pache is a designer dog, part Labrador retriever and part poodle ... she is a Labradoodle. Pache digs in the backyard and loves to go to the ranch, where she runs free and swims in the lake. Her muddy feet track the deck, she likes to bring dead birds to the back door, and she will return any ball, but she will never drop it at your feet. Jake is the liberal.

"Pache has a mind of her own," he says. "I've already lost two pairs of shoes, and she keeps me up at night twisting and turning in the bed."

Pache is more like a dog in the wild. She is happy in her dog way, but extremely "connected".

There you have it, all you will ever need to know about Cafe politics.

Clueless Politicos

As a rule, Bob understands poor Jake – Jake is just hopelessly out of touch with the real world. Jake has no clue how Bob thinks, and ends up seeming smug and condescending. Worst of all, he sometimes thinks Bob doesn't care. Jake thinks Bob has no heart, and Bob thinks Jake has no brain. The Cafe's real magic is what happened to these guys over coffee and conversation for twenty years. Who would ever know they are best friends? We should all take a lesson…

Water Street Pete was fussing and fuming. Too much rain, too many detours, too high taxes, and not enough streetlights! Pete was on a roll.

"Why can't politicians get it through their heads," Pete railed. "The general public doesn't care about their big ideas. We just want our drains working, traffic lights synchronized, roads maintained, and trash picked up!" The heads nodded around the old Cafe.

"We ought to write a Manifesto and send it out to all those politicians lining up to run for public office," Pete said, taking out a pen and pulling up a napkin. "Tell 'em what we expect right up front."

Four hours later, it was done. Here it is, uncensored and unashamed – no apologies offered.

To all Politicians: A Taxpayer's Manifesto

First, we are sick and tired of political egos. We are plumb fed up with you fighting and quarreling with each other, trying to show each other up in public. If you can't support something because you got a political feud going, then get out!

Second, we're not sure us common taxpayers can afford your sucking up to the rich anymore. When the rich pay fewer taxes than we do, something is wrong and we don't like it. If you can't represent all of us, get out.

Third, we elected you, not some high-paid consultants you can blame when something goes wrong. We're not opposed to spending some money to get good advice, but you make the decisions, and when things go wrong, you stand up and take the blame.

Fourth, get your story straight. Saying one thing on one side of the country and another on the other does not cut it with us. Get your story straight, or get out.

Fifth, get your priorities in line. We want good roads, sewers that work, adequate protection, safety nets for the truly needy, and a vision for the future. Don't trade our future for your own political gain. Represent the PUBLIC INTEREST, not your business interest, or get out.

Sixth, in case you don't know it, most of the country thinks some of our politicians act a bit goofy at times. Nobody's perfect, but you can at least refrain from being petty, bickering, uncooperative, and rude. If you can't conduct your personal and official affairs with some modicum of dignity, get out.

Seventh, we have had our fill of negative campaigning. If all you've got to run on is the mud in your hip pocket about somebody else, get out!

Eighth, treat your employees with respect. If you treat them right, they'll treat us right. Public employees are not your personal serfs. You weren't elected king or queen. Treat employees with dignity, so they can work for us, or get out!

Yours sincerely,
The North Side Cafe

Sanitary Landfills Explained

"Chickens one day, feathers the next." You'll actually hear people say things like this at the Old North Side. "I'll bet a dollar bill to a donut"… they say that too. When they cuss, it's "hell's bells," or "gall durnit."

People make a big deal out of slang used by young people. Kids once said things like, "cowabunga dude" or "chill out." But if you know what "getting your ears lowered," "going to submarine races" or "fruit and a drag and a stone turn-off" means, well, you are old.

The Old North Side has its slang, too. Here's a brief list of the latest "in" slang and their real definitions.

Election ballot: Endangered species; only counts if it is properly counted.

Political conventions: Made for TV movies about spoiled rich kids and hopelessly sentimental and naive Hollywood socialites.

Bridge building: The act of making a connection with somebody you try to rip off.

Road repair: No known meaning in most of the United States.

Cooperative government: See above.

Primary election: An old-time liar's contest. In the bigger primaries, you must develop a thirty-second commercial that will thoroughly offend everyone and leave no doubt you have no sense of propriety.

Coffee break: How young people and most retired folk spend their day.

Boss: What workers become who have no brains.

Evening news: "Honey, your supper is ready."

Vacation: A different location for the wife to cook, wash, and clean.

College graduate: Anyone who doesn't know how to change his oil, fix a lawn mower, or raise kids.

Santa Claus: Administrator of the nation's welfare program.

Good OLE boy: Anyone who drives around in a pick-up truck with beer cans on the floor.

Redneck: Anyone who throws the beer cans out the pick-up window.

Foreign cars: What college graduates can eat for supper when the economy goes to heck.

This place is run like a pool hall: Slang for congress.

Political commercial: Pointless character assassination designed to make people not want to vote.

Weekend: A chance for the wife to catch up on housework.

Political poll: Testing ground for the ignorant; a way to get the opinion of those who don't care.

Oil spill: What happens when women work on cars.

Progress: How the rich get richer.

Tax Increment Financing: Welfare for the very rich.

Recession: The lull between major sport seasons.

Planning and zoning: Hopelessly complex set of laws designed to keep anybody from doing anything that might make money.

Lawyers: The case for euthanasia.

Play-offs: The real meaning of life.

Sanitary landfill: Where North Side old-timers lived before getting married.

Meaning Behind The Saying

The boys at the Old North Side Cafe put their flag in the window. They sent checks to the New York relief fund, and last weekend, for no reason at all, old redneck Camelot Bob stood up and led them in the Pledge of Allegiance. They all stood together, put their seed hats over their hearts, and said the pledge. They said more than the words, however. You could read it in their faces and see it in their eyes. Don't ever doubt these old guys are patriots. Here is what they said, and what they meant.

I – No checking a poll on this one. Nobody else is going to do it but me.

Pledge – Promise, in the hard times, even when it costs; my word is good.

Allegiance – You will never have to worry whose side I'm on. Got your back, buddy!

To the Flag – Red, white, and blue; only a symbol, but when she waves, we think of freedom and the opportunity freedom gives to all. Stars and bars and glory!

Of the United – Out of many, one. The most astonishing political experiment of all time – and it works.

States – Fifty ways to interpret America. Mountains and deserts, forest and sea-shore, sophisticated city and backwoods rural, accented, flavored, and tinted; we stand strong, because we stand together.

And to the Republic – The miracle of representative government. We trust those we elect to build and run a government. We believe in each other enough to come together for a greater good.

For Which it Stands – Our flag stands for our right to create a more perfect union, conceived in liberty, and dedicated to the proposition that all are created equal.

One Nation – Don't get confused, we are one people, one great concept, one strength of will; if you harm one hair of one citizen, we all will waken.

Under God – Creator, Life Giver, Vishnu, Yahweh, Allah, Jehovah, Brahma, Ishtar, Loki, Prince of Peace, Great Spirit, Shiva, etc.

Indivisible – We might fuss and fight with each other on all kinds of things, but nothing is going to come between us. There is no divide and conquer. Those who have come through the fire, do not fade in the light.

With Liberty – You can knock down our buildings, you can threaten our way of life, but we have made a choice. Freedom is not negotiable. Even in the valley of the shadow of death, we are bloody, but unbowed. Liberty trumps fear any day.

And Justice – Fairness. Peace based on what is right and doing the right thing. The end does not justify the means.

For All – Red and yellow, black and white, male and female, old and young, rich and poor, believer and nonbeliever, blessed and hurting; all are precious here.

I pledge allegiance to the Flag
of the United States of America,
and to the Republic for which it stands,
one nation under God, indivisible,
with Liberty and Justice for all.

Bob Runs For President, Offers Change

It's official! Camelot Bob is running for President. He made the announcement over a honey roll and a cup of back coffee.

"Boys, I've decided to be the next president of the United States," he said, and that was it.

"President Bob," said Water Street Pete. "I like it. I'll be the V.P."

With that, Pete and the "boys" drew up Bob's campaign platform. Every plank had been carefully researched and thought out, sort of. Here it is:

Environment: Even a dog knows not to dirty where it lives. On the other hand, dogs think cute little bunnies taste just fine.

Entitlements: If government said you would get something, you should get it, but everybody above poverty should pay fair taxes. Rich people paying a lower tax rate than their secretaries is just plain wrong.

The Economy: Almost anything sells better than bombs, tanks, war planes and missiles; let's build something else.

Defense: The Oklahoma bombing showed us who our real enemy is. The enemy is hate.

Special Interest Groups: Everyone is special in a democracy. Turn off the special interest money spigot.

Abortion: Never could legislate morality; can't do it now. All the fuss just advertises abortion. When we learn to value life over life-style, abortions will go down. Till then, support adoption and care for children.

Education: One thing all the top nations have in common is how they value children. One thing all the loser countries have in common is... how they value children. Also, stop blasting schools and teachers! You don't fatten cattle by making them weak.

Supreme Court: There is only one litmus test – the best jurist gets the job!

Welfare: Jobs and their necessary training should be easier to get and more attractive than welfare checks.

Race Relations: Put minorities in positions of power. Let those who best understand the problems offer the solutions.

Foreign Policy: It is nice to be the world's rich uncle, but we better be a nice rich uncle; the bigger they are, the harder they fall!

Crime: If governments are moral, the people will follow. Opportunity trumps criminal behavior.

Juvenile Delinquency: Hold parents accountable for the behavior of their children. It costs ten times as much to put a kid in prison as it does to send a kid to Harvard. You figure it out.

Unemployment: Let's quit buying products and services from any company that gives its top executive raises for firing people. Any way you cut it, having to fire thousands of people is a sign of failure. No company downsizes to greatness.

Government: Government provides water, electricity, sewers, law enforcement, fire protection, health regulation, environmental control, taking care of those who are weak, defending our country – quit griping about paying some taxes to live in the greatest country in the world! Honor those who work in government, and good people will work in government.

Minority Rights: We are all going to need them one day.

Terrorists: Cockroach powder should do it.

Voter Apathy: Let people vote for "none of the above."

Health Care Costs: Make doctors and hospital officials pay for themselves whatever they charge for basic things like tissue paper, aspirin, tape, and food. Our economy will keep booming.

School Funding: Once again, it costs ten times more to incarcerate a child than to educate a child. We can't build enough prisons if we don't build enough schools.

Testing: Yes! Test students, teachers, administrators, parents, politicians, lawyers, and corporate executives. Publish the results.

School Choice: Let students choose schools, not schools choose students. If a student gets a voucher that does not cover the entire cost of a private school, the private school, not the student, should pay the difference.

Dirty Campaigns: Candidates who sling mud lose federal funding. Why should we pay to hear that @$&*#!

There it is. Bob for President and Pete for V.P.

A Unique View Of Life

The old boys at the Cafe are concerned they may be misunderstood. Products of WWII and the Kennedy assassination have a unique view of the world with a "colorful vocabulary." Some call it a salty, chauvinist, cynical view. You can judge for yourself.

By popular demand, here is another volume of the standard Old North Side Glossary of Familiar Terms. Enjoy.

County Budget: A complex collection of accounts designed to make citizens feel stupid if they ask where their money is going.

Helping Around the House: Lifting your feet when the wife runs the vacuum.

Reserve Funds: Tax money held in abeyance in case of dire need like tickets to a show in Las Vegas or sidewalks and streetlights on a politician's street.

Primary Election: Regional contests to see who can tell the greatest whoppers and raise the most money.

Pot Luck Dinner: Thirteen baskets of K-Fried Chicken, six tubs of Hy-Vee potato salad, and 20 wives talking about how rough their day has been.

Prostitution: An honorable profession for lawyers, insurance salesmen, most doctors, real estate agents, and phone solicitors.

Honest Politicians: The people who could not get elected.

County Government: There ain't no such thing.

Play-offs: Sport event created every four weeks to give men at least two weeks off each month from helping around the house.

Gated Communities: The country's tribute to Republican values.

Skateboards: God's punishment for the invention of asphalt.

Belief: *Nature has given women so much power that the law has* very wisely given them little. – Dr. Samuel Johnson

Malpractice Insurance: The price one pays for playing God.

City Beautification Project: Addition of as many large fast food signs as possible.

Traffic Control: Synchronized stoplights, so everyone is stopped all the time.

Taxes: How people from the Northeast pronounce Texas.

Advice: "Sometimes I wake up grumpy; other times I let her sleep."

Marriage: It is not a word, it's a sentence.

Second Car: The one the wife gets to drive.

Summer Vacation: Driving as far as you can each day before arguing about where to eat and spend the night.

Women's Liberation: Washing machine.

Hippies Back And They're Mad

by Gladstone Gus

If you like to deride all the old flower power, pinko, liberal, peace-love-and-happiness, long-haired freaks of the '60s and early '70s, you might want to quit reading right now and save your blood pressure. If you think the peace symbol is the sign of the American Chicken, flower decorated vans are brothels on wheels (if the van is rockin'...don't come a knockin'), and sitting around campfires strumming guitars, singing the songs of protest and idealism are anti-American, you are warned, STOP NOW. This rant is about bell-bottoms, hip-huggers, beads, headbands, Bob Dylan, and a whole generation of kids who took to the road to protest a war, and proclaim that all people, black and white and otherwise, were born equal.

Yes, old hippies are guilty of not caring about money every living second of their lives.

Yes, old hippies are guilty of tolerance, of letting people be, of forgiving, and trusting to a fault.

Yes, old hippies still love the land and want to protect it.

Yes, old hippies are still spiritual ("let me write the songs of a nation, and I care not who writes its laws").

Yes, old hippies still love kids (keep the baby, Faith).

Yes, old hippies still don't trust anybody over thirty, though they are all in their 50s and 60s now.

Of course, the big knock on old hippies was their occasional recreational use of drugs and their huge error of judgment concerning the soldiers who fought in Vietnam. Old hippies deeply regret the losses to drug addiction and the insults to soldiers. Interestingly enough, many old hippies are now fiercely patriotic and against drug abuse of any kind.

The trouble with old hippies is it is hard to identify them by their looks anymore. Most of them actually grew up, raised families, hold respectable jobs and became ... normal looking. Some are even rather spiffy dressers. One of them might ...gasp!... be your neighbor, and you would not even know.

The new Republican administration is frat-boy party all the way with a beer chaser...a kind of urbane hippie. The sons of money and position, they are blue blazer, button-down shirt with a striped tie. They now are enjoying a no-nonsense, bottom line, chain-of-command, 1950's management revival. Old hippies, whom they disdain, need not apply.

Here's the problem. Have you noticed that nobody wants to be a teacher anymore? Have you noticed the shortage in nurses, craftsmen, competent and fair mechanics, social workers, journalists, pastors, day-care workers, stay-at-home moms, etc.? Nobody wants to go in those professions. Nobody wants to do anything that does not make a lot of money right away. A nice sunset does not cut it; it has to be a nice sunset in Hawaii. Nobody loves their car; they lease a new one every few years. Houses do not have porches to welcome a strolling neighbor; a huge garage cuts you off from potential extraneous human contact; and McDonald's has won over mom and pop stores and cafes.

Go ahead, make fun of old hippies all you want. I'll just bet the best old teacher, carpenter, nurse, chaplain, or mom you know was once a hippie. Now that they are all retiring, just who do you suppose will do their jobs? Who will take up the "heart and soul of the country" banner? Who is going to sacrifice for peace, love, freedom, and happiness if it doesn't make money?

You are going to miss them when they're gone. Peace today.

When Johnny Comes Marching Home

by Gladstone Gus

At 7:55 a.m., December 7, 1941, Japan attacked Pearl Harbor, Hawaii. Japan's pilots sunk or damaged 19 ships and killed 2,300 people. On December 8, the United States declared war on Japan. Three days later, on December 11, war was declared on Germany and Italy. Those days are bookmarks for some.

On Sunset Street in Liberty, Missouri, December 7, 2002, was again a special day; and again, for good reason. My crusty old neighbors, Jim and George, the kids across the street, the young lady down the block, and I all hung out our American flags.

Across the street from us, red, white, and blue helium balloons bounced in the breeze from a porch rail. Another flag was on the door. Day and night, a flag waves from a lighted pole in the front yard. There was cause for celebration. Our neighbor was coming home. For over a year, he had served his country as part of the armed services in Afghanistan. Left behind were a wife and two small girls, extended family, and friends and his neighbors. Up and down my street, the neighborhood knew he was gone, and we never watched a news broadcast or heard about a skirmish that we did not think of him.

December 7, 2002, I kept busy in my front yard all morning watching cars come by my neighbor's house to get the word on his progress home.

"Yes, they are at the airport right now," a guy said.

"They were right behind my car on the interstate," somebody reported.

"They should be here any moment," came from a man in a pick-up truck.

Then their van arrived…and the door slid open. The little girls danced out; they beamed. They showed their dad the new roof, the raked yard, the poster on the door, and they hovered close just to make sure their dad was really there. It was cute, and I smiled for the fun of watching.

Then the dogs were let out. Both are large and mature, but they became puppies, licking and twirling, twisting their butts about, unable to separate themselves from their missing master. Then, everybody went inside.

I strung some more Christmas lights, and when I saw my neighbor's mom come out, I asked her how the party was going.

"It's a great party," she said, "but why don't you ask him yourself?"

And there stood my neighbor, home from Afghanistan. You could tell he had missed home cooking, but his smile was bright.

"Welcome home," I said shaking his hand. "Thanks for what you did for us."

I almost choked up on the last line. He said the neighbors had been great, and then we just stood there a moment.

Call it duty, or a job, or whatever, but my neighbor missed over a year with his wife and young children to serve his country in a very hostile place. He did this to keep my family and friends safe. I wish I had been able to say all the thanks I was feeling.

Before September 11, 2001, we used to lament that the only heroes our kids knew were rock singers, jocks, and movie stars. Now, they are everywhere. Even on the street where you live. Say "thank you" as much as you can.

JAW-JAW Is Better Than WAR-WAR

Time to dust off the peace quotes again. At least think about it!

It is easier to fight for one's principles than to live up to them. – **Alfred Adler**

Until lions have their historians, tales of the hunt shall always glorify the hunters.
– **African Proverb**

*In every child who is born, no matter what circumstances, and of no matter what parents,
the potentiality of the human race is born again. And in him, too, once more, and in each
of us, our terrific responsibility toward human life; toward the utmost idea of goodness, of the
horror of terror, and of God.* – **James Agee**

Peace begins when the hungry are fed. – **Anonymous**

*Peace is the work of justice indirectly, in so far as justice removes the obstacles to peace; but it
is the work of charity (love) directly, since charity, according to its very notion, causes peace.*
– **St. Thomas Aquinas**

That's all nonviolence is - organized love. – **Joan Baez**

*Youth is the first victim of war; the first fruit of peace. It takes 20 years or more of peace to
make a man; it takes only 20 seconds of war to destroy him.* – **King Baudouin I,
King of Belgium**

*Can I see another's woe, and not be in sorrow too? Can I see another's grief, and not seek for
kind relief?* – **William Blake**

We do not inherit the earth from our fathers. We borrow it from our children.
– **David Bower**

It is the job of thinking people, not to be on the side of the executioners. – **Albert Camus**

A spiritual person tries less to be godly than to be deeply human. – **Rev. William Sloane Coffin, Jr.**

We are, each of us, angels with only one wing, and we can only fly by embracing one another.
 – **Luciano de Crescenzo**

*No one is so foolish as to prefer to peace, war, in which, instead of sons burying their fathers,
fathers bury their sons.* – **Croesus, King of Lydia, in Herodotus' The Persian Wars**

*The hottest places in hell are reserved for those who, in times of great moral crisis, maintain
their neutrality.* – **Dante**

*Nobody was born nonviolent. No one was born charitable. None of us comes to these things
by nature but only by conversion. The first duty of the nonviolent community is helping its*

members work upon themselves and come to conversion. – **Lanza del Vasto**

What good is it to me that Mary gave birth to the Son of God fourteen hundred years ago, and I do not also give birth to the Son of God in my time and in my culture? We are all meant to be mothers of God. God is always needing to be born. – **Meister Eckhart**

Any intelligent fool can make things bigger, more complex, and more violent. It takes a touch of genius – and a lot of courage – to move in the opposite direction. – **Albert Einstein**

When I despair, I remember that all through history the way of truth and love has always won. There have been tyrants and murderers and for a time they seem invincible but in the end, they always fall -- think of it, ALWAYS! – **Mahatma Gandhi**

We may never be strong enough to be entirely nonviolent in thought, word and deed. But we must keep nonviolence as our goal and make strong progress towards it. The Attainment of freedom, whether for a person, a nation or a world, must be in exact proportion to the attainment of nonviolence for each. – **Mohandas Gandhi**

I am part and parcel of the whole and cannot find God apart from the rest of humanity. – **Mohandas Gandhi**

In all things it is better to hope than to despair. – **Johann Wolfgang von Goethe**

I am only one; but still I am one. I cannot do everything, but still I can do something. I will not refuse to do the something I can do. – **Helen Keller**

Compromise does not mean cowardice. – **John F. Kennedy**

The ultimate measure of a person is not where one stands in moments of comfort and convenience, but where one stands in times of challenge and controversy. – **Martin Luther King, Jr.**

I believe that unarmed truth and unconditional love will have the final word in reality. That is why right, temporarily defeated, is stronger than evil triumphant. – **Martin Luther King, Jr.**

One day we shall win freedom, but not only for ourselves. We shall so appeal to your heart and conscience that we shall win you in the process, and our victory will be a double victory. – **Martin Luther King, Jr.**

If you succumb to the temptation of using violence in the struggle, unborn generations will be the recipients of a long and desolate night of bitterness, and your chief legacy to the future will be an endless reign of meaningless chaos. – **Martin Luther King, Jr.**

I destroy my enemies when I make them my friends. – **Abraham Lincoln**

The belief in the possibility of a short decisive war appears to be one of the most ancient and dangerous of human illusions. – **Robert Lynd (1879-1949), Anglo-Irish essayist, journalist**

Jaw-jaw is better than war-war. – **Harold MacMillan**

I do not believe in using women in combat, because females are too fierce. – **Margaret Mead**

War does not determine who is right - only who is left. – **Bertrand Russell**

When the rich make war, it's the poor that die. – **Jean-Paul Sartre**

Fear less, hope more,
> *Whine less, breathe more,*
> *Talk less, say more,*
> *Hate less, love more,*
And all good things are yours.
– **Swedish Proverb**

The greatest disease in the West today is not HIV-AIDS or cancer, it is being unwanted, unloved, and uncared for. We can cure physical diseases with medicine, but the only cure for loneliness, despair, and hopelessness is love. There are many in the world dying for a piece of bread, but there are many more dying for a little love. The poverty in the West is a different kind of poverty - it is not only a poverty of loneliness but also of spirituality. There's a hunger for love, as there is a hunger for God. – **Mother Teresa**

Peace is not the absence of conflict but the presence of creative alternatives for responding to conflict --alternatives to passive or aggressive responses, alternatives to violence. – **Dorothy Thompson**

What good is a house, if you haven't got a decent planet to put it on? – **Henry David Thoreau**

The illiterate of the 21st century will not be those who cannot read and write, but those who cannot learn, unlearn, and relearn. – **Alvin Toffler**

Violence produces only something resembling justice, but it distances people from the possibility of living justly, without violence. – **Leo Tolstoy**

Do all the good you can,
By all the means you can,
In all the ways you can,
In all the places you can,
At all the times you can,
To all the people you can,
As long as ever you can.
     – **John Wesley**

Chapter 7

Life's Melting Pot

Here are two well-known "truths" about storytelling.

- The delicate art of survival is finding the story in your suffering.
- Stories happen most often to the people who are able to tell them.

Larry, who owns the Old North Side Cafe, can't tell a story and therefore thinks nothing significant has ever happened to him. Larry fought in Vietnam, had a marriage annulled, bought the Cafe on a whim, and remembers the exact date of every birthday for hundreds of people. He knows the old guys in the Cafe are more than a little crazy. Storytellers always are. Larry thinks they are self-absorbed, but harmless. He also knows they are stunningly cheap, grouchy, and horrendous liars.

Larry thinks just about everything the old boys say is an exaggeration or a straight-up lie. He's kept a list of what he considers to be the most outrageous tall tales. For example, here is one that drives Larry crazy.

Camelot Bob, a lover of poop stories, swears vets regularly use magnets fired into a cow's reticulum (with something called a balling gun) to collect bailing wire, nails, and bits of metal that get stuck in a cow's stomach. He swears he has seen a "cow bullet" discharged with a wristwatch and a man's ring stuck on it. Larry is appalled by such blovation.

Here is more Camelot Bob nonsense, according to Larry:

- Rats multiply so quickly, that in 18 months, two rats could have over a million descendants.
- Our eyes are always the same size from birth, but our nose and ears never stop growing. That's why old men look funny.
- Mosquitoes kill more humans than any other animal.
- Boanthropy is a rare mental disorder that causes a person to think he is an ox. One of the first recorded cases is in the book of Daniel (4:33), which tells about Nebuchadnezzar, a Babylonian king, who would eat grass.

Ridgeway Ron is the expert on all things farming and especially pigs, cows, and chickens. Here is Larry's list of Ron's questionable facts:

- Top speed for a pig is 11 miles an hour. A pig can outrun a chicken.
- It is physically impossible for pigs to look up at the sky, so even if they could fly, no pig would ever see it.
- Chickens and turkeys are capable of crossbreeding. When they do, they produce offspring that are known as turkens.
- Sheep can survive for two weeks buried in a snowstorm.
- Cows can smell odors up to five miles away.
- Twelve or more cows are known as a fink.

- Pigs can become alcoholics. Ron tells a hilarious story about a whiskey sipping pig farmer whose pet pig learned to pull out the stopper on a whiskey bottle. Apparently, the pig drank itself into a stupor, fell asleep out by the pond, and died of sunburn. True story.

Larry reports that Holly Lake Jake, who loves all forms of weather, says he has seen lightning balls, glowing lights on weather vanes, moon rainbows, and rainbow fires in the sky.

All of the above is stuff that comes up in stories, and no matter what Larry says, you never really know if it is true.

Stories help us from being overwhelmed by the staggering concepts of eternity, the fact we don't yet have much of a clue how the universe is put together, or if emotions are just chemical compounds in the brain…or something more. Stories are like cultural glue that holds things together. We can poke around the edges of reality with a good story and not get burned.

Gladstone Gus likes to talk about Einstein's theory of relativity. That gets the men into discussions about black holes, dark matter, and the mind-boggling truth that "space and time exist only in your mind."

"Neither space nor time actually exists in nature; we just made them up like we did math, music, language, tools, and, of course, love, to try to understand things," Gus says.

Then there is the stuff about ghosts and an alien abduction; Stella predicting the future; and Manor Hill Mack always living through something he knows has happened before. The truth is complicated.

In time, the Cafe itself is the story. The daily confab allows the old boys to work out their fears and hopes. The same stories the old codgers tell today are just modern versions of stories told by men huddled in caves watching inexplicable lightning storms, or scared sailors stranded on boats becalmed on silent seas.

Water Street Pete grins. He waves his fork; the men bend close to listen.

"My great-grandmother made a fortune raising dogs," Pete says. "She crossed a Pointer with a Setter and called it a Pointsetter, a popular, and now traditional Christmas pet." The men moan.

"My great Uncle Garrett thought he was cow," says Camelot Bob. "He walked around the house mooing and chewing hay."

"Didn't you take him to a psychiatrist and get him fixed?" asked the always gullible Holly Lake Jake.

"We thought about it," Bob replied, "but to be honest, we needed the milk."

Everything is superstition at the old Cafe. Everything has its kernel of truth. Only stories can hold so much.

Losers Week At The Old North Side Cafe

The men gather and contemplate steam rising from coffee cups. They run their fingers over the Formica tabletops and adjust for comfort in worn, Naugahyde bench seats.

The Cubbies lost! The Red Sox lost. Even worse, the Red Sox lost to the Damn Yankees. There are no Baseball Gods. There is no justice, or meaning, or poetry in the world. The rich always win. Those with the money think life's funny. The self-centered, the haughty, the smug, and the connected get to eat the heart of the watermelon. They move to the front of the line. They get the tickets to the big game, and their children have an easy go.

Most of us know in our hearts that Charlie Brown had it all just about right. We are all doomed! We keep kicking, but someone moves the ball. We love the red-headed girl only from afar, and we say "good grief!"

Whenever the Red Sox or the Cubbies took a lead in the series, we knew it meant an even more bitter heartbreak. Both series had to go seven games. Both had to have blown leads. It is the way the world works. We're not the Yankees; we can't go out and buy whatever we want. We don't win almost every time. We are lucky to bat .250 or not muff the easy grounder. Like the Cubbies and the Red Sox, we are survivors; backdrops to a tragic play. Each day brings us a challenge, and we muddle through without triumph or ceremony. We are the axis on which the earth spins.

You know, there are fans who went to the back yard and lifted a fist to God.

"Is this the best you can do?" they shout.

"Is this all you have?" they ask.

"Do you honestly think I will crumble just because we get beat in extra innings?"

"Do you think I care that you stacked the deck against us?"

"Do you think I care if we never can win?" they cry out.

The stars twinkle silently, and the leaves rustle; the fist drops, and the head bows, "Oh good grief."

It is then our little mundane miracle happens. Somewhere in the darkest part of the heart, a flame flickers. All those bitter defeats; the early risings and hard work at dead ends; the wishing for and longing, but never having, have only strengthened the resolve. The tirade withers to the spiritual base of all lovable losers – "Just wait till next year!"

Yes, the old boys are struggling at the Old North Side Cafe. They took out their best stuff, and once again Fate flicked them down like some old crumb. It is, however, in these moments that the camaraderie begins. There is no fire too hot to melt their hardened spirits. They lived through droughts and Depression, war, job loss, and heartbreak. No silver spoons, daddy's car, trust fund, or expensive champagne weakens these old souls.

There is an arm across the shoulder, a couple of shrugs and another sip of coffee. Eyes lift, and somehow it all begins again. God must love us in some way, because he made so many of us. Hope is our currency. Bring on another day!

When Baseball Was Fun
On Claybourn Field

Manor Hill Mack can remember the old ballpark like it was a picture. Old Man Tinsley's prized pine tree was smack in the middle of center field, and if you hit the ball in the tree, it was an automatic double. Mrs. Claybourn's house was the left field line, but if you hit her house, it was an automatic out. Kelly Creek ran through right field and created several pages of rules. Hitting the ball in the creek was an out, but hitting a ball over the creek was a home run, except after a rain, then hitting any ball to right field was two outs. First base was further than third base, and you could lead-off from first, but not from third. You could declare two different speeds for a ghost runner if you only had three people on a side. A fast runner could score on a fly ball, and the slow runner could jar the ball out of the catcher's mitt in a make-believe collision.

Games were played until somebody had to go home, and the score was always in dispute. Line-up changes occurred depending on who was batting and who could yell the loudest. When Dennis Campbell came up to bat, the center fielder was dispatched about twenty yards behind the pine tree. Dennis always hit the ball to the same place. The question was could the other team catch a high fly ball? Most of the time, they could not. If Becky Rickman, Mary Lou Morgan, or Cathy Sweet came by, the game was automatically canceled on account of hormones. The ball was usually wet (from going in the creek) and coming apart. You shared gloves. Breaking a bat for any reason was an automatic suspension. That was baseball, and it was marvelous!

Now kids play ORGANIZED BALL. The fields are immaculate. The equipment is superb. There is only one problem, and it ruins everything – parents. What used to be kid fun is now a nightmare.

First, parents are horrible, obvious, liars. They think every kid needs praise every moment. When a kid strikes out with runners in scoring position, parents say things like, "Good swing." Nobody ever said "Good swing" back on Claybourn field. They said nothing, or they said, "You'll get 'em next time." The lies wouldn't be so bad if parents would learn if they can't be yelling FOR something, to just keep their fat mouths shut.

Next comes the Parent v. Umpire/Coach eternal struggle. Nothing makes a team weaker than idiot parents who blame everything on umpires or coaches. The true jerk will even challenge an umpire to fight after a game, or corner a coach to demand (not ask) more playing time for their kid. On Claybourn field, boys fought over important stuff like Becky, Mary Lou, and Cathy. Baseball was for fun.

Finally, parents are only interested in the score – winning and losing. Mack played on a team that came one game away from the Little League World Series. He can't remember the score of that game. Parents can. They demand all-star teams and COMPETITIVE leagues. They think it builds skills and sharpens the fighting spirit to a fine edge. The other team is the enemy and must be destroyed. Mostly, it just ruins baseball for a lot of kids.

On Claybourn field, when you caught Campbell's towering shot over the pine tree, you felt great. The competition was inside yourself – the other kids were your friends. Baseball on Claybourn field was about life, solving your own problems, and learning to have fun. Please, no parents allowed.

Reverend Maple's Last Ride

When the last trees lose their leaves, Gladstone Gus takes a moment to smile. Sometimes his grin breaks into a full laugh, and it's then you know he's remembering Reverend Maple. The good preacher was already old when Gus was young. Sometimes Gus wished he knew the man in his younger years. Surely there was more to know about Reverend Maple than the way he drove. That's what made Gus smile. The stories of Reverend Maple's "driving" are endless.

First, there's the time Reverend Maple drove back from St. Joe, Missouri on the wrong side of the interstate.

"People are just so friendly," Reverend Maple said, after threatening the lives of half his small town. "Everybody honked and waved at me the whole time."

That was Reverend Maple.

Gus remembered he had a bright red Thunderbird convertible. When he weaved down Main Street, it was like Moses parting the waters. Cars pulled off on each side of the road. Some even drove up on lawns avoiding Reverend Maple. All the while, the good reverend blithely drove down his middle of the road, eating a candy bar and watching birds directly overhead.

Then there was Reverend Maple's amazing ability to clean out a prayer meeting.

On Wednesday nights, the Pastor Emeritus came to the family night supper and prayer meeting. He brought meatloaf made with carrots, and he went to the dessert end of the food table first. Reverend Maple was even known to serve himself during the prayer on those nights Vera Nold brought one of her chocolate cream pies.

After eating, folks gathered in the sanctuary to sing and pray, always keeping a watchful eye on Reverend Maple. No matter what, Reverend Maple left the prayer meeting at exactly 8:30 p.m. (his watch), and it was best to beat him out of the parking lot. Reverend Maple never looked at what was behind him when he backed out his car. Anything in his way became a statistic. Many cars carried a dent from Reverend Maple's well-worn bumper. You couldn't fault Maple's logic however. Maple figured people should know he would be backing out and keep their car out of the way.

Anyway, the church could be in the middle of a really great hymn like, "Blessed Assurance" or "The Old Rugged Cross" when Reverend Maple got up to leave. Leola, the organist, usually saw him leave first and immediately stopped playing, revealing about thirty badly off-key voices praising the "power in the blood." Hymn books crashed to the floor and a bottleneck formed at the back door. Moments later, cars were racing and tires were screeching in order to beat Reverend Maple's exit. All meetings should have a Reverend Maple.

Finally, it must be said that Reverend Maple in his later years never once knowingly obeyed a parking or street sign. He put the tickets in his glove box and left his car where he liked.

Reverend Maple died in his sleep just after the leaves fell one autumn. Gus was 15 years old. The story goes they found 36 tickets and 10 half-eaten Hershey bars in his glove box. By request, his funeral procession wound its way around his hometown. A police escort in front parted the cars to the side of the road, just like Maple's driving had once done. Reverend Maple would have liked his last ride through town.

Gus thinks about Reverend Maple each year when the leaves are gone. The way the town made allowances for the preacher was a good thing. Most courtesy is only polite, leafy cover. When the leaves fall, you can tell what's really there. Gus' hometown let a man grow old gracefully. They gave him a little extra room because he was one of their own.

Your Momma Is So Ugly She Dates Lawyers

Professional status has an ebb and flow. Once, doctors and preachers were at the top of the heap. Now, it's NASCAR power-driving speed merchants that have our hearts. Garbage collecting, once considered a distasteful profession, gained stature with the shortage of landfills and realization that "sanitary engineers" pull in higher salaries than teachers, police, fire fighters, and nurses.

Perhaps the greatest example of ebb and flow has been in the field of law. There was once a day when some people actually admired and looked up to lawyers. Now, lawyers hide their identities claiming they work in more dignified areas such as used car sales, insurance adjusting, phone solicitation, and media evangelism. On playgrounds, young children now use the word lawyer the way they once used words like cootie-face, slime-bucket, and dog-breath. "Your Momma's so ugly, she has to date lawyers," they say on the playground.

Manor Hill Mack told this one: A ship went down in the shark-infested waters of the Pacific. In a frenzied feeding, all the ship's crew and passengers were killed by the ravenous sharks, except one man, a lawyer in a Brooks Brothers suit. "Why didn't the sharks eat you?" the rescuers asked.

"Professional courtesy," the lawyer replied.

Next day it was Camelot Bob's turn. A prominent young lawyer found himself at Heaven's gate. St. Peter came out to shake his hand. "Mr. Jones," said St. Peter, "you are the first to ever break Methuselah's record for longevity. You have lived 919 years."

"I'm 46," the lawyer said.

"46? But aren't you Steven Z. Jones, the lawyer from Gladstone, Missouri?"

"Yes," he answered.

St. Peter checked his book and then slapped his hand against his forehead. "Oh, how silly of us. Now I see the mistake! We accidentally calculated your age by adding up the hours you billed to your clients!"

Even Holly Lake Jake came through with a joke.

"What do you call a smiling, sober, courteous person at a bar association convention?" Jake asked.

"I don't know," the men mumbled.

"The caterer," Jake replied.

That reminded Water Street Pete of a joke.

The United Way had never received a nickel from the town's most successful lawyer. A volunteer reminded the lawyer that his annual income was over a million dollars and asked the lawyer if he would give back to his community through the United Way. The lawyer thought for a moment and said, "Do you know that my mother is dying after a long, painful illness and has huge medical bills beyond her ability to pay?"

The United Way rep said, "Uh, no."

"Do you know my brother, a disabled veteran, is blind and confined to a wheelchair and is unable to support his wife and six children?"

The United Way rep tried to apologize, but the lawyer went on.

"Do you know my sister's husband died in a dreadful traffic accident," the lawyer's voice rising in indignation, "leaving her penniless with a mortgage and three children?"

"I had no idea," the rep said.

The lawyer then said, "...and if I don't give any money to THEM, why should I give any to you?"

At last Bob stood to defend lawyers.

"Gentlemen," he said, "we have been hard on our brothers in law. Just because they clog the justice system with petty suits, encourage greed, cheat through technicality, and use misfortune and suffering to feather their pockets is no reason to put them down. Think of the good they do. They keep sushi bars, starch companies, and hair oil manufacturers open, providing jobs for honest working people. They have raised the appreciation of women for men in other professions, and they have raised argyle to an art form. Now, I have a very important question. Do any of you know how to save a lawyer choking to death in a bar?"

There was a stone silence.

"Good," said Bob, and he sat down.

Yes, the ebb and flow has claimed another victim at the Old North Side Cafe. It isn't fair, of course. Lawyers have given much to our great American culture. Some of our brightest, most intelligent people have worked to frame a system of laws that allow us to live together in some resemblance of order.

Say, speaking of intelligence, that reminds Mack of the joke about the lawyer and the chicken in a spelling contest. "Well, the lawyer..."

Mouse Was Bigger Than He Thought

Mice are a close second for the title of "Man's Best Friend." Let me explain. Women who love to wear Mickey Mouse sweatshirts will swoon at the mere sound of a mouse. A woman's fear of mice is legendary, and it is this fear that works in a man's favor. The boys at the old Cafe know it.

Water Street Pete never changed a diaper in his life, thanks to mice. He made a deal with his wife that he would empty every mousetrap for the entirety of their marriage provided she changed every diaper. His wife jumped at the offer. Manor Hill Mack worked the same deal for ironing shirts. Women must think there is something especially virile and manly about being able to dispose of a mouse. Many are the men who have won a woman's favor over a mouse, and none more so than Camelot Bob. Here's the story.

Bob's wife was home alone at night. It was early fall, a time when mice begin seeking inside warmth. Bob's wife should have been safe, but she was not. The two cats who adorned their house were worthless. More ornament than warrior, their primal instincts had eroded to sniffing out canned cheese and fish flavored Kibbits.

It was late in the evening when she heard the first commotion. One of the cats had cornered a mouse behind the nightstand at the side of her bed. Fear gripped her soul. It took five minutes to summon the courage to flee the room; she waited in the kitchen for Bob's return. Bob really wasn't much better than the cats, but the sight of his wife in distress signaled an ancient genetic code. The cave had been invaded. The castle must be defended. Bob puffed himself up and entered the bedroom. A plan formed.

"Get the dowel rod we use to secure the sliding glass door," he said. His wife responded instantly. Staff in hand, he re-entered the bedroom to kill the beast. His woman cringed by the kitchen door. Bob tried to calm his breathing. Every nerve ending was alive, feeding him information vital to the hunt. Bob edged the nightstand from the wall, and there it was. It was larger and furrier than he imagined. An image formed in the back of his mind – a rat! A sudden THUMP shook the house, and then it was silent. Moments later, Bob walked into the kitchen.

"Is it done?" his wife asked.

"Yes," Bob nodded.

The motion of his arm was slow and deliberate as he pulled his hand from behind his back to show his wife a ... sock! Yes, Bob had killed a dusty sock. The terrified mouse fled the room, fearing both the hunter and the sound of his stick. Bob's wife kissed her man, and they laughed together.

One pair of mice can produce thousands of offspring in a single year. A mouse can jump 12 inches straight up. Mice have been known to hide in ceilings, cereal boxes, women's shoes, kitchen drawers, and yes, toilets. They can attack without warning or mercy.

Women, take heed. Lavish your warrior man with praise and love, not to mention cooking, ironing, cleaning, slipper fetching, and yes … sex! The mice will get you if you don't.

A Bug In My Bed!

"Dad, this is not funny!" Paige said, holding up her arm. Holly Lake Jake could see his daughter was distraught. He also knew she had a serious problem. Jake had seen these welts before. "Good Lord," he thought.

"Darling, those are bedbug bites, and…." Her scream cut him in mid-sentence.

"Bedbugs! No! No!" she screamed, then collapsed in his arms.

The Old North Side coffee klatch knows bed bugs. It was a fact of life before the invention of DDT.

"How? Why? What'll I do?" Paige screamed, scratching her arm. Jake's daughter is as fastidiously clean as she is dramatic.

"First, stop scratching or it will get infected," Jake said. "You probably got them while in New York."

Jake has that right. Infestations are showing up at colleges (SWMS), hotels and motels, dressing rooms, used furniture, and offices. Our love of travel to exotic places for fun and war is making it worse.

"I hate bugs!" his daughter screamed. "I'm washing everything, buying new mattresses, pulling up carpet…" Her spittle was air-born, and her eyes were bugged.

"…Whoa Baby," Jake calmly interrupted. He had watched his mother and knew the drill – hot water and dryers, inspection, reduced clutter, vacuuming, and sealing. There was a good reason our grandparents used to say, "Cleanliness is next to Godliness." Bedbugs live months without a meal in mattress seams, box springs, baseboards, behind wallpaper, and in clutter. Thank God, they carry no known diseases.

Back at the Cafe, the boys were talking about bedbug hysteria.

"I remember igniting gunpowder on mattresses or soaking them with gasoline. Uncle Clem fumigated buildings with burning sulfur or cyanide gas," Manor Hill Mack said. *(The best-known brand was Zyklon B, which later became infamous at Auschwitz.)* Jake smiled. He pictured a rabid environmentalist locked in a room infested with bedbugs. "DDT will be making a comeback," he thought.

Good Grief! Charles Is Gone

The Old North Side grew up with the Peanuts gang and still can't believe it is over. Fifty years is a long time to be schooled every Sunday morning in Charlie Brown's University of Hard Knocks.

Here's what they learned, dark and doomed as it may be.
- The Red Baron was a World War I pilot before he was a pizza.
- The Great Pumpkin and the little red headed girl are metaphors for national politics. Pig Pen represents a natural life phase brought on by college dorms and bachelor living.
- Woodstock speaks the preferred language of all teenagers.

Now, there is nobody to explain all these truths in ways we can understand. Charlie Brown prepared the Cafe for life. He reminded us that winning is not the point, losers have a purpose, and five-cent psychiatric help may be overpriced.

What Would Charlie Brown Do (WWCBD), we could ask ourselves, before it became a catch phrase, when life challenges us.

WWCBD, we could ask as we've watched the Royals finish 92 games below .500 for three years and counting.

WWCBD, we could ask when women are a mystery or even the dog turns on us.

Linus was especially helpful in understanding that it was ok to be different, and inspired great jazz!

Marci, Lucy, Peppermint Patty, and Sally helped us understand the nuanced differences in the women the guys would eventually marry. Gus liked Sally, and thankfully, that's the kind of woman he got.

Here is the biggest lesson from the Peanuts gang. Pete and his brother once had a paper route. They carried newspapers up Hamburg Hill in St. Joseph, Missouri. The hill was especially steep and long. The papers were heavy, and the mornings were early and often cold. The only pleasure of the paper route was that before walking the hill each morning, they could read the comics before anyone. Peanuts was, of course, the favorite. It was a simple pleasure, but it carried them up the hill.

That was the great lesson. Charlie Brown and Snoopy taught Pete to take happiness where he could, and keep it simple. Many times life is a losing, uphill struggle, but little victories win the day. Those who don't understand this are, well, blockheads.

Charles Schultz gave us his simple pleasures for fifty years. Trying to come to terms with the hard truth that it's over, I wonder again, WWCBD.

"Good grief, we're doomed," he might whisper through that squiggly line serving as his befuddled mouth. And that alone is enough to keep us going back on up the hill.

Hello Mom – Get Dad On The Phone

by Gladstone Gus

Someday the images will fade. We won't see suicidal planes flying full speed into buildings full of people. We won't see strange lunar landscapes covered in dust or rumbling clouds chasing hapless citizens down New York City streets. The exact number of dead and wounded, the cost, the cold chattering of revenge – all will fade. What will remain is love, and the memory of love, each time a cell phone rings.

Stories will emerge over the next month. We will learn of heroes, courage, flinty human grit, and we will experience again the enigmatic, marvel of life. We will call our kids in faraway cities just to hear a voice. We will wipe tears as we drive to work listening to the radio or watching television at night. In an early darkness, we will awaken and reach out to touch a spouse, comforted to know we are not alone. We will remember where we were, what we were doing, and we will tell that story at different times in other places with strangers we hardly know. We will recall, with immense clarity, even the tiny details of our life on September 11, 2001. That memory will unite us. Rich or poor, regardless of where we live, our race, our religion – none of that will matter. We will share a uniting moment with an entire nation.

Like a photograph captures a single instant in a freeze frame, part of us will always be that person we once were, watching airplanes crash, and witnessing humanity holding on.

"Hello Mom, can you get Dad on the phone?"
"Mom, Dad. I just wanted you to know I love you."

You know the stories already.

People with cell phones called home from high-jacked airplanes and the top of the World Trade Towers. They knew they were about to die, and they wanted to say the three words that give meaning to life, even a life about to end. They called from beneath the rubble with directions and a final word in case things went bad.

The messages were mostly the same.
"I love you," they whispered.
"Tell the kids I love them," a father said.
"If I don't make it, remember I love you," a wife said.

Confronted with the undeniable fact that evil exists in our world, cell phones rang, and the human spirit went to the well where the water is clean. Stunned by carnage and an acrid smoke that burned lungs and stung swollen eyes, workers dug against odds, because love calls us to attempt the impossible. Those running from falling debris stopped and turned back to pick up fallen strangers. We are lifted by the unknown depth of love. At night when we watch the stars, it will help to know this.

That cell phone message is still out there, still hurtling through space, now light years away. It is a message for all eternity.

"Hello Mom, can you get Dad on the phone?"
"Mom, Dad. I just wanted you to know I love you."

Death To Sport Utility Vehicles

It happened to Manor Hill Mack Thursday afternoon before the Chief's football game. Now he is pissed.

In the valley of death that is Highway 291, between Firestone and Sutherlands Lumber Company, Mack edged his aging Ford Taurus out from the Total gas station onto the ribbon of rage that is the street. At the same moment, a red Ford Expedition turned left from Blockbuster Video. The traffic-clogged road forced the driver to attempt a lightning strike to avoid southbound traffic. The urban assault vehicle careened into Mack's lane, its bumper aimed at Mack's head. The Taurus lurched forward, starved for gas, desperate for inches to save it from the River Bend junkyard scrap heap. In the instant before certain death, Mack looked into the eye, or rather the finger, of the Expedition's driver. Road rage red, he gestured his I.Q., sperm count, and mental age equivalent. His mouth twisted in a snarl, and his Chief's red turtleneck turned pale under the flush of his face.

Mack now knows God still has plans for the Taurus and/or him. Mere inches saved them. The Expedition driver was relentless. He turned his head to trace Mack's family back to dogs, to tell him to eat in the barnyard, to suggest that he and Mack have some kind of abnormal sexual union. Crazed and puffing, he shook his fist and contemplated a daring U-turn to finish his assault. Luckily for Mack, he made the light and escaped his life and no new dents.

Sales of sport utility vehicles (over 6,000 lbs.) have jumped. Their purpose on the roadways is simple. Kill the likes of Mack to save the likes of them. They got the cash to make Mack the trash. Women who could barely drive their Honda Civic EX's are now being outfitted by their caring husbands into sport tanks. What were once "Gosh, I'm sorry" fender-benders are now trips to hospitals and funeral homes.

Bumpers on Sport Utility Vehicles do not line up with bumpers on regular cars, and that's the point. Look at the ads. One even shows a man driving his tank on the tops of other cars in rush hour traffic. Kill or be killed; it's survival of the fittest, the law of the jungle, baby.

Just last week, an after-school fistfight in Kansas City turned ugly. Instead of the time-honored tradition of using fists to settle a dispute, one boy brought a gun. The other boy is now dead. There was a rip in our cultural fabric. Fists don't usually kill. Youthful aggression could once be vented without dreadful consequence. The rules said no guns or knives.

"Now we got no rules," Manor Hill Mack moans. "Sport Utility Vehicles break the rules. They are a breach of contract. Their size, bumper, and over-engineered power are the equivalent of bringing an AK47 to a fistfight. On the street, it is simply no contest. They turn once annoying accidents into life-threatening situations."

"Here's a solution," Mack says. "A $10,000 per vehicle tax to cover the cost of my funeral would be nice. Sure, rich, testosterone-poisoned males and clueless over-the-hill drivers will still get their tanks, but the extra cost may send a few of the jerks back to their Corvettes and Volvos.

"Second, some legislation is appropriate. Even tanks can be made to have bumpers that line up with regular cars, unless the point really is to kill.

"Third, there is a Ford Expedition driver with a Chief's red turtleneck and hat somewhere tonight wracked with pain. My voodoo doll has a pin stuck in every part of his body offering a debilitating stinging sensation. Your health is gone, buster! Your next car is a wheel chair. Make it a nice big one."

Catching A Riff With The Dixie Chicks

by Gladstone Gus

It is only a word memory, but I recall my Dad talking about the Grand Ole Opry. His family was originally from Kentucky, and country/bluegrass was in their blood. As a result, I have this mythical memory of my Dad's family gathered around a huge radio in the living room on a Saturday night, listening to the country stars of the day. I know my Dad and Mom went to the Grand Ole Opry in Nashville at least twice, and I vaguely recall Dad talking about going to the Opry as a young man in the Air Force during WWII.

Lots of people in my family play the piano, but I took to the guitar at 14-years old to ease my sense of loss after a knee injury ended my dreams to play sports. My guitar has been my keeper and last line of refuge ever since. *Red River Valley* was the first song I learned to play, and I heard country music playing in my head all through those rock and roll years of the 1960s and '70s. Even after Elvis became a caricature of himself, I had his albums hidden away where Beatles, Beach Boys, and Bob Dylan fans could not find and ridicule them. I still listened. I was a fan. Songs like *Sixteen Tons, Streets of Laredo, Ring of Fire,* and *Cheatin' Heart* jangle in my subconscious, and I know the lyrics to a thousand country songs as if by magic.

There was a night in San Angelo, Texas, when a lanky cowboy band played *Cotton-Eyed Joe* and *Faded Love* so well that suddenly I could two-step as if I were born and raised in West Texas, wearing white shirts, boot jeans, huge belt buckles, a straw hat, and cowboy boots. The great counterclockwise ritual dance pulled me in and found my country soul. It was my first realization that there is magic in country music.

Last week, it was my turn to go to the Grand Ole Opry for the first time. I pretended I was my Dad, a young man escaping from the war. Or I was a true country boy on a lark to the big city, ready to party with Porter Wagner and Little Jimmy Dickens.

That night in Nashville, I was once again the lean guitar picker who knew every Elvis song by heart and sang Hank Williams tunes to the mountains when nobody else was around. Thankfully, my often-offensive sense of sophistication slipped to the floor, and I thought the rhinestones and flashy boots, the big hair and the cowboy hats, were just about right. The fiddle music, the steel guitar, and songs of lost love, broken hearts, and whiskey nights at the Grand Ole Opry rang so true to a boy who had grown up on the countryside of town.

Then, I had my moment at the Opry. They played a very strange country song from my past. Somewhere in my memory is a song about Little Jimmy Brown. It has a hold on me. Here is how it starts; maybe you will remember:

There's a village hidden deep in the valley among the pine trees half forlorn
And there on a sunny morning little Jimmy Brown was born
All the chapel bells were ringing in the little valley town
And the songs that they were singing was for baby Jimmy Brown
And the little congregation prayed for guidance from above

"Lead us not into temptation bless this hour of meditation guide him with eternal love…"

There I was at the Grand Ole Opry, sitting on the front row, singing all the lyrics to this song about the cycle of life. I had no idea I knew them so well. Jim Brown, the original singer, must be older than the hills now, but for a while, when he sang, reality lost all hold on space and time. I was my Dad, away from home and about to go to war. I was me as a little boy listening to the radio with my Mom, and I was the man who had gone to the Grand Ole Opry hoping something like this could still happen.

There is a common magic in country music. The world we live in is as messy as any Hank Williams lyric, but there is a comfort in the ordinary simplicity of "three guitar chords and the truth."

A few nights later, I embarrassed myself trying to two-step at a country bar. My magic from the Grand Old Opry was all used up. Come some summer night, however, I'll be thinking about trains and prison, lost love, wild horses, whiskey, and all night rides to the mountains in my pickup truck. I'll hear a song start with a riff on the guitar. Roy Acuff, Bill Monroe, Patsy Cline, and Ernest Tubb will sing or play a few bars; Alan Jackson and the Dixie Chicks will do some harmony, and Elvis and I will be on the radio, WSM-AM Clear Channel Frequency, from Nashville, Tennessee.

Chapter 8

Thanksgiving and Christmas

There are about 10 formative years when the deepest, strongest, and longest lasting memories of the holiday seasons are created. These early days set the baseline, and from then on everything is measured against those first celebrations.

The old codgers are sad to wake up and not be a child on Christmas morning anymore. As a child, the thrill of holiday magic permeated the very air one breathed. Santa was coming! Important adults talked about something strange and beautiful called a Virgin Birth, stars exploded, angels formed a heavenly host (whatever that was), and a sensory cacophony of tastes, aromas, sounds, touches, and sights permanently imprinted impressionable young brains.

There always is a moment of perfection that claims the holiday memory for a little child. It may be mom and dad kissing after dad gave her a new coat to wear to the family gathering. It might be walking out on the back porch on Christmas Eve and staring at a star, suddenly shadowed by what must have been a sled and reindeer. It is getting the gift you always wanted, or mom prizing your potpie tin ornament over every other present she received. For Gladstone Gus, it was going to bed in a new pair of pajamas, feeling all snug and tingly. Then, one Christmas, it is all suddenly gone. All the things you thought life should be are vanquished in childhood's end. We all must move to the constant, insistent drumbeat of "grow up!"

New and different memories of Thanksgiving and Christmas develop over the years, but they are all a pale reflection of that handful of first experiences. Among the Cafe men, there is a shared understanding of the holidays. They grew up surrounded by families they could see. Thanksgiving was family and abundance. Christmas trees were always big, and the packages beneath them seemed to flow across the room.

You have no idea what a Thanksgiving feast or Christmas Eve at Grandma's house meant to these young boys; they all grew up in love with Christmas and Thanksgiving. Somewhere, deep inside, they want to pay it forward. They want to make it real again.

Every year, the old guys go searching for those now distant feelings and memory markers. Every year, they fail. Thanksgiving is a rush of action, culminating in protruding stomachs and football games. Christmas is the journey and not the journey's end. The men make the miracles happen for others, and that sustains them. Christmas and Thanksgiving are not for the weak of heart.

Ridgeway Ron, with his farmer's crusty heart, has an interesting take on Christmas. Whenever his kids started getting squirrelly, caused trouble, or needed an attitude adjustment, he took them camping. Nothing settles a kid like going camping. No matter how self-absorbed a child might be, there comes a moment when s/he realizes they are all alone in the woods, totally dependent on dad.

Christmas and Thanksgiving, at their best, are like a great camping trip to an unknown destination where anything can happen. Everyone has a part, and if they cooperate, it can be memorable and wonderful. Similar to a soap opera, somehow things work out if you just keep at it. The secret is to keep showing up and moving forward. You discover qualities and assets in each other that amaze and delight the entire clan. Camping takes preparation and a lot work. You have to devote yourself to the children, but it works wonders to treat Christmas like a camping trip. There is even a major role for old dad. Finally, because the scars of childhood's end do not really heal, the old guys never again get that moment of perfection they once knew. However, for them, just to remember is to live again. Magic never entirely leaves the holiday, it creeps up in the dark, and can claim even the most crotchety old curmudgeon.

The Cafe is decorated for the season. Festive tunes are playing. The aromas from the great oven in the back kitchen are tantalizing blessings to all. Ghosts of holidays past are out, and the old guys are remembering how it "used to be." This is where it all gets good. Read on!

Thanksgiving For The Least Among Us

Pit-a-pat, pit-a-pat, pit-a-pat. The freezing rain lingered through the night and covered the morning with a dull, gray sheen. Fallen leaves marked the final vengeance of autumn. Bare trees glistened in the haze, waiting.

This is Cafe weather. This is huddle together, slap the back, dumb jokes, where-ya-been weather. The coffee never smells better or warms deeper. Like those little kids who make fortress tents of old sheets and pillows, the men crawl into their Cafe, and they are safe.

"How about that guy they left dead on the golf course for two hours?" asked Camelot Bob. "His buddies just played on through. Now, doesn't that beat anything you ever heard?"

"That's what happens when you move to Florida – value disorientation. Compassion fatigue sets in, and death on the course is just another hazard," said Ridgeway Ron.

"Ron, shut up!" Bob orders. "Or talk English like the rest of us."

"If I croak on the golf course, promise me you won't leave me out there for two hours while you finish your game," said Manor Hill Mack.

"Depends," said Bob, deadpan serious. "If you die on the front nine, no problem, but if it's the back nine, and I'm hot, well...." Wadded napkins bombed Bob, as usual.

The rain picked up outside, and the men drew closer. The talk wound around to the KKK, a cross burning in Liberty, and finally landed on Thanksgiving. Thanksgiving, now there is a topic. Families are gathering, birds are getting smoked, oysters dressed, bread baked, and the stockpile of toilet paper is formidable.

Mack, the ex-Gas Service Company employee, told the now legendary, and mostly untrue, story of being called out to check a gas leak on Thanksgiving Day. Mack grumbled all the way to the lady's house where the gas leak turned out to be an old dog with a digestion problem. Jake told his boyhood story about hiding the Thanksgiving goose, because he hated goose and wanted turkey. Jake blamed the disappearing goose on the dog.

Wind drove the rain harder against the plate-glass windows, and the laughter got louder. Some stories had been told so often, the men knew all by heart, but the telling never gets old. The friendship implied in their shared stories was its own Thanksgiving.

Then, after a while, the talk wore out. Men excused themselves to the rest of the day. The Cafe was mostly empty as Stella began clearing and wiping tables. She, too, knew the stories and loved them.

On Thanksgiving Day, she would open the restaurant for those who had no place to go. It was her tradition and cost her plenty. Stella is not a religious person in the traditional sense. She does remember a Bible story, however, about a man who was left for dead on the side of the road, and others passed him by. Finally, it was an outcast who gave him help.

There's also a story she remembers about doing things for "the least among us" that brings us closer to God. While the men stayed home and piled their day with food and family, Stella and her ragtag band of men and women – those not included by their own families (mostly gay); those without families – would feed anyone who asked. Nobody would be left on the side while others played through.

Stella watched the wind and rain tearing leaves from the trees and harkening winter. "Values disorientation, compassion fatigue, cultural blind spots, safe harbors" – Stella actually had never heard of most of those phrases before. But her Cafe was a safe harbor, one of few where all would be part of the celebration.

Stella knows our Thanksgiving will be most blessed when the least among us joins the feast.

Stella Serves Thanksgiving

A stiff, cold wind blew down the street. On Thanksgiving, the Old North Side is closed. The men are at home with children in houses, about to be over-filled with warmth, and the unmistakable tastes of roast turkey, hot rolls, and pumpkin pie.

Stella lowered her head into a sharp gust and counted the blocks to the Cafe. She was already cold. The kids were with their father for the holiday. Before the divorce, and before her boy's death, Thanksgiving was awful. She cooked a meal for at least 20 – turkey and all the trimmings. Rolls, cranberry sauce, and the little extras like oyster dressing and fudge made the day special. She remembered how mad she was after the feast was over. Hours and hours of hard work were reduced to 30 minutes of consumption and football games. Few said thanks. She and possibly one or two others were left to do dishes while the men lounged. Stella did not miss that part of Thanksgiving. She chided herself for her moment of self-pity. Saturday, the kids would be back for Thanksgiving with her family. Still, she felt alone. The wind blew a little harder, and she picked up her pace.

When Stella was little, Thanksgiving was a family time. Even as a child, she understood this holiday was for adults. It was their celebration of the things they stood for. The best moments came with the simple rituals like prayer and carving the turkey. Her dad had been harsh and distant at times, but on Thanksgiving, his house was always open. She remembered resenting some of the ragged looking people who came to their home, but her fathered welcomed them.

It was 4:30 a.m., and Stella knew she was behind. Little spits of snow filled the air. Her fingers ached with the cold as she unlocked the Cafe. Soon, the ritual began. The first smell of coffee, the rattling of pans, ovens warming, vegetables peeled, Stella moved with an ease that betrayed the size of the task before her. Tug showed up at 8:30 a.m. with an armload of groceries. Tug was from the church.

"Hey, I brought my TV to watch the games. Do you mind?"

"Heck no," said Stella.

By 11:30 a.m., the first of the day's guests wandered in. He was rough looking, and had a blue stocking cap, which he clutched in both hands as he stood by the door. Soon, they poured in from the cold. Mostly, they sat in silence, their eyes down. Old men, some women, and a few children; they all shared the same hunger.

"Welcome!" said Stella, bursting from the kitchen, coffee in hand. Her smile was a mile wide.

Stella and her helpers, other people who had no place to go on Thanksgiving, served about 60 that day. Tug said a prayer that made 'em all cry. She carved turkey till her hands ached. The football game was as stupid as ever. Few said thanks.

They finished washing dishes about 7 p.m. Stella stayed and cleaned the Old North Side until 10 p.m. and walked home in the dark. She bowed her head to the cold. All those years when she had so much, she never thought about those who had nothing. Becoming tender was not easy, and, at times, took the strangest of turns.

She welcomed the cold walk home. The stars were sharp pinpoints. The warmth from inside etched a smile on her face. Her lost boy was with her once again. This Thanksgiving had been a good one.

This Happens If You Eat Too Much

A massive conservation effort is underway at the Old North Side Cafe. With only days left to Thanksgiving, a vague terror has swept through local stomachs that there may not be room to hold the coming feast. These men know that in the next four days, they will damage themselves. Massive doses of moist, succulent turkey, rich steaming oyster dressing, warm home-made rolls running with butter, candied sweet potatoes and, of course, dessert (this is a holiday for pie eaters) are coming, and proper preparations must be made.

The storage problem is incredible. As a result, the collective North Side is cleaning its system, so to speak. Rigid fasting is hollowing out vast caverns once filled with a daily piece of coconut cream pie and gallons of coffee. There is even a notion that some walking will help sift and compact what is already there, to make more space.

Remember, most of these men live on the last belt notch. Many have already gone to pants with elastic waistbands (an excellent wardrobe selection for Thanksgiving Day itself) and large, bulky sweaters – dark blue, of course.

This year, Manor Hill Mack is in a special quandary. Two month ago his arteries were ballooned out and the doctors have him on a new diet. A diet is an unconceivable thing to an old Iowa farm boy.

For most of his life, eating, like most everything else on the farm, was another chore. He ate on the run. There were cows to milk, pigs to feed, chickens to check, and land to till. Even the big Thanksgiving feast was an obstacle course to the real pleasure of the day – rabbit hunting with his uncles. Unfortunately, Mack now has learned the pleasure of eating, and with no rabbits to chase or farm to mend, Mack's daily uniform is roomy, velour sweaters and stretch pants.

So, it was with hesitation that Mack eyed the Thanksgiving feast spread before him at his daughter's house. His eyes fell to the smoked turkey, positioned at center table, as the family joined hands to offer a Thanksgiving blessing. The family tradition is that each person present (including the little kids) name one thing they are thankful for. The prayer begun, Mack was still sneaking peaks at the buttered mashed potatoes and giblets gravy when it came his turn to offer thanks.

"I'm thankful for my family, that we are able to be here together and share this day," said Mack, the warm aroma of fresh baked bread drifting under his nose. Mack squeezed his granddaughter's hand to let her know it was her turn to pray. Mack grinned to himself; who knows what his precocious three-year-old grandchild would say.

"Thank you, God, for my Paw-Paw Mack," she said. Her eyes squinted tight, and now she was praying as hard as she could. "Please take care of his heart."

Mack felt her hand squeeze his, and he reached down to pat her head. She looked up at him with tears filling her eyes. Little people know so much more than we ever dream. Mack picked her up and whispered in her ear that God was taking care of him just fine. She laid a reassured head on his shoulder.

All of his life, Mack had been so busy that he missed a lot of little things, little joys, and little pleasures. He would not miss them today. This Thanksgiving, the food never tasted better. What little he ate melted in his mouth as he watched his family – little eyes devouring giant drumsticks; his children and their spouses laughing, enjoying one another; his wife, the most wonderful of all. It was a fine gathering.

Mack had a feast of the heart that day. In the end he was stuffed, but there was room for more. There always is for a true Thanksgiving.

I Heard Him On The Radio

Gray clouds hung close to the skyline. The air was damp and cold. Only the oaks still had leaves. The earth was a textured brown collage in the last days of an Indian summer. Gus watched it all speed by. This was his season. Thanksgiving was his holiday. Free of crass commercialism, Thanksgiving is what a holiday should be – food and feelings.

Heading north on the interstate, Gus couldn't resist the urge to pull off at his old stomping grounds and home. Home is the old river town of St. Joseph, Missouri, where the Pony Express originated and Jesse James was shot. "You can see the bullet hole," the old sign off the Belt Highway used to say.

Gus took the new alternate route along the river and pulled off in the north end. An old house at the end of 4th Street called him. The mist grew and the sky came closer. Carved dirt banks lined with giant cottonwoods were just as he remembered, and for a moment, Gus ached that it could still be so real. He half expected Jip, Grandpa's old black lab, to bound across the street. So many memories were here… what Thanksgiving should be.

At a big, white house atop the hill, a roasted duck was waiting. Grandma would have mincemeat pie and oyster dressing. In back, a barn was filled with ancient radio equipment. The highest point in St. Joseph was Grandpa Charley's log pole radio tower with a blue Christmas star on top. From Grandpa's ham radio room, grandchildren talked with Europe, South Africa, Iran, South America, and all points between.

"WØNMD, this is W–Zero–Nancy–Mike–Dog, go ahead," Grandpa said, and the world came back. That mystery in the airwaves was Thanksgiving to Gus.

Of course, in the present, the house was smaller and looked shabby. The barn was gone, but the tower stood. Gus was looking for the blue star when his car radio crackled. Maybe it was just a CB radio, but he heard a voice.

"Go ahead, I've got you now," a man said. Gus knew it was not a radio station.

"Roger, I've got a copy on that. We've got gray skies and cold weather here, and a turkey in the oven. How's it there? Over."

"Ugh, Roger that. We've got 85 degrees and clear skies. Turkey's on. Over."

The static crackled again, and the routine radio program returned. That was it. A broken line of geese angled across the gray sky, honking out instinct's mystery map. Did they hear the voices, too? Gus wondered and then smiled. If he had gone crazy, it was pleasant enough. He hadn't thought about Grandpa and his ham radio in a long, long time.

Back on the interstate, Gus felt he was on the world's edge. His recall of everything was so real – the smells of Grandma's kitchen, her old butcher knife, the jars she kept in the pantry, and the great silver maple in the back yard – all of it came back.

He saw the barn with its magic old microphones and vacuum tubes; so many times he had gone there alone and imagined talking to the world. The magic stayed all through the drive north to pick up his mom and bring her back Liberty.

At the table that night, a living family waited for the traditional toast and prayer to begin the feast. Only a few knew the meaning when Gus raised his glass and said, "W–Zero–Nancy–Mike–Dog, thanks for the copy; we got a good Thanksgiving going on here; you have a good one, too! Over."

Then Gus smiled. Somewhere, it's all there, all magic and alive. Those people and times we loved so much, floating on the airwaves of Thanksgiving.

Some Stories Just Go On And On

by Gladstone Gus

This story was first told many years ago. Today, you will read the rest of the story.

You could not miss Walter A. Dunn. He drove a bright orange pickup truck. On Saint Patrick's Day, he spray-painted his work boots a bright green, proudly combed his shock of bright red hair, and walked about the Downtown Square in Savannah, Missouri, handing out candy. At Christmas, he broke out a decidedly shabby Santa Claus suit and beard, the green boots, and bag of candy to spread cheer. Children sensed there was way too much kid left in this man, and so they took to him as bigger version of their own kind. Walter Dunn was my dad.

Come December, he would roar into the back driveway, rocks flying, and his bright orange truck skidding, and call me to the work of Christmas. "BOY, GET IN THE TRUCK," he said. "WE'VE GOT WORK TO DO!"

I don't know why, but the work of Christmas was always during my favorite TV show, or when I had something planned, or when I was in a sour puss mood and ready to BAH-HUMBUG Christmas. No matter the excuse, Dad insisted I go.

Walter A. Dunn was the town Gas Service Company representative, better known, to my endless embarrassment, as the town "Gas Man." My dad dug ditches, put in gas lines, checked furnaces, read meters, and solved problems as a one-man show in Savannah. One consequence of his job was he knew who could pay their gas bills, and more importantly, who could not; that is where the "Work of Christmas" comes into play. In the back of Walter's orange truck were big, plastic leaf bags full of presents. It was Christmas for the folks who would have had none without Walter.

Small, rural towns are full of four-room houses built on bare ground with a crawl space underneath. One gas space heater warmed the whole house. Worn, yellow wallpaper covered picture-less walls. Sparse, throw-covered furniture and cord-bare area rugs, now a dull gray or brown, were all there was to hold back the empty space. No house we ever visited had a Christmas tree. Walter burst into these homes, packages flying, grins churning, and hearts flapping. "SANTA SENT ME!" Walter said, and nobody questioned his word. Then, just that quick, we were gone! Behind us, kids were playing, a mother was crying, and Walter was grinning ear to ear.

Why do we forget the real joy of this season is in the giving? Why do we forget to be grateful for the things we do have? Walter Dunn was grateful for what he had, and being grateful made him good. Being good made him great.

Most every Christmas season has a moment when it all works. The family is together, or the night sky is crisp and cold and full of life. We sing a carol, and the words touch us, or we have a memory and celebrate our luck to have had a good life. We connect with the spirit of the season. At these moments, we know the greatest gift of Christmas is bittersweet.

All those years ago, Walter A. Dunn had a chance to make a difference, and so he did. A Christmas Star ornament with Walter's name hangs proudly on our tree each year. You see, our family did not have the money to buy presents for other families, but it was a sacrifice my dad made with joy. It is my memory of the real meaning of Christmas.

Here is the rest of the story.

Last year, I spoke and played guitar at a local church. I read a few columns, including the one printed here. After the program, a lady came up to me and said, "I was one of the children who got Christmas from your dad. I still remember what it meant to me." She grew up in Savannah in the early 1960's and still thinks about my dad's Christmas gift. We cried, and then we laughed, just like I am crying and laughing now. Walter's good lives on! May it be so for all of us.

The Best Lie He Ever Told

How finicky Camelot Bob let himself get talked into a part in the church's annual Christmas pageant was a nagging mystery.

"I do things for the best reason on earth," Bob likes to say. "Because I want to." He didn't really want to read scripture in the Christmas pageant, but that's what Pastor Fred somehow got him to do. Now, against his will, Bob was even using his brand new Eddie Bauer Ford Explorer to haul the Granger kids to rehearsal. This was a problem because Bob believes today's children are unruly, sassy, and need serious discipline. The Granger children needed a lot of discipline. Their feet were muddy and their fingers were sticky. They liked to make the windows go up and down, slam doors, touch glass, and (gasp) chew gum.

"No, we can't listen to another radio station! And, put on your seatbelts!" Bob shouted, using his sternest voice. His hostility was not faked.

At rehearsals, it never occurred to Bob to do anything but fume. Nothing was ever right for Camelot Bob! The director had no control, the rehearsals were inefficiently planned, and the directions were not precise. Bob's perfectionism meant he missed every pleasant moment. He missed the 5-year-old angels learning where to stand and sing. He missed it when the organist played so beautifully. Furthermore, Bob was a dreadful reader. From the tone of his voice, you would think there was a carjacking someplace instead of good news in Bethlehem.

Unfortunately, Bob's bad news was just beginning. While taking the Granger kids home that evening, the unthinkable happened.

"I don't feel so good," the youngest girls said. Before Bob could get his finger on the automatic window button, she threw up all over his pristine Eddie Bauer Explorer. Bob melted down. Barfing children are outside the experiential boundary of anal-retentive control freaks with a cleanliness fetish. All Bob could think about was the car's interior and the possibility of designer air-fresheners.

Bob helped the little girl to the front door of her house, and then realized nobody was home. His first thought was to abandon them all and go take care of his car. Instead, he carried the girl into her house.

Inside, the house was a complete mess. Dishes were unwashed and clothes were strewn everywhere. A dead plant graced the table. A stale odor of grease and mildew permeated the house.

"Where are you parents?" Bob demanded.

"Mom's at work," the oldest answered. "My dad doesn't live here anymore." It was a confession not easily said. Her eyes left Bob's and went to her younger sister. Then, the girl sat on the floor and started to cry.

Whatever it was that caused Bob to agree to read the scripture and offer his Explorer to haul kids in the first place, was now moving in for a kill. A hard memory worked its way loose in Bob's brain. Some mud was about to get dumped.

A brutal truth came to Bob and punched in hard.

This is how Bob had grown up – in squalor.
This is how he felt as a little boy – abandoned.
This was his worst nightmare – people finding out!

All the defenses of order and control Bob had built to protect himself from these memories cracked and broke away. Bob held the sick girl close. The frightened little boy that still lived in him knew exactly how she felt. Bob gave the children comfort and stayed with them till their mom got home.

Everyone noticed the change in Bob at rehearsal the next week. Bob was devoted to the angels. They even had new costumes. Bob asked the director what he could do to help, and then Bob read the scripture like it was about his own child in that lowly stable. The Granger girls all wore flashy new Eddie Bauer squall jackets.

Of course there is a whole lot more to this story, but now you know enough. Whenever anyone asks Bob why he took in the Granger family like he did, he just smiles and says, "I do things for the best reason earth. Because I want to!"

But he knows that is the best lie he ever told.

Tips For The Season

The North Side Guide to a Better Christmas

In case you have forgotten how to make the season right, the old North Side boys have thoughtfully prepared a few guidelines. Follow them all, and they guarantee a Merry Christmas.

TOYS FOR EVERYONE: No matter how old or young, people still like toys. Paddleball or expensive stereo; make sure everyone gets a toy, and Christmas will be better.

DECORATE: The minimum is a tiny tree. If you won't put up at least a picture, you deserve to be miserable. Other than that, the more you do, the more fun you and everyone else will have.

LOVE THE ONE YOU'RE WITH: It's hard, but the best way to honor those you miss by death or distance is to spread joy to the ones you have. Find somebody and share something.

COOK: Special food makes everything special. Take the time to make something. Become famous in your family for some dish. If you can't cook, buy something and say you did it.

HELP SOMEBODY: Volunteer for something, or just be nice to a friend. You won't have Christmas unless you find a way to help somebody.

FAMILY IS #1: If you have a choice, opt to be with your family. Forgive and forget.

RELIGION HAS A PLACE: In an era when people have given up on our major institutions, church included, Christmas has to be more than gifts and good feelings or you miss the point.

SURPRISE: One surprise gift is a must. Be generous, and go for it.

MAKE ONE PRESENT: Make one gift by hand – bake it, saw it, sketch it, sew it, or write it; just do it.

HOLDING AND TOUCHING: Break out the mistletoe, and use it. Christmas is for touching.

ENJOY: Attitude is everything. Enjoy your chance to go to lots of parties or cook for the family. Enjoy having 1,000 things to do. Enjoy being tired and still having a list. Hospitals and nursing homes are filled with folk who would give anything to trade places with you.

BE A GOOD "GETTER:" Giving may not be better than receiving, but it's close. When you get something, please appreciate that somebody gave you something. Show some joy!

SING: Go caroling if you can. Go to the church musical; put on some Christmas music. It will soothe the savage beast in you when you start to frazzle.

START TRADITIONS: Collect Santas, pewter goblets, Teddy bears, or coffee mugs. Have a traditional family toast, read the Christmas story or do advent wreaths. Create the traditions that will carry you through the hard times.

TELL FAMILY STORIES: Gather everyone around, and tell about Grandpa when he was young or Christmas long ago. Kids will listen.

GAG GIFTS: Give at least one each year, and watch the fun begin (DO NOT HURT ANOTHER'S FEELINGS!).

SPECIAL THINGS: Parents (children), dig through the old photo albums and find pictures of you with your child (parents). Have one enlarged and framed and give it to your son or daughter (parents). Write, "I love you" on it.

SHARE YOUR BLESSINGS: The person who dies with the most toys is still dead.

NEW PAJAMAS: Every kid should have brand new pajamas to wear to bed on Christmas Eve.

HAVE THE COURAGE TO PLAN: Somebody has to get things going. Make a plan, and see what happens. Draw names, go skating, cut a tree, string popcorn; do something with your kin.

Merry Rock'em Sock'em Christmas!

Jodi Gives Up Her Blanket

Holly Lake Jake couldn't help the smile that was breaking out across his face. He knew the prelude was a time to reflect, pray, and generally be holy, but the smile won. Up front, the children were lighting candles to begin the Advent worship service. Of course, two candles wouldn't light despite the joint bonfire three acolytes were throwing against it. Jake knew the situation was getting desperate. It was just like adults to have candles that won't light; kids can't win.

The unlit candles stirred an old memory in Jake. It was Arkansas in his youth, and Christmas at a country church. Reverend Fred had it in his mind to create a living nativity and had gone about recruiting children from the congregation for the various parts. Jake was to be a Wise Man, and his little brother a shepherd.

Conspicuously absent from the cast was Jake's little sister, Jodi. Though the Bible said there was a "multitude of angels" in the birth story, and surely the cast could take one more, still no Jodi. Jake knew why. Jodi was a problem. She forever endeared herself to Reverend Fred by walking out of his Children's Service after complaining to the entire congregation that the Birth Story was prejudiced against pigs. Jodi loved pigs, and when the preacher didn't include them in the barnyard animals present at Jesus' birth, she walked out, swinging her blanket behind.

That was another thing about Jodi…the ever-present, smelly childhood blanket. The cloth was a journal of her growing up experiences. The stains recorded her first attempts at eating, the list of hated vegetables, and her dreaded milk allergy.

The blanket was wrecked, tattered, and limp beyond recognition, but Jodi clung to it. Adults begged her to give it up, but Jodi was not ready for that. Jodi irritated much of the older congregation. She never stood to sing during hymns, kept her eyes open and head up during prayer, and constantly fidgeted. Pastor Fred knew this and wondered what to do with Jodi. Jake, the newly ordained Wise Man, quickly lorded his high status over his brother and sister. First, he ridiculed his brother for being a lowly shepherd and then mocked his blanket-bound sister for not making the Multitude of Angels cast. Ah, youth! It really isn't as sweet as we remember.

That night, Pastor Fred was nervous. A rare Arkansas cold snap had settled in Malvern. Snow was spitting, and you could tell it was just aching for a big storm. Pastor Fred hurried the congregation outside to the makeshift stable. Mary and Joseph were shivering, looking less than adoringly at the raggedy china faced doll doubling as Jesus. Finally, Joseph gave up and put on earmuffs. Jake, ever smug and self-centered, thought he looked nifty in his mother's bathrobe. He held a cigar box wrapped with gold paper.

Despite an increasing volume of falling snow, everyone got into place. Pastor Fred passed out the candles and commenced to sing *Silent Night*. Unfortunately, the wind picked up and snow came even harder. The congregation was more concerned with keeping his or her candle lit than singing. Mostly, everyone just wanted to get inside.

"*Silent night, Holy night, All is calm all is bright...*" The song started, and Pastor Fred thought he had it made. Then Jodi stepped forward. In front of God and everybody, she came strolling right into the stable and up to the manger, just staring. She hesitated only a moment before taking her blanket and putting it around the lifeless doll. Jodi stepped back a pace and sang, the snow falling, a serious look on her little girl face.

The congregation scattered on the last note, heading for shelter. Jodi stood alone in the falling snow. She was quietly crying. Pastor Fred knelt beside her, "Shall I get your blanket?" he asked. Jodi shook her head, "No."

Pastor Fred scooped her up and held her close as he carried her into the little church. Jake saw it all and hid it away. What a wonderful little sister he had. And so no one knew why Jake walked to the front of the church and helped the kids light the last candle. It was for Jodi and her blanket from all those years ago.

How To Bake A Christmas Wreath

by Gladstone Gus

The recipe read, "Cut in the butter." I had no idea what that meant, though my imagination came up with a few alternatives. Thankfully, none were close to the real meaning. I do have a set *modus operandi* for solving such problems, however. We will get to that in a moment.

First, I should explain just why my life had come to cutting in butter in the first place. Every Christmas since at least the Cuban Missile Crisis, I have savored my mother's Christmas Wreath. The Christmas Wreath is not an ordinary coffee cake. It is the stuff of youth and memories. My brother and I would sit in a warm, fragrant kitchen eating the Christmas Wreath and drinking cold milk. We licked our fingers and pressed them against the platter for the last possible crumb or bit of icing. There is no better food. This season, my mother fell and cracked her ribs, and then she got an infected tooth. There would be no Christmas Wreath if I did not take on the challenge and bake my own.

Now, about the *modus operandi* mentioned earlier. When I don't know what to do in my life, when I'm stuck, I call my wife. If she doesn't know everything, she certainly has me fooled. Fortunately, she did not mention that the last time I tried to make a coffee cake we had to use the fire extinguisher. My wife said to just drop the two sticks of butter in the huge bowl of flour, salt, sugar, and mysterious special ingredients, and use two sharp knives like a pair of scissors and cut the butter into tiny little bits. What a cool concept. Christmas Wreath and sword fighting all at the same time. I never had so much fun baking.

My wife was not available to take my phone call when it came to the drizzle of white frosting, so I called my mother. She enlightened me to the wonder of powdered sugar, milk, and heat. *Viola!* The miracle of powdered sugar frosting. I used a syrup dispenser to create the drizzle effect. Unfortunately, it was more downpour than drizzle.

I called my brother when the Christmas Wreath was ready. He came over and ate a huge portion, but he was not suitably impressed, so I talked to my father-in-law and told him he had to pinch hit for my father and properly compliment my Christmas Wreath. He did a fine job.

Christmas Day, the moment I had waited for, finally arrived. I went to the kitchen, cut a generous slice of Christmas Wreath, and poured a tall glass of cold milk. The kitchen still smelled of cookies, cinnamon, Dutch potatoes, a ham roasting in the oven, and morning coffee. I ate my coffee cake, washed it down with milk, and tasted the memory. It was so sweet. I licked my fingers to compress the last crumbs and pieces of chopped nuts. The powdered sugar frosting was magical.

I thought about my mom and all the years she made the Christmas Wreath for my brother and me. The memory never had more meaning. My busy brother came to mind and our connection from so many years. Since my father's death, my father-in-law has been his agent in my life, and I thought of both with great appreciation. Mostly, I thought of my *modus operandi*. In times of trouble, and the best of times, I call my wife. She knows how to cut the butter.

T.S. Elliot said we should not stop exploring, that if we do continue to explore, there will times we return to the place we started and know it for the first time. The truth is my Christmas Wreath was not even close to being as good as the ones my mother made. It never will be! Those days when I sat with my brother in mother's kitchen eating and laughing were a gift long in the making, now lost to time.

I can't help but hope that someday my son, or even a grandchild, will sit in his or her kitchen eating a Christmas Wreath that tastes so unusually good. I hope they, too, will one day know the love that makes it taste so fine.

Anybody Seen Christmas?

The steam drifted out of Gladstone Gus's coffee cup in a soft line, bending to the motion of his breath. Around him at their familiar table, the men were gathered. Their faces were crisp red from the new cold. Snow and spits of ice had marked the new season's arrival. Winter had come at last, bringing Christmas close behind.

This was their season. Hot coffee makes sense. Packing around tables to turn back the cold is a last line of defense. Christmas, with all its tradition and family meaning, calls these venerable icons of age to life. They remember Christmas without the hubbub of commercial madness – back before money was everything – when Christmas was in the heart.

"We were really poor," says Gus. "I remember Dad told us after Thanksgiving he wasn't sure Santa could come. In the end, Dad went to the basement every night after we went to bed and made us presents from scrap lumber. He made me an easel. It was the first time I ever realized that liking art and wanting to draw was ok. That was the best present I ever got."

"We got clothes for winter and always had a big dinner. There were so many of us, we knew we wouldn't get much for presents," offered Ridgeway Ron. "Somehow, Mother saved enough to get me a wooden airplane. When I saw that plane on Christmas morning with my name on it, it was one of the most glorious moments of my life."

The North Side stories are rich mines of emotion. Here, Christmas memories gather around lighting candles, singing, playing wise men in bathrobes, decorations, and one toy, usually not very expensive, that touched the heart. Behind it was always the personal touch that made it special.

"On Christmas Eve, we always went to church. There was a gigantic Christmas tree lit with candles, and we sang. Everybody was there! Church was what we did on Christmas. Then, almost at the end, Santa came. He knew all of us by name, and we rushed forward to greet him. In his sack, he had bags filled with candy, nuts, and fruit; my favorite was an orange. I will never forget those Christmas trees and bags of candy," said Water Street Pete.

"If the wind wasn't blowing too hard, we would go outside around the Nativity scene, light candles, and sing *Silent Night*. My mom always cried and grabbed my hand. I felt like Jesus and the angels were right there with us," said Camelot Bob.

There is a mission at the Old North Side Cafe every Christmas. You feel it when they grab your shoulder and say, "Merry Christmas." You hear it when the family gathers, and they pull out a Bible to read the Christmas Story. You see it when they take the time to play with little kids. You taste it in the pecan pies and chocolate fudge they just happen to have around. These guys know the value of simple things – a cup of coffee, some friends, the fine lines of winter, and a personal touch. They don't want the old Christmases back. They had their day. They only want it where it used to be – where it has to be to make it count – a Christmas in the heart.

Bernice Learns A Lesson

It is a well-known fact of life that any reasonable man who goes to the Cafe for coffee, conversation, and companionship does not like cats. You see, real men like dogs. They ask themselves why would anyone want an animal that coughs up fur balls and takes a bath in its own spit.

"Cats tend to act too much like women," says Manor Hill Mack, and most men seem to know what that means. Therefore, each Christmas when talk begins to lag, Holly Lake Jake is asked to tell his Christmas Cat Story. Jake swears this is a true story.

Clinton (honest, that was the cat's name well before the now famous politician) was the church cat. He was the church cat, because Ms. Bernice Tavener liked cats. Bernice was the Women's Auxiliary head, the Pastor Annoyance Committee's permanent chair, and a church choir soprano who demanded a solo at every service. Even for a soprano, Bernice's vocal chords were wound a little tight. She also looked the part. Her dresses were small tents, and her Christmas hat was an expanse of green felt topped with two turtledoves.

Though most men of the church would gladly have handed Clinton over to the notoriously dense Sipes brothers for proper disposal (the Sipes brothers liked to cook live frogs), the powerful and obnoxious Bernice Tavener would not allow it. That brings us to the Christmas Eve Pastor Presley got the idea to let a dove loose during his sermon.

"Now Leslie," said Pastor Presley, dispatching Leslie Sipes up to the organ loft. "When I say, 'Let there be peace on earth,' you let this dove (actually a pigeon) go. You got that?"

"Yes sir," Sipes said and up to the loft he went.

Pastor Presley then told Bernice to do her mandatory soprano "ooie-oooing" when he first said the words, "peace on earth."

It was set. Leslie Sipes was in the organ loft, Bernice (in her green tent and turtledove hat) was in the choir, and Pastor Presley was ready for a Christmas Eve service nobody ever would forget.

Knowing the stunning effect the dove (pigeon) would have on the congregation, Presley went full tilt. At the "peace on earth" part, Bernice started to "ooie-oooo," and Leslie Sipes, on cue, reached for the bird. Unfortunately, the bird was dead, and Clinton the cat was grinning ear to ear. Leslie Sipes began to panic.

Down below, Pastor Presley was now saying "peace" like it had three syllables. "Paw-ee-suh, I say," and his neck veins were an inch thick. "Let tharr be paw-ee-suh, on earth," Presley said and looked to the choir loft. Nothing.

"I saaaaid, let tharr be paw-ee-suh, on earth!" Presley shouted.

At that moment, Leslie Sipes became unhinged and threw Clinton over the railing as if he thought cats could fly. The cat's screech hit perfect pitch with Bernice's "o-ooing".

Clinton's flight path seemed to hone in on Bernice. From its perspective, the cat could just see the outline of two turtledoves in a green field below. It unsheathed ten sharp daggers for combat and struck! Some say it was the highest note ever achieved in operatic history. The shock waves broke windows as far away as Missouri City.

Later, Bernice personally turned the cat over to the Sipes brothers who considered it a fine Christmas present. Bernice, herself, never sang or annoyed anyone again. Pastor Presley said it was his best Christmas ever.

Daddy Battles A Dirty, Dusty, Depression

by Manor Hill Mack

The dust settled into every corner of that old house. It floated effortlessly through the morning shafts of light, coating even the dishes with a fine film of discontent. Dad had stripped wallpaper through the night, and chunks of aging plaster littered the floor. Every remodeling job always takes longer and costs more than planned. Now, Christmas was coming, and there was more to do than money or time would allow.

That was my Christmas 41 years ago. It was not to be the happiest or the best, but it would be one to remember for all the years to come.

Lurking through the dust and demands of three young children, depression was also in the air. My mom suffered from a profound sadness no Iowa farm boy was equipped to handle or understand. And, so Dad worked. Dad was a workingman who spent his days fixing furnaces and water heaters, dryers, and gas lines. At night, he remodeled the house. His way to love was to give more. And so he gave, but once the rotting wood in the termite-infested floor structure was exposed, the Christmas money went for mandatory repairs.

Anger and tears creaked in the old house with each new disappointment. The profound sadness of depression dug deep into the family, centering in my mom.

"I'm afraid there won't be much for Christmas this year," Dad told his assembled family. "Santa is having a tough year. He wanted me to let you know." We kids took the word almost too well, as if it was expected. We went back to black and white TV, and Dad went to sand the hard oak floor – more dust and disappointment.

That would have been Christmas all those years ago if not for the oak floor. Dad figured wrong and ordered too much. He took the leftover scraps to the basement, and ideas formed. Each night, instead of sleep, using the oak strips, Dad worked making gifts for his children. For my sister, he made a baby bed. My older brother got a basketball goal, and I got an easel. They were amazingly sturdy and real. Christmas morning, that's all there was. A plastic sheet sealed off the disheveled parts of the house, and for a moment kept the dust and depression at bay.

The details of the morning are long gone now, but the gifts linger. Little Cindy spent long hours singing her dolls to sleep in that marvelous bed. Tommy shot baskets and found peace. I drew slender birds lifting off through blue skies.

Depression struck Mom four more times (often at Christmas) over the next 40 years, but medicine and understanding began to catch up on her demons. There were other years when the Christmas trees were bigger than the room, and packages flowed across the floor, spilling into closets and hallways. You can't imagine the joy of those Christmas seasons. If you had asked Dad to name the best one, he would not have tried. He certainly wouldn't have thought of that dreadful old house and the mean season it spawned.

My sister has four children now, and a better mother cannot be found in Northwest Missouri. Sports paid Tommy's way through college, and to this day, offer him solace. And I love books and art and airplanes to places far away.

All of us have a fine coating of grit on our souls that keeps us both tender and tough in hard times. That old house was torn down to make a parking lot. Dad took every stick of the oak floor and used it for twenty years (he took a lot of kidding about it too!).

Families get separated by death, disease, and distance. About all Christmas can be sometimes is hope and a promise of what may come tomorrow.

Warrior King Of Light Rules

by Manor Hill Mack

Grandpa was a stern man. A child of the Great Depression, he knew the value of a warm house and enough food. Legend has it that his family was teased one Sunday at church for their ragged clothes. His young heart was cut deep, and he never attended church again, though he lived into his 70s.

Grandpa always had a boat, and he always had a dog. He served in both World Wars. The second time, he left a wife and four young children at home because the army needed his skills in ham radio.

Unlike today, when we tend to think everything is a Kodak moment, the pictures of Grandpa speak volumes. In his few photos, Grandpa stands looking into the future with tight lips and no-nonsense eyes. Mother says he danced and played cards as a young man. Another family story says he rode a motorcycle. Grandma says she was only fifteen when they married. You don't see any of this in his picture. Mother also says he worked long hours for the Light and Power Company and slept many evenings and Sunday afternoons with a newspaper pitched over his face.

His hobby was ham radio. Today, there are still some who remember W0(zero) NMD (Nancy Mike Dog), but their numbers are fewer and fewer. Each Christmas, Grandpa climbed the enormous pole tower in his backyard to place a magnificent blue star on top of his ham radio antenna. You could see it from miles away. It was a Christmas landmark in St. Joseph, Missouri.

On Christmas Eve, the family gathered at Grandma and Grandpa's house. Grandpa was not a rich man, but his gifts were. One Christmas, now so long ago that it is more emotion than fact, Grandpa gave his grandchildren ray guns. In an age when battery powered toys were scarce and hideously expensive, the ray guns were monumental toys. There were eight grandchildren in all, but only five were old enough to fully appreciate the divine significance of red, blue and gold beams piercing the darkness. With ray guns, children were invincible. No force on earth or from the stars could match this mighty weapon. The five children ran upstairs in Grandpa's cavernous old house and blasted away in the darkness.

The upstairs rampage took a nasty turn, however, when the middle grandson dived to the bed firing his blue beam at interstellar demons. The bed moaned and slid into the nightstand, crashing Grandma's cherished bedside lamp to the floor. The sound shook the house, and the terrified grandchildren waited in darkness. A light flipped on, and there was Grandpa, his lips tight and his eyes stern. "What is going on?" he demanded.

"We were saving the world, and knocked over the light," a grandchild meekly replied. Grandpa picked up the lamp and all its pieces, then he flipped the light out again. In the dark, we heard him move, and then a brilliant beam of white light from a four-battery flashlight cut the darkness.

"I am the Warrior King of Light," Grandpa announced, "come to save the planet!" Side by side, grandchildren and grandfather battled into Christmas night, romping and hiding, slamming doors, and sliding under beds. It was a glorious victory for childhood, light sabers, and life.

The grandchildren never saw the Warrior King of Light after that Christmas; it was just stern Grandpa. Still, in the cold dark of the holiday season, sometimes those grandchildren (now all grown and old) spot a blue star atop some high place and smile. The Warrior King of Light is up there waiting. They know it's true.

A Hamburg Hill Christmas

I will never think about Christmas without remembering Hamburg Hill. Hamburg Hill rose five blocks straight up from St. Joseph Avenue to reach the highest spot in the North End of St. Joseph, Missouri. Each morning around 4:30 a.m., my brother and I walked down Hamburg Hill to pick up our copies of the *St. Joseph News Press,* and then we walked back up the hill delivering the paper to our customers' front doors. About 3 p.m. each afternoon, we did it again.

My brother practically ran up the hill. He could deliver one side of Hamburg Hill, do 4th and 5th Streets, the Crowder house and then hit the Valley of the Shadow of Death (the longest part of the paper route) before I could do one side of Hamburg Hill. He was unbelievable.

In November, however, my brother started to slow down. By December, he was limping and my parents took him to a doctor. We learned he had a tumor just below his right knee. By Christmas, he needed crutches and an operation. That Christmas was a hard season. I was throwing the paper route alone. My brother was hurt. My parents were worried about cancer. Hamburg Hill seemed bigger each day.

Christmas of that year I got up extra early and trudged down Hamburg to start the route. The paper that morning was so large that delivering them would take two trips. I put as many papers as I could carry in my bag. The rest I hid in the laundromat where I folded or put rubber bands on the newspapers each day. Off I went, criss-crossing the street, hitting each front door with a newspaper as I went up the hill. I was breathing heavy and my legs were already tired. It was time to start singing.

How singing became such a big part of my life is a mystery, but in times of trouble or joy, I break into song. Maybe it was all the musicals I watched where average people broke out in song in everyday life. I thought singing was normal behavior. I started with *Hark the Herald Angels Sing* and *Oh Come All Ye Faithful.* Suddenly, I felt better. By the time I was through with the first batch of papers, I was singing *Joy to the World.* I then pointed my nose down the hill, spread my arms as if they were wings, and took off running and singing down Hamburg Hill. I expected to go airborne at any moment.

Back at the laundromat, I put the rest of the papers in my sack, the sack on my back, and headed back up the hill. *Onward Christian Soldiers,* I sang. House lights were coming on and I knew Christmas was starting in the homes with younger children. *Here Comes Santa Claus* turned into *Rudolph the Red Nosed Reindeer* as I sped up Hamburg and then turned down 4th Street. Coming back up 5th Street, I sang *Jingle Bells*, pretending I was driving a sleigh. The last leg of the route was down to the Crowder house and through the Valley of the Shadow of Death. I chose *Oh Little Town of Bethlehem* and a personal favorite, *Silver Bells*, to get me through. The stars were fading and a sliver of light crept up in the east as I finished the last paper at the end of my block. At the vacant lot next door to the Dewey house, I stopped to look down at the town. St. Joseph was all spread out before me on that Christmas morning. I think I was 10. I know I was exhausted.

You can't imagine what a goofy kid I was. I stood in the vacant lot and started to sing *Silent Night*, as if it was the most important thing in the world. I sang every word with all my heart, like I was singing it for my brother; or maybe, it was for all the children and their parents down below. Maybe I sang it just for me.

When I finished, I was worn out from walking and crying. It was then my Dad arrived. He had come looking for me, worried and wondering why throwing the route had taken so long. He never asked why I was singing all alone and crying. He just grabbed my hand and we walked home together on that Christmas morning.

My brother's tumor was not malignant. He became one of the most celebrated athletes in Northwest Missouri, and an absolute legend at William Jewell College. People sometimes wondered how his skinny-looking legs could be so powerful, but I know it was Hamburg Hill. Today, I still like to turn on the Christmas tree lights, sit on the piano bench or the wood box, play my guitar, and sing the Christmas tunes. My family knows I am goofy about these things, and they forgive me. Singing with all my heart is still important to me. I don't know why. I just learned one Christmas morning on Hamburg Hill.

Beware The Christmas Pepper

This Christmas story begins in the late fall. Water Street Pete was at the Farmer's Market buying the last few squash of the season, when he spied a little orange pepper.

"It's a hot one," the old farmer said with a wink.

"I like 'em hot," Pete said and bought a bunch.

The slightly dried peppers were still in Pete's pantry when he began fixing his famous Christmas chili. Every year, Pete went to his daughter's house for tree trimming. His grandkids decorated the tree, and Pete made chili. As you know, the real fun of decorating a tree for kids is the constant fighting over who gets to hang prized ornaments and who turns on the lights. Parents don't understand that kids would rather fight than just about anything. Pete had fought with his brother at every opportunity. They counted M&Ms to see who got the most, and drew endless lines on couches, car seats, and tables to mark their territory. Then they fought over the smallest infraction.

The greatest Christmas tree battle of all is "TINSEL WARS". Kids, tinsel, and parents do not mix. Parents believe tinsel should be "placed" on trees; kids know tinsel is to be thrown. Tinsel should fly about the room and hang in gigantic bunches.

"NO, No, no-no-no!" Pete heard his daughter say. "Put one strand on at a time."

"Why does Tommy have more tinsel..." the child interrupted grabbing from his brother.

"I do not! Give that back to me," the oldest shouted, grabbing the tinsel back.

"CHILDREN!" the mother shouted. "IT'S CHRISTMAS."

Pete closed the door to the kitchen and got out the bowls. The chili smelled especially good this year; the kids would be hungry after the big fight.

Ten minutes later, bits of tinsel could be seen in every corner of the room. The work was done. They turned out all the lights. Silent Night played softly on the stereo, and they plugged in the tree's colored candle bulbs.

"OOOHHH, AAAHHH," they all said. For a moment, nobody fought. They were a family.

"I'm hungry," said the youngest after about 15 seconds.

Naturally, the children fought over who got the biggest bowl of chili. It was to be the last such fight they would ever have. The first indication that something was wrong came as a whimper more than a scream, but the screams followed. The chili peppers from the Farmer's Market (the ones in Pete's chili that night) were the dreaded habanera – the hottest in the world. Pete's chili was just slightly hotter than Death Valley. "Eat sugar!!" Pete yelled, but the damage was done.

The story is now one of the great memories of Christmas. Seems that after grandpa's chili, the kids lost their taste for fighting. Now that tinsel has gone out of style, the only tree fight concerns where to hang the chili pepper ornaments Pete bought each of his grandkids. It was the least Pete could do to remind them of a grandpa's goof in a time that will one day be long ago and far away.

Quest For A Perfect Tree

A cold snowy rain closed the world around them as Manor Hill Mack and his family drove into the unknown. They were on a Christmas mission, a quest for a perfect Christmas tree. Perfect trees are no longer found hanging around outside supermarkets or in lots with bare light bulbs dangling above them. No, the perfect tree is fresh cut (like our ancestors used to do) from a farm where they wait in rows.

Mack had chosen the old clunker for this mission. Named the Great White Hope (because every time you get in it, you hope it starts), it was the car to face the wondrous mud-debris mix of the country and the friendly residue of dried pine needles sure to be embedded throughout the car. Old farm men love their clunkers; cars that can take abuse and still start. Cars that are not afraid of a little dirt.

"Are we there yet?" asks a little voice from the back. Mack grinned. They had only been on the road five minutes. They were heading on a twenty-minute drive to a tree farm in the middle of nowhere, located at the end of a gravel road.

In the old days, perfect trees were whatever Mack's dad said they were. Mack's dad claimed he could hear them singing. The old trees were marvels of perfection. There was the bare side for a snug fit close to the wall. There were big holes for the most prized ornaments. They were spindly and gangly, just the kind to show off tinsel and construction paper chains, but the most perfect thing about them was the price. Perfection did not exist above $4.75.

So here was Mack, driving into oblivion, braced to shell out $45 for a tree with no wall side, holes for ornaments, or space for tinsel. Today, trees are supposed to look like copies of artificial, perfect trees. Mack wondered when he had lost control.

One does not just walk into the great Christmas tree forest and calmly cut a tree. One must run into it screaming frantically, "This one, this one; no, this one, this one!"

"Here is a bare spot," they say, and a great tree is rejected. "This has a hole," says another, and a beauty is passed by. Children, sensing all the perfect trees are being cut, become even more frantic in their search.

"Nobody will look at the tree I like," says a very unhappy child. "I'm wet and cold," says another. They begin to play hide and seek in trees. At this point, Mack lifts a hand to his ear and strains to listen.

"What is it Grandpa?" say the kids.

"I hear singing," Mack says, turning toward an unknown sound.

"What is it, Grandpa?" they ask again.

"I think I hear a tree singing. It's this way." Gramps is now turning toward the part of the forest they had already come through. "Do you hear it? It's like a song."

"I hear it!" says one, and then another.

The next moment, Mack is hugging a tree right at the farm entrance.

"This is it!" he says. "This is a wonderful tree." Mack hoists the little ones up to take a real good look. Then, Mack starts singing. "O, Christmas tree, O Christmas tree…" They all hug the tree together.

"Let's get it!" Mack shouts with obvious joy.

"Let's get it!" the children shout back.

Once back at home, the decoration began.

"This tree side fits right up against the wall," cries one voice. "This bare spot is perfect for the Teddy Bear," says another. "Look how my paper chains hang on these branches," adds the smallest.

Then there's the marvelous moment of lighting. All lights in the whole house are turned off. In total darkness, the countdown begins. Three…two… one… the nine-year-old flips the switch. The tree bursts to life. Ornaments, some of them dating back 40 years, sparkle and shine.

It is a "perfect" Christmas tree!

Grandpa Charley Makes A Decision

by Holly Lake Jake

Somewhere along the river bottoms of the Grand River outside Pattonsburg, you can still see the old shack. It's a dilapidated mess now, but it was already in bad shape when Great Grandpa Charley was a boy. Somehow, the shack's story comes up at the Cafe every few years, always around Christmas.

You'll have to know the Watson family to understand why. They were poor, rural folk. There wasn't a college education in the clan, and wouldn't be for another fifty years. In summer, they fished catfish and grew watermelon. They kept a few chickens, had some mules, and a cow. Come Christmas, they would hitch up the wagon and go to Grandma Horton's house where they ate and exchanged gifts. Then, they went hunting. That takes us to the shack.

Charley, age 15, was out hunting after Christmas dinner when a storm blew up. Sleet came first, and the hunting was good. Then the clouds ripped open, and a frightening white darkness shut the forest down. That's when Charley saw the wagon pulled by an old mule. It was obvious there was a problem.

"You folk doing all right?" Charley asked.

"We been better," the man said. The answer shocked him. It was a black man's voice. Charley had a decision to make. Helping a Negro was not popular or wise.

"Where you going?" Charley asked.

"North," the man said, and Charley knew there was big trouble. The small bundle next to the man moved. It was a white woman.

"We need help," the woman said. "I'm having a baby."

Charley was struck dumb. The snow swirled, and his mind clouded. He needed to get himself home. Charley made the decision. "Follow me," he said and led them to the shack.

The snow was deep and getting deeper. Nobody talked. Charley put a fire in the stove. He was about to leave when the baby came. It was messy; it was loud, and then it was soft and silent. Charley never learned their names, but the baby was to be called James. When he left, the mother was nursing, and the father was just sitting, staring at them. Charley left them all he had. The next few days, Charley came back with food and a blanket. His mom would have died if she knew. The three left on the fourth day. There weren't many words of parting. He held James once.

Now, as Christmases drift past and Charley is long-ago dead, the story dims. Of course, there is all the obvious stuff about Mary and Joseph and no room at the inn. He was black, and they were outcasts; James would have a tough row ahead. The story has all the elements of Christmas. For Charley, those ideas never came up. Maybe they should have, but what the teenage boy remembered was that when the chance to help came, he took it.

When culture's prejudice stared him in the eye and said, "No!" Charley looked it down and said, "Yes." Charley would be like that all his life.

There is no "rest of the story." Charley didn't hear from the family again. James did not grow up to be somebody in a history book, or at least Charley never knew it, if he did. All that's left is the shack and a memory.

Along the Grand River by Pattonsburg, you can go see it. It's a Christmas reminder that the way the world is, is not how it has to be.

Chapter 9

Special Stories

Water Street Pete, Holly Lake Jake, Camelot Bob
Manor Hill Mack, Ridgeway Ron, Gladstone Gus,
City Hall Sam and Stella

They were a unique collection of individuals. While every town in the United States once had its own version of the Old North Side, each was flavored differently by local customs and characters.

Our North Side Cafe and her special crew were part of a time and a tradition quickly passing away. Men will always gather to tell their stories, but now it is a coffee bar or a grocery store restaurant where they gather. Stella can't get a job at these self-serve places, and Stella was <u>the</u> key to the Cafe's heart.

Furthermore, there are just not that many old farmers any more. The common farm background, bc it actual farming or living in a farm community, was a uniting factor at the Cafe. People who can understand what farm life was like; the communities that grew around the farm; the values and mores championed in this culture; and the kind of characters it created, are essential to an Old North Side Cafe ever existing again.

Back then, there was a strange paradox to farm life. On one hand, farms created rugged individualists who competed fiercely with one another for who had the best spread and the greatest skills. At the same time, farmers were inextricably linked to, and dependent upon, each other. When a crisis came, be it weather, injury, or family turmoil, they rode to one another's aid, no questions asked or payment expected. This "farm" mentality is crucial to the kind of relationships that existed at the North Side.

Finally, technology is creating cyber cafes where like-minded people can insulate themselves from different opinions or alternate lines of thought. Nobody likes how uncivil our culture has become, but it now seems to be true that Republicans and Democrats, liberals and conservatives, normal people and Yankee fans, no longer can coexist in the same location. It is unthinkable to sit by quietly and let a political foe have his/her say.

Not so at the Old North Side Cafe. You had to be tolerant and civil! Lord knows the terrible justice Water Street Pete or Stella would bring crashing down on anyone who got out of line. Besides, there were just not enough old guys to be that picky about things.

There always will be great human stories for telling and re-telling, no matter the time and or place. But narrative will never be quite the same as at the North Side

Cafe. Northwest Missouri between 1950 and 2005 colored these stories with the bright impression of farm life – a blending of reds, greens and golds that connect the human spirit to the earth. The pale blues and the cold greys of the tumultuous 1960s, Vietnam and Iraq Wars, Watergate, the Challenger disaster and NYC 9/11 permeated the canvas. A luminous quality of rural faith and religion, deep commitment to common good values and civility, and a sense of hope completed the portrait of these times.

This final painting is of a rich and textured Cafe with a cast of characters whose stories deserve to be remembered.

Robin Spotting

Some things are beyond understanding. This is the case with the annual Robin Spotting Contest at the Old North Side Cafe. Legend has it that Water Street Pete began the contest as a joke, sometime in the pre-Nixon era, but nobody knows for sure. Today, it is spring's premier rite of passage.

Contest rules are simple. The first man or woman (yes, Stella the waitress plays) to have a verified robin spotting after February 20 wins a dinner paid for by the North Side gang. Ridgeway Ron once won and took the entire gang to the Athena Greek Restaurant on Broadway where they then dined on dolmas, Slovakian duck, pita bread, and baklava. That they had to leave early because of an "incident" with a belly dancer is never mentioned and will remain thus now. If this sounds like an idle spring pastime, you're wrong.

Despite the fact that many robins stay in the area for the entire winter, the competition is keen. The bragging rights are immense. The robin spotting ritual verifies once again that aging men enter a second childhood with behaviors more immature and juvenile than any displayed by delinquents at the local theater on a Friday night.

"Boys, you can make my reservation now for the Peppercorn Duck Club," predicted Camelot Bob. "These are the eyes of a hunter – eyes accustomed to the wild. The first robin is mine." The year he really did win, the men had to go to the Golden Ox to watch Bob devour two pounds of well-done prime American beef. The gluttonous ritual took 18 minutes, five Moosehead beers, and one noxious Havana Regal cigar. The whole dinner cost more than most of their first cars!

Ridgeway Ron had fed birds all winter, and exchanged numerous phone conversations with the executive director of the bird sanctuary just outside of town. He was sure his intellectual approach would net him the first robin.

The key to winning the Robin Spotting Contest was verification. There must be a signed witness of unquestionable character able to verify any sighting. Naturally, that leaves out any city or county politician, weathermen, doctors, lawyers, insurance salesmen, or preachers. You also could not count wives, relatives, or children under 10. This, of course, was a problem for Manor Hill Mack, who was related to almost everybody in town.

Anyway, with March about to poke its head around the corner, the contest was off to its usual bit of squabbles. Holly Lake Jake announced he had purchased, and perfected, a robin birdcall. With that announcement, Jake pitched his head back, took out his bird whistle, and let loose the most authentic sounding robin song a man ever heard. The North Side was in shock.

"Boys, we'll be going down to Bryant's Barbeque on Brooklyn Street to eat our spring feast. I'll be having a slab of ribs, order of fries, couple dozen pickles, and at least two frosty mugs of beer," smiled Jake. "I'll enjoy watching you pay." A defeated silence rolled across the North Side.

"That ain't fair," complained City Hall Sam, who was already taking early morning walks, complete with verification pad. "You're manipulating nature when you call birds. This is supposed to be a natural sighting. Calling robins is unnatural!" Men grunted their approval. "Unnatural," they shouted.

"The winners tell jokes, and the losers cry deal," said Jake whistling the prettiest little robin song you ever heard.

At that point, a new and deeper resolve swept over the North Side. Each man decided this would be the year he won. Clearly, the use of calls is sneaky and underhanded. Right must prevail! And so, on Ash Wednesday 2004, the gauntlet was thrown down. Roving packs of wrinkled men would soon be scouring back alleys, wormy lawns, and wooded creeks searching for robins.

Give these crazed men a wide berth! If there are two things that make immature boys or feisty old men work up a sweat, it's the thought of winning a stupid contest, and then eating themselves into submission. Let spring's siren song be heard!

Part 2

It is hard to understand how a little thrush can become so important. Legend says that a robin picked a thorn from the crown of Christ as he made his way to Calvary. A drop of blood fell from the thorn to the bird's breast, dyeing it red. An Old English tale calls a robin the "pious bird with the scarlet breast." That being said, and despite the bleak March forecast this year, the North Side is ready for spring. The annual Robin Spotting Contest is that last little push to take these men to warmer days.

This year, however, with Holly Lake Jake using a birdcall to imitate the ringing notes of the robin, the old boys are miffed, and Jake is feeling some peer pressure to give up his birdcall. So they sit at the North Side, robins on their minds, wondering exactly what day in March Osama Bin Laden will be captured. The Cafe crew thinks the government knows exactly where Bin Laden is, and we are just waiting for a spring thaw and a good news week to make the capture. Then, a topic even more important than terrorists came up.

"I heard a kindergarten teacher spotted a robin down by Sugar Creek," said Bob, as a hush fell across the table.

"Was she sure it was robin?" asked Mack.

"Kindergarten teachers know what robins look like," said Bob.

So, there were robins out there. Now the contest took on a new dimension. Time was running out. Jake reached for his robin caller and eyed the pine tree outside. It took several seconds before he noticed the pocket was empty. Then the realization swept over him that the whistle was missing.

"Has anybody seen my whistle?" Jake asked. There was stone silence; grown men shifted their eyes up and over like little boys caught with stolen candy. "Who's got my whistle?" demanded Jake.

"You mean that little red, plastic robin whistle you keep on a yellow string?" asked Bob. Jake nodded. "I ain't seen it," said Bob with a grin.

Jake was about to respond when Stella pitched the missing whistle onto the table. "You dropped this," she said. "I ought to keep it, 'cause it isn't fair you're using it." The fierce eye of disapproval bore down on Jake as he pulled the call from the table and put it in his pocket. "I won't use it," he said.

That night, Stella walked home listening for the sound of spring. Working all day left little time for robin spotting. "It would teach these guys a lesson if a woman won the contest," she laughed to herself. Just then, a distinct sound cut the night. She looked up, and a smile the size of a North Side slice of coconut cream pie cut across her face. "A woman will win this year," she said out loud, "and you can take this woman's word to the bank."

Across town, Camelot Bob was searching the skies with his new $1,200 binoculars from L.L. Bean. Water Street Pete had hired fifth graders to search the skies for him. Ridgeway Ron not only tromped through a creek behind his house, but knowing robins are fruit and bug eaters who like to live in open spaces near people, he took to hiking toward the Odd Fellows Home. Robins often return to the same nesting site year after year, a behavior the Cafe crowd understands. Holly Lake Jake was on the telephone with the local bird sanctuary asking where to find robins.

Manor Hill Mack not only put out birdfeed at his house, but, not wanting to take a break from searching for robins, he did it again … Mack pulled up to a fast food drive-in window, and while searching the horizon for a robin, ordered into the trash bin. (Don't laugh, most of the Cafe crowd does this. Still, there is a self-conscious moment about asking a waste can for a burger). In Manor Hill Mack's eyes, this was the year he would win the annual North Side Robin Spotting Contest! He would not be denied the honor of having his friends pay for a healthy meal of hand-choked Stroud's chicken, his prize for spotting the first redbreast of spring. Of course, the irony of eating a bird for seeing one is lost on Mack.

Stella sighed; no woman had a chance against such odds.

Part 3

Robin spotting contests are now in full swing across the Northland. An academic sub-contest has broken out at William Jewell College. Hospital employees are searching for the first robin. Elementary school children are included, and at least one businessman on the town square has his eyes on the lookout. He thinks he has already won.

Robins are out there; they have been all winter. The trick is official verification.

Nowhere is the competition so keen as at the Old North Side Cafe. Men like Camelot Bob, Holly Lake Jake, and Ridgeway Ron are taking robin spotting seriously this year. Bob even made a third L.L. Bean order thinking a $120 three-layer Windstopper fabric jacket in forest green would give him the edge. Others are hiking daily, calling the bird sanctuary for advice, enlisting spotters, and putting out bird feed.

The men at the North Side should have been concerned when Stella came tearing into the Cafe, blathering something about hearing a robin "...a gift from God... singing just to her."

"Sure Stella," said Bob in his condescending style. "You don't know the difference between a robin and a sparrow."

Stella bristled. "Come on, I'll show you," she said, and a line filed outside.

"Well, where is it?" asked Bob. "I don't see a bird anywhere."

"He must be around somewhere," Stella answered. "I heard him!"

"What did he sound like?" asked Ron.

"Like a robin," said Stella. "You know, a thrush. Like this," and she whistled....

"Oh that sound. I heard it too," Holly Lake Jake said, lifting his robin whistle in his mouth and offering the sweetest song springtime ever heard.

"That's it!" cried Stella, her face lighting up like a beacon. "That is the exact sound!" Then it hit her. She was a victim of another vicious North Side gag. The men started stomping around, giggling like little boys who just heard an underwear joke.

"Did it sound just like that whistle? Oh, how could that be?" asked Bob. "Good job Stella, but the contest is to find a robin, not Jake's whistle."

"Maybe robins are using whistles now too," laughed Water Street Pete. Oouugh! A rage began to well up in Stella.

"Listen here you gum-flapping old goats, if you tricked me ...." It was no use, however. The joke was on Stella and she had fallen for it hook, line, and sinker.

Just then, Stella changed faces, and a coy grin worked its way across her jaw.

"Boys, I think we'll be going to dinner at the North Side Cafe right here in the Northland. You old coots will be cooking up and serving me a real gourmet dinner, and I'll expect all of you to be on your best behavior: coats, wives, and ties."

"Stella, dear woman, that was not a real robin that whistled at you," smiled Bob. "You just stick with serving coffee. When I win, we'll be going out to eat some manly burnt meat and drink cold beer."

Stella never lost her smile for she was about to have her day. "The whistle may be fake, but that robin sitting on the fence back over there is as real as the fat in your brain, Bob," said Stella.

Sure enough, there was a robin sitting on the fence. The bright, red-breasted male robin had come to challenge Jake's whistle.

At the Old North Side Cafe a few days later, Stella tipped a glass of fine wine to all the men and their wives.

Bob Gets His Hair Done

Bob had reason to appreciate his hair. At age five, he had ringworm. The doctors shaved his head and forced him to wear a stocking cap treated with a foul smelling ointment. Each night under a spotlight, his mother plucked the contaminated white hairs out of his head with a pair of tweezers. Between tears, Bob kept muttering, "Someday."

At age eight, his dad bought hair clippers as a money saving venture. Every two weeks, dad appeared, clippers in hand, saying, "Bobby, come here. Daddy wants to cut your hair."

Bob hit the door the moment he saw the clippers, and the race was on. Soon, the whole neighborhood was involved. "Bobby, you come back here this instant!" screamed dad.

Bob hid in the bushes beside the steps of the Lutheran church at the top of the hill. Dad always found him there and dragged him by his ear to the Den of Torture. The Den of Torture was the kitchen. Dad's clippers were cheap and pulled out as many hairs as they cut. Therefore, the strategy was simple – cut as much as he could, as fast as he could, before the child broke into complete hysterics. The 45-second burr cut left Bob with interesting tufts on the top of his head and the inevitable cut on his ear. Butch Wax in hand, Bob tried to salvage the massacre. "Someday," Bob said.

In high school, Bob found the comforts of the beauty shop. Here, a kind woman gently washed his hair before cutting it with scissors. She stopped periodically, to hold up a mirror and ask him how it looked. Men did not go to the beauty shop in those days. The haircut was a favor from the mother of a friend; Bob went in the evenings when nobody knew. When the stylist moved away, Bob went back to the anguish of the village barber. With a slap and a buzz, he walked out with a new set of white walls thinking to himself, "Someday."

As a wise adult male, Bob just would not go to a beauty shop. Sissy prima donnas went to beauty salons. Real men took the buzz. Who wanted to sit around women with curlers in their hair talking about recipes and bad sex? Bob might have lived this pitiful macho existence forever if not for his wife. Tired of his griping, she made an appointment for him at the Big Apple Beauty Salon. She knew just how to lure him in. "You'll look so much more handsome with your hair styled," she purred. After 45 minutes of hair inspection, Bob decided to go.

When Bob entered the Big Apple, two women were having their nails done. "My husband thinks he's some kind of macho Republican sex machine," whined one of the women. "Actually, I think Al Gore's a lot more interesting."

Bob was about to head out when he was frozen by the sound of the sexiest voice he had ever heard.

"You must be Bob," said an astonishing pile of red hair. "Have a seat honey; I'll be with you in a minute."

The face turned, and Bob was smitten. She was gorgeous beyond his wildest imaginings. Ten minutes later, he was sitting in a chair, her fingers running through his hair. She tilted his head back, and it brushed her ample bosom. The place smelled like the beauty shop of his youth.

"So, what will it be?" she asked. Bob faltered, then said just a trim.

"We don't get many full heads of hair like yours in here," she said. "Usually, men are too arrogant and macho to come here. It's nice to meet a man who has some sensitivity." Bob gulped as she lowered him down to shampoo his hair.

Part 2

Camelot Bob has found himself at the Big Apple Beauty Salon where the shapely Pauline is preparing to cut his hair. As an avowed conservative, Reagan-loving Republican and chauvinist, Bob could not be more out of place than in the zany Big Apple Beauty Salon.

Bob realized the mess he was in when he looked at the next chair. There, an incredibly handsome young man in black dancing slippers, gold lame pants, and a puffy black and white checked shirt was finishing a Mohawk haircut on what appeared to be a nine- or ten-year old boy. Bob was aghast. So it was here that such debauchery occurred. He wondered what the boy's parents would think. Bob would sue if such a thing happened to his child.

"This is radical, truly bogus," the boy said, eyeing his Mohawk. "What do you think mom, gnarly huh?" Out of the corner stepped a skinny woman with multiple bracelets on each arm and a Gucci bag. "It looks fine," she said. "Can we go now?"

"Sure Mom, but I need some colored gel to really make it crank." With that, the woman paid about $80 and left dragging what appeared to be a multicolored Osage Indian behind her.

"Do many children get their hair cut like that?" asked Bob, his horror clearly displayed.

"Not too many, some still like spikes, burrs, or rat tails," smiled Pauline. "Would you like a different look? Louis, come here and look at this man's hair," she said.

With that, the young man in the gold lame pants walked over and started flipping Bob's hair.

"I think a wave would be nice. You could do a few close rods across the top."

"Oh, I like that," whispered Pauline with what seemed a sexual innuendo. "How about it, Bob?"

"I think I just want a trim. I like a neat look like John Ashcroft or Orrin Hatch," whispered Bob.

"Oh you can't be serious," said Pauline, putting both her hands in his hair and massaging the scalp. "Hair like this is a treasure. Properly styled, it could make you look ten years younger." With that, Pauline batted her moist brown eyes in the mirror and ran a caring finger across Bob's temple. "You'll be so handsome," she said and wanton pleasure filled her voice.

Three hours later, Bob walked out of the Big Apple Salon with a permanent wave across the top of his head. His hair was at least an inch and a half taller now and would never need combing again. All he would do in the morning is run his hands through the wet hair, and it would fall naturally into place. Under his arm, he carried a package of hair essentials. There was an odd looking comb with only six or seven big teeth in it. There was Avocado-Passion Fruit Enriched Shampoo, Palm Oil Conditioner, and an all-natural Silk Treatment Spray for those irritating windy days. The whole package was a bargain at $119.99. At that moment, the boy with the rainbow Mohawk charged forward on his skateboard.

"Radical, Mister!" he exclaimed in absolute awe. "Your hair really cranks."

At 6:00 a.m. the next morning, Bob called Harvey the Barber and asked for a special appointment. For the next two weeks, bald Bob never took off his Royals baseball cap.

Camelot Bob, recognizing his vulnerability, was now more intolerant than ever of kids, minorities, Democrats, liberals, and weakness. He was still positive, however, that every problem the country knew could be traced back to John and Robert Kennedy. But for a moment, in the Big Apple Beauty Salon, there was a chink in Bob's armor. The beautiful Pauline was touched, too. She sent Bob a perfumed letter. Alas, that's a story for another day.

Jake Goes South Making Memories

Holly Lake Jake was happy for the silence. New Orleans had worn out his two young grandsons, and they were sleeping in the back of the station wagon. Night was creeping up now, and they were heading east to Gulf Port.

Water is relentless in the bayou country of the Gulf Coast. Incredible bridges span huge stretches of marsh and mud with their wandering water trails. Jake had a rare moment of pleasure. Those two boys in the back were the world to him; a magical link with immortality. They made the world make sense. Here they were, traveling through the South, looking for adventure and finding their share. Grandparents should take these journeys, Jake believed. He didn't understand people who got wrapped up in themselves and were happy enough to have their grandkids hundreds of miles away. Life truly had saved the best for last in the mysterious bond between grandchildren and grandparents.

"I'm hungry," said the 8-year-old, yawning and stretching at the same time. "Let's eat." Eight-year olds must eat at least eight times a day. They should be cows, just left to graze at will. Furthermore, they have no sense of proportion. They always want a quarter-pound hamburger with cheese, large fries, and a drink … and feel slighted if you won't buy it. Two bites, three fries, and five sips later, they are full. More precisely, they are sick. They say things like, "If I take another bite, I will throw up all over the car." Jake once sat at the table for two-and-a-half hours choking down liver and peas on behalf of starving children in some far-away country. Wasting three-fourths of a cheeseburger and $5.89 did not sit well with him.

"You just ate two hours ago," said Jake, but his blinker light was already on. Jake had strict travel rules you stop to eat or go to the bathroom on demand, and you always stay at a hotel with a pool. It was Jake's revenge from having to pee in mason jars and stay at roach motels when he was young.

Hours later, they pressed on past Biloxi in the dark. All the motels looked too garish, and Jake felt like driving. MISTAKE! North of Biloxi, toward the Alabama capital of Montgomery, is a swamp. Worse yet, it is below the gnat line where thousands of little bugs visit your eyes any moment you are outside. Nobody much lives here, and motels just don't exist. Jake was tired, and the driving was hard. The youngest of the two boys crawled into the front seat and sat close to his grandpa.

"When are we going to get there?" he asked, a little bit afraid.

"It won't be long now," Jake lied, and squeezed the boy's knee.

The older boy patted Jake on the arm and asked if he was, "Doing ok?"

"No problem," Jake said.

Through the darkness they went, and Jake felt how much those boys needed him. Back home, kids get a little sassy now and then. They act grown up and distant. They are smart-aleck and careless. Sometimes it's hard to believe this generation of kids needs anything, especially love. Jake knew better. Children need love more than anyone might ever guess. All kids do. Jake and the boys huddled close, looking for a safe port in the long night. The youngest fell asleep as the Alabama darkness spread out before them like a giant sea. The other talked quietly; the conversation keeping them both awake until they reached an open motel. That night was one of the best memories of those boys Jake would ever have.

Holly Lake Jake sensed it was time to go home. His tour of the South was about over. They had made Atlanta, Georgia, when his two grandsons started asking questions.

"What do you think Mom is doing right now?" asked the 8-year-old. "How long will it take us to get home?" asked the 14-year-old.

It was Atlanta that did it. The new Athens, home of the 1996 Olympics, the Jewel of the South, is a dud. Atlanta is schizophrenic. It is part Old South hospitality and charm; part new age frenzy. It's a glitzy wonderland, home of Coca Cola, CNN, and Chops. The result is the stereotype of a spoiled cheerleader. All charm and promise outside, and vicious like a junkyard dog underneath. Ted Turner is happy to charge a small fortune for a tour of CNN and treat you like a goat while doing it. Coca-Cola charges another fortune to show you its advertising. Meanwhile, the Martin Luther King area is, well, shabby. The Carter Museum is set off like a stepchild.

Atlanta's heart needs a valve job. At Peach Tree Center, you can walk enclosed areas anywhere and never set foot on the street. Good thing; there is some serious violence out there. Since Rodney King, people are in no mood for small talk in their panhandling. "I'm hungry, give me money," they say, and it is more than a request. If not for Stone Mountain, one might wish Atlanta would follow Atlantis into the sea. Georgia would not have fared well at all if Jake and the boys had not stopped for church in Comer.

Comer is outside Athens – home of the Bulldogs and the famous Varsity Restaurant, where grease still means something. The heart of Georgia is alive and well at the Comer Baptist Church. Here, Jake and his boys were not Yankee invaders, they were friends. Preacher Tom reminded everyone to come to Vacation Bible School, and people did. In the patriotic South, Preacher Tom told the congregation that America's might was not in its fist, but in its heart; that greatness came not from what you had, but what you gave. People are like that in Comer. Folks make their living from chickens, lumber, service trades, and farms; but they make their lives from each other. So it was Sunday after church when Jake and the boys headed home, with lightness in their hearts and outlooks. Their tour of the South was over.

The glory of travel is coming home. To have seen and done, to hear the sounds of life in other places, taste the food, and experience the difference, gives home a point of reference. The rainstorm in Jackson, laughter in New Orleans, long drive in Alabama, and nightmare in Atlanta would all be balanced with every day at home. On a great adventure, a grandpa and his two grandkids had seen the South, and come home standing (much to the relief of the women in their lives).

Fifty years from now, when Jake is reduced to a granite marker, two boys might think of him and smile. They might carry on a tradition. They might just remember that family and relationships are the most important things around.

Taking A Son To Study Law

by Gladstone Gus

It was a hail of a trip!

Thinking it would prove more scenic and maybe save some time, my son and I left the safe and reliable Interstate to take the two-lane blacktop roads across Kansas on our trip to Phoenix and Tucson. At Wichita, we turned west on old Highway 54 heading for Tucumcari, New Mexico. There we would again hook up with the Interstate. Our plan when we left Wichita, just after 5:30 p.m., was to drive to Liberal, Kansas. We would find a hotel and spend the night.

This detour would be more than across Kansas, however; we would detour through time, too. Driving into the night across Kansas is a family tradition. We are usually on our way to Colorado and the mountains, and Kansas is an annoyance at best. On this night, however, with a generally full moon shining in the driver's side window from the south, Kansas turned spacious with farm house and grain elevator etchings along the horizon. Radio stations carry the full spectrum of music, from country to western music. Grain and hog prices, and radio garage sales joined static to complete the spectrum of wireless entertainment. Crossing Kansas at night, Highway 54 becomes an endless repetition of white lines, telephone poles, all night Pepsi machines, and empty spaces.

I drove, and we talked. We remembered our other trips. Because I was lucky enough to be a schoolteacher, I had time in the summers to go on adventures. Zach, and then Matthew and I drove off to Niagara Falls, New Orleans, Seattle, Atlanta, and all points in between. Sometimes, we made up our route according to whim and the state's color on the map. We followed two basic rules: we slept only in motels with a swimming pool and ate hamburgers at least once a day. It does not take much more than that to keep kids happy.

Our actual conversation from that crossing-Kansas night is already fading in time. We talked about graduate school, music, the Royals, Republican bad breath, and ancient history. I told him about all my drives across the plains on Highway 36 until I noticed he was sleeping.

At midnight, we made Liberal, Kansas. The main attraction in Liberal is Dorothy's House and a theme park dedicated to the Wizard of Oz. The house is a replica of the original used on the set of the famous movie. Tonight, however, the main attraction was the Holiday Inn Express. Located off the main the drag, we had to cross the river and follow a labyrinth of bad signage to get there.

The Holiday Inn Express was not open. It looked like it had been bombed. Actually, a recent hailstorm had wrecked that place and most of Liberal, Kansas as well. Roofers, insurance agents, hawkers, and construction crews filled every other available motel. We had to drive on. My son took the wheel after I forgot to push in the clutch to stop. He could tell I was tired.

Here is where the adventure began. We were worn out, and there was no place to stay. I asked an extraordinary looking lady with beautiful blonde hair and albino red eyes where we might find room. She said we had best find another town. At a convenience store, the clerk turned pale when we asked where the next town might be. He swallowed hard and then choked up the name "Guymon", like it was some kind of penal colony at the edge of civilization.

Guymon, Oklahoma, has a population of about 10,500, is 312 feet above sea level, and the area code is 580. That's the interesting stuff. In Guymon, we found a room at a motel with no pool, a grain elevator view, and a manager who spoke only nine words of English – none of which related to the motel business. At breakfast, the milk was five days outdated, and the most edible offering. A sign above the counter read, "DO NOT SPIT IN THE SINK." We left Guymon knowing this was a trip we would remember for many years to come.

Part 2

The Pythagorean Theorem states that for a right triangle with legs a and b and hypotenuse c, $a^2 + b^2 = c^2$. One plan had been to drive on Interstate 35 down from Kansas City to Oklahoma City and then go west on Interstate 40. Oklahoma City was the right angle. Our alternate route, Highway 54, was the hypotenuse c in the equation. Using geometry learned in high school, we deduced not only how many miles we saved by cutting across Kansas, but we also created a formula comparing our current speed with how fast we would need to travel if we had gone through Oklahoma City.

"According to my calculations, though our speedometer says we are driving 75 mph, we are actually going 103 mph," I said, after some quick figuring on the back of an Arby's roast beef bag. Yes, I am a nerd who does things like that. If you were riding in a car going from Guymon, Oklahoma, to Tucumcari, New Mexico, and points west, you would find ways to occupy your mind as well. We laughed as my son raced the car past 110 mph, relatively speaking.

"Tucumcari (Two-Come-Carry) Tonight," read the weathered signs. At one time, Tucumcari, New Mexico, claimed to have 2,000 motel rooms. In my youth, I remember motels shaped like tee-pees, and I wanted desperately to stay in one. Tucumcari was a stopping point on the famous Route 66, the Mother Road, according to novelist John Steinbeck. "Everyone has, or will, sleep in Tucumcari at least one night in his or her life," wrote somebody in a rip-off of an earlier saying about Times Square in New York City.

Tucumcari is an old railroad town clinging to Route 66 nostalgia for its meaning. Just outside of the town is Tucumcari Mountain. It has an interesting story. The Legend of Tucumcari Mountain has supposedly been handed down "from mouth-to-mouth" by Indian tribes, reports travel writer Dan Phillips.

An Apache chief knew he was about to die and ordered two young rivals to fight for the right to become chief. As an extra-added benefit, the chief proclaimed the winner would also marry his daughter, Kari. And so it was that Tonopah and Tocom fought for the hand of Kari, the daughter of Wantonomah. But Kari loved Tocom and hated Tonopah. When Tonopah killed Tocom, Kari revenged Tocom by killing Tonopah. Kari, lovesick and distraught, then killed herself. When the old chief sees his daughter is dead, he plunges a knife into his heart, crying in agony, "Tocom-Kari." The old chief's dying utterance lives on today with a slight change to Tucumcari, and the scene of the tragedy is now Tucumcari Mountain.

We are pleased to leave Tucumcari and drive west toward Gallup, then on to Flagstaff, Arizona. My son, who is on his way to start law school in Tucson, Arizona, is driving. I am awed by his manliness to drive six hours without stopping, but my 54-year-old bladder is screaming. At a fast food restaurant, I am so dazed by it all, I hand a kid a $50 bill thinking it is $5. My son catches the error and scolds me.

"Just remember, old man, the first time I see you drool it's the old folks' home for you," my son says. It is a very old joke between us, and we laugh.

We are driving almost 14 hours today, and the car is quiet. I watch the mile markers roll by and feel the loss. Each mile takes us closer to the end of this great trip, this time I share with my son. We are in the same car, going the same direction, but my son is still beginning, and I am going the other way. No fancy math or thinking thing relieves the mile-by-mile and hour-by-hour in the car, but it is a fitting metaphor that we are driving into the desert.

We get our first glimpse of the great saguaro cactus on the last leg into Phoenix. Zach says that each arm of a saguaro takes fifty years to grow. Saguaros, some 20-feet tall with up to five arms, stand like crosses welcoming us to the Valley of the Sun. That night in Phoenix, we stay with relatives and rest for the final push into Tucson. I see on the Internet that the bloody story I read about Tucumcari is entirely false, made up by marketers. Tucumcari Mountain was actually named from an earlier Indian word, which meant woman's breast.

Tomorrow we go to Tucson.

Part 3

"Lawyer: An individual whose principal role is to protect his clients from others of his profession."

I have been faithful to my beliefs all these years. Time after time, I have excoriated lawyers and the law profession. I think lawyers encourage frivolous, unnecessary, and costly lawsuits. Lawyers have taught us not to trust each other and to go too quickly to court to settle our differences. I have heard lawyers brag that sexual harassment suits were their new cash cows. I was seated at a table with them as they bragged about shameless billing practices. Lawyer tricks and chicanery make a mockery of justice and the law. Lawyers freely admit they are trained to trust nobody, manipulate truth, and do whatever they can for a client, even if they know s/he is guilty.

What do you call a lawyer with an IQ of 40?
Answer: Your Honor.

How many lawyers does it take to grease a combine?
Answer: Only one if you run him/her through slowly.

So, over the years I have written a yearly lawyer joke column, and I must say, it seems to be a favorite. Even lawyers write me now and then with their own new joke. Other lawyers have been less appreciative and have inferred that my mother sleeps under a porch, and I should take all future meals in a barnyard, then after eating, die a miserable death. I take it all in stride. It is the work of a crusader to be passionate and steadfast in the face of seemingly impossible odds. Surely, there are a few lawyers, somewhere, who are not totally soulless.

What do you have when you bury six lawyers up to their necks in sand?
Answer: Not enough sand.

What do you call 20 lawyers skydiving from an airplane?
Answer: Skeet.

But now, something has happened that changes everything. Tomorrow, in Tucson, my first-born son is to begin law school at the University of Arizona. It is hot, 110 in the shade, and forget that dry heat nonsense.

I could not be more proud of a young man. I am thrilled to know I can still learn a few things, and I have learned there must be something beautiful and worthy about practicing law if a young man like Zachary wants to pursue it as a career. Does that mean I'll give lawyers a second chance? Yes. Does it mean I'll stop with the lawyer jokes?

When lawyers die, why are they buried in a hole 24 feet deep?
Because down deep, they are all nice guys.

Mack's Mulberry Madness

The bright sun of a June day illuminated the sidewalk. Manor Hill Mack found the day's rhythm as his morning walk carried him past the first blooms of summer. A furious squawking up ahead ripped through the air. Mack recognized it at once. Mulberry madness! The mulberry tree's seedy black berries are a bird's delight, and reason for ferocious territorial feuds.

That mulberry tree brought back a memory. Suddenly, it was a new summer. Mack was a young boy, and the mulberry tree was in a fencerow by the river on his grandfather's farm. Mack had some crusts of bread in a handkerchief and an old canteen. These were days of exploration. A young boy with the day before him, and a farm on which to romp, was off to discover his world. Young Mack had heard mulberries could cause diarrhea or worse yet, make you drunk. But he ate them anyway. He was fearless in this world.

"Squawk, squawk, squawk!" the birds' squabbles brought Mack back to his walk. The memories swirled in his head, and he smiled at how nice it was to be a kid off on an adventure. That was the beginning. That's how it started. Mack had a hankering for adventure, but he didn't know where it came from. Things were ending for him now. The farms were gone; superhighways ripped 'em up. People got better use for land than loving it. Everything seemed used up.

Mack was explaining his mulberry story back at the Cafe when a man and his boy walked in.

"You guys on vacation?" Stella asked. They looked weary.

"On our way back," the man told Stella.

"Where to?" Stella asked.

"Alaska," the man said. "We got some driving to do."

Before you could say Harry Truman, Stella had the pair telling their life stories. They lived on the Kenai Peninsula, southwest of Anchorage. He worked oil; the boy was a fishing guide on the Kenai River. They were taking some time to drive to the Florida Keys and back. Mack listened in awe as they talked about Alaska.

"You throw back the 35-pound salmon," the younger man said. "Moose still wander down the main street."

Then Mack noticed an odd coincidence. The older man's hat had the word "Mulberry" on it – "Mulberry Fishing Guide."

That night, Mack dreamed he was on a river. Maybe it was the river on Grandpa's farm. There was a mulberry tree, and bluejays were squawking. Something moved in the river. It was a silver drift along the current-side bank. Mack watched as a huge salmon leaped from the water high into the air. Then, as if flying, it came to the mulberry tree and ate. Gorged on the seedy berries, the fish slipped back in the water. The fish leaped again. This time it landed at Mack's feet. Mack had a salmon feast. Crusts of bread and water from his old canteen completed the meal.

The dream did not scare Mack, but it made him think. Was there one more great adventure for this old man?

"You've been watching too much fishing on the TV," Camelot Bob told Mack the next day when he heard they were supposed to drop their summer plans and go to Alaska.

"You're going, too," said Mack. "There ain't no doubt. You watch – you'll go. We got us a sign."

The men laughed, but Mack grinned. They had been called, and they would go. Mulberry madness had struck again.

Part 2

Manor Hill Mack has either gone crazy or been chosen for a mission. Mack knew he was "called" to Alaska, but the ridicule of his friends made him feel like an old fool. Mack was too poor to up and go on such a journey, let alone take along his friends. The teasing cured Mack for a short time. On Saturday next, however, he found a jar of mulberry preserves at the Farmer's Market which got him thinking again.

That night, he looked up the word "mulberry" in his ancient encyclopedia. Now the story turns strange.

The baseball card was there, just where Mack had left it in 1952 – in with the "M's," so he would find it again. Mulberry was a call to adventure, but also a clue for how Mack would pay for his Alaska trip.

Topps made the first true baseball cards in 1951. Inside the wrapper was caramel, instead of gum. In 1952, Topps made the most prized baseball card of all time. Today, that card, in good condition, is worth over $30,000. If you have one, you are rich.

Manor Hill Mack took that very baseball card in his hands and studied the picture of his childhood hero. It was all there. You could see it even in this early picture – the incredible power and speed, the boyish charm, the gritty determination that marked the heart of the greatest baseball player who had ever played the game, or ever would. Mack felt his heart thumping wildly. He held in his hand a mint condition, 1952 Mickey Mantle Topps baseball card. No rubber band had ever been wrapped around it. It had never been clipped to a bicycle spoke to create an engine sound. It was perfect, just like the day young Mack had put it there all those years ago.

Mickey Mantle was a dream come true. He and Willie Mays came up in the same year, 1951. Together, they would revitalize baseball. Number 6, Babe Ruth, had passed the torch to Number 3, Joe DiMaggio, who retired in 1952. Now, Number 7, Mickey Mantle, would carry the torch again. (All three numbers would be retired forever when Mickey left the game in March of 1969.)

Mack first saw Mickey play in Independence, Kansas, and then again in Joplin, Missouri. When Mickey's first run at the Major Leagues turned sour, he was briefly sent back to Kansas City. Mack caught his game.

Mickey Charles Mantle was named for his father's favorite ballplayer, Mickey Cochrane (even though Cochrane's real first name was Gordon). Injured as a kid playing football, Mantle played hurt his entire life. Legend has it that he tore a cartilage in 1951 when he stepped on a drain pipe, chasing a fly ball hit by Willie Mays and caught by Joe DiMaggio. Mickey hit a lifetime total of 536 home runs, and in 1956 led the league in batting average, runs batted in, and home runs. He lost a batting title the following year when his .365 average was topped by Ted Williams's .388.

Though Mantle was often intentionally walked, Roger Maris, who batted in front of him, was not. In fact, Maris was not given a single free pass the year he hit 61 home runs. That's how much other teams feared Mantle. Another legend says Mantle's legs were so powerful they left deep holes in the infield when he took off to steal a base. His 1953 home run blast in Washington traveled 565 feet. Run, hit, catch, and throw; Mickey did it all, and he did it in pain. Nobody ever did it better.

Mack held the card up to the light. He and the Commerce City Comet were young together. Mickey gave Mack some of the great thrills of his life. Maybe he would give Mack and the boys one more great adventure.

Part 3
Sometimes things work out. The old magic that takes young kids to the right fishing hole or opens doors to old barns where time stands still has its way of coming back.

Manor Hill Mack didn't understand all that was happening to him. He just knew he was supposed to go to Alaska and fish for salmon. Somewhere in Alaska he would find something he lost a long time ago when he was young. He felt he would find it, just like he found the 1952 Mickey Mantle baseball card that paid the way. He would know it when he did, just like he knew the mulberry tree that first sent him on this mission, and then took him to the letter "M" in his encyclopedia. Something was leading him.

Back at the Cafe, Mack was given prophet status. The teasing took a new turn.

"Mack, got any idea what stock I should buy or heard any voices concerning tonight's game?" Camelot Bob asked. Bob was strangely serious. Holly Lake Jake searched through every book in his library thinking he might find his own treasure. He did find a Playboy centerfold his son left in an ancient copy of Creatures of the South Seas, and a speeding ticket he had hidden from his wife.

Mack's wife was taking Mack's new wealth from the baseball card in stride. She also took half the profits, but it was her idea and her encouragement for what came next.

Two days after Mack sold his Mickey Mantle card, he handed Jake and Bob plane tickets for Alaska. They would fly through Seattle to Anchorage, and from there travel west on the Kenai Peninsula to Soldotna. They would fish for salmon on the famous Kenai River and witness a sun that does not set. They would talk as friends in front of a fire, and listen to the squalls of cold ocean rains.

Somewhere in Alaska something was waiting. Mack wanted his friends close by. Others from the Cafe were invited, but they could not go. It was to be the three of them.

"Why do I feel like I'm going with Moses to the Promised Land?" joked Bob. "I'm telling you now, if we find any tablets or a golden calf, I'm coming home right then."

Jake was more philosophical, "Mack, I think you are one card short of a full deck. But, being the gracious friend that I am, I will spend your money with great abandon."

Mack counted the days and wondered if there would be another "sign" before they left. He got it at the airport. The Cafe regulars came to see the three off.

"Don't do too much male bonding. Your wives might get jealous," said Water Street Pete.

Somebody gave Mack a drum to beat when they were out in the wilderness, saying that's what real men were doing these days. For the first time, Mack got scared. What in the world was he doing? Suddenly, being chosen for a mission didn't seem so glamorous. What if he was going up to Alaska to die? Mack was about to have a full-blown anxiety attack when Stella, the Cafe waitress, stepped forward.

"You'll need this," she said handing Mack a brown paper bag. Inside were three bottles of Bryant's Bar-B-Q sauce, and a New York Yankee's baseball cap with the word "Mulberry" carefully embroidered just under the logo.

It was his "sign". The hat was perfect. Up in Alaska, something was stirring, as if it knew Mack was at last on the way.

Part 4

Mack was at the Midnight Sun Resort and Fishing Camp when he collapsed.

Breakfast was eggs, bacon, pancakes, and potatoes. Mack was on his third cup of coffee when he laid his head on the table, dangerously close to the pool of boysenberry syrup that had run off his pancakes onto his napkin. Three days of no nights had worn Mack to the nub. Perpetual sunshine had blocked his brain sleep cues, and the result was Mack playing whiffle ball in a parking lot at 2 a.m. Breakfast is served at 3 a.m., so you can be on the river and ready to fish at 4 a.m. The syrup was now oozing onto Mack's cheek, and he got a big taste of sugar. By that time, Camelot Bob had grabbed him by the collar and yanked him back up into a sitting position.

"Wake up you old fool," Bob said. "We got fishing to do."

Fishing for salmon is different. You bounce a heavy ball of bait off the bottom of a river. The salmon swimming up the river are no longer eating; in fact, the redder the salmon get, the closer they are to dead. They only strike the bait, because some deep primal instinct forces them to attack one more time.

Mack was bouncing his bait on the bottom of the river about 5:15 a.m. when he was struck. "Fish on! Fish on!" men started yelling. They held a big fishing net upright in the boat as a clear sign that all the fishermen around the area were to reel in their lines.

Mack panicked. He started reeling in as the line was spooling out. The big salmon was making a 300-yard run up the river. Mack was holding on for dear life. About 45 minutes later, Mack had learned to reel in after the line was drug out. It took another 45 minutes, and a second 200-yard run down river to get the fish into the boat. The fish was a monster!

"Keep the line tight," the guide yelled in Mack's ear just as the full length of the salmon came parallel to the boat. "It's 60 pounds if it's a pound," the guide yelled. "Keep the line tight! Hot damn! We got us a trophy fish!!"

The guide grabbed the net. Mack was awash in adrenalin. At last, the small farm boy was about to measure up. This was his fish; his prophecy was fulfilled. Just that quick, Mack let the line go slack. The fish turned its head to the side and spit out the hook. The giant fish was gone.

You could feel the agony in the boat. At first, Mack was the least struck. He had no idea what he had just lost. Then, he saw the eyes of the guide, then Jake, then Bob. Mack knew he had just missed the winning extra point in the championship game of life. In the end, the salmon gods gave all three men two fish, the legal limit. Two were over 30 pounds. Mack got a lesson in keeping his line tight.

For another week, they fished and hiked; then it was time to go home. Mack was already practicing his "fish that got away" story. Jake and Bob would make sure it was properly humiliating.

"The only real losers are the people who never play the game," the guide finally said to Mack. "That was the biggest fish I've seen on this river in a long time." With that, he took the New York Yankees hat off of Mack's head and pinned a pink salmon pin at the end of the word "mulberry".

"Did the guys put you up to this?" Mack asked, and the guide said, "Put me up to what?"

"Nothing," Mack said and thanked him for the pin. That was all Mack needed to know and more than he expected. On the day he left Alaska, Mack tipped his hat to the next-to-last great adventure of his life. Everything he had expected, and more, had come to pass.

Mack went home with no answers, but with a lot fewer questions. Do we find ourselves or create ourselves? Are our stories already written, and we tell them as best we can, or do we make them up as we go? What does it mean to really live your life? Mack didn't know and didn't care. He was just happy for his chance to have played the game.

Part 5

It was time to say good-bye to Alaska, the great land. Manor Hill Mack knew he would never be able to explain the adventure back home – you never can. "Alaska is different," he will say. Heads will nod, pretending to understand.

How do you explain a state four times bigger than Texas where nobody lives? Every person in Alaska could move to Missouri and create only the third largest city in the state. How do you explain gigantic chunks of blue ice breaking off glaciers and crashing into the ocean? How do you explain that the killer whales, sea otters, puffins, and porpoises you see in museums are only a small hint at what it is like to see them in real life?

A pod of killer whales swam with Mack's boat. The dorsal fin of the larger male split the ocean like a sail, arching up and down through the water. Suddenly, Mack realized <u>he</u> was the new thing in Alaska. The whales swam by the boat to see him. A sea otter lounged on his back 200 yards from shore with an Alaskan king crab lunch resting on his belly. It was a scene so comical and filled with delight that you could forget for a moment that the seas below are a world of such appalling violence that its food chain reads like a menu.

Alaska is different; it does not forgive mistakes. Tourists who do not respect Alaska's weather die every year. Moose, reject horses on stilts, meander onto highways at will and stand placidly waiting for motorists to crash cars into them. Motorists do. The tides can change as much as 20 feet in a few hours, circling and drowning unsuspecting tide pool hikers. Alaska is different.

Then there is fishing. To every poor soul struck dumb by the great Fish God, Alaska is Nirvana. It is Heaven. It is the pot of gold at the rainbow's end. Every hook in the Kenai River has a chance of hauling in a world record. For a king salmon, that would be around 98 pounds.

"There are a lot of fish in here," said Joe Haines, Mack's river guide. "Somebody is going to get bit. We're going to get bit."

Silver salmon run the Kenai so thick you can see them. Fishermen line the banks and cast in syncopation, so the lines won't tangle. The catch is 10-18 pounds each; fish carcasses also line the banks. They make good fillets when the fishing frenzy ends.

On the ocean floor, 400-pound halibut prowl the depths, their eyes physically twisted to the top of their heads to look up. Once hooked, it is like pulling a refrigerator to the surface to land one. The biggest must be killed with a .410 shotgun before being meat-hooked into the boat. Captain Scott of K-Bay Charters took Mack and his friends into the teeth of a giant halibut run. All told, they hauled in almost 1,000 pounds of fish. On the way to shore, the men sat in the galley telling stories of fish and the sea as two giant halibut flopped on the back deck, too large to fit in the meat locker. That night, they dropped cubes of halibut meat into boiling, sugared salt water. When the cooked meat floated to the surface, it tasted for all the world like lobster.

The adventure ended. From his southbound Delta flight, Mack could see the tips of the continent's largest mountains poking holes into the clouds. Back home, Mack's dog was throwing up and would need to go to the vet, the basement was flooding again, the treasured hollyhocks were all bent down, and the grass desperately needed mowing. Nothing was different.

Still, those who are called to Alaska never come home all the way again. That much was changed. Nothing is really over until we die. Mack put his NY mulberry hat with the salmon pin on a new hook by the kitchen door. He would see it every morning on his way out the door to the Old North Side Cafe.

Dust In The Wind

Camelot Bob used a knife! Unlike his buddies who punctuated their comments by shaking a fork for effect, Bob's exclamation point of choice was a Cafe knife. He held it in his fist with the tip of the knife pointing at somebody, and then uttered his famous words: "I am only going to say this once." Usually, Bob would go on to say that same thing over and over again in the next five or six sentences; but the men all agreed, the knife worked! They all listened as if Bob would stab them and never say his important thing again.

Just why he said it, where it came from, what it really meant, was and is a mystery. Bob certainly didn't know. He just found himself picking up his knife and pointing it at people around the table. Then he said, "I am only going to say this once. Listen up! None of us is getting out of this alive. Our moments have piled up, and there's no real future left for us. We are steadily and unalterably becoming part of the past. That is all life ever is."

Bob did not know it, but he was predicting the Cafe's end and offering a truth about storytelling. He accurately understood that the gradual accumulation of moments meant the Cafe was about to collapse from its own weight.

Every day, each of us lives a special few moments. Some mean more than others. Little things take on meanings that have just a bit more resonance, and we remember them. A cold burst of wind from an open door can mark an entire season. A woman comes in the Cafe with her wedding dress on; or a soldier and his son share a piece of pie. Smells and sounds and images stick in our mind. Then there are those moments when we realize age has crept up and planted wrinkles and dark spots on everyone's faces. Other moments, and these are the best, we seem to feel we are where we are supposed to be, and doing the work things we were always meant to do.

These random moments, over time, grow into something that is new, different and detached from the pointless rattle and empty spaces that often fill up daily life. This new thing is never noticed in the present. It cannot be captured in a plot, and it defies the endless argument that "everything always happens for a reason."

Over time, a parallel cafe is created. This "other" cafe contains a larger reality that is altogether different from the one the men lived and talked about every day. Perhaps a random collection of stories, seemingly unconnected in time, can carry truths that are bigger and more important than any of us can ever know.

Back to the Old North Side. The sunlight of a bright fall day illuminates a spectrum of dust particles floating above the Liar's Table, offering endless possibilities for observation. Nobody noticed the dust particles, however. The men were desperate to understand why Bob was still pointing his knife at them, and what he had just said. Bob dropped the knife and didn't explain his strange pronouncement. The moment just lingered in the air.

These cafe stories, homilies and essays are not a novel. They are like small, one-act plays. They existed for a single moment, and can never be repeated exactly the same again – never! The "moments" from these stories that pile up in the reader's mind will eventually form their own reality and meaning. This is where an authentic, but different, Old North Side Cafe still exists.

Artifacts And Last Testaments
Let's Play "Remember When?"

The Old North Side Cafe's coffee cup philosophers lean over the edge of current reality to look for truth and a moment of meaning. Water Street Pete is usually the leader of such movements. A hardened realist, Pete knows truth when he sees it and can smell a fool's breath before he speaks. "The world has changed around us boys," Pete says, gazing to a ceiling tile for effect. "We were lucky to grow up when we did."

Ah, the smell of cherished old half-truths permeates the North Side. It is a soothing balm. Even in the safety of a small northwest Missouri cafe, the men can hear the storms of change raging outside. For solace and comfort, they huddle close and retreat to the cozy den of "remember when." Here is a smattering of their philosophical gems. For full effect, huddle close as you read – go back and "remember when" with them.

Remember when:
- car loans did not outlast the car?
- "talk radio" reported on crop prices?
- the church potluck supper was more than three boxes of K-Fried Chicken, two bags of chips, a three-bean salad from Price Chopper, and a box of Nabisco cookies?
- four people could go to the movies for what the popcorn costs today?
- parent-teacher conferences were for helping students, not blaming teachers?
- a lawn service was a sunrise service in the park?
- the gun you feared most was a radar gun?
- insurance paid for the medicine doctors prescribed?
- truckers drove slower than you?
- kids wanted frozen TV dinners, because they were different?
- home cooking was actually done at home?
- grocery shopping didn't require a loan, five-page store map, and tool kit to fix the broken cart?
- kids watched TV when they were bored, instead of being bored because they couldn't watch TV?
- kiss-and-tell was not a political sport?
- girls pierced their ears and men lifted weights?
- the Christmas season started after Thanksgiving?
- you knew you had it better than you parents ever did?

And so the day spun itself into evening, and the men went home full of the past and girded to face the present. Let the change storm rage. It cannot touch nor diminish the gilded memories at the Old North Side Cafe.

Denouement

Camelot Bob worries about death and taxes and the worry gets worse every year. Holly Lake Jake does not worry about dying. He says, "I just want to live enough," whatever that means. The guys at the Cafe understand that some people think they are immortal precisely because they don't know they're already dead. By the time you read this, the Cafe will have hopefully restocked its shelves with another round of characters. The old boys who graced a century's end will be gone. Forgetting and "who cares," will eventually take care of everything. Let's move on.

It is a little known fact that Heaven's entrance exam is not about accomplishment. Nobody cares if you were president of this, head of that, won this award, or got your name on a stack of rocks. "Nope, in Heaven, the entrance exam is like a medical inspection. They check for scars. Those with the most scars are the first to get in." That is what Jake used to say. His curmudgeonly cronies would hear Jake say this and then moan and roll their eyes. Jake was such a sissy boy. Pete sometimes wanted to stab him with that fork.

One day at the Cafe, Ridgeway Ron, the farmer with the stubby fingers, got the guys talking about threshing machines and old farm life. The boys started telling their stories and time collapsed. Pretty soon, they were laughing and talking about washing off the wheat chaff down at the creek on a hot summer day. They told "stupid chicken" stories, "good dog" tales, and how a man was once gunned down in broad daylight in front of an entire town in Northwest Missouri, but nobody was ever charged with murder. Stella, as always, teased Bob relentlessly. Mack, Jake, Sam and Gus all told amazing stories about county fairs, spider bites, and income tax evasion. The day wore on and then ended. The paradigm, the pattern, call it what you will, but it is always there. Things end, and not much is relevant in a year or two.

"The past is a bucket of ashes," Pete would say. "Our job is to clean out the fire pit and get ready for tomorrow night."

The old guys built their fires and then shoveled out the pit. They laid in the wood of controversy, challenge, example, bonding, and expectation. Somebody, someday, if we ever learn to tell stories again, will discover fire again. They will have to keep the fires up on their own.

The Cafe men cleaned up pretty well after themselves, and they knew enough to leave when the party was over. On the way out the door, the old men slapped backs and grinned the goofy smiles of little boys trotting off to bed. Their great day was over.

"Those who get to actually live their brief moment, don't mind paying the price of admission," the Boss Hawg liked to say. And so, the good old boys end with their usual charm.

"See you in the funny papers."

Epilogue

Manor Hill Mack comes back from Alaska with a new sense of peace, joy, and purpose. He gets three more good years with the love of his life at his side. In the evenings, they watch reruns of the old TV show MASH (always were too busy before) and then have a ceremonial dish of ice cream before going to bed. These are happy days for them. Mack dies watching a Royals baseball game. The entire town will come to his funeral. You just can't help but hope there is a heaven where softball is the major sport. Mack is the umpire and all the kids who never got a chance on our side of life are lining up to play for the first time. "Plaaaaaaay Baaaaaallllll!" Mack orders to the assembled teams. Oh, what a day that will be!

Camelot Bob will go into the hospital with a minor scrape on his toe, develop a staph infection, and then watch helplessly as first one leg is cut off, and then the other, in order to save his life. Modern medicine, and the horrific new infections it has created, will kill Bob. He dies terribly disfigured by numerous amputations. He is the first of the crew to go, and the men begin a tradition that will survive till the last man (or Stella) is gone. Holly Lake Jake came up with the idea. After the memorial service, they come together for a moment of silence and then they put their hands together in the center of the circle. They look closely at one another and say "Amen" together. Their presence is their prayer.

Ridgeway Ron will steadily lose his memory and sit silently, staring at a blank wall in a nursing home. Jake and Gus visit regularly and tell him story after story, always believing some part of him still can hear and understand. Even in his severely compromised state, Ron's good heart and sweet personality stand out. Ron never fusses or acts out in anger. He endures with a dignity that reflects how he has lived. All the ladies at the home love Ron. Sometimes, for no apparent reason, he just smiles.

Holly Lake Jake stays connected to his intellect and God by taking up Quantum Mechanics and reading every book he can find on the subject. Inspired by the Einstein quote, "*There are only two ways to live your life. One is as though nothing is a miracle. The other is as though everything is a miracle,*" Jake becomes a layman philosopher proficient in probabilities and good guessing. He never stops looking for, wondering about, or serving his church and God.

Water Street Pete, the Boss Hawg, dies of bacon. (He would <u>heartily</u> approve of that joke). His overeating catches up with him. He endures every known medical procedure for heart disease developed over 50 years of medical research. He will still be on a transplant list when he finally goes to the other side. Every man at the Cafe remembers Pete holding up his fork like a scepter, and hears his voice filleting any erroneous nonsense. He was a force of nature. More than anyone else, they talk about Pete when they talk about the Cafe.

Stella will move to Tucson, Arizona. She happily lives in a trailer park, and her grandkids often come to visit. The Cafe now stays empty on Thanksgiving – nobody has a dinner for the homeless and disenfranchised. That does not mean, however, that the legacy has ended. You cannot count the number of people who now will include a stranger in their holiday celebrations because Stella planted that seed in them. Stella seems to never wear out, and she will always have a charisma that puts people at ease and makes them feel welcomed. She appears bent on living out her days serving others, especially a group of old guys who meet each morning up in the clubhouse to drink, God forbid, tea. Already, they all love Stella.

Gladstone Gus and his wife find ways to stay involved in the lives of young people. They both strive to support the things that provide education, hope and sustenance to children and parents. They bought insurance to help pay for the day they move to an extended care facility because they never wanted to be a bother to anyone. Gus will eventually endure the steady stream of forgetfulness, broken hips, and doctor visits that mark the end of life. The naps will get longer and the bones more brittle. Gus, too, will one day pass the torch to the new cafe.

By now you know Gus is my representative in this book. I wish I could be more like him; and, of course, like Jake as well.

Let the people say, "Amen."

Made in the USA
San Bernardino, CA
13 April 2014